BEST SELLERS

BEST SELLERS

from Reader's Digest
Condensed Books

The Reader's Digest Association
Pleasantville, New York

READER'S DIGEST CONDENSED BOOKS

Editor: John T. Beaudouin
Executive Editor: Joseph W. Hotchkiss
Managing Editor: Anthony Wethered
Senior Editors: Ann Berryman, Doris E. Dewey (Copy Desk), Noel Rae,
Robert L. Reynolds, Jane Siepmann, Jean N. Willcox, John S. Zinsser, Jr.
Associate Editors: Istar H. Dole, Marcia Drennen, Frances Travis, Patricia Nell Warren
Art Editors: William Gregory, Marion Davis, Thomas Von Der Linn
Art Research: Katherine Kelleher
Senior Copy Editors: Olive Farmer, Anna H. Warren
Associate Copy Editors: Jean E. Aptakin, Catherine T. Brown, Estelle T. Dashman,
Alice Murtha, Barbara P. Stafford
Research Editor: Linn Carl

SPECIAL PROJECTS
Executive Editor: Stanley E. Chambers
Senior Editors: Marion C. Conger, Sherwood Harris, Herbert H. Lieberman
Associate Editors: Elizabeth Stille, John Walsh

The original editions of the books in this volume are published and
copyrighted as follows:

The Odessa File, published at $7.95 by The Viking Press, Inc.
© 1972 by Danesbrook Productions Ltd.

P.S. Your not listening, published at $5.95 by Richard W. Baron Publishing Co., Inc.
© 1972 by Eleanor Craig

CONTENTS

THE ODESSA FILE

THE ODESSA FILE

A barbarous international organization
stood in his way, but if the
infamous SS officer still lived,
Peter Miller would hunt him down—
or die trying

A CONDENSATION OF THE BOOK BY
FREDERICK FORSYTH
ILLUSTRATED BY ARTHUR SHILSTONE

The Odessa's Sinister Mission

by Frederick Forsyth

The ODESSA of the title is a word composed of six initial letters, which stand for *Organisation Der Ehemaligen SS-Angehörigen* (Organization of Former Members of the SS).

The SS was the army within an army, devised by Hitler, commanded by Himmler, and charged with the security of the Third Reich. In effect it carried out Hitler's ambition to rid Germany of all elements he considered to be "unworthy of life," to enslave the "subhuman races of the Slavic lands," and to exterminate every Jew on the Continent.

Before the SS was destroyed, its most senior members made secret provision to disappear to a new life. Vast sums of SS gold were deposited in foreign banks, false identity papers were prepared, escape channels opened up. When the Allies finally conquered Germany, the bulk of the mass murderers had gone.

The Odessa was the organization formed to effect their escape. When this was accomplished, the ambitions of these men developed. Their aim was and remains fivefold: to rehabilitate former SS men into the professions of the new Federal Republic, to infiltrate political life, to stultify the course of justice in West Germany when it operates against a former *Kamerad,* to see that former SS men established themselves in industry, and finally to convince the German people that the SS killers were in fact ordinary patriotic soldiers in no way deserving of persecution.

In all these tasks, backed by its considerable funds, the Odessa has been measurably successful, and in none more so than in reducing official retribution through the West German courts to a mockery. Changing its name several times, the Odessa has sought to deny its own existence, with the result that many Germans are inclined to say it does not exist. The short answer is: it does, and the *Kameraden* of the death's-head insignia are still linked within it.

1

THERE was a thin robin's-egg-blue dawn coming up over Tel Aviv when the intelligence analyst finished typing his report. He stretched the cramped muscles of his shoulders, lit another filter-tipped cigarette, and read the concluding paragraphs.

Corroborative details arriving in this office indicate the sub-stantial accuracy of the location of the factory. If the appropriate action is taken, it may safely be assumed the West German au-thorities will concern themselves with its dismantlement.

It is therefore recommended that the facts be placed soon in the hands of these authorities, ensuring an attitude at the highest level in Bonn that will make certain the continuance of the Wal-dorf deal.

Once this is accomplished, the Right Honorable members of the Committee may be assured the project known as Vulcan is in the process of being dismantled and the rockets will never fly in time. If and when war with Egypt comes, that war will be fought and won by conventional weapons, which is to say by the republic of Israel.

The man on whose debriefing the report was based stood at the same hour in prayer fifty miles to the east at a place called Yad Vashem, but the analyst did not know this. He did not know precisely how the information in his report had been obtained, or how many men had died before it reached him. He did not need to know.

EVERYONE seems to remember with great clarity what he was doing on November 22, 1963, at the moment he heard President Kennedy was dead. The President was hit at 12:30 in the afternoon, Dallas time, and the announcement that he was dead came at about 1:30 Central Standard Time. It was 2:30 in New York, 7:30 in the evening in London, and 8:30 on a chilly, sleet-swept night in Hamburg.

Peter Miller was driving back into town after visiting his mother at her home in Osdorf, a suburb of the city. He always visited her on Friday evenings. He would have called her if she had a telephone, but as she did not, he drove out to see her. That was why she refused to have a telephone.

He was listening to music broadcast by Northwest German Radio. At eight thirty the music stopped and the voice of the announcer came through, taut with tension.

"Attention! Here is an announcement. President Kennedy is dead. I repeat, President Kennedy is dead."

"My God," Miller breathed. He eased down on the brake pedal and swung to the right-hand side of the road. All along the broad, straight highway other drivers were also pulling to the side, as if driving and listening to the radio had suddenly become mutually exclusive—which in a way they had.

The light music on the radio had stopped, replaced by a funeral march. At intervals the announcer read snippets of further information as they were brought in. The details began to fill in: the open-car ride into Dallas, the rifleman in the window of the Texas School Book Depository. No mention of an arrest.

As a reporter, Miller could imagine the chaos in the newspaper offices of the country as every staff man was called back to help put out a crash edition. He wished in a way he were back on the staff of a daily newspaper, but since he had become a free lance three years earlier he had specialized in feature stories inside Germany, mainly connected with crime, the police, the underworld. His mother accused him of mixing with "nasty people," and his arguments that he was becoming one of the most successful reporter-investigators in the country availed nothing.

As the reports came through, Miller leaned back on the comfortable leather upholstery of his Jaguar, trying to think of an angle that could be chased up inside Germany. The reaction of the Bonn government would be covered out of Bonn by the staff men; the memories of Kennedy's visit to Berlin the previous June would be covered from there. He didn't see anything he could ferret out to sell to the picture magazines that were his best customers.

It is always tempting to wonder what would have happened if . . . Usually it is a futile exercise, but it is probably accurate to say that if Miller had not pulled to the side of the road for half an hour he would not have seen the ambulance, or heard of Salomon Tauber or Eduard Roschmann, and forty months later the republic of Israel would probably have ceased to exist.

He finished his cigarette and threw the stub away. At a touch of the button the 3.8-liter engine beneath the long sloping hood of the Jaguar XK 150 S thundered once and settled down to its habitual and comforting rumble. Miller flicked on the headlights and swung out into the growing traffic stream along Osdorf Way.

He had got as far as the traffic lights on Stresemannstrasse when he heard the ambulance behind him. It came past him on the left, the wail of the siren rising and falling, then it swung across Miller's nose and down to the right into Daimlerstrasse. Miller reacted on reflexes alone. He let in the clutch, and the Jaguar surged after the ambulance, twenty yards behind it.

It was probably nothing, but one never knew. Ambulances meant trouble, and trouble could mean a story, particularly if one were first on the scene. Miller always carried a small Yashica camera with flash attachment in the glove compartment of his car.

The ambulance twisted into the narrow streets of the suburb of Altona and drew up in front of a crumbling rooming house, where a police car already stood. Its blue roof light sent a ghostly glow across the faces of the bystanders around the door.

A burly police sergeant in a rain cape roared at the crowd to stand back and make a gap in front of the door for the ambulance. Its driver and attendant climbed down, ran around to the back, and eased out an empty stretcher. After a brief word with the sergeant the pair hastened upstairs.

Miller pulled the Jaguar to the opposite curb twenty yards down the road. He climbed out and strolled over to the sergeant.

"Mind if I go up? I'm press." He waved his press card.

"And I'm police," said the sergeant. "Nobody goes up. Those stairs are narrow enough as it is, and none too safe. The ambulance men will be down right away. You can wait and check at the station later."

A man Miller recognized came down the stairs and emerged onto the pavement. They had been in school together at Hamburg Central High. The man was now a junior detective inspector in the Hamburg police, stationed at Altona Central.

"Hey, Karl."

The young inspector caught sight of Miller and his face broke into a grin. He nodded to the sergeant.

"It's all right, Sergeant. He's more or less harmless."

Miller shook hands with Karl Brandt.

"What are you doing here?" Brandt asked.

"Followed the ambulance."

"Damned vulture. What are you up to these days?"

"Same as usual. Free-lancing."

"Making quite a bundle out of it by the look of it. I keep seeing your name in the picture magazines."

"It's a living. Hear about Kennedy?"

"Yes. Hell of a thing. They must be turning Dallas inside out tonight. Glad it wasn't on my turf."

Miller nodded questioningly toward the dimly lit hallway back of Brandt.

"A suicide. Gas. Neighbors smelled it coming under the door."

"Not a film star by any chance?" asked Miller.

"Yeah. Sure. They always live in places like this. No, it was an old man. Looked as if he had been dead for years anyway."

Brandt watched as the two ambulance men came down the hall-way with their burden; then he turned around and said, "Make some room. Let them through."

The two men walked out onto the pavement and around to the open doors of the ambulance. Brandt followed them, with Miller at his heels. As the ambulance men reached the door of the ve-hicle, Brandt said, "Hold it," and flicked back the corner of the blanket above the dead man's face. He remarked over his shoulder, "Just a formality. My report has to say I accompanied the body to the ambulance and back to the morgue."

The interior lights of the ambulance were bright, and Miller caught a two-second look at the face of the suicide. His only im-pression was that he had never seen anything so old and ugly. A few strands of lank hair were plastered over the otherwise naked scalp, and the face was hollowed out to the point of emaciation. The lips hardly existed, and both upper and lower were lined with vertical creases. To cap the effect, two pale and jagged scars ran down the man's face, from the temples to the corners of the mouth.

After a quick glance Brandt stepped back as the ambulance attendant rammed the stretcher into its berth. The vehicle surged away, and the crowd started to disperse.

Miller looked at Brandt and raised his eyebrows. "Charming."

"Yeah. Well, I must get back to the station. See you, Peter."

Miller drove back toward the Altona railroad station, picked up the main road into the city center, and twenty minutes later swung into the underground garage off Hansaplatz, not far from the build-ing where he had his penthouse apartment.

Keeping the car in an underground garage all winter was one of the extravagances he permitted himself. Also, he liked his fairly expensive apartment because it was high and he could look down on the bustling boulevard of the Steindamm. Of his clothes and food he thought nothing, and at twenty-nine, just under six feet, with the rumpled brown hair and brown eyes that women go for, he didn't need expensive clothes.

The real passions of his life were sports cars, reporting, and Sigrid Rahn, though he sometimes shamefacedly admitted that if it came to a choice between Sigi and the Jaguar, Sigi might have to find her loving somewhere else.

He stood and looked at the Jaguar in the lights of the garage after he had parked it. Miller could seldom get enough of looking at that car. Even approaching it in the street he would stop and admire it, occasionally joined by a passerby who would pause to remark, "Some car, that."

Normally a young free-lance reporter does not drive a Jaguar XK 150 S. Spare parts were almost impossible to come by in Hamburg, the more so as the XK series had gone out of production in 1960. He maintained it himself, spending hours on Sundays in overalls under it or half buried in the engine. He had hardened up the independent suspension on the two front wheels, and as the car had stiff suspension at the back, it took corners steady as a rock. Just after buying it he had had it resprayed black with a long wasp-yellow streak down each side.

It was late when Miller unlocked the door of his apartment, and although his mother had fed him at six, he was hungry again. He scrambled some eggs and listened to the late news. It was all about Kennedy and heavily accented on the German angles, since there was little more coming through from Dallas. The police were still searching for the killer. He switched off the radio and got into bed, wishing Sigi were home. He always wanted to snuggle up to her when he felt depressed. But the cabaret at which she danced did not close till nearly four in the morning, often later on Friday nights, when the provincials and tourists were thick down the Reeperbahn.

So he smoked another cigarette and fell asleep to dream of the hideous dead face of the old man in the slums of Altona.

WHILE Peter Miller was eating his scrambled eggs at midnight in Hamburg, five men were sitting drinking in a house attached to a riding school outside Cairo. The time there was one in the morning. The five men were in a jovial mood because of the news from Dallas which they had heard almost four hours earlier. Two of the guests and the host were Germans, the other two Egyptians. The host was proprietor of the riding school, a favorite meeting place of the cream of Cairo society and the several-thousand-strong German colony.

Sitting in the leather easy chair by the shuttered window was Peter Bodden, formerly an expert on Jews in the Nazi propaganda ministry of Dr. Joseph Goebbels. Bodden had taken the Egyptian name of El Gumra. On his left was another Goebbels man, Max Bachmann. Both were still fanatical Nazis. Of the Egyptians, one was Colonel Shamseddine Badrane, personal aide to Marshal Abdel Hakim Amer, who later became vice-president of Egypt. The other was Colonel Ali Samir, head of the Moukhabarat, the Egyptian secret intelligence service.

Peter Bodden raised his glass toward the ceiling. "So Kennedy the Jew-lover is dead. Gentlemen, I give you a toast."

The reference to Kennedy as a Jew-lover baffled none of the five men in the room. On March 14, 1960, while Dwight Eisenhower was still President of the United States, the Premier of Israel, David Ben-Gurion, and the Chancellor of Germany, Konrad Adenauer, had met at the Waldorf-Astoria Hotel in New York.

The two statesmen had signed a secret agreement whereby West Germany was to open a credit account for Israel to the tune of fifty million dollars a year. Ben-Gurion, however, soon discovered that to have money was one thing, to have a secure and certain source of arms was quite another. Six months later the Waldorf agreement was topped off with another, signed by the defense ministers of Germany and Israel, under which Israel would be able to use the money to buy weapons in Germany.

Adenauer, aware of the vastly more controversial nature of the second agreement, delayed implementing it for months. Then in November 1961 he was in New York to meet the new President, John Fitzgerald Kennedy, and Kennedy put the pressure on. He did not wish arms to be delivered to Israel from the United States, but he wanted them to arrive somehow. Israel needed fighters, transport planes, 105-mm howitzer artillery pieces, armored cars, personnel carriers, and tanks. And Germany had all of these, mainly of American make. So the deal was pushed through.

German tanks started to arrive at Haifa in late June, 1963, and the former members of the SS found out about them. Their organization, Odessa, promptly informed the Egyptians, with whom its agents in Cairo had the closest links.

In late 1963 things started to change. On October 15 Adenauer, "the Granite Chancellor," went into retirement. His place was taken by Ludwig Erhard, a good vote-catcher as the father of the German economic miracle, but weak and vacillating in matters of foreign policy.

Even while Adenauer was in office there had been a vociferous group inside the West German cabinet in favor of shelving the Israeli arms deal. The old chancellor had silenced them with a few terse sentences, and such was his power that they stayed silenced. But as soon as Erhard took the chair they opened up again. While Erhard dithered, the determination of John Kennedy that Israel should get her arms via Germany was unremitting.

And then Kennedy was shot. The big question in the small hours of the morning of November 23 was simply: Would President Lyndon Johnson take the American pressure off Germany and let the indecisive chancellor in Bonn renege on the deal? In fact he did not, but there were high hopes in Cairo that he would.

The host at the convivial meeting outside Cairo that night, having filled his guests' glasses, turned back to the sideboard to top up his own. Wolfgang Lutz, born at Mannheim in 1921, was a former major in the German army, who had emigrated to Cairo in 1961 and started his riding academy. Blond, blue-eyed, hawk-faced, he was a favorite among both the influential political figures of Cairo and the expatriate German—and mainly Nazi—community along the banks of the Nile.

He turned to face the room and gave a broad smile. If there was anything false about that smile, no one noticed. But it *was* false. He had been born a Jew in Mannheim, but had moved to Palestine at the age of twelve. He was a major, but in the Israeli army. He was also the top agent of Israeli Intelligence in Egypt.

Lutz could hardly wait for his guests to depart, for he desperately wished to get his transmitter out of the bathroom scales and send a message to Tel Aviv. He raised his glass to the four smiling faces. "Death to the Jew-lovers," he toasted, forcing his own smile. "*Sieg Heil.*"

PETER MILLER woke the next morning just before nine and shifted luxuriously under the enormous feather comforter that covered the double bed. Even half awake he could feel the warmth of the sleeping figure of Sigi, and he snuggled closer to her.

Sigi, still fast asleep after only four hours in bed, grunted in annoyance. "Go away," she muttered. Miller sighed, slipped out of bed, and padded into the living room to pull back the curtains. The steely November light washed across the room. He yawned and went into the kitchen to brew the first of his innumerable cups of coffee.

Sigi was twenty-two, and at school had been a champion gymnast who, so she said, could have gone on to Olympic standing if her bust had not developed to the point where it got in the way. On leaving school she became a teacher of physical training at a girls' school. The change to striptease dancing came for the simplest of reasons: it paid five times a teacher's salary.

Miller had seen her by chance on a visit to Madame Kokett's bar just below the Café Keese on the Reeperbahn. She was a big girl, five feet nine, with a figure to match. She stripped to the music with her face set in the usual bedroom pout of strippers. Miller had sipped his drink without batting an eyelid.

But when the applause started, the girl had bobbed a shy, half-embarrassed little bow and given a big sloppy grin like a half-trained bird dog which, against all the betting, has just brought back a downed partridge. It was the grin that got Miller. He asked the bartender if she would like a drink, and she was sent for.

To his surprise Miller found she was a very nice person to be around, and asked if he might take her home after the show. With obvious reservations, she agreed. She emerged from the cabaret clad in a most unglamorous duffel coat.

Miller played his cards coolly. They just had coffee and talked. She finally unwound from her tension and began chatting gaily.

He learned she liked pop music, art, walking along the banks of the Alster lakes, keeping house, and children. They started, then, going out together on her one free night a week.

After three months Miller took her to his bed, and later suggested that she move in. Sigi, who had a single-minded approach to the important things of life, had already decided she wanted to marry Peter Miller, and the only problem was whether she should try to get him by sleeping in his bed or not. Sensing his ability to fill the other half of his mattress with other girls if the need arose, she decided to accept his invitation and make his life so comfortable that he would want to marry her. They had been together for six months by this late November morning.

MILLER carried the radio into the bathroom and listened to the news while he shaved and showered. A man had been arrested for the murder of President Kennedy. There were no news items on the entire program but those connected with the Kennedy assassination.

After drying off, he went back to the kitchen and made more coffee. He was halfway to the living room with it when the phone rang. It was Karl Brandt.

"Peter? Look, it's about this dead Jew."

Miller was baffled. "What dead Jew?"

"The one who gassed himself last night in Altona."

"I didn't know he was Jewish," said Miller. "What about him?"

"I want to talk to you. Not on the phone. Can we meet?"

Miller's mind clicked into gear immediately. "How about lunch?" He mentioned a small restaurant on Gänsemarkt.

"Good," said Brandt. "I'll be there at one o'clock."

Throughout lunch Karl avoided his subject, but when the coffee came he said simply, "The man last night."

"Yes," said Miller. "What about him?"

"You know what the Nazis did to the Jews during the war and even before it?"

"Of course. They rammed it down our throats at school."

At the time Miller had accepted what the teachers said without even knowing what was being talked about. Later it had been difficult to find out what the teachers had meant. There was nobody to ask, nobody who wanted to talk. Only with coming manhood had he read a little about it, and although what he read disgusted him, he could not feel it concerned him.

It was another time, another place, a long way away. He had not been there when it happened, his father had not been there, his mother had not been there. Something inside him had persuaded him it was nothing to do with Peter Miller, so he had asked for no names, dates, details. He wondered why Brandt should be bringing the subject up.

Brandt stirred his coffee, not knowing how to go on. "That old man last night," he said at length. "He was a German Jew. He was in a concentration camp."

Miller thought back to the death's-head on the stretcher the previous evening. Was that what they ended up like? It was ridiculous. The man must have been liberated by the Allies eighteen years earlier and had lived on to die of old age. But the face kept coming back. He had never before seen anyone who had been in a camp—at least, not knowingly. For that matter he had never met one of the SS mass killers, he was sure of that. One would notice, after all.

"What about it?" he asked the detective.

For answer Brandt took a brown paper-wrapped parcel out of his attaché case and pushed it across the table. "The old man left a diary. Actually, he wasn't so old. Fifty-six. It seems he wrote notes at the time and stored them in his foot wrappings. After the war he transcribed them all. They make up the diary."

Miller looked at the parcel with scant interest. "Where did you find it?"

"It was lying next to the body. I picked it up and took it home. I read it last night. It was horrible. I had no idea it was that bad—the things they did to them."

"Why bring it to me?"

Now Brandt was embarrassed. He shrugged. "I thought it might make a story for you."

"Who does it belong to now?"

"Technically, Tauber's heirs. We'll never find them. So I suppose it belongs to the police department. But they'd just file it. You can have it, if you want it. Just don't let on that I gave it to you. I don't need any trouble in the department."

Miller paid the bill, and the pair walked outside.

"All right, I'll read it. But I don't promise to get steamed up about it. It might make an article for a magazine."

Brandt turned to him with a half smile. "You're a cynical bastard," he said.

"No," said Miller, "it's just that, like most people, I'm concerned with the here and now. What about you? After ten years in the police I'd have thought you'd be a tough cop. This thing really upset you, didn't it?"

Brandt was serious again. He looked at the parcel under Miller's arm and nodded slowly. "Yes. Yes, it did. I just never realized it was so terrible. And by the way, it's not all past history. That story ended here in Hamburg last night. Good-by, Peter."

The detective turned and walked away, not knowing how wrong he was.

2

PETER MILLER took the brown parcel home and arrived there just after three. Settled in his favorite armchair, with the inevitable cup of coffee at his elbow and a cigarette going, he opened it. The diary consisted of a hundred and fifty typewritten pages in a loose-leaf folder with stiff cardboard covers. It had apparently been banged out on an old machine, for some of the letters were distorted or faint; and it seemed to have been typed over a period of years, for most of the pages bore the unmistakable tinting of old paper. But there was a preface of new pages at the front of the typescript and a sort of epilogue at the back. Both were dated November 21, two days previously.

The opening paragraphs surprised Miller, for the language was clear and precise German, the writing of a well-educated and cultured man. On the outside of the front cover a square of white paper had been pasted, and on it had been written in large capitals THE DIARY OF SALOMON TAUBER.

Miller settled deeper in his chair and began to read.

My name is Salomon Tauber, I am a Jew and about to die. I have decided to end my own life because it has no more value. Those things that I have tried to do with my life have come to nothing; for the evil that I have seen has survived and flourished and only the good has departed. The friends that I have known, the sufferers and the victims, are all dead, and only the persecutors are all around me. I see their faces on the streets in the daytime, and in the night I see the face of my wife, Esther, who died long ago. I have stayed alive this long only because there was one thing I wished to do, and now I know I never shall.

I bear no hatred or bitterness toward the German people, for they are a good people. Peoples are not evil; only individuals are evil. The English philosopher Burke was right when he said, "I do not know the means for drawing up the indictment of an entire nation." The Bible relates how the Lord wished to destroy Sodom and Gomorrah for the evil of those who lived there, but among them was one righteous man, and because he was righteous he was spared. Therefore guilt is individual, like salvation.

When I came out of the concentration camps of Riga and Stutthof, when I survived the Death March to Magdeburg, when the British soldiers liberated my body there in April 1945, leaving only my soul in chains, I hated the Germans. I asked then, as I had many times over the previous four years, why the Lord did not strike them down, every last man, woman, and child. And when He did not, I hated Him too, crying that He had deserted me and my people, whom He had led to believe were His chosen people.

But with the passing of time I have learned again to love;

25

to love the rocks and the trees, the sky above and the river flowing past the city, the stray dogs and the cats, and the children who run away from me because I am so ugly. They are not to blame. There is a French adage, "To understand everything is to forgive everything." When one can understand people's fear and greed and ignorance, one can forgive. But one can never forget.

There are some men whose crimes surpass comprehension and therefore forgiveness, and here is the failure. For they are still among us—in the cities, in the offices, lunching in the canteens, smiling, shaking hands, calling decent men *Kamerad*. That they should live on, not as outcasts but as cherished citizens, this is the failure.

Lastly, as time passed, I have come again to love the Lord, and to ask His forgiveness for the things I have done against His laws, and they are many.

Shema, Yisrael, Adonai elohenu, Adonai echad.
[*Hear, O Israel, The Lord is our God, The Lord is One.*]

The diary began with twenty pages in which Tauber described his boyhood in Hamburg. By the late 1930s he was married to a girl named Esther and was working in Hamburg as an architect. He was spared being rounded up before 1941 owing to the intervention of his employer. Finally he was taken, in Berlin, while on a journey to see a client. After a period in a transit camp he was packed with other Jews into a boxcar on a cattle train bound for the east.

I cannot remember the date the train finally rumbled to a halt in a railway station. I think it was six days and seven nights after we were shut up in the car in Berlin. Suddenly the train was stationary, the slits of white light told me it was daytime outside, and my head swam from exhaustion and the stench.

There were shouts outside, the sound of bolts being drawn back, and the doors were flung open. As brilliant daylight rushed into the car men threw arms over their eyes and screamed with the pain. Half the car emptied itself onto the platform in a tumbling mass of stinking humanity. As I had been standing at the rear of the car to one side of the centrally placed doors, I avoided this and stepped down upright to the platform.

The SS guards who had opened the gates, mean-faced, brutal men who jabbered and roared in a language I could not understand, stood back with expressions of disgust. Inside the boxcar thirty-one men lay trampled on the floor. They would never get up again. The remainder, starved, half blind, steaming and reeking from head to foot, struggled upright on the platform. Our tongues, blackened and swollen, were gummed to the roofs of our mouths from thirst, and our lips were split and parched.

Along the platform forty other cars from Berlin and eighteen from Vienna were disgorging their occupants, about half of them women and children. Many of the women and most of the children were naked, smeared with excrement, and in as bad shape as we were. Some women carried the lifeless bodies of their children in their arms as they stumbled out into the light.

The guards ran up and down the platform, clubbing the deportees into a sort of column prior to marching us into the town. But what town? And what was the language these men were speaking? Later I was to discover that this town was Riga and the SS guards were local Latvians, as fiercely anti-Semitic as the SS from Germany, but of a much lower intelligence, virtually animals in human form.

There were a few German SS officers standing in the shade of the station awning. One stood aloof on a packing crate, surveying with a thin but satisfied smile the several thousand human skeletons who emptied themselves from the train. He was tall and lanky, with pale hair and washed-out blue eyes.

Later I was to learn he was a dedicated sadist, known as "the Butcher of Riga." It was my first sight of Waffen SS Captain Eduard Roschmann.

At five o'clock on the morning of June 22, 1941, Hitler's 130 divisions, in three army groups, had rolled across the border to invade Russia. Behind each army group came SS extermination squads, charged by Hitler, Himmler, and Heydrich with wiping out the Communist commissars and the rural Jewish communities, and penning the large urban Jewish communities into the ghettos of each major town. The army took Riga, capital of Latvia, on July 1. By August 1 the SS had begun the extermination program that would make Ostland (as the Germans renamed the three occupied Baltic States) Jew-free.

Then it was decided in Berlin to use Riga as the transit camp to death for the Jews of Germany and Austria. In 1938 there were 320,000 German Jews and 180,000 Austrian Jews, a round half million. By July 1941 tens of thousands had been dealt with in the concentration camps, notably Sachsenhausen, Mauthausen, Ravensbrück, Dachau, Buchenwald, Belsen, and Theresienstadt. But the camps were getting overcrowded. Work was begun to expand or begin the six extermination centers of Auschwitz, Treblinka, Belzec, Sobibor, Chelmno, and Maidanek. Until they were ready, however, a place had to be found to finish off as many Jews as possible and "store" the rest. The obscure lands of the east seemed an excellent choice for the purpose.

The Riga ghetto lay at the northern edge of the city, with open countryside to the north. There was a wall along the south face; the other three sides were sealed off with rows of barbed wire. There was one gate, on the northern face, through which all exits and entries had to be made. From this gate, running down the center of the ghetto, was Mase Kalnu Iela, or Little Hill Street. To the right-hand side of this (looking from south to north) was the Blech Platz, or Tin Square, where selections for execution took place, along with roll call, selection of slave-labor parties, floggings, and hangings. The gallows, with its eight steel hooks and permanent nooses swinging in the wind, stood in the center of this. It was occupied every night, and frequently several shifts had to be processed before Roschmann was satisfied with his day's work.

The whole ghetto must have been just under two square miles, a township that had once housed 15,000 people. After we arrived transports continued to come day after day, until the population of our part of the ghetto soared to 40,000, and with the arrival of each new transport a number of the inhabitants had to be executed to make room for the newcomers.

As summer merged into autumn and autumn into winter, conditions grew worse. Each morning the entire population was assembled on Tin Square. These were mainly men, for women and children were exterminated on arrival in far greater percentages than the work-fit males. We were divided into work groups that left the ghetto each day in columns, to work twelve hours at forced labor in the growing host of workshops nearby.

I had told them early on that I was a carpenter, which was not true, but as an architect I had seen carpenters at work and knew enough to get by. I guessed, correctly, that there would always be a need for carpenters, and I was sent to a nearby lumber mill.

Before marching to work in the mornings we were given a half liter apiece of so-called soup, mainly water, sometimes with a knob of potato in it. We had another half liter, with a slice of black bread and a moldy potato, on returning to the ghetto at night. Bringing food into the ghetto was punishable by hanging. Nevertheless, to take that risk was the only way to stay alive.

As the columns trudged back through the gate each evening, Roschmann and his cronies would do spot checks. At random they would order people to strip. If food was found on them, they would stay behind while the others marched to Tin Square for roll call. Then Roschmann and the other SS guards would stalk down the road, followed by the condemned people. The males among them would mount the gallows and wait with ropes around their necks during roll call. Then Roschmann would walk along and kick the chairs out from under them, one by one, grinning up at the faces above him. Sometimes he would pretend to kick the chair away, only to pull his foot back in time, laughing uproariously.

Sometimes the condemned men would pray to the Lord, sometimes they would cry for mercy. Roschmann liked this. He would pretend he was slightly deaf, cocking an ear and asking, "Can you speak up a little? What was that you said?"

When it was a woman who was caught with food, she was made to watch the hangings of the men first, especially if one was her husband or brother. Afterward Roschmann made her kneel in front of the rest of us while the camp barber shaved her bald, and then she was taken to the cemetery outside the wire. There she was made to dig a shallow grave, and kneel beside it while Roschmann fired a bullet from his Luger into the base of her skull. Word came from the Latvian guards that he would often fire past the woman's ear. She would fall into the grave with shock, only to have to climb out and go through it all again. The Latvians were brutes, but Roschmann managed to amaze them for all that.

There was one certain girl at Riga who helped the prisoners at her own risk. She was Olli Adler—from Munich, I believe. Her sister Gerda had already been shot in the cemetery for bringing in food. Olli was a girl of surpassing beauty and took Roschmann's fancy. He made her his concubine—the official term was housemaid, because relations between an SS man and a Jewish girl were banned. She used to smuggle medicines into the ghetto when she was allowed to visit it, having stolen them from the SS stores. This, of course, was punishable by death. The last I saw of her was when we boarded the ship at the Riga docks.

By the end of that first winter I was certain I could not survive the hunger and cold and damp, the overwork, and the constant brutalities. My strong frame had been whittled down to skin and bones. In the mirror I saw a haggard, stubbled old man. I was just thirty-five and I looked double that; my will to live had dissipated. Then something happened in March that gave me another year of willpower.

I remember the date even now. It was March 3, 1942, the day of the second Dünamünde convoy. About a month earlier we had seen the arrival of a strange van. It was about the size of a long single-decker bus, but without windows. It parked just outside the ghetto gates, and at morning roll call Roschmann announced that there was a new fish-pickling factory at the town of Dünamünde, about eight miles north of Riga. It involved light work, he said, good food, and good living conditions. Because the work was so light, the opportunity was open only to old men and women, the frail, the sick, and the small children.

Roschmann walked down the lines, selecting those to go, and the old and sick were eager to show themselves. Finally over a hundred were selected, and all climbed into the van. The doors were slammed shut, and the van rolled away, emitting no exhaust fumes. Later, word filtered back that there was no fish-pickling factory at Dünamünde; the van was a gassing van. So a Dünamünde convoy meant death by gassing.

On March 3 the whisper went around that there was to be another Dünamünde convoy, and sure enough, at morning roll call Roschmann announced it. But there was no pressing forward to volunteer, so with a wide grin Roschmann began to stroll along the ranks, tapping on the chest with his quirt those who were to go. He started at the rear rank, where he expected to find the weak and the old. There was one old woman who had foreseen this and stood in the front rank. She must have been sixty-five, but she had rouged her cheeks and painted her lips, hoping to pass for a young girl.

Reaching her, Roschmann stopped, stared, then grinned.

31

"Well, what have we here?" he cried. "Don't you want a nice little ride to Dünamünde, young lady?"

Trembling with fear, the old woman whispered, "No, sir."

"And how old are you, then?" boomed Roschmann as his SS friends began to giggle. "Seventeen? Twenty?"

The old woman's knees began to tremble. "Yes, sir," she whispered.

"Well, I always like a pretty girl," cried Roschmann. "Come out where we can all admire your beauty."

He hustled her to the center of Tin Square. "Now, since you're so young and pretty, perhaps you'll dance for us, eh?"

His cronies were laughing fit to bust. The woman shook her head. Roschmann's smile vanished. "Dance," he snarled.

She made a few little shuffling movements, then stopped. Roschmann fired his Luger into the sand an inch from her feet. "Dance . . . dance . . . dance, you hideous Jewish bitch," he shouted, firing each time he said dance. He made her leap higher and higher, until at last she fell to the sand, unable to rise. He fired his last three slugs in front of her face, blasting the sand up into her eyes. Then, with no more ammunition left, he shouted "Dance" again and slammed his boot into her belly.

All this had happened in complete silence, until the man next to me started to pray. He was a Hasid, small and bearded, in the rags of his long black coat. He began to recite the *Shema* in a quavering voice that grew steadily louder.

I too began to pray, silently, that the Hasid would be quiet. But he would not.

"*Shema, Yisrael . . .*"

"Shut up," I hissed out of the corner of my mouth.

"*Adonai elohenu . . .*"

"Will you be quiet! You'll get us all killed."

"*Adonai echa-a-a-ad.*"

Like a cantor he drew out the last syllable in the traditional way. At that moment Roschmann stopped shouting at the old woman and lifted his head like an animal scenting the wind.

"Who was that talking?" he screamed, striding toward me. "You—step out of line." I stepped forward. His face, twitching like a maniac's, changed as he looked at me, and he gave his quiet, wolfish smile that struck terror into even the Latvian SS men.

His hand moved so quickly no one could see it. I felt only a thump down one side of my face, and a tremendous bang as if a bomb had gone off next to my eardrum; then the quite distinct but detached feeling of my own skin splitting like rotten calico from temple to mouth. His hand moved again, and the other side of my face ripped open. He had a two-foot quirt, with a steel core in the handle and plaited leather thongs. It could split hide like tissue paper.

Warm blood was dripping off my chin in two red fountains. Roschmann pointed to the old woman sobbing in the square.

"Pick up that old hag and take her to the van," he barked.

And so it was that I picked up the old woman and carried her to the gate and the waiting van, pouring blood onto her from my chin. As I set her down in the van she gripped my wrist with a strength I would not have thought she still possessed. She pulled me down, and with a handkerchief that must have come from better days she stanched some of my flowing blood. She looked up at me, her face streaked with mascara, tears, and sand, but with dark eyes bright as stars.

"Jew, my son," she whispered. "Swear to me that you will live. You must live, so that you can tell them outside what happened to our people here. Promise me, swear it by the Torah."

And so I swore that I would live, somehow. Then I stumbled back down the road into the ghetto, and halfway there I fainted.

Shortly thereafter I made two decisions. One was to keep a secret diary, nightly tattooing words and dates into the skin of my feet and legs, hidden by my ragged foot wrappings, so that one day I would be able to give precise evidence against those responsible for what was happening.

The second decision was to become a *kapo*. The decision

was hard, for *kapos* were camp police who herded their fellow Jews to work, and often to execution. They carried pickaxe handles and sometimes, under the eye of a German SS officer, used them to beat their fellow prisoners. Nevertheless, on April 1, 1942, I went to the chief of the *kapos* and volunteered, thus becoming an outcast. There was no point in explaining why I had done it: that one *kapo* more or less would make no difference; but that one single surviving witness might make all the difference, not to save the Jews of Germany, but to avenge them.

I should describe here the method of execution of those unfit for labor, for in this manner between 70,000 and 80,000 Jews were exterminated under Roschmann's orders at Riga. When the cattle train arrived at the station with a new consignment of prisoners, usually about 5000 strong, close to 1000 were already dead from the journey. The new arrivals—say 4000—were then lined up on Tin Square and the selections for extermination took place, not merely among them but among us all. From the new arrivals the old, the diseased, most of the women, and almost all the children were set on one side as unfit. The remainder were then counted. If there were 2000 of them, then 2000 of the existing inmates whose health had been worked to ruins would be picked out by Roschmann's quirt to die, so that 4000 had arrived and 4000 went to execution hill. That way there was no overcrowding.

At first these victims were marched to the High Forest, just outside the town, where they dug the enormous open ditches into which they fell when the Latvian SS mowed them down. The remaining Riga Jews filled in enough earth to cover the bodies, adding one more layer of corpses to those underneath. When the ditch was full, a new one was started. All those killed on execution hill were stripped at the graveside. The gold, silver, and jewelry were taken in charge by Roschmann personally.

In August 1942 I was standing in Tin Square as Roschmann went around making his selections from a transport that had just come in from Bohemia. The new arrivals were already shaved bald, and it was not easy to tell the men from the women, except for the shift dresses the women wore. There was one woman, thin as a rake and coughing, who caught my attention. Something about her rang a bell in my mind.

Arriving opposite her, Roschmann tapped her on the chest and passed on. Most of those selected that evening were marched to the High Forest. But there was a gassing van at the gates, and a group of about a hundred of the frailest were detached from the crowd. SS Lieutenant Krause pointed to five of us *kapos*. "You," he shouted, "take these to the Dünamünde convoy."

Among the limping, crawling, coughing people we escorted to the van was that thin woman. She knew where she was going—they all did—but like the rest she stumbled obediently to the rear of the van. She was too weak to climb up, for the tailboard was high off the ground, so she turned to me for help. We stood and looked at each other in stunned amazement. Behind me I heard somebody approach, and the two *kapos* at the tailboard straightened to attention, scraping their caps off with one hand. Realizing it must be an SS officer, I did the same. The woman just stared at me unblinking. The man behind me came forward. It was Captain Roschmann. Those pale blue eyes glared at me, then flickered to the woman, and the slow, wolfish smile spread across his face.

"Do you know this woman?" he asked.

"Yes, *Herr Kapitän*," I answered.

"Who is she?" he asked. I could not reply.

"Is she your wife?" he went on. I nodded dumbly.

He grinned even more widely. "Well now, my dear Tauber, where are your manners? Help the lady up into the van."

I stood there unable to move. He put his face closer to mine. "You have ten seconds to pack her in or you will go yourself."

Slowly I held out my arm and Esther leaned upon it. With this assistance she climbed into the van. She looked down at

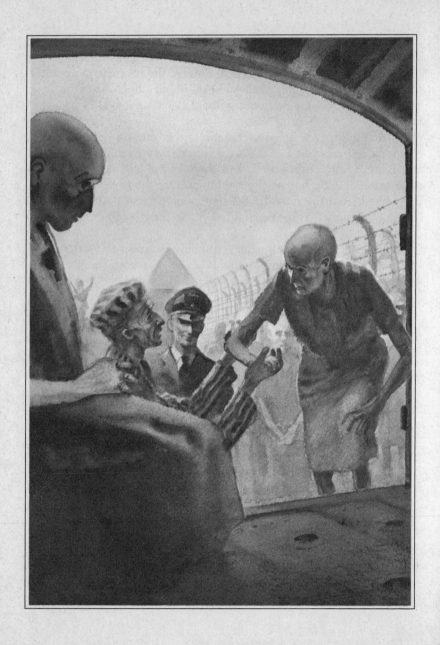

me, and two tears rolled down her cheeks. She did not say anything; we never spoke throughout. Then the doors were slammed, and the van rolled away. The last thing I saw was her eyes looking at me.

I have spent twenty years trying to understand the look in her eyes. Was it love or hatred, contempt or pity, bewilderment or understanding? I shall never know.

Roschmann turned to me, still grinning. "You may go on living until it suits us to finish you off, Tauber. But you are dead as of now."

And he was right. That was the day my soul died inside me. It was August 29, 1942.

Peter Miller read on late into the night. Several times he sat back in his chair and breathed deeply for a few minutes to regain his calm. Once, close to midnight, he laid the folder down and made more coffee. Tauber had now come to the spring of 1944, to the moment when Soviet troops had cut the whole of Ostland off from the Reich, marching south of the Baltic States right through to the Baltic Sea. The Wehrmacht generals, who had seen the trap closing on them, had argued and pleaded with Hitler to pull back the forty-five divisions inside the enclave. Hitler's reply had been his parrot-cry, "Death or Victory." Cut off from resupply, 500,000 soldiers fought with dwindling ammunition to delay a certain fate.

That spring, when the Russians were pushing westward, the Riga ghetto was finally liquidated. Most of its 30,000 remaining inhabitants were marched to the High Forest. About 5000 were transferred to the camp of Kaiserswald, while behind them the ghetto was fired, and then the ashes were bulldozed. Of what had been there, nothing was left but hundreds of acres of ashes.

For twenty pages Tauber described his struggle to survive starvation, disease, and brutality in Kaiserswald. Roschmann was not there. Apparently he was still in Riga, for Tauber went on to tell how in October 1944 the SS, panic-stricken at the thought of being taken alive by the Russians, prepared for a desperate evacuation of Riga by sea, taking along a handful of the surviving prisoners as their passage ticket back to the Reich. This became fairly common practice for the SS staff of the concentration camps as the Russian advance swept on. So long as they could still claim they had a task to perform important to the Reich, they could continue to outrank the Wehrmacht and avoid the terrible prospect of being required to face Stalin's divisions in combat. This "task," which they allotted to themselves, was to escort back into the still safe heart of Germany the few remaining wretches from the camps they had run. Sometimes the charade became ridiculous, as when the SS guards outnumbered their tottering charges by as many as ten to one.

It was in the afternoon of October 11 that we arrived, by now barely 4000 strong, at the Riga docks. In the distance we could hear a strange *crump*, as if of thunder—Russian mortars landing in the suburbs. The dock area was crawling with officers and men of the SS. There must have been more of them than there were of us. We were lined up in rows against one of the warehouses and thought we were to die under the machine guns. But this was not to be. Apparently the SS troops were going to use us as their alibi to escape from the Russian advance. Berthed alongside Quay Six was a freighter, the last one out of the encircled enclave. As we watched, the loading began of some of the hundreds of German army wounded who were lying on stretchers in warehouses farther along the quay.

It was almost dark when Captain Roschmann arrived. He stopped short when he saw the wounded being put aboard. "Stop that!" he shouted to the stretcher-bearers. He strode across the quay and slapped one of them in the face, then rounded on us prisoners. "You scum," he roared. "Get up on that ship and get these men off. That ship is ours."

Prodded by the gun barrels of the SS, we were about to begin carrying the stretchers back ashore when another shout stopped us. An army captain was running down the quay.

"Who ordered these men to be off-loaded?"

Roschmann came up behind him. "I did. This boat is ours."

The captain spun around. "This ship was sent to pick up army wounded," he said. "And army wounded is what it will take." He shouted to the orderlies to resume the loading.

Roschmann was trembling—with anger, I thought. Then I saw he was scared. He began to scream, "Leave them alone! I have commandeered this ship in the name of the Reich." But the orderlies obeyed the Wehrmacht captain. I could see the captain's face, gray with exhaustion, as he made to march past Roschmann to supervise the loading.

From one of the stretchers a voice shouted, in Hamburg dialect, "Good for you, Captain. You tell the swine." Then the Wehrmacht captain was abreast of Roschmann. The SS officer grabbed his arm and slapped him across the face. I had seen Roschmann slap men a thousand times, but never with the same result. The captain shook his head, bunched his fist, and landed a haymaker of a right-fisted punch on Roschmann's jaw. Roschmann went flat on his back in the snow, a small trickle of blood coming from his mouth, and the captain moved on toward his orderlies.

As I watched, Roschmann drew his Luger and fired between the army captain's shoulders. Everything stopped at the crash from the pistol. The captain staggered and turned. Roschmann fired again, and the bullet caught the captain in the throat. He was dead before he hit the quay. I saw something fly off from around his neck as the bullet struck. I never knew the captain's name, but what he had worn was the Knight's Cross with oak-leaf cluster.

Miller read with astonishment turning to doubt, disbelief, a deep anger. He read this page a dozen times before he went on.

Roschmann, Tauber recorded, ordered the prisoners back to unload the Wehrmacht wounded. Then 4000 survivors of Riga were packed into the ship's two holds, so cramped they could hardly move. The hatches were battened down above them, the SS streamed aboard, and the ship sailed hastily before the Russian dawn patrol could spot and bomb it. It took three days to reach Danzig, well behind German lines. Three days in a pitching, tossing hell belowdecks, without food or water, during which a quarter of the prisoners died.

Riga fell to the Russians on October 14, while they were at sea. From Danzig the prisoners were taken by barge to the concentration camp of Stutthof. There thousands more died of malnutrition, but somehow Tauber stayed alive. Then, in January 1945, as the Russians closed in, the survivors of Stutthof were driven through winter snow on the notorious Death March toward Berlin. Tauber survived even this, and finally, at Magdeburg prison, west of Berlin, the SS ran for safety and abandoned the remaining prisoners to the bewildered old men of the Home Guard. Unable to feed the prisoners, and terrified of what the advancing Allies would say when they found them starving, the Home Guard permitted them to go scrounging for food in the surrounding countryside.

The last time I had seen Eduard Roschmann was on the Danzig quayside. But I was to see him once again. It was on April 3, 1945. I had been out that day, with three others, toward Gardelegen, and we had gathered a small sackful of potatoes. We were trudging back with our booty when a car came up behind us. Inside were four SS officers, evidently making their escape. Sitting beside the driver, pulling on the uniform jacket of an army corporal, was Eduard Roschmann.

He did not see me. But I saw him. There was no doubt about it. All four men were apparently changing their uniforms. As the car disappeared past us, a garment was thrown from a window. We reached the spot a few minutes later and stooped to examine it. It was the jacket of an SS officer, bearing the silver twin-lightning symbols of the Waffen SS and the rank of captain. Roschmann of the SS had disappeared.

Twenty-four days after this, there was a hammering on the

locked gates of the prison. The old guard went to open them. The man who stepped through, cautiously, with a revolver in his hand, was evidently an officer, in a uniform I had never seen before. He was accompanied by a soldier in a flat round tin hat who carried a rifle. They just stood there in silence, looking around the courtyard.

In one corner were stacked about fifty corpses, those who had died in the past two weeks and whom no one had the strength to bury. Others, half alive, lay around the walls trying to soak up a little of the spring sunshine, their sores festering and stinking.

The two men looked at each other, then at the seventy-year-old Home Guardsman. He looked back, embarrassed. Then he said, "Hello, Tommy."

The officer said quite clearly in English, "You Kraut pig."

And suddenly I began to cry.

The English put me in the hospital, but I left and hitchhiked home. When I saw everything in ruins, I finally, belatedly, collapsed completely.

The diary ended with two more clean white sheets of paper, evidently recently typed, which formed the epilogue.

I have lived in this little room in Altona since 1947. After I came out of the hospital I began to write the story of what happened to me and to the others at Riga. Looking back, it was all a waste of time and energy, the battle to survive and to be able to write down the evidence. Others have already done it so much better. I wish I had died in Riga with Esther.

I know I will never see Eduard Roschmann stand before a court, never give evidence to that court about what he did.

Once a woman came to see me. She said she was from the reparations office and that I was entitled to money, that it was my right to be recompensed for what was done. I said I did

41

not want money. They sent someone else to see me, and I refused again.

One of the British doctors asked me why I did not emigrate to Israel. How could I explain that I can never go up to the Holy Land, not after what I did to Esther, my wife? I think about it often, but I am not worthy to go.

But if ever these lines should be read in the land of Israel, will someone there please say *Kaddish* for me?

Salomon Tauber
Altona, Hamburg
November 21, 1963

———————

Peter Miller lay back in his chair for a long time, staring at the ceiling and smoking. Just before five in the morning Sigi came in from work. She was startled to find him awake.

"What are you doing up so late?" she asked.

"Been reading," said Miller.

Later they lay in bed as the first glint of dawn picked out the spire of St. Michaelis, Sigi drowsy, Miller staring up at the ceiling, silent and preoccupied.

"Penny for them," said Sigi after a while.

"Just thinking."

"I know. What about?"

"The next story I'm going to cover."

"What are you going to do?" she asked.

"I'm going to track a man down."

3

WHILE Peter Miller and Sigi slept in Hamburg, a giant Argentine Coronado airliner entered final approach for a landing at Barajas airport, Madrid. Sitting in a window seat in the third row of the first-class passenger section was a man in his early sixties with iron-gray hair and a trim mustache.

His passport identified him as Senor Ricardo Suertes, citizen of

Argentina, and the name was his own grim joke against the world. For *suerte* in Spanish means luck, and luck in German is *Glück*. The airline passenger had been born Richard Glücks, later to become a full general of the SS, head of the Reich Economic Administration Main Office and Hitler's inspector general of concentration camps. On the wanted lists of West Germany and Israel, he was number three, after Martin Bormann—Hitler's dreaded deputy— and the former chief of the Gestapo, Heinrich Müller. The role Glücks had played was unique. He had been a mastermind of the elimination of the Jews, and yet had never pulled a trigger.

Of the crimes against humanity committed on the German side between 1933 and 1945, probably ninety-five percent can be laid at the door of the SS. Of these nearly ninety percent can be attributed to two SS departments. These were the Reich Security Main Office (RSHA) and the Reich Economic Administration Main Office.

The economic bureau was involved because the intention was to exterminate every Jew on the face of Europe, and most of the Slavic races also, and to make them pay for the privilege. The Jews were first robbed of their businesses, houses, bank accounts, furniture, cars, and clothes. They were shipped to slave-labor camps and death camps with what they could carry, assured they were destined for resettlement. On the camp square their suitcases were taken from them, along with the clothes they wore.

Out of the luggage of six million people, millions of dollars' worth of booty was extracted, for the European Jews of the time habitually traveled with their wealth upon them. From the camps, entire trainloads of gold trinkets, jewels, silver ingots, gold dollars, and bank notes of every description were shipped back to the SS headquarters inside Germany. Throughout its history the SS made a profit on its operations. A part of this profit, in the form of gold bars, made up the fortune on which the Odessa was later based. Much of this gold still lies in vaults beneath the streets of Zurich.

The second stage of the exploitation lay in the living bodies of the victims. Those unfit for work were exterminated. Those able to work were hired out, either to the SS's own factories or to German industrial concerns such as Krupp, Thyssen, and von Opel, at three

43

marks a day for unskilled workers, four marks for artisans. As much work as possible was extracted from them for as little food as possible. Hundreds of thousands died in this manner.

The third stage of the exploitation lay in the corpses. The dead left behind wagonloads of shoes, socks, shaving brushes, spectacles, jackets, and trousers. They also left their hair, which was turned into felt boots for the winter fighting, and their gold teeth and fillings, which were later melted down to be deposited as gold bars in Zurich.

In charge of the entire economic, or profit-making, side of the extermination of fourteen million people was the man in seat 3-B on the airliner that night.

Glücks preferred not to risk his liberty by returning to Germany after his escape. He had no need to. Handsomely provided for out of the secret funds, he could live out his days comfortably in South America. His dedication to the Nazi ideal secured him a high and honored place among the fugitive Nazis in Argentina, from whence the Odessa was ruled.

From the airport Glücks took a cab to the Zurburán Hotel. He had showered and shaved and had ordered breakfast when, at nine o'clock on the dot, three soft knocks—a pause—and two more knocks sounded at his door. He opened and quickly closed it behind the new arrival.

"*Sieg Heil!*" The man flashed up his right arm in salute.

General Glücks raised his own right hand. "*Sieg Heil!*" He waved his visitor to a seat.

The man facing Glücks was the chief of the Odessa network inside West Germany. To the citizens of his city he was a brilliantly successful lawyer in private practice. His Odessa code name was Werewolf.

General Glücks finished a cup of coffee and lit a large Corona. "You have probably guessed the reason for this sudden visit," he said. "As I dislike remaining on this continent longer than necessary, I will get to the point. Kennedy is now dead, and there must be no failure to extract the utmost advantage from this event. Do you follow me?"

"Certainly, in principle, General. But specifically?"

"I refer to the secret arms deal between Bonn and Tel Aviv. You know about the weaponry flowing from Germany to Israel?"

"Yes, of course."

"And you know also that our organization is doing everything in its power to assist the Egyptian cause?"

"Certainly. We have organized the recruiting of numerous German scientists to that end."

General Glücks nodded. "Good. Now, Arab protests have led to the formation of a group in Germany strongly opposed to the arms deal. So far Erhard has not called off the shipments. What Kennedy wants, Erhard gives him. But Kennedy is now dead." The SS general jabbed the glowing tip of his cigar at his subordinate. "For the rest of this year, therefore, our main political action within Germany will be to whip up public opinion against this arms deal and in favor of Germany's true and traditional friends, the Arabs."

"Yes, yes, that can be done."

"Your job will be to coordinate press publicity through the pamphlets and magazines we secretly support, advertisements in major newspapers, lobbying of civil servants and politicians."

"To promote feeling against Israel today will be difficult."

"The angle," said Glücks tartly, "is simply that Germany must not alienate eighty million Arabs—a perfectly permissible practical viewpoint. Funds, of course, will be made available. Erhard must be subjected to constant pressure at every level. If we can cause policy in Bonn to change course, our stock in Cairo will rise sharply."

Werewolf nodded, seeing his plan of campaign taking shape before him. "It shall be done," he said.

"Excellent," replied General Glücks.

"General, we spoke of our scientists in Egypt—"

"Ah yes, the second prong in our plan to destroy the Jews once and for all. You know about the rockets of Helwân, of course. Do you know what they are really for?"

"Well, I assumed of course—"

"That they would be used to throw high explosive onto Israel?"

General Glücks smiled broadly. "You could not be more wrong. I think the time is ripe to tell you why the rockets and the scientists are so vitally important."

He leaned back and told his subordinate the real story behind the rockets of Helwân.

AFTER the war, when King Farouk still ruled Egypt, thousands of Nazis and former members of the SS had found a sure refuge along the sands of the Nile. Among these were a number of scientists. Even before the coup d'état that dislodged Farouk, two German professors, Paul Görke and Rolf Engel, were charged with studies for a rocket factory. The project went into abeyance when Naguib and then Nasser took power. After the defeat of Egypt in the 1956 Sinai campaign, the new dictator vowed that one day Israel would be totally destroyed. But it wasn't until 1961, when Nasser got Moscow's final "No" on heavy rockets, that the Görke–Engel project was revitalized—with a vengeance. Within the year, Factory 333 was built and opened at Helwân, south of Cairo.

To open a factory is one thing; to design and build rockets is another. Long since, the senior supporters of Nasser, mostly with pro-Nazi backgrounds, had been in touch with the Odessa. And from the Odessa came the answer to the Egyptians' problem. What Nasser needed, they pointed out, was something remarkably similar to the V-2s that Wernher von Braun and his team had built at Peenemünde to pulverize London. And many of the Peenemünde team were still available.

Late in 1961 the Odessa appointed a chief recruiting officer in Germany, and he in turn employed as his legman a former SS sergeant, Heinz Krug. With the salaries they could offer, they were not short of choice recruits. Many of the scientists who worked at the Institute for Aerospace Research in Stuttgart were frustrated because the Paris agreement of 1954 forbade Germany to indulge in research or manufacture in nuclear physics and rocketry. The prospect of research money and the chance to design real rockets was too tempting. Among the recruits who left for Egypt in early 1962 were Professor Wolfgang Pilz, Dr. Eugen Sänger and his wife,

Irene, Dr. Josef Eisig, and Dr. Kirmayer, all experts in aerodynamics, propulsion fuels, and the design of warheads.

General Glücks paused, drew on his cigar, and returned to the immediate problem. "The key of a guided missile, however, lies in the teleguidance system, and *that* we have been unable to furnish to the Egyptians. By ill luck we could not persuade a single expert in guidance systems to emigrate to Egypt.

"But we promised Egypt rockets, and have them she will. President Nasser is determined there will one day be another war between Egypt and Israel, and war there will be. Just think. If, when all the Soviet weaponry has failed, our scientists' rockets could win that war, we would then have achieved the double coup of ensuring a safe home for our own people in an eternally grateful Middle East and the final destruction of the Jew-pig state—thus fulfilling the last wish of the dying Führer. It is a mighty challenge, and we must not fail."

With awe and some puzzlement Werewolf watched his senior officer pacing the room. "Forgive me, General, but will four hundred medium warheads really finish off the Jews once and for all?"

Glücks gazed at the younger man with a triumphant smile. "But what warheads! You do not think we are going to waste mere high explosive on these swine! Some will contain concentrated cultures of bubonic plague. Others will explode high above the ground, showering Israel with irradiated cobalt sixty. Within hours they will all be dying of the plague or of gamma-ray sickness. *That* is what we have in store for them."

"It's brilliant," Werewolf breathed.

"Brilliant, yes. Provided we of the Odessa can equip those rockets with systems which direct them to the exact locations where they must explode. To this end we have started a factory in West Germany, run by a man whose code name is Vulcan. It manufactures transistor radios as a front. But in its research department a group of scientists is devising the teleguidance systems that will one day be fitted to the rockets of Helwân."

"Why don't they simply go to Egypt?" asked the other.

Glücks smiled again. "I told you that none of our guidance experts would emigrate. The men who now work in Vulcan's factory believe they're working on a contract for the Defense Ministry in Bonn."

"How on earth was that arranged?"

"Quite simply. The Paris agreement forbids Germany to do rocket research, so the men under Vulcan were sworn to secrecy by a genuine official of the Defense Ministry, who also happens to be one of us. They are all prepared to work for Germany, though not for Egypt. The cost of such research is stupendous. It has made enormous inroads into our secret funds. Now do you understand the importance of Vulcan?"

"Of course," replied the Odessa chief from Germany. "But if anything happened to him, could not the program go on?"

"No. Vulcan is chairman and managing director of the company, sole shareholder, and paymaster. No one else knows the true nature of the research. The men in the closed-off section are believed to be working on microwave circuits for the transistor market. The secrecy is explained as a precaution against industrial espionage. The only link between the factory and the research is Vulcan. If he went, the entire project would collapse."

"Can you tell me the name of the factory?"

General Glücks mentioned a name.

The other man stared at him in astonishment. "But I know those radios," he protested.

"Of course. It's a bona fide radio factory. Here, look."

General Glücks handed the man from Germany a photograph.

Werewolf stared at it, then turned it over and read the name on the back. "Good God, I thought he was in South America."

"On the contrary. He is Vulcan. At the present time his work has reached a most crucial stage. Now, your instructions. If you should get a whisper of anyone asking inconvenient questions about this man, that person is to be—discouraged. One warning. Then a permanent solution. Do you follow me, *Kamerad?* No one, repeat, no one is to get anywhere near exposing Vulcan."

The SS general rose. His visitor did likewise.

"That will be all," said Glücks. "You know what to do."

4

"But you don't even know if he's alive." Peter Miller and Karl Brandt were sitting in Miller's car outside the house of the detective inspector. Miller had found him at Sunday lunch.

"No. So that's the first thing I have to find out. If Roschmann's dead, obviously that's the end of it. Can you help me?"

Brandt slowly shook his head. "Sorry, I can't."

"Why not?"

"Look, why can't you just make a story out of the diary?"

"Because there's no story in it," said Miller. "What am I supposed to say? 'Surprise, surprise, I've found a loose-leaf folder in which an old man who just gassed himself describes what he went through during the war.' There have been hundreds of memoirs written since the war. No editor in Germany would buy it."

"So what are you going on about?" asked Brandt.

"Simply this. Get a major police hunt started for Roschmann on the basis of the diary, and I *have* got a story."

Brandt tapped his cigarette ash into the dashboard tray. "There won't be a major police hunt. Peter, you may know journalism, but I know the Hamburg police. Our job is to keep Hamburg crime-free now, in 1963. Nobody's going to detach overworked detectives to hunt a man for what he did in Riga twenty years ago."

"But you could at least raise the matter?" asked Miller.

"No. Not me. I don't intend to jeopardize my career."

"Why should this jeopardize your career? Roschmann's a criminal, isn't he? Police forces are supposed to hunt criminals."

Brandt crushed out his stub. "There's a sort of feeling in the police that to start probing into the war crimes of the SS can do a young policeman's career no good. Nothing comes of it anyway. The request would simply be denied. But the fact that it was made goes into a file. Then bang goes your chance of promotion. Nobody mentions it, but everyone knows it."

Miller sat and stared through the windshield. "All right. If that's the way it is," he said at length. "But I've got to start somewhere. Did Tauber leave anything else behind when he died?"

"Well, there was a brief note, in which he said he left his effects to a friend of his, a Herr Marx."

"Well, that's a start. Where's this Marx?"

"How the hell should I know?" said Brandt.

"Didn't you look for him?"

Brandt sighed. "Have you any idea how many Marxes there are in Hamburg? Anyway, what the old man left wasn't worth ten pfennigs."

"That's all, then?" asked Miller. "Nothing else?"

"Not a thing. If you want to find Marx, you're welcome to try."

"Thanks. I will," said Miller.

THE next morning Miller visited the house where Tauber had lived. The door was opened by a middle-aged man wearing a pair of stained trousers supported by string, and a collarless shirt.

"Morning. Are you the landlord?"

The man looked Miller up and down and nodded.

"A man gassed himself here a few nights back," said Miller.

"Are you from the police?"

"No. The press." Miller showed his press card.

"I ain't got nothing to say."

Miller waved a ten-mark note. "I only want to look at his room."

"I've rented it."

"What did you do with his stuff?"

"It's in the backyard. I'll show you."

The pile of junk was lying in a heap under the thin rain. There were a battered typewriter, a few clothes, some books, a fringed white silk scarf. He went through everything in the pile, but there was no address book.

"Do you have any tenant by the name of Marx?" Miller asked.

"Nope." The landlord regarded him sourly.

"Did you ever see Tauber with anybody? With a friend?"

"No. Not surprised, the way he kept mumbling to himself. Crazy."

For three days Miller quartered the area, asking up and down the streets, checking tradesmen, the milkman, and the postman.

Most people remembered seeing the old man shuffling along, head down, wrapped in an ankle-length overcoat. But none had seen him talk to anyone else.

It was Wednesday afternoon when he found the urchins playing football.

"What, that old Jew? Mad Solly?" said one of them in answer to Miller's question. "Yes, I seen him once with a man. Talking, they was. Sitting and talking."

"Where was that?"

"On the grass bank along the river. On one of the benches."

"How old was he, the other one?"

"Very old. Lot of white hair."

Miller wandered to the Elbe River and stared down the length of the grass bank. There were a dozen benches, all empty. In the summer they'd be full of people watching the ocean liners come in and out. Now, on his left, half a dozen North Sea trawlers were drawn up at the wharves, discharging their fresh-caught mackerel and herring. As a boy he had loved this fishing port. He liked the fishermen—gruff, kindly men. He thought of Roschmann, and wondered how the same country could produce them both.

His mind came back to Tauber. Where could he have met his friend Marx? It was not until he was back in his car and had stopped for gas that the answer came—as so often—from a chance remark. The pump attendant pointed out there had been a price increase, and added that money went less and less far these days. He left Miller staring at the open wallet in his hand.

Money. Where did Tauber get his money? He didn't work, he had refused reparations payments, yet he paid his rent and had not starved. A disability pension, perhaps.

Miller drove around to the Altona post office.

"Can you tell me when the pensioners collect their money?" he asked the lady behind the grille marked PENSIONS.

"Last day of the month, of course," she said.

Miller was back on Friday morning, watching the old men and women begin to filter through the doors of the post office. Just before eleven an old man with a shock of white hair like candy floss came out and looked around as if searching for someone. After a few minutes he turned and began to walk in the direction of the riverbank. Miller followed.

The old man settled himself on a bench. Miller approached slowly from behind. "Herr Marx?"

The old man turned. "Yes," he said gravely, "I am Marx."

"My name is Miller."

Marx inclined his head.

"Are you—er—waiting for Herr Tauber?"

"Yes, I am," said the old man.

"May I sit down?"

"Please."

Miller sat beside him. "I'm afraid Herr Tauber is dead."

"I see," the old man said simply.

Miller told him about the events of the previous Friday night. They sat in silence for several minutes, and then Miller said, "You don't seem surprised. That he killed himself."

"No," said Marx, "he was a very unhappy man."

"He left a diary, you know."

"Yes, he told me once about that."

"Were you in Riga, too?"

The man looked at him with sad old eyes. "I was in Dachau."

"Look, Herr Marx, I need your help. In his diary your friend mentioned a man, an SS officer, called Roschmann. Captain Eduard Roschmann. Did he ever mention him to you?"

"Oh, yes. That was really what kept him alive. Hoping one day to give evidence against Roschmann."

"That's what he said in his diary. I read it after his death. I'm a press reporter. I want to try and find Roschmann. Bring him to trial. Do you understand?"

"Yes."

"But there's no point if Roschmann is already dead. Can you remember if Herr Tauber ever learned whether Roschmann was still alive and free?"

"Captain Roschmann is alive," Marx said simply, "and free."

Miller leaned forward earnestly. "How do you know?"

"Because Tauber saw him last month."

"Last month?" repeated Miller. "Did he say how?"

Marx sighed. "Yes. He was walking late at night, as he used to do when he could not sleep. He was passing the State Opera House just as people came out. Wealthy people, men in dinner jackets, women in furs and jewels. One was Roschmann. He climbed into a taxi with two others and they drove off."

"Now listen, Herr Marx, this is very important. Was he absolutely sure it was Roschmann?"

"Yes, he said he was."

"He hadn't seen him for almost nineteen years. How could he be sure?"

"He said he smiled, and once you had seen Roschmann smile you never forgot it. He said he would recognize that smile among a million others, anywhere in the world."

THAT evening Peter Miller paid his usual Friday visit to his mother. She was a short, plump, matronly person who had never quite resigned herself to the idea that all her only son wanted to be was a reporter.

As she dried the dishes after dinner, he told her what he had been doing and mentioned his intention to track down Eduard Roschmann. She was aghast. "It's bad enough your covering the doings of those nasty criminals, without getting mixed up with those Nazi people. I don't know what your dear father would have thought—"

"Mother, during the war did you suspect what was going on? What the SS did to people?"

"Horrible things. Terrible. The British made us look at the films after the war. But it won't get better for talking about it. Your father—"

"Look, Mother, until I read that diary I never asked what it was that they did, that we were all supposed to have done. Now I'm beginning to understand. And it wasn't my father who did it, or you, or me. That's why I want to find this man, this monster. It's right that he should be brought to trial."

She was close to tears. "Please, Peterkin, leave them alone."

Peter Miller turned to face the mantelpiece, dominated by a photograph of his dead father in his captain's uniform. He stared out of the frame with a kind, rather sad smile. Peter remembered when he was five years old, and his father had taken him to Hagenbeck's Zoo. And he remembered how his father came home after enlisting in 1940, how his mother had cried, and how he had thought that women were stupid to cry over such a wonderful thing as a father in uniform; and the day in 1944—he was eleven then—when an army officer had come to tell his mother that her war-hero husband had been killed.

The black-edged column of names in the newspaper was different that day in late October, for halfway down was the entry: "Fallen for Führer and Fatherland. Miller, Erwin, Captain, on October 11. In Ostland."

"I mean," said his mother behind him, "do you think your father would want his son digging into the past, trying to drag up another war-crimes trial? Do you think that's what he'd want?"

Miller spun around and kissed her lightly on the forehead.

"Yes, Mutti. I think that's exactly what he'd want."

He let himself out, climbed into his car, and headed back into Hamburg, his anger seething inside him.

HANS HOFFMANN was one of West Germany's wealthiest and most successful magazine publishers. His formula was simple—tell it in words and make it shocking, then back it up with pictures that make those of his competitors look as if they'd been taken by novices with their first box Brownies. It worked. His chain of eight magazines had made him a multimillionaire. But *Komet*, the news and current-affairs magazine, was still his favorite, his baby.

That Wednesday afternoon Hoffmann closed the diary of Salomon Tauber after reading the beginning, leaned back, and looked at the young reporter. "I can guess the rest. What do you want?"

"There's a man mentioned in there called Eduard Roschmann," said Miller. "SS captain. Commandant of Riga ghetto. Killed eighty thousand men, women, and children. I want to find him."

"How do you know he's alive?"

Miller told him briefly.

Hoffmann pursed his lips. "Pretty thin evidence."

"True. But I've brought home stories that started on less."

Hoffmann grinned, recalling Miller's talent for ferreting out stories that hurt the Establishment. "If the police can't find this man Roschmann, what makes you think you can?"

"Are the police really looking?" asked Miller.

Hoffmann shrugged. "So what do you want from me?"

"A commission to give it a try. If nothing comes of it, I drop it."

Hoffmann put his elbows on the desk and rested his chin on his knuckles. "Miller, you're a good reporter. I like the way you cover a story; you've got style. That's why you get a lot of work from me. But you don't get this one."

"But why? It's a good story."

"Listen, you think this is a story everyone will want to read. *No one* will want to, and I'll tell you why. Before the war just about everyone in Germany knew at least one Jew. The fact is, before Hitler, we didn't hate Jews. We had the best record of treatment of our Jewish minority of any country in Europe. Better than France or Spain, infinitely better than Poland and Russia.

"Then Hitler started. Telling people the Jews were to blame for the first war, unemployment, everything else that was wrong. People didn't know what to believe. So when the vans took the Jews away, they kept quiet. They got to believing the voice that shouted the loudest. Because that's the way people are, particularly Germans. We're a very obedient people.

"For years people haven't asked what happened to the Jews. They just disappeared. Now you want to bring it all up again, what happened to their next-door neighbors. These Jews"—he tapped the diary—"were people they knew, and they stood and watched them taken away for your Captain Roschmann to deal with. You couldn't have picked a story they'd want to read less."

Miller sat and digested this. "There's another reason you want me to drop it, isn't there? Not just the public reaction."

Hoffmann eyed him keenly. "Yes," he said.

"Are you afraid of them—still?" asked Miller.

Hoffmann shook his head. "No. I just don't go looking for trouble. That's all."

"What kind of trouble?"

"Have you ever heard of a man called Hans Habe?"

"The novelist? Yes, what about him?"

"He used to run a magazine in the early 1950s. A good one too— *Echo of the Week* it was called. He ran a series of exposés of former SS men living in freedom in Munich."

"What happened to him?"

"One day he got more mail than usual. Half the letters were from his advertisers, withdrawing their custom. Another was from his bank, saying it was foreclosing on his overdraft, as of that minute. Within a week the magazine was out of business."

"So what do the rest of us do? Keep running scared?"

"I don't have to take that from you, Miller." Hoffmann's eyes snapped. "I hated the bastards then. I do now. But I know my readers. They don't want to know about Eduard Roschmann."

"All right. I'm sorry. But I'm still going to cover it."

"If I didn't know you, Miller, I'd think there was something personal in this. Anyway, how are you going to finance yourself?"

"I've got some savings." Miller rose to go.

"Best of luck," said Hoffmann, rising. "I tell you what I'll do. The day Roschmann is arrested, I'll commission you to cover the story. But while you're digging for him, you're not carrying the letterhead of my magazine around as your authority."

Miller nodded. "I'll be back," he said.

5

WEDNESDAY morning, December 4, the heads of the five branches of the Israeli Intelligence apparatus, the Mossad, met for their regular informal weekly discussion.

On his way to this meeting the controller of the Mossad, General Meir Amit, was a deeply worried man. The cause of his worry was a piece of information that had reached him in the small hours. A fragment of knowledge to be added to the immense file on the rockets of Helwân. The general leaned back in his limousine and considered the history of those rockets.

THE Israeli Mossad had learned of the existence of the rockets in 1961. From the moment the first dispatch came through from Egypt, they had kept Factory 333 under surveillance. They were well aware of the influx of German scientists. It was a serious matter then; it became infinitely more serious in the spring of 1962.

In May of that year Heinz Krug, the German recruiter of the scientists, first approached the Austrian physicist Dr. Otto Yoklek in Vienna. Instead of allowing himself to be recruited, the Austrian made contact with the Israelis. He told the Mossad that the Egyptians intended to arm their rockets with warheads containing irradiated nuclear waste and cultures of bubonic plague.

So important was the news that the then chief of the Mossad, General Issar Harel, flew to Vienna to talk to Yoklek himself. He was convinced the professor was right, a conviction corroborated by the news that the Cairo government had just purchased a quantity of radioactive cobalt equal to twenty-five times Egypt's possible requirement for medical purposes.

On his return Issar Harel urged Premier David Ben-Gurion to allow him to begin a campaign of reprisals against the German scientists who were either working in Egypt or about to go there. The old premier was in a quandary. On the one hand he realized the hideous danger the new rockets presented; on the other hand the army wanted the German tanks and guns, due to arrive in Israel at any moment. Israeli reprisals on the streets of Germany might just persuade Adenauer to shut off the arms deal. Ben-Gurion compromised. He authorized Harel to undertake a discreet campaign to discourage German scientists from going to Cairo.

But Harel went beyond his brief. On September 11, 1962, recruiter Heinz Krug disappeared. His wife claimed he had been kidnapped by Israeli agents, but the Munich police found no evidence of this. In fact, a group led by a shadowy figure called Leon had abducted him and dumped his body in a lake.

The campaign then turned against the Germans already in Egypt. On November 27 a registered package addressed to Professor Wolfgang Pilz arrived in Cairo. It was opened by his secretary, and in the ensuing explosion the girl was maimed and blinded for life. On November 28 another package arrived at Factory 333. Five dead and ten wounded in the mail room. The next day a third package was defused without an explosion.

By February 1963 the reprisal campaign was making headlines in Germany. In March, Heidi Görke, daughter of Professor Paul Görke, pioneer of Nasser's rockets, received a telephone call at her home in Freiburg, Germany. A voice suggested she meet the caller at a hotel in Basel, just over the Swiss border.

Heidi informed the German police, who tipped off the Swiss. They planted a bugging device in the room reserved for the meeting and heard two men warn Heidi and her brother to persuade their father to get out of Egypt if he valued his life. The two men were arrested in Zurich the same night. One agent was Yosef Ben-Gal, Israeli citizen. It was an international scandal. The men were tried in Basel in June. The trial went well. Professor Yoklek testified as to the warheads and the Egyptian intent to commit genocide. Shocked, the judges acquitted the two accused.

But back in Israel there was a reckoning. In a rage, Ben-Gurion rebuked General Harel for the lengths to which he had gone. Harel, who had become a legend in his own lifetime and relished it, handed in his resignation. To his surprise, Ben-Gurion accepted it. At the end of June, General Meir Amit became chief of Intelligence. His instructions remained the same. With no alternative, he resumed the terror campaign against the scientists already inside Egypt.

Guarded by Egyptian troops, these Germans lived in the suburb of Maadi, seven miles south of Cairo. To get at them Meir Amit used his top agent, the riding-school owner, Wolfgang Lutz, who in September 1963 began taking the suicidal risks that would lead to his eventual undoing.

The German scientists, badly shaken, began to get death threats mailed from Cairo. On September 27 a letter blew up in the face of

Dr. Kirmayer. For Dr. Pilz this was the last straw. He left Cairo for Germany. Others followed, and the furious Egyptians were unable to stop them.

THE man in the limousine that December morning knew, of course, that his agent—the supposed Nazi, Lutz—was the sender of the explosives. But he also knew that the genocide program was not being halted. General Amit flicked his eye over the decoded message he had received. It confirmed simply that a virulent strain of bubonic bacillus had been isolated in the contagious-diseases laboratory of Cairo Medical Institute, and that the budget of the department involved had been increased tenfold.

HAD Hans Hoffmann been watching he would have been forced to give Miller full marks for cheek. After leaving the office, Miller took the elevator to the fifth floor and dropped in to see Max Dorn, the magazine's legal-affairs correspondent.

"I've just been to see Herr Hoffmann," he said. "Now I need some background. Mind if I pick your brains?"

"Go ahead," said Dorn, assuming Miller was on a *Komet* story.

"Who investigates war crimes in Germany?"

"Well, basically it's the various attorney generals' offices of the states of West Germany."

"You mean, they *all* do it?"

Dorn leaned back in his chair. "There are ten states in West Germany. In each state attorney general's office there is a department responsible for investigation into what are called 'crimes of violence committed during the Nazi era.' Each state capital is allocated a certain area as its special responsibility. Munich, for instance, is responsible for Dachau, Buchenwald, Belzec, and Flossenburg. Most crimes in the Soviet Ukraine and the Łódź area of former Poland come under Hanover. And so on."

"Who do the Baltic States come under?" Miller asked.

"Hamburg," said Dorn promptly.

"You mean if there had ever been a trial of anyone for crimes in Riga, it would have been here?"

"Yes. Though the arrest could have been made anywhere."

"Has there ever been a trial in Hamburg of anyone guilty of crimes committed in Riga?" Miller asked.

"Not that I remember," said Dorn.

"Would it be in the clippings library?"

"Sure. If it happened since 1950, when we started the clippings."

"Mind if we look?" asked Miller.

"No problem."

The library was in the basement, tended by five archivists in gray smocks. It was almost half an acre of gray steel shelves and filing cabinets.

"What do you want?" Dorn asked Miller as the chief librarian approached.

"Roschmann, Eduard," said Miller.

"Personal index section," said the librarian. He opened a cabinet and flicked through it. "Nothing on Roschmann, Eduard."

"Do you have anything on war crimes?" Miller asked.

"Yes," said the librarian. "This way." They went along a hundred yards of cabinets.

"Look under Riga," said Miller.

The librarian mounted a stepladder and foraged. He came back with a red folder labeled RIGA—WAR-CRIMES TRIAL. Miller opened it. Two pieces of newsprint fluttered out. Miller picked them up. Both were from the summer of 1950. One recorded that three SS privates had gone on trial for brutalities committed at Riga between 1941 and 1944. The other recorded that all three had been sentenced to long terms of imprisonment.

"Is that it?" asked Miller.

"That's it," said the librarian.

It was nearly a week before Miller could get an appointment in the Hamburg attorney general's office.

The man he confronted was nervous, ill at ease. "You must understand I have only agreed to see you as a result of your persistent inquiries," he began.

"That's nice of you all the same," said Miller. "I want to inquire about a man whom I assume your department must have under permanent investigation—Eduard Roschmann."

"Roschmann?" said the lawyer.

"SS Captain Roschmann. Commandant of Riga ghetto from 1941 to 1944. I want to know if he's alive, if he has ever been arrested, and if he has ever been on trial."

The lawyer was shaken. "Good Lord, I can't tell you that."

"Why not? It's a matter of public interest."

"I hardly think so," the lawyer said. "Otherwise we would be receiving constant inquiries of this nature. Actually, so far as I can recall, yours is the first inquiry we've ever had from . . . a member of the public."

"Actually, I'm a member of the press," said Miller.

"That may be. But I'm afraid we are not empowered to give information regarding the progress of our inquiries."

"Well, that's not right, to start with," said Miller.

"Oh, come now, Herr Miller, you would hardly expect the police to give you such information about *their* criminal cases."

"I would. In fact, I do. The police are customarily very helpful in issuing bulletins on whether an early arrest may be expected. Certainly they'd tell a journalist if their main suspect was, to their knowledge, alive or dead."

The lawyer smiled thinly. "All I can say is that all matters concerning the area of responsibility of my department are under constant inquiry. *Constant*, I repeat. And now I really think, Herr Miller, there is nothing more I can do to help you."

IT TOOK Miller a week to get ready for his next move. He spent it reading books concerned with the war along the eastern front and the camps in the occupied eastern territories. It was the librarian at his local library who mentioned the Z Commission.

"It's in Ludwigsburg," he told Miller. "I read about it in a magazine. The Z Commission—Z for *Zentral*—is the only organization in the country that hunts Nazis on a nationwide, even an international level."

"Thanks," said Miller. "I'll see if they can help me."

Miller went to his bank the next morning and drew out all he had, leaving ten marks to keep the account open.

He kissed Sigi, telling her he would be gone for a week, maybe more. Then he took the Jaguar from its underground home and headed south toward the Rhineland. The first snows had started, whistling in off the North Sea, slicing in flurries across the autobahn as it swept south of Bremen and into the flat plain of Lower Saxony. He paused once for coffee, then pressed on across North Rhine–Westphalia. He stuck to the fast lane as always, pushing the Jag close to a hundred miles an hour.

By six in the evening he was beyond the Hamm Junction, and the glowing lights of the Ruhr began to be dimly discernible to his right through the darkness. When the autobahn was on an overpass he could look down and see factories and chimneys stretching away into the December night, lights aglow from a thousand furnaces churning out the wealth of the economic miracle. Fourteen years ago, as he had traveled through it by train toward his school holiday in Paris, it had been rubble.

LUDWIGSBURG is a little market town in the rolling pleasant hills of Württemberg, eight miles north of Stuttgart. Set in a quiet road off the High Street is the home of the Z Commission, an underpaid, overworked group of men dedicated to hunting down the Nazis and the SS who were guilty of mass murder. Even though the statute of limitations had eliminated all SS crimes with the exception of murder and mass murder, the Z Commission still had 170,000 names in its files.

There were eighty detectives and fifty investigating attorneys on the staff. The lawyers were mainly taken from private practice, to which they would one day return. The detectives worked solely because they were dedicated to the task. They knew their careers were finished. For detectives prepared to hunt the SS in West Germany, there would be no promotion in any other police force in the country.

Quite accustomed to having their requests for cooperation ignored, to seeing their loaned files unaccountably become missing, or their quarry disappear after an anonymous tip-off, the Z men worked on at a task they realized was not in accordance with the wishes of the majority of their fellow countrymen.

Miller found the commission at 58 Schorndorferstrasse, a large house inside an eight-foot-high wall. Two massive steel gates barred the way to the drive. When he pulled the bell handle a shutter slid back and a face appeared. "Please?"

"I would like to speak to one of your investigating attorneys," said Miller.

"Which one?" said the face.

"Anyone will do. Here is my press card."

The man shut the hatch and went away. When he came back, it was to open the gate, lead Miller to the front door, and pass him over to another porter, who showed him into a small waiting room. "Someone will be with you directly," he said, and shut the door.

The man who came three minutes later was in his early fifties, mild-mannered and courteous. He handed Miller back his press card and asked, "What can I do for you?"

Miller explained briefly about Tauber and Eduard Roschmann.

"Fascinating," the lawyer said.

"The point is, can you help me?"

"I wish I could," said the man, and for the first time since he had started asking questions about Roschmann in Hamburg, Miller believed he had met an official who genuinely would like to help him. "But the point is I am bound hand and foot by the rules that govern our continued existence here. Which are that no information may be given out about any wanted SS criminal to anyone other than a person officially representing one of a specific number of authorities."

"In other words, you can tell me nothing?" said Miller.

"Please understand," said the lawyer, "this office is under constant attack. Not openly—no one would dare. But privately, within the corridors of power, we are incessantly being sniped at. We are allowed no latitude where the rules are concerned."

"Have you, then, a newspaper-clippings reference library?"

"No, we don't."

"Is there in Germany any such file open to the public?"

"Only those compiled by newspapers and magazines. *Der Spiegel* is reputed to have the most comprehensive. And *Komet* has a very good one."

"I find this rather odd," said Miller. "Where in Germany today does a citizen inquire about investigation into war crimes and get material on wanted SS criminals?"

"I'm afraid a citizen can't," the lawyer said uncomfortably.

"All right," said Miller. "Where are the archives in Germany that refer to the men of the SS?"

"There's one set here, in the basement," said the lawyer. "All photostats. The originals of the entire card index of the SS were captured in 1945 by an American unit. At the last minute a group of the SS tried to burn their records. They got through about ten percent before the American soldiers stopped them. The rest were all mixed up. It took the Americans two years to sort them out. Since then the entire SS index has remained in Berlin; even we have to apply to the Americans if we want something more. Mind you, they're very good about it; no complaints at all about cooperation from that quarter."

"And that's it? Just two sets in the whole country?"

"That's it. I repeat, I wish I could help. If you should get anything on Roschmann, we'd be delighted to have it."

Miller said, "If I find anything, there are only two authorities that can do anything with it. The attorney general's office in Hamburg, and you. Right?"

"Yes, that's all," said the lawyer.

"And you're more likely to do something positive with it than Hamburg." Miller made it a flat statement.

The lawyer gazed fixedly at the ceiling. "Nothing that comes here that is of real value gathers dust on a shelf."

"Okay. Point taken," said Miller, and rose. "One thing, between ourselves, are you still looking for Eduard Roschmann?"

"Between ourselves, yes."

"And if he were caught, there'd be no problems about getting a conviction?"

"None at all. He'd get hard labor for life."

"Give me your phone number," said Miller.

The lawyer took out a card and wrote on it. "My name and two phone numbers. Home and office. You can get me day or night. In every state police force there are men I can call and know I'll get action. There are others to avoid. So call me first, right?"

Miller pocketed the card. "I'll remember that."

"Good luck," said the lawyer.

IT's A long drive from Stuttgart to Berlin, and it took Miller most of the following day. Fortunately it was dry and crisp, and the Jaguar ate the miles northward past the sprawling carpet of Frankfurt to Hanover. Here Miller followed the branch-off to the border with East Germany. There was an hour's delay at the Marienborn checkpoint while he filled out the inevitable forms, and while the customs men and the green-coated People's Police poked around, in and under the Jaguar. There was a further delay at the entry into West Berlin, where again the car was searched, and his overnight case emptied onto the customs bench. Eventually he was through, and the Jaguar roared toward the glittering ribbon of the Kurfürstendamm, brilliant with Christmas decorations. It was the evening of December 17.

He decided not to go blundering into the American document center the same way he had into the attorney general's office in Hamburg and the Z Commission in Ludwigsburg. Without official backing, he had come to realize, no one got anywhere with Nazi files in Germany.

So in the morning he called Karl Brandt in Hamburg.

Brandt was aghast. "I don't know anyone in Berlin."

"Well, think. You must have come across someone from the West Berlin force at one of the colleges you went to."

"I told you I didn't want to get involved."

"You *are* involved. Either I get a look at that archive officially, or I breeze in and say you sent me."

"I'll have to think," said Brandt, stalling for time.

"I'll give you an hour," said Miller, and slammed down the receiver. When he called back, Brandt was angry, frightened, and clearly wishing he had kept that diary to himself.

"There's a man I was at detective college with. I didn't know him well, but he's with Bureau One of the West Berlin force."

"What's his name?"

"Schiller. Volkmar Schiller, detective inspector."

To Miller's great relief, Detective Inspector Volkmar Schiller was about his own age and seemed to have his own cavalier attitude to red tape. Miller explained briefly what he wanted.

"I don't see why not," said Schiller. "The Americans are pretty helpful to us. Because we're charged with investigating Nazi crimes, we're in there almost every day."

They took Miller's Jaguar and drove out to 1 Wasserkäferstieg, in the suburb of Zehlendorf, Berlin 37. The building was a long, low, single-story affair set amid the trees.

"Is that it?" said Miller incredulously.

"That's it," said Schiller. "Not much, is it? The point is, there are eight floors below ground level. That's where the archives are stored, in fireproof vaults."

Inside the front door was the inevitable porter's lodge. The detective proffered his police card. He was handed a form, which he filled out, and they were led into a larger room, set out with rows of tables and chairs. After a quarter of an hour a clerk quietly brought them a file. It was about an inch thick, stamped with the single title: ROSCHMANN, EDUARD.

Volkmar Schiller rose. "If you don't mind, I'll be on my way," he said. "If you want anything photostated, ask the clerk."

Miller rose and shook hands. "Many thanks."

"Not at all."

Ignoring the other three or four readers hunched over their desks, Miller put his head between his hands and started to peruse the SS dossier on Eduard Roschmann.

It was all there. Nazi party number, SS number, application forms filled out and signed by the man himself, medical record, self-written life story, officer's commission, promotion certificates, right up to April 1945. There were also two photographs, one full face, one profile. They showed a man with hair close shorn, a pointed nose, a lipless slit of a mouth, and a grim expression. Miller began to read. . . .

Eduard Roschmann was born on August 25, 1908, in the Austrian town of Graz, son of a highly respectable brewery worker. He attended college to try to become a lawyer, but failed. In 1931, at the age of twenty-three, he began work in the brewery where his father had a job, and in 1937 rose to the administrative department. That year he joined the underground Austrian Nazi party and the SS, both then banned organizations in neutral Austria. A year later Hitler annexed Austria and rewarded the Nazis with swift promotions all around.

In 1939, at the outbreak of war, he volunteered for the Waffen SS; he was trained in Germany and served in a Waffen SS unit in the overrunning of France. In December 1940 he was transferred to Berlin—here somebody had written in the margin, "Cowardice?" —and in January 1941 was assigned to the SD, the Security Service of the RSHA. In August 1941 he became commandant of the Riga ghetto. He returned to Germany by ship in October 1944 and, after handing over what was left of the Jews of Riga to the SD of Danzig, reported to Berlin headquarters.

The file ended there, presumably because the SS clerk in Berlin reassigned himself rather quickly in May 1945.

Attached to the back of the bunch of documents was a sheet bearing the typewritten words: "Inquiry made about this file by the British Occupation authorities in December 1947."

Miller took from the file the self-written life story, the two photographs, and the last sheet. With these he approached the clerk. "Could I have these photocopied, please?"

"Certainly." Another man who had been reading in the room also tendered two sheets for copying.

Ten minutes later there was a rustle behind the clerk, and two envelopes slid through an aperture. The clerk glanced quickly inside one of the envelopes. "The file on Eduard Roschmann?" he queried.

"For me," said Miller, and extended his hand.

"These must be for you," the clerk said to the other man, who was glancing sideways at Miller.

The man took his envelope and they walked to the door. Outside, Miller ran down the steps and climbed into the Jaguar.

An hour later he rang Sigi. "I'm coming home for Christmas," he told her.

Two hours later he was on his way. As his car headed for Hamburg, the other man sat in his tidy flat off Savignyplatz, dialing a number in West Germany. He introduced himself briefly to the man who answered.

"I was in the document center today. There was a man in there reading the file of Eduard Roschmann. He had some pages photocopied. After the message that went around recently, I thought I'd better tell you."

There was a burst of questions from the other end.

"No, I couldn't get his name. He drove away in a long black sports car. Yes, it was a Hamburg license plate."

He recited the number slowly for the man at the other end.

"Well, I thought I'd better. I mean, one never knows with these snoopers. Yes, thank you. Merry Christmas, *Kamerad*."

6

CHRISTMAS DAY was on the Wednesday of that week, and it was not until after the Christmas period that the man who had received the news about Miller passed it on. When he did, it was to his ultimate superior.

The man who took the call, on a strictly private wire, thanked his informant, put down the phone, leaned back in his leather-padded chair, and gazed out the window at the snow-covered rooftops.

"Damn and damn and damn," he whispered. "Why now?"

He thought back to his meeting with SS General Glücks in Madrid almost five weeks earlier, and to the general's warning about the importance of maintaining at any cost the security of the radio-factory owner who, under the code name Vulcan, was now at the crucial point in preparation of guidance systems for the Egyptian rockets. Alone in Germany Werewolf knew that Vulcan was Eduard Roschmann.

He glanced down at the jotting pad on which he had scribbled the number of Miller's license, and pressed a buzzer on his desk. His secretary's voice came through from the next room.

"Hilda, what was the name of that private investigator we employed last month on the divorce case?"

"One moment . . . It was Memmers, Heinz Memmers."

"Give me his telephone number, will you? . . . No, don't ring him. Just give me the number."

He noted it down, then rose and crossed the room to a wall safe. From the safe he took a thick book and flicked through the pages until he came to Memmers. There were only two listed, Heinrich and Walter. He ran his finger along the page opposite Heinrich, usually shortened to Heinz. He noted the date of birth, worked out the age of the man in late 1963, and recalled the face of the private investigator. The ages fitted. He jotted down two other numbers listed for Heinz Memmers and picked up the telephone.

After a dozen rings a gruff voice said, "Memmers Private Inquiries."

"Is that Herr Heinz Memmers?"

"Yes, who is speaking?"

"Tell me, does the number 245,718 mean anything to you?"

There was dead silence, broken only by a heavy sigh as Memmers digested the fact that his SS number had just been quoted to him. His voice came back, harsh with suspicion. "Should it?"

"Would it mean anything to you if I said that my own number had only five figures in it—*Kamerad?*"

The change was electric. Five figures meant a very senior officer indeed. "Yes, sir," said Memmers.

"Good," said Werewolf. "Now, some snooper has been inquiring into one of the *Kameraden.* I need to find out who he is. I have his license number." Werewolf read it slowly. "Got that?"

"Yes, *Kamerad.*"

"I want to know the name, address, profession, family, social standing—the normal rundown. How long would that take you?"

"About forty-eight hours," said Memmers.

"There is to be no approach made to the subject. He must not know inquiry has been made. Is that clear?"

"Certainly. It's no problem."

"Very well, then. I'll ring you back on Monday."

MILLER set off from Hamburg the same afternoon. This time his destination was Bonn, the small town on the river's edge that Konrad Adenauer had chosen as the capital of the Federal Republic. Just south of Bremen his Jaguar crossed Memmers' Opel speeding north to Hamburg. Oblivious of each other, the two men flashed past on their separate missions.

It was dark when Miller entered the single long main street of Bonn and drew up beside a traffic policeman.

"How can I get to the British embassy?" he asked.

The policeman pointed straight down the road. "Follow the tramlines. As you are about to leave Bonn and enter Bad Godesberg, you'll see it on your left."

Miller nodded his thanks and drove on. Outside the embassy, he parked in one of the slots provided for visitors.

He walked through the glass doors and found himself in a small foyer. "I would like to speak with the press attaché, please," he said in his halting English, and proffered his press card.

"I don't know if he's still here. I'll try him." The receptionist dialed a number on the house telephone. Miller was in luck.

The press attaché, he was glad to see, was in his mid-thirties and seemed eager to help. "What can I do for you?"

"I am investigating a story for a newsmagazine," Miller lied. "It's about a former SS captain, one of the worst, a man still sought by our own authorities. Can you tell me how I can check whether the British ever captured him, and if so, what happened to him?"

The young diplomat was perplexed. "Good Lord, I'm sure I don't know. I mean, we handed over our records and files to your government in 1949."

Miller decided to avoid mentioning that the German authorities had all declined to help. "True," he said. "But my inquiries for the period after 1949 indicate he has not been put on trial in the Federal Republic. However, the American document center in West Berlin reveals that a copy of the man's file was requested by the British in 1947. There must have been a reason for that, surely?"

"Yes, one would indeed suppose so," said the attaché. He furrowed his brow in thought.

"So who would the British investigating authority have been?" asked Miller.

"Well, the investigations were carried out by the provost marshal, and the trials were prepared by the legal branch. But the files of both were handed over in 1949."

"Surely copies must have been kept by the British?"

"I suppose they were," said the attaché. "But they'd be filed away in the archives of the army by now."

"Would it be possible to look at them?"

The attaché appeared shocked. "Oh, I very much doubt it. I suppose bona fide research scholars . . . but I don't think a reporter would be allowed to see them—no offense meant, you understand?"

"I understand," said Miller. He rose, and so did the attaché.

"I don't really think the embassy can help you."

"Okay. One last thing. Was there anybody here then who is still here now?"

"Oh, no, they've all changed many times. Wait a minute, though, there's Anthony Cadbury. The sort of senior British press chap. Married a German girl. I think he was here just after the war. You might ask him."

"Fine," said Miller. "Where do I find him?"

"Well, it's Friday. Probably at his favorite place by the bar in the Cercle Français, in Bad Godesberg, just down the road."

MILLER found it, a hundred yards from the bank of the Rhine. Cadbury was not there, but the barman told Miller that if he did not come in that evening, he would almost certainly be there for prelunch drinks the following day.

Miller checked into the Dreesen Hotel nearby; then he dined

at the Cercle Français, hoping the Englishman would turn up. At eleven he went back to the hotel to sleep.

Cadbury walked into the bar of the Cercle Français a few minutes before twelve the following morning, greeted a few acquaintances, and seated himself at his favorite corner stool. After he had ordered a drink, Miller rose and went over to him.

"Mr. Cadbury?"

Bright blue eyes under shaggy gray eyebrows surveyed Miller warily. "Yes."

"My name is Miller. Peter Miller. I am a reporter from Hamburg. May I talk with you a moment, please?"

Anthony Cadbury gestured to the stool beside him. "I think we had better talk in German, don't you?" he said, dropping into the language. "What can I do for you?"

Starting at the beginning, Miller told the story from the moment of Tauber's death. The London man did not interrupt once. When Miller had finished, Cadbury gestured to the barman to fill his own glass and bring another beer for Miller.

"Cheers," said Cadbury. "Well, now, you've got quite a problem. I must say I admire your nerve."

"Nerve?" said Miller.

"It's not quite the most popular story to investigate among your countrymen, in their present state of mind," said Cadbury, "as you will doubtless find out in the course of time."

"I already have," said Miller.

"I thought so," said the Englishman, and grinned suddenly. "A spot of lunch? My wife's away for the day."

Over lunch Miller asked about Cadbury's years in Germany.

"I came in as a war correspondent with Montgomery's army. About your age then. The headquarters was at Lüneburg. From then on, I just sort of stayed. Covered the end of the war, all that, then the paper asked me to remain."

"Did you cover the zonal war-crimes trials?" asked Miller.

Cadbury nodded while he chewed his steak. "The ones held in the British Zone. The star criminals in our zone were Josef Kramer and Irma Grese. Heard of them?"

"No, never."

"Well, they were called the Beast and Beastess of Belsen. Did you hear about Belsen?"

"My generation wasn't told much about all that," Miller said.

Cadbury shot him a glance. "But you want to know now?"

"We have to know sooner or later. May I ask you something? Do you hate the Germans?"

Cadbury considered the question for a minute. "Just after the discovery of Belsen, a crowd of journalists went up for a look. I've never been so sickened in my life. In war you see terrible things. But nothing like Belsen. At that moment, yes, I hated them all."

"And now?"

"No. Not any longer. I married a German girl in 1948, and I live here. I wouldn't if I still felt the way I did in 1945."

"What caused the change?"

"Time. The passage of time. And the realization that not all Germans were Josef Kramers. Or Roschmanns. Mind you, I still can't get over a sneaking sense of mistrust for German people of my generation."

"And my generation?"

"You're better," said Cadbury. "Let's face it, you have to be better."

"Will you help me on Roschmann? Nobody else will."

"If I can," said Cadbury. "What do you want to know?"

"Do you recall him being put on trial in the British Zone?"

"No. I'm certain there was no trial of Roschmann in the British Zone of Germany. I'd remember the name."

"But why would the British authorities have requested a photocopy of his career from the Americans in Berlin?"

"I don't know how he would have come to the attention of the British. At that time nobody knew about Riga. We got no information from the east. Yet that was where the overwhelming majority of the mass murders took place. We were in an odd position. Eighty percent of the crimes against humanity were committed east of what is now the Iron Curtain, but about ninety percent of the men responsible were in the three Western zones. Hundreds of guilty men slipped through our hands because we didn't know what they had done a thousand miles to the east."

"As for Roschmann," said Miller, "where would one start to look, among the British records?"

"Well, we can start with my own files. They're back at my house. Come on, it's a short walk."

Cadbury's study was lined with file boxes along two walls. Besides these, there were two gray filing cabinets in one corner.

He gestured to the cabinets. "This one is stuffed with files on people, in alphabetical order. The other concerns topics, listed under subject headings. We'll start with the first one."

There was no folder with Roschmann's name on it.

"All right," said Cadbury. "Now for subject headings. There's one for Nazis, another for SS. A large section, headed JUSTICE, has subsections about trials. Then there's the war-crimes one. Let's start."

It took them until nightfall to wade through those four files. Eventually Cadbury rose with a sigh.

"I'm afraid I have to go out to dinner tonight," he said. "The only things left to look through are these." He pointed to the boxes.

Miller closed the file he was holding. "What are those?"

"Those," said Cadbury, "are nineteen years of dispatches from me to the paper. That's the top row. Below them are nineteen years of clippings from the paper of news stories and articles about Germany and Austria. That's quite a lot to get through. Fortunately tomorrow is Sunday."

"It's very kind of you to take so much trouble," said Miller.

Cadbury shrugged. "I have nothing else to do this weekend. Meet me for a drink in the Cercle Français about eleven thirty."

It was in the middle of Sunday afternoon that they found it. Anthony Cadbury suddenly shouted, "Eureka!" It was one of his own dispatches, dated December 23, 1947.

"The paper didn't use it," he said. "Who wants to know about a captured SS man just before Christmas?" He laid the sheet on the desk for Miller to read.

> *British Military Government, Hanover*—A former captain of the notorious SS has been arrested by British military authorities at Graz, Austria, and is being held pending further investigation.
>
> The man, Eduard Roschmann, was recognized on the streets of the Austrian town by a former inmate of a concentration camp, who alleged Roschmann had been the commandant of the camp in Latvia. After identification, Roschmann was arrested by members of the British Field Security Service in Graz.
>
> A request has been made to Soviet zonal headquarters at Potsdam for further information about the concentration camp in Riga, Latvia, and a search for further witnesses is under way, the spokesman said. Meanwhile the captured man has been positively identified as Eduard Roschmann from his personal file stored by the American authorities in their SS index in Berlin.

Miller read the brief dispatch four or five times. "You got him," he breathed.

"I think this calls for a drink," said Cadbury.

MEMMERS was in his office on Monday morning at nine sharp. The call from Werewolf came through at half past.

"So glad you called, *Kamerad*," said Memmers. "I got back from Hamburg late last night."

"You have the information?"

"Certainly." Memmers read from his notes. "The owner of the car is a free-lance reporter, Peter Miller. Aged twenty-nine, about six feet tall, brown hair, brown eyes. Widowed mother lives in Osdorf. He lives in an apartment in Hamburg." Memmers read off Miller's address and telephone number. "He lives there with a girl, a striptease dancer, Miss Sigrid Rahn. He works mainly for the picture magazines. Apparently does very well. Specializes in investigative journalism. Like you said, *Kamerad*, a snooper."

"Any idea who commissioned him on this inquiry?"

"No, that's the funny thing. Nobody seems to know what he is doing at the moment. I checked with the girl by phone, claiming to be from a magazine. She said she did not know where he was, but expected a call this afternoon."

"Anything else?"

"Just the car. It's very distinctive. A black Jaguar, British model, with a yellow stripe down the side."

Werewolf thought for a minute. "Could you find out where he is now?" he asked.

"I think so," said Memmers. "I could call the girl back this afternoon, saying I needed to contact Miller urgently."

"Yes, do that," said Werewolf. "I'll call you at four."

THAT Monday morning Cadbury rang Miller at the Dreesen Hotel at ten thirty.

"Glad to get you before you left," he said. "I've got an idea. Meet me at the Cercle Français this afternoon around four."

At noon Miller rang Sigi to tell her where he was.

When they met, Cadbury ordered tea. "If Roschmann was captured and identified as a wanted criminal," he said, "his case would have come under the eyes of the British legal officials in our zone of Germany at the time. Have you ever heard of a man called Lord Russell of Liverpool?"

"No, never," said Miller.

"He was the legal adviser to the British military governor during the occupation. Later he wrote a book called *The Scourge of the Swastika*. Didn't make him terribly popular in Germany, but it was quite accurate. He's retired now, lives in Wimbledon. I could give you a letter of introduction."

"Would he remember so far back?"

"He was reputed to have a memory like a filing cabinet. If he prosecuted the Roschmann case, I'm sure he'd remember every detail."

Miller nodded. "Yes, I could fly to London to talk to him."

Cadbury stood up, reached into his pocket, and produced an envelope. "I have the letter ready. Good luck."

WEREWOLF's phone rang just after four.

"His girl friend got a call from him," said Memmers. "He's in Bad Godesberg, staying at the Dreesen Hotel."

Werewolf put the phone down and thumbed through an address book. In a moment he called a number in the Bonn–Bad Godesberg area.

MILLER went back to the hotel to call Cologne airport and book a flight to London for the following day, Tuesday, December 31. The receptionist pointed to a chair in the bay window overlooking the Rhine.

"There's a gentleman to see you, Herr Miller."

Miller saw a middle-aged man holding a black homburg and a rolled umbrella. He strolled over. "You wanted to see me?"

The man sprang to his feet. "Herr Peter Miller?"

"Yes."

The man bowed in the short, jerky manner of old-fashioned Germans. "My name is Schmidt. Dr. Schmidt."

"What can I do for you?"

"I am told you are a journalist. Yes?" Dr. Schmidt smiled brightly. "You have a reputation for being very tenacious."

Miller remained silent.

"Some friends of mine heard you are presently engaged on an inquiry into events that happened—well, let us say, a long time ago. A very long time ago."

Miller stiffened. "An inquiry about a certain Eduard Roschmann," he said tersely. "So?"

"I just thought I might be able to help you." The man fixed his eyes kindly on Miller. "Captain Roschmann is dead."

"Indeed?" said Miller. "Can you tell me when he died?"

"Ah yes, of course." Dr. Schmidt seemed happy to oblige. "He was killed in Austria fighting the Americans in early 1945. His body was identified by several people who had known him."

"He must have been a remarkable man," said Miller.

Dr. Schmidt nodded. "Well, indeed, some of us thought so."

"Remarkable," Miller said, "to have been the first man since Jesus Christ to rise from the dead. He was captured alive by the British in December 1947 at Graz in Austria."

The doctor's eyes reflected the glittering snow along the balustrade outside the window. "Miller, you are being very foolish. Permit me to give you a word of advice. Drop this inquiry."

Miller eyed him. "I suppose I ought to thank you," he said.

"Perhaps you ought," said the doctor.

"You make me sick, *Herr Doktor*. You and your whole stinking gang. You are filth on the face of my country. So far as I am concerned, I'll go on asking questions till I find him."

He turned to go, but the elder man grabbed his arm. They stared at each other from a range of two inches.

"You're not stupid, Miller. But you're behaving as if you were. It's almost as if you had some personal stake in this matter."

"Perhaps I have," said Miller, and walked away.

7

MILLER knocked on the door of a house in a quiet street of the London borough of Wimbledon. Lord Russell himself answered, a man in his late sixties wearing a cardigan and a bow tie.

"Mr. Anthony Cadbury gave me a letter of introduction to you," Miller said. "I hoped I might have a talk with you, sir."

Lord Russell gazed at him with perplexity. "Cadbury?"

"A British newspaper correspondent," said Miller. "He covered the war-crimes trials of Josef Kramer and the others from Belsen."

"Yes, Cadbury, newspaper chap. I remember. Haven't seen him in years. Well, don't let's stand here. Come in, come in."

Without waiting for an answer, he turned and walked back down the hall, and Miller followed. He hung his coat on a hook, at Lord Russell's bidding, and they went into the sitting room, where a welcoming fire burned in the grate.

Miller held out the letter from Cadbury. Lord Russell took it, read it quickly, and raised his eyebrows.

"Humph. Help in tracking down a Nazi? Is that what you came about? Well, sit down, sit down. No good standing around."

They sat in armchairs on either side of the fire.

"How come a young German reporter is chasing Nazis?"

"I'd better explain from the beginning," said Miller.

"I think you better had," said the peer. While Miller talked he filled his pipe, lit it, and was puffing contentedly away when the German had finished.

"I hope my English is good enough," said Miller at last, when no reaction came from the retired prosecutor.

Lord Russell seemed to wake from a private reverie. "Oh, yes, yes, interesting, very interesting. And you want to try and find Roschmann. Why?" He shot the question, and Miller found the old man's eyes boring into his own.

"The man should be brought to trial," he said stiffly.

"Humph. The question is, will he be?"

Miller played it straight back. "If I can find him, he will be. The point is, my lord, do you remember him?"

Lord Russell seemed to start. "Remember him? Oh, yes, I remember him. Or at least the name. Wish I could put a face to the name. There were so many of them."

Miller took the photocopies of Roschmann's two pictures from his breast pocket. Lord Russell gazed at them, then rose and began to pace the sitting room.

"Yes," he said at last, "I've got him. I can see him now. We got him in Graz. His file was sent on to me in Hanover. You say your man Tauber saw him on April third, 1945, driving west through Magdeburg in a car with several others?"

"That's what he said in his diary."

"All right, young man, I'll fill in what I can. . . ."

ROSCHMANN and his SS colleagues made it as far as Munich before the end of April, then split up. Roschmann was in the uniform of a corporal of the German army, by this time with papers in his own name but describing him as an army man.

The American army columns now sweeping through Bavaria were concerned with rumors that the Nazi hierarchy intended to shut themselves up in a fortress at Berchtesgaden and fight it out to the last man, so they paid scant attention to the hundreds of wandering German soldiers. Traveling by night across country, hiding by day in woodsmen's huts and barns, Roschmann crossed into Austria and headed for the sanctuary of his hometown. He had almost made it to Graz when he was challenged by a British patrol on May 6. Foolishly he tried to run for it. As he dived into the undergrowth by the roadside, a hail of bullets cut through the brushwood, and one passed clean through his chest, piercing one lung. After a quick search in the darkness the British Tommies passed on, leaving him undiscovered in a thicket. From there he crawled to a farmer's house half a mile away. Still conscious, he told the farmer the name of a doctor in Graz, and for three months he was tended by friends, first at the farmer's house and then in the town itself. When he was fit enough to walk, the war was three months over and Austria under four-power occupation. Graz was in the heart of the British Zone.

All captured German soldiers were held by the British for two years in prisoner-of-war camps, and Roschmann, deeming a British camp the safest place to be, gave himself up. So from August 1945 to August 1947, while the hunt for the worst of the wanted SS murderers went on, he remained there at ease. He was using the name of a friend who had been killed in North Africa. Since the Allies had neither the time nor the facilities to conduct a probing examination of army corporals, the name was accepted as genuine. By the summer of 1947 Roschmann was released, and felt it safe to leave the custody of the camp. He was wrong.

One of the survivors of Riga, a native of Vienna, had sworn his own vendetta against Roschmann. This man haunted the streets of Graz, waiting for Roschmann to return to his home, the parents he had left in 1939, and the wife he had married while on leave in 1943, Hella Roschmann.

From his release in August, Roschmann worked as a laborer in the fields outside Graz. Then, on December 20, 1947, he went home for Christmas. The old man was waiting.

Within an hour two British sergeants of the Field Security Service, puzzled and skeptical, arrived at the house and knocked. After a quick search they discovered Roschmann under a bed. Had he brazened it out, he might easily have talked the sergeants into disbelieving the old man's story. But hiding was the giveaway. He was led off to be interviewed by Major Hardy of the FSS, who promptly had him locked up while a request went off to Berlin to check the American index of the SS.

Confirmation arrived in forty-eight hours, and the Americans asked for Roschmann to be transferred to Munich to give evidence at Dachau, where the Americans were putting other SS men on trial. The British agreed, and on January 8, 1948, Roschmann, accompanied by two British sergeants, was put on a train bound for Salzburg and Munich.

LORD RUSSELL paused in his pacing, crossed to the fireplace, and knocked out his pipe.

"Then what happened?" asked Miller.

"He escaped," said Lord Russell.

"He *what?*"

"He escaped. He jumped from the lavatory window of the moving train, after complaining the prison diet had given him diarrhea. By the time his two escorts had smashed in the lavatory door, he was gone into the snow. They never found him. He had evidently made contact with one of the organizations which helped ex-Nazis escape."

"So—where does one go from here?" Miller asked.

Lord Russell blew out his cheeks. "Your own people, I suppose."

"Which ones?" asked Miller, fearing he knew the answer.

"As it concerns Riga, it should be the Hamburg attorney general's office," said Lord Russell.

"I've been there; they didn't help."

Lord Russell grinned. "Not surprised, not surprised. Have you tried Ludwigsburg?"

"Yes. They were nice, but not very helpful. Against the rules," said Miller.

"Well, that exhausts the official lines of inquiry. There's only one other man. Have you ever heard of Simon Wiesenthal?"

"Wiesenthal? Yes, vaguely. The name rings a bell, but I can't place it."

"He lives in Vienna. Jewish chap who spent four years in a series of concentration camps. Decided to spend the rest of his days tracking down Nazi criminals. No rough stuff, mind you. He just keeps collecting information. When he's convinced he has found one, he informs the police. If they don't act, he gives a press conference and puts them in a spot. Needless to say, he's not terribly popular with officialdom. He reckons they are not doing enough to bring known Nazi murderers to justice, let alone chase the hidden ones."

"Wasn't he the man who found Adolf Eichmann?" asked Miller.

Lord Russell nodded. "And several hundred others. If anything is known about your Eduard Roschmann, he'll know it. I'd better give you a letter. He gets a lot of visitors."

He went to the desk and swiftly wrote a few lines.

"Good luck, you'll need it," he said as he showed Miller out.

THE NEXT morning Miller flew back to Cologne, picked up his car, and set off on the two-day run to Vienna.

He made it by midafternoon of January 3. He drove straight into the city center and asked his way to Rudolfsplatz. At number 7, the list of tenants showed the Documentation Center to be on the fourth floor. He mounted, and knocked at the cream-painted wooden door. From behind it someone looked through the peephole before the lock was drawn back. A pretty blond girl stood in the doorway.

"Please?"

"My name is Miller. Peter Miller. I would like to speak with Herr Wiesenthal. I have a letter of introduction."

He gave it to the girl, who smiled and asked him to wait.

A minute later she reappeared. "Please come this way."

Miller followed her down a passage to an open door. As he entered a man rose to greet him.

"Come in," said Simon Wiesenthal.

He was a burly man over six feet tall, wearing a thick tweed jacket. He held Lord Russell's letter in his hand.

The office was small and crammed with books. The desk stood away from the window, and Miller took the visitor's chair in front of it. The Nazi-hunter of Vienna seated himself behind it.

"My friend Lord Russell tells me you are trying to hunt down a former SS killer," he began without preamble.

"Yes, that's true."

"May I have his name?"

"Roschmann. Captain Eduard Roschmann."

Simon Wiesenthal exhaled in a whistle. "The Butcher of Riga? One of my top fifty wanted men. May I ask why you are interested in him?"

Miller started to explain briefly. Wiesenthal held up his hand. "I think you had better begin at the beginning. What about this diary?"

With the man in Ludwigsburg, Cadbury, and Lord Russell, this made the fourth time Miller had had to tell his tale. Each time it grew a little longer, another period having been added to his knowledge of Roschmann's life story. He began again and went through until he had described the help given by Lord Russell. "What I have to know now," he ended, "is where did he go when he jumped from the train?"

"Have you got the diary?" Wiesenthal asked. Miller took it out of his briefcase and laid it on the desk.

Wiesenthal examined it appreciatively. "Fascinating." He looked up and smiled. "All right, I accept the story."

"Was there any doubt?" Miller asked.

Simon Wiesenthal eyed him keenly. "There is always a little doubt, Herr Miller. Yours is a very strange story. I still cannot follow your motive for wanting to track Roschmann down. Are you sure there's nothing personal in this?"

Miller ducked the question. "People keep suggesting that. Why should it be personal? I'm only twenty-nine years old. All this was before my time."

"Of course." Wiesenthal glanced at his watch and rose. "It is five o'clock, and I would like to get home to my wife. Would you let me read the diary over the weekend?"

"Certainly," said Miller.

"Good. Then please come back on Monday morning and I will fill in what I know of the Roschmann story."

MILLER ARRIVED ON Monday at ten and found Simon Wiesenthal attacking a pile of letters. He gestured the reporter to sit down. "I read the diary. Remarkable document."

"Were you surprised?" asked Miller.

"Not by the contents. We all went through much the same sort of thing. But it's so precise. Tauber would have made a perfect witness. He noticed everything, even the small details. And noted them—at the time. That is very important to get a conviction before German or Austrian courts. And now he's dead."

"Herr Wiesenthal, you're the first Jew I have ever had a long talk with who went through all that. Tauber said there was no such thing as collective guilt. But we Germans have been told for twenty years that we are all guilty. Do you believe that?"

"No," said the Nazi-hunter flatly. "Tauber was right."

"How can you say that, if we killed all those millions?"

"You, personally, were not there. You did not kill anyone." Wiesenthal regarded him intently. "Do you know about the sections of the SS that really were responsible for the killing?"

"No."

"Then I'd better tell you. You've heard about the Reich Economic Administration Main Office, charged with exploiting the victims before they died?"

"Yes, I read something about it."

"Its job was in a sense the middle section of the operation," said Herr Wiesenthal. "When the economic exploitation was over, finishing the victims off was the task of the Reich Security Main Office, the RSHA. The rather odd use of the word 'Security' stems from the quaint Nazi idea that the victims posed a threat to the Reich, which had to be made secure against them.

"The RSHA was divided into several departments; one of these was the dreaded Security Service and Security Police, headed first by Reinhard Heydrich, assassinated in Prague in 1942, and later by Ernst Kaltenbrunner, executed by the Allies. Their teams devised the tortures used to make suspects talk."

Roschmann, Miller remembered, had been in the Security Service at Riga.

"Another department was the Gestapo," Wiesenthal went on, "headed by Heinrich Müller, who's still missing. The Jewish section was headed by Adolf Eichmann. Other departments were the Criminal Police and the Foreign Intelligence Service.

"If one is going to specify guilt, therefore, that's where it rests—on those economic and security offices of the SS—and the numbers involved are thousands, not the millions who make up contemporary Germany. The theory of the collective guilt of sixty million Germans suits the SS extremely well. Even today they hide behind it. They realize that so long as it's accepted, nobody will start to look for specific murderers—at least, not look hard enough."

Miller digested this. "The reason Tauber apparently had for killing himself—do you believe it?"

"I believe he was right in thinking no one would believe that he saw Roschmann on the steps of the Opera."

"But he didn't even go to the police," said Miller.

After a pause Simon Wiesenthal replied, "No. I don't think it would have done any good. Not in Hamburg, at any rate."

"What's wrong with Hamburg?"

"You went to the state attorney general's office there?"

"Yes, I did. They weren't terribly helpful."

"I'm afraid the attorney general's department in Hamburg has a certain reputation in this office," Wiesenthal said. "Take for example the SS General Bruno Streckenbach. In 1939 he led an extermination squad in Nazi-occupied Poland. At the end of 1940 he was head of the security sections of the SS for the whole of Poland. Thousands were exterminated during that period. Just before the invasion of Russia he helped to organize the extermination squads that went in behind the army.

"Then he was promoted to deputy chief of the entire RSHA under Heydrich. When Heydrich was killed by the Czech partisans—that was the killing that led to the reprisal at Lidice, you know—he became deputy under Kaltenbrunner. As such he had all-embracing responsibility for extermination squads throughout the Nazi-occupied eastern territories until the end of the war."

Miller looked stunned. "They haven't arrested him?"

For answer Simon Wiesenthal rummaged in a drawer and produced a sheet of paper. He folded it down the center from top to bottom, and handed it to Miller so that only the left side of the sheet showed. "Do you recognize those names?"

Miller scanned the list of ten names with a frown. "Of course. These are all senior police officers of the Hamburg force. Why?"

"Spread the paper out," said Wiesenthal.

Miller did so. Fully expanded, the sheet had additional columns showing the Nazi-party card numbers, SS numbers, ranks, and promotion dates for each man listed.

Miller looked up. "My God," he said.

"Yes. Streckenbach was their commanding officer once."

AFTER a lunchtime break Wiesenthal took up the Roschmann story from the day he escaped from British custody, January 8, 1948. He had already been in touch with a Nazi escape organization called the Six-Point Star, nothing to do with the Jewish symbol, but so called because it had tentacles in six major Austrian cities. After jumping from the train into deep snow he staggered as far as a peasant's cottage and took refuge there. The following day he crossed the border into Upper Austria, walked to Salzburg province, and contacted the Six-Point Star. They took him to a brick factory, where he passed as a laborer while arrangements were made with the Odessa for a passage south to Italy.

At that time the Odessa was in close contact with the French Foreign Legion, into which scores of former SS soldiers had fled. So one day a car with French license plates and a Foreign Legion driver drove Roschmann and five other Nazi escapers over the Italian border to Merano, where the Odessa representative paid the driver, in cash, a hefty sum per head.

From Merano, Roschmann was taken to Rimini, where he had the five toes of his right foot amputated, for they were rotten with frostbite, the result of his wandering through the snowy night of January 8. His wife, in Graz, got a letter in October from Rimini, in which for the first time he used the new name he had been given, Fritz Bernd Wegener.

Shortly afterward he was transferred to the Franciscan monastery in Rome. When his papers were ready he set sail from Naples for Buenos Aires. There he was received by the Odessa and lodged with a German family called Vidmar. Early in 1949 he was advanced the sum of fifty thousand American dollars out of the Bormann funds in Switzerland, and went into business as an exporter of South American hardwood timber to Western Europe. The firm was called Stemmler and Wegener.

He engaged a German girl as his secretary, Irmtraud Sigrid Müller, and in early 1955 he married her, although his first wife, Hella, still lived in Graz. Soon afterward Roschmann saw that the writing was on the wall for the Perón regime, and that if Perón fell, much of the protection accorded to ex-Nazis might be removed. So, with his new wife, Roschmann left for Egypt.

He spent three months there in the summer of 1955, and came to West Germany in the autumn. Nobody would have known a thing but for the anger of a woman betrayed. Hella Roschmann had written her husband in care of the Vidmar family in Buenos Aires. The Vidmars replied that he had married his secretary and gone back to Germany. Furious, the wife informed the police and asked for the arrest of Fritz Wegener on a charge of bigamy.

"Did they get him?" asked Miller.

Wiesenthal shook his head. "No, he disappeared again. Certainly under a new set of papers, and almost certainly in Germany. You see, that's why I believe Tauber could have seen him."

"Is it worth contacting Hella Roschmann?" asked Miller.

"I doubt it. Roschmann is not likely to reveal his whereabouts to her again. Or his new name. He must have acquired his new papers in a devil of a hurry."

"Who would have got them for him?" asked Miller.

"The Odessa, certainly."

"Just what is the Odessa? You've mentioned it several times."

"You've never heard of them?" asked Wiesenthal.

"No. Not until now."

Simon Wiesenthal glanced at his watch. "You'd better come back in the morning. I'll tell you all about them."

8

"I REMEMBERED something overnight that I forgot to tell you yester-day." And Peter Miller went on to recount the incident of Dr. Schmidt, who had accosted him at the Dreesen Hotel and warned him off the Roschmann inquiry.

Wiesenthal pursed his lips and nodded. "You're up against them, all right. It's most unusual for them to take a step like that with a reporter, particularly at such an early stage. I wonder what Rosch-mann is up to that could be so important."

Then for two hours the Nazi-hunter told Miller about the history of the Odessa.

WHEN the Allies stormed into Germany in 1945 and found the concentration camps with their hideous contents, they not unnat-urally rounded on the German people to demand who had carried out the atrocities. The answer was the SS—but the SS were nowhere to be found.

Where had they gone? Either underground, inside Germany and Austria, or abroad. And it was no spur-of-the-moment flight. What the Allies failed to realize until much later was that each had meticulously prepared his disappearance beforehand. While the Nazis and the SS were screaming at the German people to fight on, they themselves prepared for comfortable exile. The SS bullied the German army into battle, to take unbelievable casual-ties from the Russians, for six months after defeat was inevitable, to give them time to complete their own escape plans. The SS stood behind the army, shooting and hanging some of the army men who took a step backward. Thousands of the Wehrmacht died in this way. It casts an interesting light on the so-called SS patriotism that, from Heinrich Himmler down, each tried to save his own skin at the expense of all the other Germans.

Just before the final collapse the SS all over the country quit their posts, stuffed their beautifully forged papers into the pockets of new civilian clothes, and vanished. They left the old men of the

Home Guard to meet the British and the Americans at the gates of the concentration camps, and the exhausted Wehrmacht to go into prisoner-of-war camps.

The Odessa was the organization of men that was formed just before the end of the war to take charge of getting wanted Waffen SS members out of Germany. To this end, the Odessa had established close links with Juan Perón. Argentina issued seven thousand passports "in blank," so that the refugee merely had to fill in a false name, add his own photograph, get it stamped by the Argentine consul, and board ship for Buenos Aires or the Middle East.

SS refugees poured through Austria into the South Tirol and were shuttled from safe house to safe house along the route to Genoa, or, like Roschmann, to Rimini and the Franciscan monastery in Rome. Often with the help of charitable organizations like Caritas, Red Cross travel documents and prepaid steamship tickets were procured. Just how many SS murderers passed to safety will never be known, but they were well over eighty percent of those who would have faced death sentences.

The Odessa had succeeded in its first job. Now, having established itself comfortably on the proceeds of mass murder, transferred from Swiss banks, it sat back and watched the deterioration of relations between the Allies of 1945. With the establishment in May 1949 of a new republic of West Germany, the leaders of the Odessa set themselves five new tasks.

The first was the infiltration of the SS into every profession in the new Germany. Throughout the late forties and fifties former members of the SS slipped into lawyers' and doctors' offices, onto judges' benches, and into the police forces and local government. From these positions they were able to protect each other from investigation and arrest, advance each other's interests, and generally ensure that investigation and prosecution of former *Kameraden* went forward as slowly as possible, if at all.

The second task was to infiltrate the mechanisms of political power. Avoiding the high levels, former Nazis slipped into the grass roots of the ruling party at ward level. It may be a coincidence, but no one with a record of calling for vigorous investigation of SS crimes has ever been elected in the Christian Democratic or the Christian Socialist parties. One politician expressed it with crisp simplicity: "It's a question of election mathematics. Six million dead Jews don't vote. Five million former Nazis can and do, at every election."

The aim of this infiltration was simple. It was to slow down or stop the prosecution of former members of the SS. In this the Odessa had a great ally—the secret knowledge in the minds of hundreds of thousands that they had either helped in what was done, albeit in a small way, or had known what was going on and remained silent. Years later, respected in their communities, they could hardly relish the mention of their names in a faraway courtroom where an SS man was on trial.

The third task the Odessa set itself was to infiltrate business and industry in order to take full advantage of the staggering "economic miracle" of the fifties and sixties. Bankrolled from the Zurich deposits, former SS men developed businesses of their own, whose profits help keep Odessa's funds flourishing.

The fourth task was, and still is, to provide the best possible legal defense for any SS man forced to stand trial. In every SS court case, defense lawyers have been among the most brilliant and the most expensive in Germany, regardless of the defendant's income; but no one ever asks who pays the bills.

The fifth task is propaganda. This takes many forms, from encouraging the dissemination of right-wing pamphlets to lobbying for the statute of limitations to end all legal culpability of the SS. Efforts are made to assure the Germans of today that the death figures of Jews, Russians, Poles, and others in the camps were but a tiny fraction of those quoted by the Allies—one hundred thousand dead Jews is the usual figure mentioned.

But the main object of Odessa propaganda is to persuade seventy million Germans—and they've had a large degree of success doing it —that the SS men were patriotic soldiers, like the Wehrmacht, and that solidarity among former comrades must be upheld. This is the weirdest ploy of all, for the Wehrmacht regarded the SS with repugnance, while the SS treated the Wehrmacht with contempt. Five thousand of the Wehrmacht were executed by the SS after the July 1944 plot against Hitler, in which fewer than fifty were implicated. And, as I've said, millions of young Wehrmacht men were hurled into death or captivity so that SS men could live prosperously elsewhere. How former members of the army, navy, and air force can conceivably regard ex-SS men as *Kameraden* is a mystery. Yet herein lies the real success of the Odessa, which has, by and large, succeeded in stultifying West German efforts to bring to trial the mass murderers.

WHEN Wiesenthal had finished, Miller laid down the pencil with which he had made notes. "I hadn't the faintest idea," he said.

"Few people have," conceded Wiesenthal. "The term Odessa is hardly ever mentioned in Germany nowadays. The new word is the Comradeship, just as the Mafia in America is called *Cosa Nostra*. But the Odessa is still in Germany, and will be while there is still an SS criminal to protect."

"And you think these are the men I'm up against?"

"I'm sure of it. Dr. Schmidt's warning could not have come from anyone else. Be careful; these men can be dangerous."

Miller's mind turned to something else. "When Roschmann's first wife gave away the Wegener name, how would the Odessa get him the new passport you said he must now have?"

"They probably have a forger somewhere who turns them out."

"So if one found the passport forger, one might find Roschmann."

Wiesenthal shrugged. "One might. But to do that one would have to penetrate the Odessa. Only an ex-SS man could do that."

"Then where do I go from here?" said Miller.

"I should think your best bet would be to try and contact some of the survivors of Riga. Look—" He flicked open Tauber's diary. "There's reference here to an Olli Adler who was in Roschmann's company during the war. It may be she survived and came home to Munich."

Miller nodded. "If she did, where would she register?"

"At the Jewish Community Center. It contains the archives of the Jewish community of Munich. I'd try there."

"Do you have the address?"

Simon Wiesenthal checked in an address book. "Reichenbachstrasse, number twenty-seven." He rose and escorted Miller to the door. "Good luck," he said, "and let me know how you get on."

THE morning of January 9, Miller drove into Munich and found 27 Reichenbachstrasse. He went to the inquiry desk on the third floor and, while he waited for someone to come, glanced around the room. There were rows of books, all new, for the original library had long since been burned by the Nazis. There was a rack of newspapers, some in German, others in Hebrew. A short dark man was scanning the front page of one of the latter.

"Can I help you?" The inquiry desk was now occupied by a dark-eyed woman in her mid-forties.

Miller made his request: Any trace of an Olli Adler, who might have reported back to Munich after the war?

"Where would she have returned from?" asked the woman.

"From Riga."

"Oh, dear," said the woman. "I don't think we have anyone listed who came back here from Riga. But I'll look."

She went into a back room, and returned after five minutes.

"I'm sorry. There is nobody listed under that name."

"Would there be anybody else left in Munich who was at Riga? The man I'm really trying to find is the former commandant."

There was silence in the room. Miller sensed that the man by the newspaper rack had turned around to look at him.

"It might be possible there is someone. But I'd have to go through the whole list of survivors. Could you come back tomorrow?"

"Yes," he said. "I'll come back. Thank you."

MILLER was in the street, reaching for his car keys, when he heard someone step up behind him.

"Excuse me," said a voice. He turned. The man facing him was the one who had been at the newspaper rack.

"You are inquiring about the commandant of Riga?" asked the man. "Would that be Captain Roschmann?"

"Yes, it would," said Miller. "Why?"

"I was at Riga. Perhaps I can help you." The man was short and wiry, somewhere in his forties, with button-bright brown eyes. "My name is Mordecai, but people call me Motti. Shall we have coffee and talk?"

They adjourned to a nearby coffee shop. Miller described his hunt so far, and the man listened quietly. "Mmmm," he said finally. "Quite a pilgrimage. Why should a German want to track down Roschmann?"

"Why shouldn't a German be angry at what was done?"

Motti shrugged. "It's unusual for a man to go to such lengths, that's all. About Roschmann's last disappearance—you really think he has a passport provided by the Odessa?"

"I've been told so. And it seems the only way to find the man who forged it would be to penetrate the Odessa."

Motti considered the young man in front of him for some time. "What hotel are you staying at?" he asked.

Miller told him he had not checked in yet, but planned to go to one he had stayed at before. At Motti's request he went to the telephone and called the hotel.

When he got back to the table, Motti had gone. There was a note under the coffee cup. It said: "Whether you get a room there or not, be in the residents' lounge at eight tonight."

THAT same afternoon Werewolf read the written report that had come in from Dr. Schmidt in Bonn. The last words General Glücks had spoken to him in Madrid virtually robbed him of any freedom of action. "A permanent solution" had been the order, and he knew what that meant. Nor did the phraseology Dr. Schmidt had used leave him room for maneuver: "A stubborn young man, truculent and headstrong, and with an undercurrent of personal hatred for the *Kamerad* in question, Eduard Roschmann, for which no explanation seems to exist. Unlikely to listen to reason, even in the face of personal threat."

Werewolf sighed and dialed a number in Düsseldorf.

After several rings a voice said simply, "Yes?"

"There's a call for Herr Mackensen," said Werewolf.

The voice at the other end said, "Who wants him?"

Instead of answering the question directly, Werewolf gave the identification code.

There was a pause, then: "This is Mackensen," said the voice.

"There is work to be done. Get over here by tomorrow morning."

"When?" replied Mackensen.

"Be here at ten," said Werewolf. "Tell my secretary your name is Keller."

In Düsseldorf, Mackensen went into his bathroom to shower and shave. He was a big, powerful man, a former sergeant of the SS division Das Reich, who had learned his killing when hanging French hostages in Tulle and Limoges back in 1944. After the war he had driven a truck for the Odessa, running human cargo into the South Tirol. In 1946, stopped by an American patrol, he had slain all four occupants of the jeep, two of them with his bare hands.

He had been employed later as a bodyguard for senior men of the Odessa, and in the mid-1950s he had become the Odessa executioner. By January 1964 he had fulfilled twelve such assignments.

THE call came on the dot of eight. It was taken by the reception clerk, who put his head around the corner of the residents' lounge, where Miller sat watching television.

He recognized the voice on the phone.

"Herr Miller? It's me, Motti. I have friends who may be able to help you. Would you like to meet them?"

"I'll meet anybody who can help me," said Miller.

"Good," said Motti. "Leave your hotel and turn left down Schillerstrasse. Two blocks down on the same side is Lindemann's coffee shop. Meet me there right away."

Miller took his coat and walked out through the doors. Half a block from the hotel something was jabbed into his ribs from behind, and a car slid up to the curb.

"Get into the back seat, Herr Miller," a voice breathed.

The door nearest him swung open, and Miller ducked his head

and got in. The back seat contained another man, who moved over to make room. He felt the man behind him enter the car also.

His heart was thumping as the car slid from the curb. He recognized none of the men. The one to his right produced a sort of black sock and said, "I am going to bind your eyes."

Miller felt the sock being pulled over his head until it covered his nose. He recalled what Simon Wiesenthal had told him: "Be careful; these men can be dangerous."

They drove for about half an hour, then the car slowed and stopped. He was eased out of the back seat, and with a man on each side was helped across a courtyard. For a moment he felt the cold night air on his face, then he was indoors again. A voice said. "Take off the bandage," and the sock was removed.

The room he was in was evidently belowground, for there were no windows. It was well decorated and comfortable. There was a long table with eight chairs around it, close to the far wall. Motti stood smiling, almost apologetically, beside the table. The two men who had brought Miller in offered him a chair and sat down at his left and right. Across the table was another man—about sixty, Miller thought—lean and bony, with a hollow-cheeked, hook-nosed face and the eyes of a fanatic. It was he who spoke.

"Welcome, Herr Miller. I apologize for the strange way in which you were brought to my home. The reason for it was that if you decide to turn down my proposal, you can be returned to your hotel without knowing our place of meeting.

"My friend here," he gestured to Motti, "informs me that for reasons of your own you are hunting a certain Eduard Roschmann. And that to get closer to him you might be prepared to attempt to penetrate the Odessa. We might be prepared to help you."

Miller stared at him in astonishment. "Are you telling me you are not from the Odessa?" he said.

The man leaned forward and drew back the sleeve of his left wrist. On the forearm was tattooed a number in blue ink. "Auschwitz." He pointed to the men at Miller's sides. "Buchenwald and Dachau." He pointed at Motti. "Riga and Treblinka. Herr Miller, there are some who think the murderers of our people

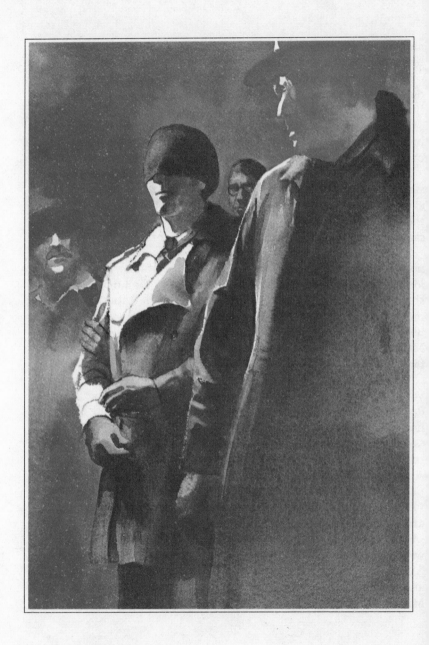

should be brought to trial. I and my group do not agree. We stayed on in Germany after 1945 with one object, and one only, in mind. Revenge. We don't arrest them, Herr Miller; we kill them like the swine they are. My name is Leon."

Leon interrogated Miller for four hours before he was satisfied of the reporter's genuineness. When he finished, he leaned back and surveyed the young man. "Are you aware how risky it is to try and penetrate the Odessa?"

"I can guess," said Miller. "For one thing, I'm too young."

"There would be no question of using your own identity. There is a list of former SS men, and Peter Miller's name is not on it. And you will have to age—ten years at least. You will have to take on, completely, the identity of a man who really was in the SS."

"Do you think you can find such a man?" asked Miller.

Leon shrugged. "It would have to be one whose death cannot be checked out by the Odessa. In addition you will have to pass all the Odessa tests. That means living for five or six weeks with a former SS man who can teach you the phraseology, the behavior patterns. Fortunately, we know such a man."

Miller was amazed. "Why should he do such a thing?"

"He is a former SS captain who sincerely regretted what was done. Later he was inside the Odessa and passed information about wanted Nazis to the authorities. He would be doing so still, but he was caught and was lucky to escape with his life. Now he lives under a new name, in a house outside Bayreuth."

"What else would I have to learn?"

"Everything about your new identity. Where the man was born, his date of birth, how he got into the SS, where he trained, where he served, his unit, his commanding officer, his entire history from the end of the war onward. You will also have to be vouched for by a guarantor. That will not be easy. A lot of time and trouble will have to be spent on you, Herr Miller."

"What's in this for you?" asked Miller suspiciously.

Leon rose and paced the carpet. "The worst of the SS killers are living under false names," he said. "We want those names."

"Have you ever tried to get your own men inside the Odessa?" asked Miller.

Leon nodded. "Twice," he said.

"What happened?"

"The first was found floating in a canal without his fingernails. The second disappeared without trace. Do you still want to go ahead?"

Miller ignored the question. "If you are so efficient, why were they caught?"

"They were both Jewish," said Leon shortly. "We tried to get the tattoos from the concentration camps off their arms, but they left scars. Besides, they were both circumcised. By the way, are you circumcised?"

"Does it matter?" inquired Miller.

"Of course. If a man is circumcised it does not prove he's a Jew; many Germans are circumcised as well. But if he is not, it more or less proves he is not a Jew."

"I'm not," said Miller.

Leon nodded with pensive satisfaction. "Certainly that improves your chances. That just leaves the problem of changing your appearance and training you to play a very dangerous role."

It was long past midnight. Leon looked at his watch. "Motti, I think a little food for our guest."

Motti grinned, and disappeared through the door.

"You'll have to spend the night here," said Leon to Miller. "Give me your keys and I'll have your car brought around. It will be better out of sight for the next few weeks. We'll take care of your hotel bill and luggage. In the morning you must write your mother and girl friend, explaining that you'll be out of touch for a while. Understood?"

Miller nodded and handed over his car keys.

"Tomorrow we will drive you to Bayreuth and you will meet our SS officer. His name is Alfred Oster. Meanwhile, excuse me. I have to start looking for your new identity."

He rose and left. Motti soon returned with a plate of food, then left Miller to his cold chicken, potato salad, and growing doubts.

FAR AWAY TO THE NORTH, in Bremen General Hospital, an orderly was patrolling his ward in the small hours of the morning. At the end of the room was a tall screen. The orderly, a man called Hartstein, peered around at the man in the bed behind it. He lay very still. The orderly checked the pulse. There was none.

Something the patient had said earlier in delirium caused the orderly to lift his left arm. Inside the armpit a number was tattooed—his blood group, a sure sign that the patient had once been in the SS.

Orderly Hartstein covered the dead man's face and glanced into the drawer of the bedside table. He drew out the driver's license that had been placed there along with the man's other personal possessions when he had been brought in after collapsing in the street. It showed he was thirty-eight, date of birth June 18, 1925. The name was Rolf Günther Kolb.

The orderly slipped the driver's license into his pocket and went off to report the death to the night physician.

SHORTLY before noon Peter Miller and Motti, accompanied by the driver of the previous night, set off for Bayreuth, in the heart of the area nicknamed the Bavarian Switzerland. Once in the back of the car, the black sock was again pulled over his head. He was pushed to the floor and kept blindfolded until they were well clear of Munich. They lunched at a wayside inn at Ingolstadt, pressed on to skirt Nuremberg to the east, and were at Bayreuth an hour later.

In January, Bayreuth is a quiet little place, blanketed by snow. They found the cottage of Alfred Oster on a byroad a mile beyond the town, and there was not another car in sight as the small party went to the front door.

The former SS officer was a big, bluff man with blue eyes and a fuzz of ginger-colored hair. Despite the season, he had the healthy tan of men who live in the sun and the mountain air.

Motti handed Oster a letter from Leon. The Bavarian read it

and nodded, glancing sharply at Miller. "Well, we can always try. How long can I have him?"

"Until he's ready," said Motti, "and until we can devise a new identity for him. We will let you know."

A few minutes later Motti left, and Oster led Miller into the living room. "So, you want to be able to pass as a former SS man, do you?" he asked.

Miller nodded. "That's right."

"Well, we'll start by getting a few basic facts right. I don't know where you did your military service, but I suspect it was in that ill-disciplined, democratic, wet-nursing shambles that calls itself the new German army. Here's the first fact. The new German army would have lasted exactly ten seconds against any crack regiment of the British, Americans, or Russians during the last war.

"Here's the second fact. The Waffen SS were the toughest, best-disciplined, fittest bunch of soldiers who ever went into battle in the history of this planet. Whatever they did can't change that. *So smarten up, Miller.* So long as you are in this house, this is the procedure.

"When I walk into a room you leap to attention. And I mean *leap!* You smack those heels together and remain at attention until I am five paces beyond you. When I say something to you that needs an answer, you reply: *'Jawohl, Herr Hauptsturmführer.'* And when I give an order or an instruction, you reply: *'Zu befehl, Herr Hauptsturmführer.'* Is that clearly understood?"

Miller nodded.

"Heels together!" roared Oster. "I want to hear the leather smack. All right, since we may not have much time, we'll press on. Before supper we'll tackle the ranks, from private up to full general. You'll learn the titles, mode of address, uniform, and collar insignia of every rank that ever existed in any branch of the SS.

"After that I'll put you through the full political-ideological course that you would have undergone at Dachau SS training camp. Then you'll learn the marching songs, the drinking songs, and the various unit songs. I can get you as far as your departure from training camp for your first posting. Beyond that, Leon has to tell me what unit you were supposed to have joined, who was your commanding officer, what happened to you at the end of the war, how you have passed your time since 1945. However, the first part of the training will take from two to three weeks.

"By the way, don't think this is a joke. Once inside the Odessa, if you make one slip you'll end up in a canal. Believe me, I'm no milksop, but after betraying the Odessa, even I am running scared. That's why I live here under a new name."

For the first time since he had set off on his one-man hunt for Eduard Roschmann, Miller wondered if he had not gone too far.

MACKENSEN reported to Werewolf on the dot of ten. Werewolf seated the executioner in the client's chair opposite his desk and lit a cigar.

"There is a certain person, a newspaper reporter, inquiring about the whereabouts of one of our *Kameraden*," he began. The executioner nodded with understanding. Several times before, he had heard briefings begin in the same way.

"The man he is seeking is of absolutely vital importance to us and to our long-term planning. The reporter himself seems to be intelligent, tenacious, ingenious, and wholly committed to a sort of personal vendetta against the *Kamerad*."

"Any motive?" asked Mackensen.

Werewolf's puzzlement showed in his frown. He tapped ash from his cigar before replying. "We cannot understand why there should be a vengeance motive, but evidently there is," he murmured. "The man he is looking for commanded a ghetto in Ostland. Some, mainly foreigners, refuse to acknowledge our justification for what was done there. The odd thing about this reporter is that he is neither foreign nor Jewish. He's a young German, Aryan, son of a war hero—nothing in his background to suggest such a depth of hatred toward us, nor such an obsession with tracing one of our *Kameraden*, despite a firm and clear warning to stay off the matter. It gives me some regret to order his death. Yet he leaves me no alternative."

"Whereabouts?"

"Not known. A good place to start would be his own apartment, where his girl friend lives with him. If you represent yourself as a man sent by one of the magazines for which he works, the girl will probably talk to you. He drives a noticeable car. You'll find the details here." Werewolf handed him a sheet of paper.

"I'll need money," said Mackensen. Werewolf pushed a wad of ten thousand marks across the desk.

"And the orders?" asked the killer.

"Locate and liquidate," said Werewolf.

IT WAS January 13 before news of the death in Bremen four days earlier of Rolf Günther Kolb reached Leon in Munich. The letter from his North German representative enclosed the dead man's driver's license.

Leon checked that Kolb was on the SS list and that he was not on the West German wanted list. Then he went to Motti. "Here's the man we need," he said, handing him Kolb's driver's license. "He was a staff sergeant at the age of nineteen, promoted just before the war ended. They must have been very short of material. Kolb's face and Miller's don't match, but the height and build fit. So we'll need a new photograph. That can wait. To cover the photograph we'll need a replica of the stamp of the Bremen auto-license bureau. See to it."

When Motti had gone, Leon dialed a number in Bremen and gave further orders.

MACKENSEN sipped a cocktail in the bar of the Schweizerhof Hotel in Munich and considered his problem: Miller and his car had vanished. A thorough man, Mackensen had even contacted the main Jaguar agents for West Germany and obtained from them a series of publicity photographs of the Jaguar XK 150 sports car, so he knew what he was looking for. Inquiries at Miller's flat had led to a conversation with the handsome and cheerful girl friend. She had produced a letter from him, postmarked Munich, saying he would be staying there for a while.

Mackensen had checked every Munich hotel, public and private parking space, and gas station. There was nothing. The man he sought had disappeared as if from the face of the earth.

Having finished his drink, Mackensen eased himself off his barstool and went to the telephone to report to Werewolf. Although he did not know it, he stood less than a mile from the black Jaguar with the yellow stripe, which was parked in the walled courtyard of the antique shop where Leon lived and ran his small and fanatic organization.

In Bremen General Hospital a man in a white coat strolled into the registrar's office. He had a stethoscope around his neck, almost the badge of a new intern.

"I need a look at the medical file on one of our patients, Rolf Günther Kolb," he told the file clerk.

The woman did not recognize the intern, but there were scores of them working in the hospital. She found the Kolb chart and handed it to him. The phone rang, and she went to answer it.

The intern sat down and flicked through the file. It revealed that Kolb had collapsed in the street and been brought in by ambulance. An examination had diagnosed cancer of the intestine in a terminal state. A decision had been made not to operate. The patient had been put on a series of drugs, and later on pain-killers. The last sheet in the file stated simply: "Patient deceased on January 9. Cause of death: carcinoma of the large intestine. Body delivered to the municipal mortuary January 10."

The new intern eased that sheet out and inserted in its place one of his own. This one read: "Despite serious condition of patient, the carcinoma responded to treatment and went into remission. On January 16 patient was transferred at his own request to the Arcadia Clinic, Delmenhorst, for convalescence."

The intern gave the file back to the clerk, thanked her with a smile, and left. It was January 22.

Three days later Leon filled in the last section of his private jigsaw puzzle. A ticket agent reported that a certain bakery proprietor in Bremerhaven had booked a winter cruise for himself and his wife. The pair would tour the Caribbean for four weeks, leaving from Bremerhaven on Sunday, February 16. It was a small ship, not served by ship-to-shore telephone. Leon knew the man to have been a colonel of the SS during the war and a member of the Odessa after it. He ordered Motti to go out and buy a book of instructions on the art of making bread.

WEREWOLF was puzzled. For nearly three weeks he had had his representatives in the major cities of Germany on the lookout for a man called Miller and a black Jaguar sports car. Several telephone calls had been made to a girl called Sigi, purporting to come from the editor of a major picture magazine, but the girl had said she did not know where her boy friend was. Inquiries had been made at his bank, but he had cashed no checks since November. In short, he had disappeared. It was already January 31, and Werewolf felt obliged to make a phone call.

FAR away, high in the mountains, a man put down his telephone half an hour later and swore softly and violently. It was a Friday evening, and he had barely returned to his weekend manor for two days of rest.

He walked to the window of his elegantly appointed study and looked out. The light from the window spread over the thick carpet of snow on the lawn, the glow reaching away toward the pine trees that covered most of the estate.

The call he had taken disturbed him. He had told the caller there had been no one spotted near his house, no one hanging around his factory; but he was worried. Miller? Who the hell was Miller? The assurances on the phone that the reporter would be taken care of only partly assuaged his anxiety. The seriousness with which the caller and his colleagues took the threat posed by Miller was indicated by the decision to send him a personal bodyguard the next day, to stay with him until further notice.

He drew the curtains of the study, shutting out the winter landscape. The thickly padded door cut out all sounds from the rest of the house. The only sound in the room was the crackle of fresh pine logs on the hearth; the cheerful glow was framed by the great fireplace with its wrought-iron vine leaves and curlicues.

The door opened, and his wife put her head around. "Dinner's ready," she said.

"Coming, dear," said Eduard Roschmann.

THE next morning, Saturday, a party from Munich arrived at Oster's house. The car contained Leon and Motti, the driver, and a man with a black bag.

In the living room Leon said to the man carrying the bag, "You'd better get up to the bathroom and set out your gear." The man nodded and went upstairs.

The others sat at the table, and Leon asked, "How is he so far?" Miller might as well not have been there.

"Pretty good," said Oster. "I gave him a two-hour interrogation yesterday, and he could pass."

Leon handed a driver's license to Miller. The place where the photograph had been was now blank. "That's who you are going to become," he said. "Rolf Günther Kolb, born June 18, 1925. That would make you nineteen at the end of the war, and thirty-eight now. You were born and brought up in Bremen. You joined the Hitler Youth at the age of ten and the SS in January 1944 at eighteen. Both your parents were killed in an air raid in 1944."

"What about his career in the SS?" asked Oster.

"We don't know Kolb's career with the SS," Leon said. "It couldn't have been much, for he's not on any wanted list and nobody's ever heard of him. In a way that's just as well, for the chances are the Odessa have never heard of him either. But he'd have no reason to seek help from the Odessa unless he were being pursued. So we have invented a career for him. Here it is."

When he had finished reading the papers Leon gave him, Oster nodded. "It's good. It would be enough to get him arrested if he were exposed."

Leon grunted with satisfaction. "We have also found a guarantor for him. A former SS colonel from Bremerhaven is going on a sea cruise on February 16. He owns a bakery. When Miller presents himself as Kolb, after February 16, he will have a letter from this man assuring the Odessa that Kolb, who had been his employee, is genuinely a former SS man and genuinely in trouble. By that time the baker will be on the high seas and uncontactable. By the way"—he handed Miller a book—"you can learn baking as well."

He did not mention that the bakery owner would be away for only four weeks, and that after that Miller's life would hang by a thread.

"Now my friend the barber is going to change your appearance somewhat," Leon told Miller. "After that we'll take a new photograph for the driver's license."

In the upstairs bathroom the barber cut Miller's hair until his white scalp gleamed through the stubble. The rumpled look was gone. His eyebrows were plucked almost entirely away. "Bare eyebrows make the age almost unguessable within six or seven years," said the barber. "There's one last thing. You're to grow a mustache. It adds years, you know. Can you do that in a couple of weeks?"

"I guess so," Miller said, gazing at his reflection. He looked in his mid-thirties already.

When they got downstairs, Miller was told to stand up against a white sheet, and Motti took several photographs of him.

"I'll have the license ready within three days," he said.

The party left, and Oster turned to Miller. "Right, Kolb," he said, having already ceased to refer to him in any other way, "you were trained at Dachau, transferred to Flossenburg in July 1944. In April 1945 you commanded the squad that executed Admiral Canaris and other army officers suspected of complicity in the July 1944 assassination attempt on Hitler. Okay, let's get down to work, Sergeant."

THE man who sat in the window seat of the Olympic Airways flight from Athens to Munich that mid-February day seemed quiet and withdrawn. He had been born in Germany thirty-three years earlier, as Josef Kaplan, son of a Jewish tailor, in Karlsruhe. He had been three years old when Hitler came to power, seven when his parents had been taken away in a black van; he had been hidden in an attic for another three years until, at the age of ten in 1940, he too had been discovered and taken away. He had used the resilience and ingenuity of youth to survive in a series of concentration camps until 1945.

Two years later, aged seventeen and hungry as a rat, with that creature's mistrust of everyone and everything, he had come on a ship to a new shore many miles from Karlsruhe and Dachau. There he had taken the name of Uri Ben-Shaul.

The passing years had given him a wife and two children and a major's commission in the army, but had never eliminated the hatred he felt for the country to which he was traveling that day. He had agreed to swallow his feelings, to take up again, as he had done twice before, the façade of easy amiability that was necessary to effect his transformation back into a German. The Mossad had provided the other necessities: the passport, letters, cards—all the documentary paraphernalia of a citizen of a West European country—and the clothes and luggage of a German commercial traveler.

As the heavy clouds of Europe engulfed the plane, he reconsidered his mission. To follow a man named Peter Miller, to keep an eye on him—a young German four years his junior—while that man sought to do what several others had tried to do and failed: to infiltrate the Odessa. To check on the young man's findings and ascertain if he could trace the recruiter of the new wave of German scientists headed for Egypt to work on the rockets. Then to report back with the sum total of what the young man had found out before he was "blown," as he was bound to be.

He would do it; he did not have to enjoy doing it. Fortunately, no one asked him to like becoming a German again.

THE next day Oster and Miller had their last visit from Leon and Motti. With them was a new man, introduced simply as Josef.

"By the way," Motti told Miller, "I drove your car up here today. I've left it in a public parking lot down in the town, by the market square." He tossed Miller the keys, adding, "Don't use it when you go to meet the Odessa. It's too noticeable. And you're supposed to be only a bakery worker. When you go, travel by rail."

Miller nodded, but privately he regretted being separated from his beloved Jaguar.

"Here is your driver's license, complete with your photograph as you now look. You can tell anyone who asks that you drive a Volkswagen, but you have left it in Bremen, as the number could identify you to the police.

"The man who, unknown to him, is your guarantor, left from Bremerhaven on a cruise ship this morning. He was an SS colonel, is now a bakery owner and your former employer. His name is Joachim Eberhardt. Here is a letter from him to the man you are going to see. The paper was taken from his office. The signature is a perfect forgery. The letter tells its recipient that you are a good former SS man now fallen on misfortune, and asks him to help you acquire a new identity."

"Who's the man I have to present myself to?" Miller asked.

Leon handed him a sheet of paper. "That is his name and his address in Nuremberg. We are certain that he is very high up in the Odessa. He may have met Eberhardt, who is a big wheel in the Odessa in North Germany. Here is Eberhardt's photograph. Study it, in case your man asks for a description of him. I think you should probably present yourself next Thursday morning."

Miller nodded. "All right. Thursday it is."

"Remember," said Leon, "that we want to know who is recruiting rocket scientists for Egypt. And we want the Odessa's list of their top men in Germany. One last thing. Stay in touch. Use public telephones and phone this number whenever you get anything." He passed Miller a card. "Memorize and destroy it."

Twenty minutes later the group was gone.

ON THE way back to Munich, Leon and Josef sat in the back seat of the car in silence, the Israeli agent hunched in his corner. "Why so gloomy?" Leon said finally. "Everything is going well."

Josef glanced at him. "How reliable is this man Miller?"

"Reliable? He's the best chance we've ever had for penetrating the Odessa. You heard Oster. He can pass for a former SS man anywhere, provided he keeps his head."

"I'm supposed to watch him at all times," Josef grumbled. "I ought to be reporting back on every man he talks to. I wish I'd never agreed to let him go off alone. He's an amateur. Supposing he doesn't check in?"

Leon's anger was barely controlled. It was evident they had been through this before. "Now listen one more time. This man is *my* agent. I've waited years to get someone where he is now—a non-Jew. I'm not having him exposed by someone tagging along behind him."

BACK in Bayreuth, Miller stared out of the window at the falling snow. He had no intention of checking in by phone. He had no interest in rocket scientists. He had only one objective—Eduard Roschmann.

10

ON THE evening of Wednesday, February 19, Peter Miller bade farewell to Alfred Oster. He walked the mile to the railway station and there bought a one-way ticket to Nuremberg. As he passed through the ticket barrier toward the windswept platform the collector told him, "I'm afraid you'll have quite a wait, sir. The Nuremberg train will be late tonight."

Miller was surprised. German railroads made a point of honor of running on time. "What's happened?" he asked.

"There's been a large snowslide down the track. We've just heard the plow's broken down. The engineers are working on it."

Years in journalism had given Miller a deep loathing of waiting rooms. He had spent too much time in them, cold, tired, and uncomfortable. In the small station café he sipped a cup of coffee, and his mind went back to his car.

Surely, if he parked it on the other side of Nuremberg, several miles from the address he had been given . . . ? If, after the interview, they sent him on somewhere else by another means of transport, he would leave the Jaguar in a garage. No one would find it before the job was done. Besides, he reasoned, it wouldn't be a bad thing to have another way of getting out fast if the occasion required.

He thought of Motti's warning about its being too noticeable. But there was no reason for him to think anyone in Bavaria had ever heard of him or his car. To use it might be a risk, but to be stranded on foot was a greater one. He walked out of the station. Within ten minutes he was behind the wheel of the Jaguar and heading out of town.

When he arrived in Nuremberg, Miller parked his car in a side street, checked into a small hotel two blocks away, near the main station, and walked through the King's Gate into the old walled city.

Lights from the streets and windows lit up the quaint pointed roofs and decorated gables of the medieval town. It was hard to realize that almost every brick and stone of what he saw around him had been meticulously reconstructed since 1945. Old Nuremberg had been reduced to rubble by the Allied bombs.

He found the house he was looking for two streets from the square of the main market, almost under the twin spires of St. Sebald's Church.

He then walked back to the market square, looking for a place to have supper. After strolling past two or three traditional eating places, he noticed smoke curling up into the frosty night sky from the red-tiled roof of a small sausage house. It was a pretty little place, and inside, the warmth and good cheer hit him like a wave. He ordered the specialty of the house, the small spiced Nuremberg sausages, and treated himself to a bottle of the local wine to wash them down.

After his meal he dawdled over coffee, gazing at the logs flickering in the open fire. For a long time he wondered why he should bother to risk his life in the quest for a man who had committed crimes twenty years before. He almost decided to let the matter drop, to shave off his mustache, grow his hair again, and go back to Hamburg and the bed warmed by Sigi. Then when the bill came he reached for his wallet, and his fingers touched a photograph. He pulled it out and gazed at the rattrap mouth and the pale eyes that stared back at him from above the collar with the black tabs and the silver lightning symbols. After a while he held the photograph over the candle on his table. The picture was soon reduced to ashes. He would not need it again. He could recognize the face when he saw it.

MACKENSEN was confronting an angry and baffled Odessa chief at about the same time.

"How the hell *can* he be missing?" snapped Werewolf. "He can't vanish off the face of the earth. His car must be one of the most distinctive in Germany, visible half a mile off, and all you can tell me is that he hasn't been seen. . . ."

Mackensen waited until the outburst of frustration had spent itself. "Nevertheless, it's true. I've had his girl friend, his mother, and his colleagues interviewed. They all know nothing. He must have gone to ground."

"We have to find him," said Werewolf. "He must not get near to this *Kamerad*. It would be a disaster."

"He'll show up," said Mackensen with conviction. "Sooner or later he has to break cover. Then we'll have him."

Werewolf considered the logic of the professional hunter and nodded slowly. "Very well. Stay close to me. Check into a hotel here in town and we'll wait it out."

JUST before nine the following morning Miller rang a brilliantly polished doorbell. The door was opened by a maid, who showed him into an opulently furnished living room and went to fetch her employer.

The man who entered the room ten minutes later was in his mid-fifties, his medium-brown hair touched with silver at the temples. He was self-possessed and elegant, and gazed at his visitor without curiosity, assessing at a glance the inexpensive trousers and jacket of a working-class man. "And what can I do for you?" he inquired calmly.

"Well, *Herr Doktor*, I hoped you might be able to help me."

"Come now," said the Odessa man, "I'm sure you know my office

113

is not far from here. Perhaps you should go there and ask my secretary for an appointment."

"Well, it's not actually professional help I need," said Miller. He had dropped into the vernacular of Hamburg working people. He was obviously ill at ease. "I have here a letter of introduction from the man who suggested I come to you, sir."

The Odessa man took the letter without a word, and cast his eyes quickly down it. He stiffened slightly. "I see, Herr Kolb. Perhaps we had better sit down."

He spent several minutes looking speculatively at his guest, a frown on his face. Suddenly he snapped, "What did you say your name was?"

"Kolb, sir."

"First names?"

"Rolf Günther, sir."

"Do you have any identification on you?"

"Only my driver's license."

"Let me see it, please."

Miller placed the driver's license in his hand. The lawyer flicked it open and glanced over it at Miller, comparing the photograph and the face.

"What is your date of birth?" he snapped.

"My birthday? Oh . . . er . . . June eighteenth, sir."

"The year, Kolb."

"Nineteen twenty-five, sir."

The lawyer considered the driver's license for another few minutes. "Wait here," he said suddenly.

He traversed the house and entered his office at the rear, which was reached by clients from a back street. He went in, opened a wall safe, and took out a thick book.

He knew the name Joachim Eberhardt, but had never met the man. He was not completely certain of Eberhardt's last rank in the SS. The book confirmed the letter. Joachim Eberhardt, promoted colonel of the Waffen SS on January 10, 1945. He flicked over several more pages and checked against Kolb. Rolf Günther, staff sergeant as of April 1945. Date of birth 6/18/25. He closed the book, replaced it, and locked the safe. Then he returned to the living room and settled himself again.

"It may not be possible for me to help you. You realize that, don't you?"

Miller bit his lip and nodded. "I've nowhere else to go, sir. Herr Eberhardt said if you couldn't help me no one could."

The lawyer sighed. "You'd better tell me how you got into this mess in the first place."

"Well, sir, I was in Bremen. I live there, and until this happened I worked for Herr Eberhardt in the bakery. Well, I was walking in the street one day about four months back, and suddenly got very sick. I felt terribly ill, with stomach pains. I fainted on the pavement. So they took me away to the hospital."

"Which hospital?"

"Bremen General, sir. They did some tests, and they said I had cancer. In the intestine. Only apparently it was caught at an early stage. They put me on a course of drugs, and after some time the cancer went into remission."

"So far as I can see, you're a lucky man."

"Yes, well, then this Jewish hospital orderly kept staring at me. It was a funny sort of look, see? He had a sort of 'I know you' look on his face."

"Go on." The lawyer was showing increasing interest.

"So about a month ago they said I was ready to be transferred to a convalescent clinic. But before I left the hospital, I remembered the Jew-boy. He was an inmate at Flossenburg."

The lawyer sat upright. "You were at Flossenburg?"

"Yes, and I remembered this orderly from then. He was in the party of inmates that had to burn the bodies of Admiral Canaris and the others we hanged for trying to assassinate the Führer."

"You were one of those who executed Canaris and the others?"

Miller shrugged. "I commanded the execution squad."

The lawyer smiled. "That certainly would get you into bad trouble with the present authorities. Go on with your story."

"I was transferred to this clinic and I didn't see the Jewish orderly again. Then last Friday I got a telephone call. The man wouldn't give his name. He just said that a certain person had informed those swine at Ludwigsburg who I was, and there was a warrant being prepared for my arrest."

"Probably a friend on the police force of Bremen," the lawyer said. "What did you do?"

Miller looked surprised. "Well, I got out. I didn't go home, in case they were waiting for me there. I didn't even go and pick up my Volkswagen. On Saturday I went to see the boss, Herr Eberhardt. He was real nice to me. He said he was leaving for a winter cruise the next morning, so he gave me the letter and told me to come to you."

"Why did you think Herr Eberhardt would help you?"

"Well, I didn't know that he had been in the war till about two years back, when we were having the staff party. We all got a little drunk, and I went to the men's room. There was Herr Eberhardt washing his hands and singing the 'Horst Wessel Song.' So I joined in. There we were, singing it in the men's room. Then he clapped me on the back and said, 'Not a word, Kolb,' and went out. I didn't think any more about it till I got into trouble. Then I thought—well, he might have been in the SS like me. So I went to him for help."

"What was the name of the Jewish orderly?"

"Hartstein, sir."

"And the convalescent clinic you were sent to?"

"The Arcadia Clinic, at Delmenhorst."

The lawyer made a few notes on a sheet of paper and rose. "Stay here," he said, and crossed the passage to his study. He rang the Eberhardt bakery first.

Eberhardt's secretary was most helpful.

"I'm afraid Herr Eberhardt is away, sir. . . . No, he can't be, sir; he has gone on his usual winter cruise to the Caribbean. . . . Yes, in four weeks, sir."

The lawyer thought briefly of asking her if Kolb had worked there, but dismissed it as unwise to arouse a secretary's curiosity if Kolb was who he said he was. He then called Bremen General Hospital instead and asked for the personnel office.

"This is the Department of Social Security, Pensions Section," he said. "I want to confirm that you have a ward orderly on the staff by the name of Hartstein."

There was a pause while the girl at the other end went through the staff file. "Yes, we do," she said. "David Hartstein."

"Thank you," said the lawyer, and hung up. He dialed the same number again and asked for the registrar's office.

"This is the secretary of the Eberhardt Baking Company," he said. "I want to check on the progress of one of our staff who has been in your hospital with a tumor in the intestine. His name is Rolf Günther Kolb."

There was another pause. "He's been discharged," the caller was told. "He was transferred to a convalescent clinic."

"Excellent," said the lawyer. "Can you tell me which clinic?"

"The Arcadia, at Delmenhorst," said the girl.

The lawyer next dialed the Arcadia Clinic. A girl answered. After hearing the request she covered the mouthpiece and murmured to the doctor by her side, "There's a question about that man you mentioned to me, Kolb."

The doctor took the telephone. "This is the chief of the clinic, Dr. Braun," he said. "Can I help you?"

At the name, the secretary shot a puzzled glance at her employer. Without batting an eyelid he listened to the voice from Nuremberg and replied smoothly, "Herr Kolb discharged himself last Friday afternoon. Most irregular, but there was nothing I could do to prevent him. . . . Yes, he was transferred here from Bremen General. A tumor, well on the way to recovery." He listened for a moment, then said, "Not at all. Glad I could be of help to you."

The doctor, whose real name was Rosemayer, hung up and then dialed Munich. Without preamble he said, "Someone's been on the phone asking about Kolb. The checking up has started."

Back in Nuremberg the lawyer replaced the phone and returned to the living room. "Right, Kolb, you evidently are who you say you are. However, I'd like to ask you a few more questions. Are you circumcised?"

Miller stared back blankly. "No, I'm not," he said.

"Show me, Staff Sergeant," snapped the lawyer.

Miller shot out of his chair, ramrodding to attention. *"Zu Befehl,"* he responded. He held the position for three seconds, then un-zipped his fly.

"Well, at least you're not Jewish," the lawyer said amiably.

Miller stared at him. "Of course I'm not Jewish."

The lawyer smiled. "There have been cases of Jews trying to pass themselves off as *Kameraden*. They don't last long. Now I'm going to shoot some questions at you. Where were you born?"

"Bremen, sir."

"Were you in the Hitler Youth?"

"Yes, sir. Entered at the age of ten in 1935, sir."

"When were you inducted into the SS?"

"Spring 1944, sir. Age eighteen."

"Where did you train?"

"Dachau SS training camp, sir."

"You had your blood group tattooed under your right armpit?"

"No, sir. And it would have been the left armpit."

"Why weren't you tattooed?"

"Well, sir, we were due to pass out of training camp in August 1944. But in July a group of army officers involved in the plot against the Führer were sent down to Flossenburg, and troops were taken immediately from Dachau to increase their staff. I and about a dozen others went straight there. We missed our tattooing, but the commandant said it was not necessary, as we would never get to the front, sir."

The lawyer nodded. No doubt the commandant had been aware in July 1944 that the war was drawing to a close.

"Did you get your dagger?"

"Yes, sir. From the hands of the commandant."

"What are the words on it?"

" 'Blood and Honor,' sir."

"What was the book of marching songs from which the 'Horst Wessel Song' was drawn?"

"Time of Struggle for the Nation, sir."

"What was your uniform?"

"Gray-green tunic and breeches, jackboots, black collar lapels, black belt, and gunmetal buckle, sir."

"The motto on the buckle?"

"A swastika ringed with the words 'My honor is loyalty.'"

The lawyer lit a cigar and strolled to the window. "Now you'll tell me about Flossenburg camp, Staff Sergeant Kolb. How large was it?"

"When I was there, sir, three hundred twenty-eight yards square. It had a big roll-call area. God, we had fun—"

"Stick to the point," snapped the lawyer. "What was the population in late 1944?"

"Oh, about sixteen thousand inmates, sir."

"Where was the commandant's office?"

"Outside the wire, sir, halfway up a slope above the camp."

"Which was the number of the political department?"

"Department two, sir."

"Where was it?"

"In the commandant's block."

"One last question, Staff Sergeant. When you looked up, from anywhere in the camp, what did you see?"

Miller looked puzzled. "The sky," he said.

"Fool, I mean what dominated the horizon?"

"Oh, you mean the hill with the ruined castle on it?"

The lawyer nodded and smiled. "All right, Kolb, you were at Flossenburg. Now, how did you get away?"

"Well, sir, it was on the march. We all broke up. I found an army private wandering around, so I hit him on the head and took his uniform. The Yanks caught me two days later. I did two years in a prisoner-of-war camp. They thought I was in the army, sir."

The lawyer exhaled cigar smoke. "Did you change your name?"

"No, sir. I threw my papers away, because they identified me as SS. But I didn't think to change the name. I didn't think anyone would look for a staff sergeant. Nothing would have happened if that orderly hadn't spotted me, and after that it wouldn't have mattered what I called myself."

"True. Now repeat the oath of loyalty to the Führer."

It went on for another three hours. It was past lunchtime when at last the lawyer professed himself satisfied.

"Just what do you want?" he asked Miller.

"Well, sir, with them all looking for me, I'm going to need a set of papers showing I am not Rolf Günther Kolb. I can change my appearance, grow my hair and mustache longer, and get a job in Bavaria or somewhere. I mean, I'm a skilled baker, and people need bread, don't they?"

The lawyer threw back his head and laughed. "Yes, my good Kolb, people need bread. Very well. I'll do what I can. You need a new passport. Have you got any money?"

"No, sir. I'm dead broke. I've been hitchhiking."

The lawyer gave him a hundred-mark note. "I'll send you to a friend of mine in Stuttgart who will get you a passport. Check into a commercial hotel, then go and see him. He's called Franz Bayer, and here's his address. If you need a little more money, he'll help you out. But stay under cover until you have the passport. Then we'll find you a job in southern Germany, and no one will ever trace you."

Miller took the hundred marks and the address of Bayer with embarrassed thanks. "Oh, thank you, *Herr Doktor*, thank you."

The maid showed him out, and he walked back to his car. He was speeding toward Stuttgart while the lawyer was telling Bayer to expect Rolf Günther Kolb in the early evening.

Miller arrived after dark and found a small hotel in the outer city that had a garage around in back for the car. From the hall porter he got a town plan and found Bayer's street in the suburb of Ostheim. Following the map he drove down into the bowl of hills that frames the center of Stuttgart and parked a quarter mile from Bayer's house. As he stooped to lock the driver's door he failed to notice a middle-aged lady coming home from her weekly meeting of the Hospital Visitors Committee.

At eight that evening the lawyer in Nuremberg thought he had better ring Bayer and make sure Kolb had arrived safely. It was Bayer's wife who answered.

"Oh, yes, the young man and my husband have gone out to dinner somewhere. Such a nice young man," Frau Bayer burbled on. "I passed him as he was parking his car—"

"Excuse me, Frau Bayer," the lawyer cut in. "The man did not have his Volkswagen with him. He went by train."

"No, no," said Frau Bayer. "He came by car . . . a long black sports car, with a yellow stripe down the side—"

The lawyer slammed down the phone, then raised it and dialed a hotel in Nuremberg. He was sweating slightly. He asked for a room number, and a familiar voice said, "Hello."

"Mackensen," barked Werewolf, "get over here fast. We've found Miller."

11

FRANZ BAYER was fat and round and jolly. He welcomed Miller when he presented himself just before eight o'clock.

Miller was introduced to his wife and then she bustled off to the kitchen.

"Well now," said Bayer, "no doubt you'd like some food. Tell you what, we'll go into town and have a really good dinner. . . . Nonsense, my boy, the least I can do for you."

Ten minutes later they were in Bayer's car heading toward the city center.

IT WAS at least a two-hour drive from Nuremberg to Stuttgart, even if one pushed the car hard. And Mackensen pushed that night. He arrived at Bayer's house at half past ten.

Frau Bayer, alerted by another call from Werewolf, was a trembling and frightened woman. Mackensen's manner was hardly calculated to put her at ease. "When did they leave?"

"About eight," she quavered.

"Did they say where they were going?"

"No. Franz just said he was taking the young man into town for a meal. Franz loves dining out. His favorite place is the Three Moors on Friedrichstrasse," she said.

"What did the young man look like?"

"Oh, brown hair and mustache. Tall, I'd say."

"You said you saw him parking his car. Where was this?"

She described the location of the Jaguar, and how to get to it from her house.

"So they went into town in your husband's car? Its make and license number?"

Armed with all the information he needed, Mackensen left Frau Bayer and drove to the parked Jaguar. He examined it closely, certain he would recognize it again, then climbed back into his Mercedes and headed for the center of Stuttgart.

IN A small hotel in the back streets of Munich a cable was delivered to Josef in his room. He slit the envelope and scanned the lengthy contents. It began:

CELERY 481 MARKS 53 PFENNIGS, MELONS 362 MARKS 17 PFENNIGS, ORANGES 627 MARKS 24 PFENNIGS, GRAPEFRUIT 313 MARKS 88 PFENNIGS . . .

Ignoring the words, Josef wrote down the figures in a long line, then split them into groups of six figures. From each six-figure group he subtracted the date, February 20, 1964, which he wrote as 22064. In each case the result was another six-figure group. It was a simple book code, based on the paperback edition of a well-known dictionary. The first three figures in the group represented the page in the dictionary; the fourth figure could be anything from one to nine. An odd number meant column one, an even number column two. The last two figures indicated the number of words down the column from the top. He worked steadily for half an hour, then slowly read the message through.

Thirty minutes later he was in Leon's cellar. The revenge-group leader read the message and swore. "I'm sorry," he said at last. "I couldn't have known."

Unknown to either man, three fragments of information had come into the possession of the Mossad in the previous six days. One was from the resident Israeli agent in Buenos Aires to the effect that someone had authorized the payment of one million German marks to a figure called Vulcan "to enable him to complete the next stage of his research project."

The second, from a Jewish employee of a Swiss bank known to handle transfers of Nazi funds, noted that one million marks had been transferred from a Beirut bank and collected by a man named Fritz Wegener.

The third item came from an Egyptian colonel in a security position at Factory 333 in Cairo. He reported that the rocket project was lacking only a reliable teleguidance system, and that this was being constructed in a factory in West Germany and was costing the Odessa millions of marks.

The three fragments, among thousands of others, had been processed by a computer in Tel Aviv. Where a human memory might have failed, the whirring microcircuits had linked the three items, had recalled that, up to his exposure by his wife in 1955, Eduard Roschmann had used the name of Fritz Wegener, and had reported accordingly.

Josef turned on Leon. "I'm not moving out of range of that telephone from now on. Get me a powerful motorcycle and protective clothing. Have both ready within the hour. If and when your precious Miller checks in, I'll have to get to him fast."

"If he's exposed, you won't get there fast enough," said Leon. "No wonder they warned him off. They'll kill him if he gets within a mile of his man."

As Leon left the cellar, Josef ran his eye over the message from Tel Aviv again. It said:

Red alert new information indicates vital key rocket success German industrialist operating your territory. Code name Vulcan. Probably Roschmann. Use Miller instantly. Trace and eliminate. Cormorant

Josef sat at the table and meticulously began to clean and arm his Walther PPK automatic. From time to time he glanced at the silent telephone.

OVER DINNER BAYER had been the genial host, roaring with laughter as he told his own favorite jokes. Every time Miller tried to get the talk around to his passport, Bayer clapped him on the back. "Leave it to me, old boy, leave it to old Franz."

One thing Miller had developed from eight years as a reporter was the ability to drink and keep a clear head. By the dessert course they had demolished two bottles of excellent cold hock, and Bayer, squeezed into his tight horn-buttoned jacket, was perspiring in torrents. He called for a third bottle of wine.

Miller pretended to be worried that it would prove impossible to get a passport for him. "You'll need photographs of me, won't you?" he asked with concern.

Bayer guffawed. "Yes, a couple of them. No problem. You can get them taken in one of the booths at the station."

"What happens then?" asked Miller.

Bayer leaned over and placed a fat arm around his shoulders. "Then I send them away to a friend of mine, and a week later back comes the passport. No problem, old chap, stop worrying."

Miller was afraid to push him further. The fat man paid for the meal finally and they headed for the door. It was half past ten.

"I suppose that's the end of what Stuttgart has to offer in the way of night life," observed Miller.

"Ha, silly boy. That's all you know. There's the Moulin Rouge, the Balzac, the Imperial, and the Sayonara. Then there's the Madeleine. . . ." Bayer led the way to his car.

MACKENSEN reached the Three Moors at quarter past eleven.

"Herr Bayer?" said the headwaiter. "Yes, he left a while ago."

"He had a guest? Tall, with short brown hair and a mustache?"

"That's right."

Mackensen slipped a twenty-mark note into the man's hand without difficulty. "It's vitally important that I find him. Do you know where they went from here?"

"I confess I don't," said the headwaiter. He called to one of the junior waiters. "Hans, you served Herr Bayer and his guest. Did they mention if they were going on anywhere?"

"No," said Hans. "I didn't hear anything."

Mackensen asked for a copy of the tourist booklet *What's Going On in Stuttgart*. He headed for the first cabaret on the list.

MILLER and Bayer sat at a table for two in the Madeleine. Bayer, on his second large whiskey, stared with popeyes at a generously endowed young woman gyrating her hips in the center of the floor. It was well after midnight, and he was very drunk.

"Look, Herr Bayer," whispered Miller. "How soon can you—"

Bayer draped his arm around Miller's shoulders. "Look, Rolf, old buddy, I've told you. You don't have to worry, see? Just leave it to Franz." He flapped a pudgy hand in the air. "Waiter, another round."

When Miller finally got the Odessa man away from the club, it was after one in the morning and Bayer was unsteady on his feet.

"I'd better drive you home," Miller said as they approached Bayer's car. He took the keys from Bayer's coat pocket and helped the unprotesting fat man into the passenger seat. He slammed the door, walked around to the driver's side, and climbed in. At that moment a gray Mercedes slewed around the corner behind them and stopped twenty yards up the road.

Mackensen, who had visited five nightclubs, stared at the license plate of the car moving away from the curb. It was the number Frau Bayer had given him. He let in his clutch and followed.

Miller drove, not back to Bayer's house, but to his own hotel. On the way Bayer dozed, his head nodding forward. Outside the hotel Miller nudged him awake. "Come on, Franz, old mate. Let's have a nightcap."

The fat man stared about him. "Must get home," he mumbled. "Wife waiting."

"Come on, just a little drink to finish the evening. We can have a noggin in my room and talk about the old times."

Bayer grinned drunkenly. "Great times we had, Rolf."

"Great," Miller said as he helped Bayer out of the car.

Down the street the Mercedes had doused its lights and merged with the gray shadows.

Behind his desk the night porter seemed to be dozing. Bayer started to mumble.

"Ssssh," said Miller, "got to be quiet."

"Got to be quiet," repeated Bayer, tiptoeing like an elephant toward the stairs. Fortunately for Miller, his room was on the second floor, or Bayer would never have made it. He opened the door, flicked on the light, and helped Bayer into an armchair.

Outside, Mackensen stood across from the hotel. At two in the morning there were no lights burning. When a light came on he noted it was on the second floor, on the right side of the hotel.

He debated whether to go up and hit Miller as he opened his bedroom door. Two things decided him against it. The night porter, waked by Bayer's heavy tread, was puttering around the foyer. And the fat man was too drunk to be capable of getting out of the hotel in a hurry. If the police got Bayer, there would be bad trouble with Werewolf. Despite appearances, he was a much-wanted man under his real name.

Across from the hotel was a building halfway through construction. The frame and the floors were in place, with a rough concrete stairway leading up to the second floor. He could wait there and try for a window shot. Mackensen walked purposefully back to his car to get the hunting rifle which was locked in the trunk.

BAYER was taken completely by surprise when the blow came. Miller had never had occasion to use the blows he had learned in the army, and he was not entirely certain how effective they were. The vast bulk of Bayer's neck caused him to hit as hard as he could.

It was hard enough. By the time the dizziness had cleared from Bayer's brain, both his wrists were lashed tightly to the arms of the wooden chair with two of Miller's ties, and his own tie had been pulled off his neck to secure his left ankle to the foot of the chair.

"What the . . . ?" he growled thickly as Miller bound the right ankle with the telephone cord.

As comprehension began to dawn, he looked up owlishly at Miller. Like all of his kind, Bayer had one nightmare that never quite left him. "You'll never get me to Tel Aviv. You can't prove anything. I never touched you people—"

The words were cut off as a rolled-up sock was stuffed in his mouth and Miller's woolen scarf was wound around his face.

Miller drew up a chair and sat astride it, his face two feet from his prisoner's. "Listen, you fat slug. For one thing, I'm not an Israeli agent. For another, you're not going anywhere. And you're going to talk. Understand?"

For answer Franz Bayer stared back above the scarf. His eyes were red-tinged, like those of an angry boar.

Miller looked around, spotted the bedside lamp, and brought it over. "Now, Bayer, or whatever your name is, I'm going to take the gag off. You are going to tell me the name and address of the man who makes the passports for the Odessa. If you attempt to yell, you get this right across the head."

He eased off the scarf and pulled the sock out of Bayer's mouth, keeping the lamp poised in his right hand.

"You bastard," hissed Bayer. "You'll get nothing out of me."

He hardly got the words out before the sock went back into his bulging cheeks. Miller set the lamp on the floor and replaced the scarf.

"No?" said Miller. "We'll see. I'll start on your fingers."

He took the little finger and ring finger of Bayer's right hand and bent them backward. Bayer threw himself about in the chair and Miller took off the gag again.

"I can break every finger on both your hands, Bayer," he whispered. "After that I'll take the bulb out of the table lamp, and you know what I'll do with the socket."

Sweat rolled in torrents off Bayer's face. "No, not the electrodes."

"You know what it's like, don't you?"

Bayer closed his eyes and moaned softly. He knew too well what it was like, but not on the receiving end.

"Talk," whispered Miller. "The forger, his name and address."

Bayer slowly shook his head. "I can't," he whispered. "They'll kill me."

Miller replaced the gag. He took Bayer's little finger, closed his eyes, and jerked once. The bone snapped. Bayer heaved in his chair and vomited into the gag. Miller whipped it off before the fat man could drown in the evening's highly expensive food and drink. "Talk," he said. "You've got nine fingers to go."

Bayer swallowed, eyes closed. "Winzer. Klaus Winzer."

"He's a professional forger?"

"He's a printer."

"Where? Which town?"

"They'll kill me."

"I'll kill you if you don't tell me. Which town?"

"Osnabrück," whispered Bayer.

Miller replaced the gag, went to his attaché case, and took out a road map. Osnabrück was a four- or five-hour drive to the north. It was already nearly three in the morning of February 21.

Across the road Mackensen shivered in the half-completed building. The light still shone in the hotel room opposite. He flicked his eyes constantly from the illuminated window to the front door. If only Bayer would come out, he thought, he could take Miller alone. Or if Miller came out, he could take him farther down the street.

In his room Miller quietly packed his things. He needed Bayer to remain quiescent for at least six hours, so he spent a few minutes tightening the bonds and the gag that held the fat man immobile and silent, then eased the chair onto its side so he could not raise an alarm by rolling the chair over with a crash. The telephone cord was already ripped out. He took a last look around and left the room, locking the door behind him.

He was almost at the top of the stairs when a thought came to him. The night porter might have been awake enough to have seen them both mount the stairs. What would he think if only one came down, paid his bill, and left? Miller retreated and headed for the back of the hotel. At the end of the corridor was a window looking out onto the fire escape. He slipped the catch and stepped out onto the ladder. Seconds later he was in an alley back of the hotel, and off at a stride to where he had left his Jaguar, a quarter mile from Bayer's house, three miles away. He was desperately tired, but he had to reach Winzer before the alarm was raised. It was almost four in the morning when he climbed into the Jaguar, and half past four before he was on the autobahn, streaking north.

ALMOST as soon as Miller had gone, Bayer, by now completely sober, began to struggle to get free. He tried to lean forward far enough to use his teeth on the ties that bound his wrists. But his fatness prevented his head getting low enough, and the sock in his mouth forced his teeth apart. ·

Finally he spotted the table lamp lying on the floor. The bulb was still in it. It took him an hour to inch the overturned chair across the floor and crush the light bulb.

It may sound easy to use a piece of broken glass to cut wrist bonds, but it isn't. It was seven in the morning, and light was beginning to filter over the roofs of the town, before the first strands binding his left wrist parted. It was nearly eight before Bayer had one wrist free.

By that time Miller's Jaguar was boring around the Cologne Ring to the west of the city, with another hundred miles to go before Osnabrück. It had started to rain, an evil sleet running in curtains across the slippery autobahn, and the mesmeric effect of the windshield wipers almost put him to sleep. He slowed down to a steady eighty miles per hour rather than risk running off the road into the muddy fields on either side.

With his left hand free, Bayer took only a few minutes to rip off his gag, then lay whooping in great gulps of air. He unpicked the knots on his right wrist, then released his feet. His first thought was the door, but it was locked. Then the telephone, but it was ripped out. Finally he staggered on numb feet to the window, ripped back the curtains, and jerked the window open.

In his shooting niche across the road Mackensen was almost dozing, in spite of the cold, when he saw the curtains of Miller's room pulled back. Snapping the Remington up into aiming position, he waited until the window was opened, then fired straight into the face of the figure.

Bayer was dead before his reeling bulk tumbled backward to the

floor. Without a second look across the road, Mackensen ran. The crash of the rifle might be put down to a car backfiring for a minute, but not longer. He regained his car, stowed the gun in the trunk, and drove off. But he suspected he had made a mistake. The man he was to kill was tall and lean. The figure at the window was fat. He was sure it was Bayer he had hit.

Not that it was too serious a problem. Seeing Bayer dead on his carpet, Miller would be bound to flee. Therefore he would run to his Jaguar, parked three miles away. Mackensen did not begin to worry until he saw the empty space where the Jaguar had stood the previous evening.

Mackensen would not have been the chief executioner for the Odessa if he had been the sort who panicked easily. He had been in too many tight spots before. He sat at the wheel of the Mercedes for several minutes while he digested the fact that Miller could now be hundreds of miles away. If Miller had left Bayer alive because he had got nothing from him, there was no harm done; he could take Miller later. If Miller had got something from Bayer, Werewolf alone would know what information Bayer had to give. There was nothing to do but call Nuremberg.

When Werewolf heard the news, he went into the transports of rage that Mackensen had feared. "You'd better find him, you oaf, and quickly."

Mackensen explained that to find Miller he needed to know what kind of information Bayer could have supplied.

"Dear God," Werewolf breathed, "the forger. He's got the name of the forger."

"What forger, Chief?" asked Mackensen.

Werewolf pulled himself together. "I'll warn the man," he said crisply. "This is where Miller has gone." He dictated an address to Mackensen. "You get the hell up to Osnabrück like you've never moved before. If Miller's not at that house, keep searching the town for the Jaguar. And this time don't leave that car. It's the one place he always returns to."

He slammed down the phone, and then picked it up again and dialed Osnabrück.

12

KLAUS WINZER had had one of the strangest careers of any man to have worn the uniform of the SS. Born in 1924, he was the son of Johann Winzer, a pork butcher of Wiesbaden, a large, boisterous man who from the early 1920s onward was a trusting follower of Adolf Hitler and the Nazi party.

To his father's disgust Klaus grew up small, weak, nearsighted, and peaceful. At only one thing did he excel: in his early teens he fell in love with the art of handwriting and the preparation of illuminated manuscripts, an activity his disgusted father regarded as an occupation for sissies.

The war came, and in the spring of 1942 Klaus was called up for the draft. Failing to pass the medical even for an army desk job, he was sent home. For his father this was the last straw.

Johann Winzer went to Berlin to see an old friend who had risen high in the SS, in the hope the man might obtain for his son an entry into some branch of service to the Reich. The man asked if there was anything the young Klaus could do well. Shamefacedly, Johann admitted his son could prepare illuminated manuscripts, and the friend asked if Klaus would do an illuminated address on parchment, in honor of an SS major.

At the presentation in Berlin, everyone admired the beautiful manuscript, and a certain officer of the RSHA asked who had done it and requested that young Klaus Winzer be brought to Berlin. Before he knew what was happening, Klaus was inducted into the SS, made to swear oaths of loyalty and secrecy, and told he would be transferred to a top-secret project. His father, though bewildered, was in seventh heaven.

The project was basically quite simple. The SS was trying to forge hundreds of thousands of British five-pound notes and American hundred-dollar bills. It was for his knowledge of papers and inks that they wanted Klaus.

The idea was to flood Britain and America with phony money, thus ruining the economies of both countries. In early 1943, when the watermark for the British fivers had been achieved, the printing project was transferred to Sachsenhausen concentration camp, where graphic artists among the inmates worked under the direction of the SS. Winzer's job was quality control, for the SS did not trust their prisoners not to make a deliberate error in their work. Toward the end of 1944 the project was also used to prepare the forged identity cards that the SS officers would use when Germany collapsed.

At the end of the war Klaus Winzer sadly went back home to Wiesbaden. To his astonishment, having never lacked for a meal in the SS, he found civilians almost starving. His mother explained that all food had to be bought with ration cards issued by the Americans. Klaus took to his room for a few days, and when he emerged, it was to hand over to his astounded mother enough ration cards to feed them all for six months.

A month later Klaus Winzer met Otto Klops, the king of the black market of Wiesbaden, and they were in business. Winzer turned out ration cards, gasoline coupons, zonal passes, driver's licenses, PX cards; Klops used them to buy food, gasoline, tires, soap, cosmetics, and clothing, which he sold at black-market prices. By the summer of 1948 Klaus Winzer was a rich man.

But that October the authorities reformed the currency, and with it the German economy. The populace, no longer needing the black marketeers as goods came on the open market, denounced Klops; and Winzer, ruined, had to flee. Taking one of his own zonal passes and some forged references, he drove to the headquarters of the British Zone at Hanover and applied for a job in the passport office of the military government.

Two months later he was in a beer hall when a man named Herbert Molders confided that he was being sought by the British for war crimes and needed to get out of Germany. But only the British could supply passports to Germans, and he dared not apply. Winzer murmured that it might be arranged but would cost money.

Molders produced a diamond necklace which he had obtained from a concentration-camp inmate, and a week later Winzer prepared the passport. He did not even forge it. He did not need to.

The system at the passport office was simple. In section one, applicants turned up with all their documentation and filled out a form. Section two examined the documents for forgery and checked the wanted list; if the application was approved, the documents, signed by the head of the department, were passed to section three. Section three, on receipt of the note of approval from section two, took a blank passport from the safe where they were stored, filled it out, and stuck in the applicant's photograph.

Winzer got himself transferred to section three. He filled out an application form for Molders in a new name, wrote out an "application approved" slip from the head of section two, forging that British officer's signature. Then he walked into section two, picked up the application forms and approval slips waiting to go on to section three—there were nineteen that day—and slipped the Molders papers in with them. In the routine way, he took the sheaf of papers to Major Johnstone of section three. The major checked that there were twenty approval slips, so he took twenty passports from his safe and handed them to Winzer. Winzer duly stamped them, passed on nineteen of them to nineteen happy applicants, and put the twentieth in his pocket.

That evening Klaus gave Molders his new passport and went home with a diamond necklace. He had found his new métier.

Each week thereafter, armed with a photograph of one nonentity, Winzer carefully filled out a passport application and slipped it in with the regular sheaf of forms and approval slips. So long as the numbers tallied, he got a bunch of blank passports in return. All but one went to genuine applicants. The blank one went home with Klaus. All he needed then was the official stamp. He took it for one night, and by morning had his own casting of the stamp of the passport office of the state government of Lower Saxony.

In sixty weeks he had sixty blank passports. He resigned his job, sold the diamond necklace in Antwerp, and started a nice little printing business in Osnabrück.

He would never have got involved with the Odessa if Molders had kept his mouth shut. But Molders, now in Madrid, boasted about him. From then on, whenever an Odessa man was in trouble, Winzer supplied the new West German passport; by the spring of 1964 he had used forty-two out of his stock of sixty.

But the cunning little man had taken one precaution. It occurred to him that one day the Odessa might wish to dispose of his services, and of him. So he kept a record. He never knew the real names of his clients; to make out a false passport in a new name it was not necessary. But he made two copies of every photograph sent to him, pasted the original in the passport he was sending back, and kept the copies. Each photograph was pasted onto a sheet of paper, and beside it was typed the new name, the address, and the new passport number.

This file was his life insurance. There was a copy in his house, and one with a lawyer in Zurich. If the Odessa ever threatened him, he would warn them that if anything happened to him his lawyer would send the copy to the West German authorities. They, armed with the photographs, would soon compare them with their rogues' gallery, and exposure of the wanted Nazis would take no more than a week. It was a foolproof scheme to ensure that Klaus Winzer stayed alive and in good health.

This, then, was the man who sat quietly munching his toast and jam that Friday morning when the phone rang. The voice at the other end was first peremptory, then reassuring.

"There is no question of your being in any trouble with us at all," Werewolf assured him. "It's just this damn reporter. We have a tip that he's coming to see you. It's all right. We have one of our men coming up behind him, and the whole affair will be taken care of within the day. But you must get out of there at once. Now here's what I want you to do. . . ."

Thirty minutes later a very flustered Klaus Winzer explained to his housemaid that instead of going to the printing plant that morning he had decided to take a vacation in the Austrian Alps.

MILLER found a filling station at the Saarplatz at the western entrance to Osnabrück. He pulled up and climbed wearily out.

"Fill her up," he told the attendant, and headed for the phone booth. He found two listings for Klaus Winzer, one marked "printer," the second "res." for residence. As it was nine twenty, he rang the printing plant.

The man who answered said, "I'm sorry, he's not in yet. He'll no doubt be along soon. Call back in half an hour."

Miller thanked him, and headed for the suburb of Westerberg, where Winzer lived.

The house was in an obviously prosperous area. Miller left the Jaguar at the end of the drive and walked to the front door.

The maid who answered it smiled brightly at him.

"Good morning. I've come to see Herr Winzer," he told her.

"Oooh, he's left, sir. You just missed him by about twenty minutes. He's gone off on vacation."

Miller fought down a feeling of panic. "Vacation? That's odd at this time of year. Besides"—he invented quickly—"we had an appointment this morning."

"Oh, what a shame," said the girl. "He went off very suddenly. He got this phone call in the library, then, 'Barbara,' he said, 'I'm going on vacation!' He told me to call the plant and say he's not coming in for a week. That's not like Herr Winzer at all."

"Do you know where he went?" Inside Miller hope began to die.

"No. He just said he was going to the Austrian Alps."

"No forwarding address? No way of getting in touch with him?"

"No, that's what's so strange."

"Could I speak to Frau Winzer, please?" Miller asked.

Barbara looked at him archly. "There isn't any Frau Winzer."

"So he lives here alone, then?"

"Well, except for me. I mean, I live in. It's quite safe. From that point of view." She giggled.

"I see. Thank you," said Miller, and turned to go.

"You're welcome," said the girl, and watched him go down the drive and climb into the Jaguar, which had already caught her attention. She sighed for what might have been, and closed the door.

Miller felt the weariness creeping over him, accentuated by this final disappointment. He had got so close—only twenty minutes from his target. He surmised Bayer must have wriggled free and rung Winzer. Desperate for sleep, Miller drove to the Theodor-Heuss-Platz, parked in front of the station, and checked into the Hohenzollern Hotel across the square.

They had a room available at once, so he went upstairs, undressed, and lay on the bed. There was something nagging in the back of his mind, some tiny detail of a question he had left unasked. It was still unsolved when he fell asleep at half past ten.

MACKENSEN made it to the center of Osnabrück at half past one. On the way into town he had checked Winzer's house, but there was no sign of a Jaguar. At the Theodor-Heuss-Platz his face split in a grin. He phoned Werewolf and found him in a better mood.

"I reached Winzer in time," Werewolf said. "I just phoned his house to check, and the maid told me he had left town barely twenty minutes before a young man with a black sports car came inquiring after him."

"I've got some news too," said Mackensen. "The Jaguar is parked right here on the square. Chances are he's sleeping it off in the hotel, and I can take him in his room."

"Hold it," warned Werewolf. "I've been thinking. For one thing, don't do it in Osnabrück. The maid has seen him and his car and would probably report to the police. I can't have any attention directed to our forger. One other thing—does Miller carry an attaché case?"

"Yes," said Mackensen. "He had it with him last night."

"The point is," said Werewolf, "he has now seen me and knows my name and address. He knows of my connection with Bayer and the forger. And reporters write things down. That attaché case must not fall into the hands of the police."

"I've got you. You want the case as well?"

"Either get it or destroy it."

"The best way to do both would be for me to plant a bomb in the car. Linked to the suspension, so it will detonate when he hits a bump at high speed."

"Excellent," said Werewolf. "Can you do it?"

Mackensen grinned as he thought of the killing kit in the trunk of his car; it was an assassin's dream and included nearly a pound of plastic explosive and two electric detonators. "Sure, no problem. I'll have to wait until dark—" He stopped talking, gazed out of the window and barked into the phone, "Call you back."

He called back in five minutes. "Sorry. I just saw Miller, attaché case in hand, get into his car and drive off. I checked the hotel, and he's left his bags, so he'll be back. I'll get on with the bomb and plant it tonight."

MILLER woke up just before one, mildly elated. He had remembered what was troubling him. He drove back to Winzer's house.

"Hello, you again?" The maid beamed.

"I was just passing on my way back home," said Miller, "and I wondered—how long have you been in service here?"

"Oh, about ten months. Why?"

"Well, who looked after Herr Winzer before you came?"

"His housekeeper, Fräulein Wendel."

"Where is she now?"

"Oh, in the hospital. Dying of cancer, I'm afraid. That's another thing makes it so funny that Herr Winzer dashed off like that. He goes to visit her every day. He's devoted to her. She was with him for a long time—since 1950, I think."

"What hospital is she in?" asked Miller.

She gave him the name of an exclusive private sanatorium.

Miller presented himself there at three that afternoon.

MACKENSEN spent the early afternoon buying the rest of the ingredients for his bomb. "The secret of sabotage," his instructor had once told him, "is to keep the requirements simple. The sort of things you can buy in any shop."

With his purchases made, he took a room in the Hohenzollern Hotel overlooking the square, so that he could keep an eye on the parking area to which he was certain Miller would return.

Seated at the table in front of the window, with a pot of black coffee to stave off his tiredness, he went to work.

It was a simple bomb, involving plastic explosive, a transistor battery, and electric detonators. The trigger mechanism consisted of two six-inch lengths of hacksaw blade, bound parallel to each other, one and a quarter inches apart, but under tension, ready to close. To prevent their touching, he lodged a light bulb between the open jaws, fixing it in place with a generous blob of glue. Glass does not conduct electricity. Should the trigger be subjected to sudden pressure, the bulb would shatter, the two lengths of steel would close together, and the electric circuit from the battery would be complete.

His bomb device finished, he stowed it in the bottom of the wardrobe, along with the materials he'd need to attach it to Miller's car. Then he settled down at the window to wait.

13

THE DOCTOR glanced with little favor at the visitor. Miller, who hated collars and ties, and avoided wearing them whenever he could, had on a white nylon turtleneck and over it a black crewneck pullover. Over both he wore a black blazer. For hospital visiting, the doctor's expression clearly said, a collar and tie would be more appropriate. "Her nephew?" he repeated with surprise. "I had no idea Fräulein Wendel had a nephew."

"Obviously I would have come sooner, had I known of my aunt's condition, but Herr Winzer only phoned me this morning."

"Herr Winzer is usually here himself about this hour."

"I understand he's been called away for some days," said Miller blandly. "He asked me to visit my aunt in his stead."

"Strange," the doctor murmured. "He has been regular as clockwork since she was brought in. Well, he had better be quick if he wishes to see her again. She is very far gone, you know."

Miller looked sad. "So he told me on the phone."

"As her relative, of course you may spend a short time with her. But I must ask you to be brief. Come this way."

The doctor led Miller down several passages and stopped at a door, which he opened. "She's in here. Don't be long, please."

The room was in semidarkness, and until his eyes became accustomed to the dull light, he failed to distinguish the shriveled form of the woman in the bed. So pale was her face that she almost merged with the bedclothes. Her eyes were closed.

"Fräulein Wendel," he whispered, and the eyelids fluttered open.

She closed them again and began to mutter incoherently. Something about "all dressed in white, so very pretty."

Miller leaned closer. "Fräulein Wendel, can you hear me?"

The dying woman was still muttering. Miller caught the words " . . . each carrying a prayer book, so innocent."

Miller frowned in thought; then he understood. In her delirium she was trying to recall her First Communion—she was a Roman Catholic.

She opened her eyes again and stared at him, taking in the white band around his neck, the black material over his chest, and the black jacket. To his astonishment two tears rolled down the parchment cheeks. With surprising strength her hand gripped his wrist, and she said quite distinctly, "Bless me, Father, for I have sinned."

A glance down at his own shirtfront made him realize the mistake the woman had made. He debated for two minutes whether to leave her, or to risk his immortal soul and have one last try at locating Roschmann. He leaned forward. "My child, I am prepared to hear your confession."

Then, in a tired mumble, her life story came out: how she had grown up ugly, had realized there would be no marriage for her, and in 1939 had been posted, an embittered woman, as a wardress in a camp called Ravensbrück. As she told of her days of power and cruelty, tears rolled down her cheeks.

"And after the war?" Miller asked softly.

There had been years of wandering—abandoned by the SS, hunted by the Allies, working as a scullery maid, and sleeping in Salvation Army hostels. Then in 1950 she met Winzer, staying in a hotel in Osnabrück where she was a waitress while he looked for a house to buy. He asked her to come and keep house for him when he bought it.

"Is that all?" asked Miller when she stopped.

"Yes, Father."

"My child, you know I cannot give you absolution if you have not confessed all your sins."

"That is all, Father."

Miller drew a deep breath. "And what about the forged passports for the SS men?"

"I did not make them, Father," she said.

"But you knew about them, about the work Klaus Winzer did."

"Yes." The word was a low whisper.

"He has gone now. He has gone away," said Miller.

"No. Not gone. Klaus would not leave me."

"He has been forced to run away. Think, my child. Where would he go?"

The emaciated head shook slowly. "I don't know, Father. If they threaten him, he will use the file. He told me he would."

Miller started. "What file, my child?"

They talked for another five minutes. Then there was a soft tap on the door and Miller rose to go.

"Father . . ." The voice was plaintive, pleading. He turned. She was staring at him, her eyes wide open. "Bless me, Father."

The tone was imploring. Miller sighed. It was a mortal sin. He hoped somebody somewhere would understand. He made the sign of the cross. *In nomine Patris, et Filii, et Spiritus Sancti, ego te absolvo a peccatis tuis.*

The woman sighed deeply, closed her eyes, and passed into unconsciousness.

Outside in the passage the doctor was waiting to escort him back to the entrance hall.

"Thank you for letting me see her," said Miller at the front door. "There is one thing, Doctor. We are all Catholics in our family. She asked me for a priest. Will you see to it?"

"Certainly," said the doctor. "Thank you for telling me."

It was late afternoon when Miller drove back into the Theodor-Heuss-Platz and parked the Jaguar. He crossed the road and went up to his room. From two floors above, Mackensen watched his arrival. Taking the bomb in his suitcase, he went out to his car. He maneuvered it into a place where he could watch the hotel entrance and the Jaguar, and settled down to another wait.

In his room Miller began calling friends in the underworld of Hamburg, trying to locate a man called Viktor Koppel, a skillful safecracker whose court case he had once covered and who thought himself indebted to Miller. He found Koppel at half past seven, in a bar with a crowd of friends, and it took a bit of prompting before he remembered Miller.

"I need a spot of help," said Miller.

The man in Hamburg sounded wary. "I ain't got much on me, Herr Miller."

"I don't want a loan," said Miller. "I want to pay you for a job. Just a small one."

Koppel's voice was full of relief. "Oh, I see, yes, sure. Where are you?"

Miller gave him his instructions.

OUTSIDE, Mackensen decided to start on the Jaguar at midnight if Miller had not emerged.

But Miller walked out of the hotel at eleven fifteen, crossed the square, and entered the station. Mackensen was surprised. He wondered idly why Miller should want to take a train.

At eleven thirty-five his problem was solved. Miller came back out of the station accompanied by a small, shabby man carrying a black leather bag. The pair approached a taxi, climbed in, and drove off. Mackensen decided to give them twenty minutes and then start on the Jaguar.

The square was almost empty. Mackensen slipped out of his car and crossed to the Jaguar, opened the hood, and lashed the explosive charge to the inside of the engine compartment directly in front of the driver's seat. Sliding under the car, he wired the rear end of the trigger mechanism to a handy support bar. The open jaws of the trigger, held apart by the glass bulb, he jammed between two coils of the stout spring that formed the right front suspension.

When it was firmly in place, unable to be shaken free by normal jolting, he came back out from under. He estimated that the first time the car hit a bump at speed, the retracting suspension on the right front wheel would force the open jaws of the trigger together, crushing the glass bulb and making contact between the two electrically charged hacksaw blades. When that happened, Miller and his incriminating documents would be blown to pieces.

Returning to the Mercedes, Mackensen curled up on the back seat and dozed. He had done, he thought, a good night's work.

MILLER ordered the taxi driver to take them to the Saarplatz, paid him, and dismissed him. It was only when the taxi had disappeared that Koppel opened his mouth. "I hope you know what you're doing, Herr Miller. It's strange, a reporter being on a caper like this."

"Koppel, there's no need to worry. What I'm after is a bunch of documents kept in a safe inside the house. I'll take them, and you get anything else there is on hand. Okay?"

"Well, all right. Let's get it over with."

"There's one last thing. The place has a live-in maid," said Miller. "So we'll wait until we know she's asleep."

They walked the mile to Winzer's house, cast a quick look around, and darted through the gate. They hid in rhododendron bushes facing the windows of what looked like the study.

Koppel made a tour of the house, leaving Miller to watch the bag of tools. When he came back he whispered, "The maid's still got her light on. Window at the back under the eaves."

For an hour they sat shivering in the bushes. Then Koppel made another tour and reported the girl's light was out. They sat for ninety minutes more before Koppel squeezed Miller's wrist, took his bag, and padded through moonlight toward the windows.

Fortunately for them, the area beneath the windows was in shadow. Koppel flicked on a pencil flashlight and ran it around the window frame. There was a good burglarproof window catch, but no alarm system. He opened his tool bag, and with remarkable skill used a diamond-tipped glass cutter to cut a perfect circle on the surface of the glass just below the window catch, performed some final magic with sticky tape and a suction cup, and then with a rubber hammer gave the cut circle of windowpane a sharp tap. At the second tap there was a crack, and he pulled the disk out and placed it on the ground.

Reaching through the hole, Koppel unscrewed the burglar catch and eased up the lower window. He was through it as nimbly as a fly, and Miller followed more cautiously.

Koppel whispered, "Keep still," and Miller froze while the burglar closed the window, drew the curtains, and shut the door to the passage. He again flicked on his flashlight. It swept around the room, picking out a desk, a wall of bookshelves, a deep armchair, and a fireplace surrounded with red brick.

"This must be the study," Koppel muttered. "Do you know where the lever is that opens the brickwork?"

"I don't know," muttered Miller back, imitating the burglar, who had learned the hard way that a murmur is far more difficult to detect than a whisper. "You'll have to find it."

"It could take ages," said Koppel.

He sat Miller in the chair, warning him to keep his gloves on. He slipped a band around his head, with the pencil flashlight fixed into it, and inch by inch he went over the whole of the brickwork, feeling with sensitive fingers for bumps or cracks. Then he started again, probing this time clockwise with a palette knife. At half past three the knife blade slipped between two bricks, there was a low click, and a section of brick, two feet by two feet in size, swung an inch outward. Behind this false front the thin beam of Koppel's headlamp picked out a small wall safe.

Koppel now slipped a stethoscope on, held the listening end where he judged the tumblers would be, and began to ease the first ring through its combinations.

It took forty minutes until the last tumbler fell over. Gently Koppel eased the safe door back and turned to Miller, the beam from his head darting over a table containing a pair of silver candlesticks and a heavy old snuffbox.

Without a word Miller took the light from Koppel's headband and used it to probe the safe. On the bottom shelf were several bundles of bank notes, which he passed to the grateful burglar. The upper shelf contained only one object, a buff manila folder. Miller pulled it out and riffled through the sheets inside. There were about forty of them. Each contained a photograph and several lines of type. At the eighteenth he paused and said out loud, "I'll be damned!"

"Quiet," muttered Koppel with urgency.

Miller handed the flashlight back to Koppel. "Close it."

Koppel stuffed the bank notes in his pocket, slid the safe door closed, and twirled the dial until the figures were in their original order. Then he eased the brickwork back into place and pressed it firmly home.

He put the candlesticks and snuffbox gently into his black leather bag; then, switching off his light, he slid the window up and hopped through. Miller, with the file stuffed inside his sweater, joined him. He pulled the window down and they headed for the shrubbery. When they emerged from the bushes onto the road, Miller had an urge to run.

"Walk slowly," said Koppel. "Just walk and talk like we were coming home from a party." It was close to five o'clock, but the streets were not wholly deserted, for the German workingman rises early to go about his business.

There was no train to Hamburg before seven, but Koppel said he would wait in the café and warm himself with a coffee and a double whiskey. "A very nice little job, Herr Miller," he said. "I hope you got what you wanted."

"Oh, yes. Thanks. I got it all right," said Miller.

"Well, mum's the word. Bye-bye, Herr Miller." The little burglar nodded and strolled into the station café. Miller crossed the square to the hotel, unaware of the red-rimmed eyes that watched him from a parked Mercedes.

It was too early to make the calls he needed to, so Miller allowed himself three hours of sleep and asked to be awakened at nine thirty. The phone shrilled promptly, and he ordered coffee and rolls, which arrived just as he had finished a hot shower. Over coffee he sat and studied the Odessa file, recognizing about half a dozen of the faces but none of the names. The names, he told himself, were meaningless.

Sheet eighteen was the one he came back to. The man was older, the hair longer, a sporty mustache covered the upper lip. But the ears were the same—that feature that is more individual to each owner than any other. And the narrow nostrils, the tilt of the head, the pale eyes were all the same. The name was a common one. What fixed his attention was the address. From the postal district, it had to be the center of the city, and that would probably mean an apartment house.

At ten o'clock he called information for the city named on the sheet of paper. He asked for the number of the superintendent for the apartment house at that address. It was a gamble, and it came off. It *was* an apartment house, and an expensive one.

He called the superintendent and explained that he had been trying to get one of the tenants but there was no reply, which was odd because he had been asked to call at that hour. Was the phone out of order?

The man at the other end was most helpful. The *Herr Direktor* would probably be at the factory. What factory was that? Why, his own, of course. The radio factory. He mentioned its name.

"Oh, yes, of course, how stupid of me," said Miller.

The girl who answered his next call gave him the boss's secretary, who told him that the *Herr Direktor* was at his country house and would be back on Monday. No, she was sorry, the house number was private. The man who finally gave Miller the country address and private telephone number was an old contact, the industrial correspondent of a Hamburg newspaper. Miller took out his map of Germany and located the area where the estate must be. He got out Winzer's picture of Roschmann and stared at it. He'd heard of the man, a big Ruhr industrialist. And he'd seen his company's radios in the stores.

It was past noon when he packed his bags and settled his bill. He was famished, so he treated himself to a large steak in the hotel dining room. During his meal he decided to drive the last section of the chase that afternoon and confront his target the next morning. He could have called the lawyer with the Z Commission in Ludwigsburg then, but he wanted to face Roschmann first.

It was nearly two when he emerged, stowed his suitcase in the trunk of the Jaguar, tossed the attaché case onto the passenger seat, and climbed behind the wheel.

He failed to notice the Mercedes that tailed him to the edge of Osnabrück.

Mackensen watched the Jaguar accelerate down the southbound lane of the autobahn. Then he went to a roadside telephone booth. "He's on his way," he told Werewolf. "Within fifty miles he'll be in pieces you couldn't identify."

"Excellent," purred the man in Nuremberg. "You must be tired, my dear *Kamerad*. Go and get some sleep."

Miller made those fifty miles, and more. For Mackensen had overlooked one thing. His trigger device would certainly have detonated quickly if it had been jammed into the cushion suspension system of a continental sedan. But the Jaguar was a British sports car, with a far harder suspension system. As it tore down the autobahn toward Frankfurt, the heavy springs above the front wheels retracted slightly, crushing the light bulb between the jaws of the bomb trigger. But the electrically charged lengths of steel failed to touch each other. On the hard bumps they flickered to within a millimeter of contact before springing apart.

Unaware of how close to death he was, Miller made the trip to Frankfurt in three hours, then turned off toward Königstein and the wild, snow-covered forests of the Taunus mountains.

14

IT WAS dark when the Jaguar slid into the small spa town. Miller figured he was less than twenty miles from his goal. He decided to find a hotel and wait till morning. Just to the north lay the mountains, quiet and white under a thick carpet of snow. An icy wind gave promise of more snow during the night.

At the corner of Hauptstrasse and Frankfurtstrasse Miller found a hotel, the Park, and obtained a room. It was during supper that the nervousness set in. He noticed that his hands were shaking as he raised his wineglass. Partly it was exhaustion; partly delayed reaction from the tension of the break-in with Koppel. But mainly, he knew, it was the sense of the impending end of the chase, the confrontation with the man he had sought through so many by-ways, coupled with the fear that something might still go wrong.

He thought of the doctor in Bad Godesberg who had warned him off the pursuit; and of the Jewish Nazi-hunter of Vienna who had said, "These men can be dangerous." He wondered why they had not struck at him yet. Perhaps they had lost him, or decided that, with the forger in hiding, he would get nowhere.

And yet he had the file, Winzer's secret explosive evidence. He had pulled off the greatest journalistic coup he had ever heard of, and was about to settle a score as well. He grinned to himself, and the passing waitress thought it was for her. She swung her bottom as she passed his table next time, and he thought of Sigi. He felt that he needed her as he never had before.

He ran over his plan as he finished his wine. A simple confrontation; a telephone call to the Z Commission lawyer at Ludwigsburg; the arrival thirty minutes later of a police van to take the man away for imprisonment, trial, and a life sentence.

He thought it over and realized he was unarmed. Would Roschmann really be alone, confident that his new name would protect him from discovery? Supposing he had a bodyguard?

During Miller's military service one of his friends had stolen a pair of handcuffs from the military police and had given them to him as a trophy of a wild night in the army. They were in a trunk in the Hamburg flat. He also had a gun, locked in a desk drawer, a small Sauer automatic, bought quite legally when he had been covering an exposé of Hamburg's vice rackets in 1960.

He found a public phone—safer than the hotel, he suddenly thought—and called Sigi at the club where she worked. Above the clamor of the band in the background, he had to shout to make her hear. He cut short her stream of questions and told her what he wanted. She protested that she couldn't get away, but something in his voice stopped her.

"Are you all right?" she shouted.

"Yes, I'm fine. But I need your help. Please, darling, don't let me down. Not now, not tonight."

"I'll come," she said simply. "I'll say it's an emergency."

He told her to call an all-night car-rental firm he had used.

"How far is it?" she asked.

"About three hundred miles. You can make it in five hours. Or six. You'll arrive about five in the morning."

"All right, expect me." There was a pause. "Peter, darling . . ."

"What?"

"Are you frightened of something?"

The time signal started, and he had no more coins. "Yes," he said, and hung up the receiver as they were cut off.

In the hotel foyer he asked the night porter for a large envelope, and after some hunting the man produced a stiff brown one. Miller also bought enough stamps to send the envelope by first-class mail. Back in his room he opened his attaché case, which he had carried throughout the evening, and took out Salomon Tauber's diary, the papers from Winzer's safe, and two photographs. He read again the pages in the diary that had sent him off on this hunt.

Finally he wrote on a sheet of plain paper a brief message, explaining the sheaf of documents. The note, along with Winzer's file and the remaining photograph of Roschmann, he placed inside the envelope, addressed it to the Ministry of Justice in Bonn, sealed and stamped it. The envelope and the diary went back into his attaché case, which he slid under the bed. The second photograph he put into the breast pocket of his jacket.

He carried a small flask of brandy in his suitcase, and he poured a measure into a glass. His hands were trembling, but the fiery liquid relaxed him. He lay down on the bed, his head spinning slightly, and dozed off.

In the underground room in Munich, Josef paced the floor angrily. At the table Leon and Motti gazed at their hands. It was forty-eight hours since the cable had come from Tel Aviv. Their attempts to trace Miller had brought no result. A friend in Stuttgart had informed Leon that the local police were looking for a young man in connection with the murder of a citizen called Bayer. The description fitted Miller, but fortunately the name from the hotel register was neither Kolb nor Miller.

"At least he had the sense to register under a false name," said Leon. "He must have known, after killing Bayer, that he had blown his cover and so abandoned the search. Unless he got something out of Bayer that led him to Roschmann."

"Then why the hell doesn't he check in?" snapped Josef. "Does the fool think he can take Roschmann on his own?"

Motti coughed quietly. "He doesn't know Roschmann has any real importance to the Odessa," he pointed out.

"Well, if he gets close enough, he'll find out," said Leon.

"And by then he'll be a dead man," Josef said. "Why doesn't the idiot call in?"

THE phone lines were busy elsewhere that night. Klaus Winzer had called Werewolf, and the news was reassuring.

"Yes, I think it's safe for you to go home," Werewolf had said. "The reporter has by now certainly been taken care of."

The forger had thanked the Odessa chief, and set off for the comfort of his large bed at home in Osnabrück.

MILLER was awakened by a knock at the bedroom door. When he opened it he saw the night porter standing there, Sigi behind him. Miller explained that the lady was his wife, who had brought him some important papers from home. The porter, a simple country lad, took his tip and left.

Sigi threw her arms around him as he shut the door. "Where have you been? What are you doing here?"

He silenced her in the simplest way, and by the time their lips parted Sigi's cold cheeks were flushed and burning.

He took her coat and hung it on the hook behind the door. She started to ask more questions.

"First things first," he said, and pulled her down onto the bed with its thick feather comforter.

She giggled. "You haven't changed."

An hour later Miller filled a glass with brandy and water. Sigi sipped a little, and Miller took the rest.

"So," said Sigi, "would you mind telling me why the mysterious letter, why the six-week absence, why that awful skinhead haircut, and why a room here in an obscure hotel?"

Miller rose, crossed the room, and came back with his attaché case. He seated himself on the edge of the bed and talked for nearly an hour, starting with the discovery of the diary. As he talked, she grew more and more horrified.

"You're mad," she said when he had finished. "Stark, staring, raving mad. All this to get a rotten old Nazi? Why, Peter?"

"I just had to do it," he said defiantly.

She sighed heavily. "All right, so now you know who he is and where he is. You just come back to Hamburg, pick up the phone, and call the police. They'll do the rest."

Miller did not know how to answer her. "It's not that simple," he said at last. "I'm going up there this morning."

"To his house? What for?" Her eyes widened in horror.

"Don't ask me why, because I can't tell you. It's just something I have to do."

Her reaction startled him. She sat up with a jerk and glared at him. "That's what you wanted the gun for," she threw at him. "You're going to kill him—"

"I'm not going to kill him—"

"Well, then, he'll kill you. You're going up there alone against him and his mob, all to make a story for your idiotic magazine readers. You don't even think about me, you rotten, horrible—" She started crying. "Look at me, you great stupid oaf. I want to get married. I want to be Frau Miller. I want to have babies. And you're going to get yourself killed—" She jumped off the bed, ran into the bathroom, slammed the door behind her, and locked it.

Miller's cigarette burned down to his fingers. He had never seen her so angry, and it shocked him. He thought over what she had said as he listened to the tap running in the bathroom. Stubbing out the cigarette, he crossed to the bathroom door. "Sigi."

There was no answer.

"Sigi."

The taps were turned off.

"Sigi, please open the door."

There was a pause; then the door was unlocked. "What do you want?" she asked.

"Sigrid Rahn, will you marry me?"

"Do you mean it?" She looked as if she didn't believe it.

"Yes, I do. I never really thought of it before. But then, you never got angry before."

"Gosh," she said. "I'll have to get angry more often."

AT SEVEN twenty a.m. Winzer arrived at his house. He was stiff and tired, but glad to be home. The maid, Barbara, was not yet up. When she did appear, she told him of her discovery on Saturday morning of the broken window and the missing silverware. She had called the police, and they had been positive the neat, circular hole was the work of a professional burglar. She had told them Winzer was away, and they said they wanted to see him when he returned, just for routine questions about the missing items.

Winzer listened, his face paling, a single vein throbbing steadily in his temple. He dismissed Barbara to the kitchen to prepare coffee, went into his study, and locked the door. It took him thirty seconds of frantic scratching inside the empty safe to convince himself that the file of forty Odessa criminals was gone.

As he turned away from the safe, the hospital called to inform him that Fräulein Wendel had died during the night. For two hours Winzer sat before the unlit fire, oblivious of the cold seeping through the newspaper-stuffed hole in the window, as he tried to think what to do. Barbara's repeated calls that breakfast was ready went unheeded. Through the keyhole she could hear him muttering, "Not my fault, not my fault at all."

AT NINE Miller showered, finishing off with several minutes under the ice-cold spray. The depression and anxiety of the night before had vanished. He felt fit and confident.

He dressed in ankle boots and slacks, a thick pullover, and his blue duffel jacket. It had deep slit pockets at each side, big enough for the gun and handcuffs, and a breast pocket for the photograph. He took the handcuffs from Sigi's bag and examined them. There was no key, and the manacles were self-locking.

He opened and examined the gun. The magazine was full. He worked the breech several times, smacked the magazine into the grip, pushed a round into the chamber, and set the safety catch to "On." He stuffed the card with the phone numbers of the Z Commission lawyer in Ludwigsburg into his trouser pocket.

Sigi was fast asleep, and he wrote a message for her to read when she awoke: "My darling. I am going now to see the man I have been hunting. I have a reason for wanting to look into his face and be present when the police take him. By this afternoon I will be able to tell you what it is. But just in case, here is what I want you to do. . . ."

The instructions were precise. He wrote down the telephone number in Munich she was to call, and the message she was to give. He ended: "Do not under any circumstances follow me. You could only make matters worse. If I am not back by noon, or have not called you in this room by then, call that number, give that message, check out of the hotel, mail the envelope at any box in Frankfurt, then drive back to Hamburg. Don't get engaged to anyone else in the meantime. All my love, Peter."

He propped the note on the bedside table by the telephone, along with the large envelope containing the Odessa file, and three fifty-mark bills. Tucking Tauber's diary under his arm, he slipped out. At the reception desk, he asked the porter to give his room a call at eleven thirty.

Miller went to the parking lot back of the hotel, climbed into the Jaguar, and pressed the starter. While the engine was warming up he brushed the snow off the hood, roof, and windshield.

Back behind the wheel, he slipped into gear and drove onto the main road. The fresh snow that had fallen during the night acted as a sort of cushion under the wheels. After a glance at the map, he set off down the road toward Limburg.

15

THE MORNING was gray and overcast, and the wind keened off the mountains. The road wound upward out of town and was soon lost in the sea of trees that make up the Romberg Forest. Miller turned off toward Glashütten, skirted the flanks of the towering Feldberg mountain, and took a road leading down to the village of Schmitten. After another twenty minutes of careful driving, he began to look for the gateway to a private estate. When he found it, he headed into the driveway.

Two hundred yards up it, a branch from a massive oak had fallen in the night, bringing down with it a thin black pole which now lay squarely across the drive. Rather than get out and move the pole, Miller drove carefully forward, feeling the bump as it passed under the front and then the rear wheels.

The car moved on and emerged into a clearing which contained a villa, fronted by a circular area of gravel. He climbed out of the car in front of the main door and rang the bell.

WHILE Miller was climbing out of his car, Klaus Winzer made his decision and called Werewolf. The Odessa chief was brusk and irritable, for it was long past the time he should have heard on the news of a sports car being blown to pieces, apparently by an exploding gas tank, on the autobahn south of Osnabrück. As he listened, his mouth tightened in a thin, hard line.

"You fool, you unbelievable, stupid little cretin! Do you know what's going to happen to you if that file is not recovered?"

In his study in Osnabrück, Klaus Winzer replaced the receiver. He took an old but serviceable Luger from the bottom drawer of his desk; the lead slug that tore his head apart was not a forgery.

WEREWOLF sat and gazed in something close to horror at the silent telephone. He thought of the men for whom it had been necessary to obtain passports through Klaus Winzer, and the fact that each of them was destined for arrest and trial if caught. The exposure of the dossiers would step up the pursuit of wanted SS men. The prospect was appalling.

But his first priority was the protection of Roschmann. Three times he dialed the private number and three times he got a busy signal. Finally he tried through the operator, who told him the line must be out of order.

He rang the Hohenzollern Hotel in Osnabrück and caught Mackensen about to leave. In a few sentences he told the killer of the latest disaster and where Roschmann lived. "It looks as if your bomb hasn't worked. Get down there faster than you've ever driven. Hide your car and stick to Roschmann. There's a body-guard called Oskar as well. If Miller goes straight to the police, we've all had it. But if he goes to Roschmann, take him alive and make him talk. We must know what he's done with those papers before he dies."

"I'll be there at one o'clock," Mackensen said.

THE door opened at the second ring.

Years of good living had put weight on the once lanky SS officer. He looked the picture of middle-aged, upper-middle-class, pros-perous good health. He surveyed Miller without enthusiasm.

"Yes?" he said.

It was several seconds before Miller could speak.

"My name is Miller," he said, "and yours is Eduard Roschmann."

Something flickered in the man's eyes, but he spoke smoothly. "This is preposterous. I've never heard of Eduard Roschmann."

Behind his calm façade the former SS man's mind was racing. Recalling his conversation with Werewolf weeks before, he over-came his first impulse to shut the door in Miller's face.

"Are you alone in the house?" asked Miller.

"Yes," said Roschmann truthfully.

"I'm coming in," said Miller flatly.

Roschmann turned and strode down the hallway and through an open door, with Miller at his heels. It was a comfortable room, evidently the study, with a thick, padded door that Miller closed behind him. A log fire burned in the grate.

"Where is your wife?" asked Miller.

Roschmann shook his head. "She has gone away for the weekend to visit relatives," he said. That much was true. And she had taken one of the cars. What Roschmann did not mention was that the other was in the garage for repairs, and his chauffeur-bodyguard, Oskar, had bicycled to the village half an hour earlier to report that the telephone was out of order. What was occupying his racing mind was how to keep Miller talking until Oskar returned.

When he turned to face Miller, the young reporter's right hand held an automatic pointed straight at his belly.

Roschmann covered his fright with bluster. "You threaten me with a gun in my own house?"

"Then call the police," said Miller. "They'll identify you, *Herr Direktor*. The face is still the same, also the bullet wound in the chest, and the scar under the left armpit where you no doubt tried to remove the Waffen SS blood-group tattoo."

Roschmann let out the air in his lungs in a long sigh. "What do you want, Miller?"

"Sit down," said the reporter. "There in the armchair where I can see you. And keep your hands on the armrests. Don't give me an excuse to shoot, because I'd dearly love to."

Roschmann sat in the armchair, his eyes on the gun.

Miller perched on the edge of the desk, facing him. "So now we talk," he said.

"About what?"

"About Riga. About eighty thousand people—men, women, and children—whom you had slaughtered there."

Roschmann began to regain his confidence. "That's a lie. There were never eighty thousand disposed of in Riga."

"Seventy thousand? Sixty?" asked Miller. "Do you really think it matters precisely how many thousands you killed?"

"That's the point," said Roschmann eagerly. "It doesn't matter. Look, young man, I don't know why you've come after me. But I can guess. Someone's been filling your head with a lot of sentimental claptrap about so-called war crimes and suchlike. It's all nonsense. How old are you?"

"Twenty-nine."

"You were in the army for military service?"

"Yes."

"Then you know. In the army a man's given orders; he obeys them. He doesn't ask whether they are right or wrong."

"You weren't a soldier," said Miller quietly. "You were an executioner. A murderer. So don't compare yourself with soldiers."

"Nonsense," said Roschmann. "We were soldiers like the rest. You young Germans—you don't know what it was like. . . ."

"So tell me, what was it like?"

Roschmann leaned back—the immediate danger had passed. "What was it like? We ruled the world, the Germans. We had beaten every army they could throw at us. For years they had looked down on us, and then we showed them we were a great people. You youngsters don't realize what it is to be proud of being a German.

"It lights a fire inside you. When the flags were waving and the whole nation was united behind one man, we could have marched to the ends of the world. That is greatness, young Miller. And we of the SS were the elite, still are the elite.

"Sensible people should forget the stupid things people tell about what happened to a few Jews in a few camps. They make a big fuss because we had to clean up the pollution of the Jewish filth that impregnated German life. We had to, I tell you. It was a mere sideshow in the great design of a German people, pure in blood and ideals, ruling the world as is their right, *our* right, Miller, *our* destiny. For make no bones about it, we are the greatest people in the world."

Despite Miller's gun, Roschmann rose from his chair and paced the carpet.

"You want proof? Look at Germany today. In 1945, utterly destroyed. And now? Rising again, increasing each year in her industrial and economic power. Yes, and military power. One day we will be as mighty as ever. It will take time, but the ideals will be the same, and the glory the same. And what brings this about? Discipline, harsh discipline—the harsher the better. And management. For we can manage things. Look at our factories, churning out power and strength each day to build Germany's might.

"And who do you think did all this? People who mouth platitudes over a few miserable Jews? Or cowards who try to persecute patriotic German soldiers? *We* did this—the same men who were heroes twenty, thirty years ago—we brought this prosperity back to Germany."

He turned from the window and faced Miller, his eyes alight. But he also measured the distance to the heavy iron poker by the fire. Miller noticed the glance.

"Now you come here, a representative of the young generation, full of your idealism, hunting me down with a gun. You think that's what they want, the people of Germany?"

Miller shook his head. "No, I don't," he said shortly.

"Well, there you are, then. If you turn me in to the police, they might make a trial out of it, but that is not certain, with all the witnesses scattered or dead. So put your gun away and go home. Read the true history of those days, learn that Germany's greatness stems from patriots like me."

Miller observed with rising disgust this man who paced the carpet, seeking to convert him. After some seconds he asked, "Have you ever heard of a man called Tauber?"

"Who?"

"Salomon Tauber. He was a German, too. Jewish. He was in Riga from the beginning to the end."

Roschmann shrugged. "I can't remember him. Who was he?"

"Sit down," said Miller. "And this time stay down."

Roschmann shrugged and went back to the armchair. Confident now that Miller would not shoot, his mind was concerned with how to trap him before he could get away.

"Tauber died in Hamburg last November," Miller said. "He gassed himself. Are you listening?"

"Yes. If I must."

"He left behind a diary. It was an account of what happened to him, what you and others did to him, in Riga and elsewhere. But mainly in Riga. He came back to Hamburg, and he lived there for eighteen years, because he was convinced you were alive and would never stand trial. I got hold of his diary."

"The diary of a dead man is not evidence," growled Roschmann.

"It is for me. There's a page of it I want you to read."

Miller opened the diary and pushed it into Roschmann's lap. "Pick it up," he ordered, "and read it—aloud."

Roschmann read the passage in which Tauber described Roschmann's murder of a German army officer wearing the Knight's Cross with oak-leaf cluster.

"So what?" he said at the end of it. "The man struck me. He disobeyed orders. I had the right to commandeer that ship."

Miller tossed a photograph onto Roschmann's lap. "Is that the man you killed?"

Roschmann looked at it and shrugged. "How should I know? It was twenty years ago."

There was a slow click as Miller thumbed the hammer back and pointed the gun at Roschmann's face. "Was that the man?"

Roschmann looked at the photograph again. "All right. So it was. So what?"

"That was my father," said Miller.

The color drained out of Roschmann's face. He whispered, "You didn't come about the Jews at all."

"No. I'm sorry for them, but not that sorry."

"But how could you know from that diary who the man was?"

"My father was killed on October 11, 1944, in Ostland," said Miller. "For twenty years that was all I knew. Then I read the diary. It was the same day, the same area, the two men had the same rank. Above all, both men wore the Knight's Cross with oak-leaf cluster, the highest award for bravery in the field. There weren't that many of those awarded, and very few to mere army captains."

Roschmann stared at the gun as if mesmerized. "You're going to kill me. You mustn't do that, not in cold blood. You wouldn't do that. Please, Miller, I don't want to die."

Miller leaned forward and began to talk. "I've listened to your twisted mouthings till I'm sick to my guts. Now you're going to listen to me while I make up my mind whether you die here or rot in some jail.

"You had the nerve, the damned crass nerve, to tell me that you, you of all people, were a patriotic German. I'll tell you what you are. You and all your kind are the worst filth that was ever elevated from the gutters of this country to positions of power. And for twelve years you smeared my country with your dirt.

"What you did revolted the whole of civilized mankind and left my generation a heritage of shame that's going to take us all our lives to live down. You used the German people until they could not be used anymore, and then you quit while the going was good. You weren't even brave. You were the most sickening cowards ever born. You murdered millions for your own profit and in the name of your maniacal power lust, and then you ran and hid like the dogs you are. And as for daring to call army soldiers and others who really fought for Germany *Kameraden,* that's a damned obscenity. Patriotism! You don't know what the word means.

"I'll tell you one other thing, as a German of the generation you so despise. This prosperity we have, it's got nothing to do with you. It's got to do with millions who do a hard day's work and never murdered anyone in their lives."

Miller pulled the telephone over, took the receiver off the cradle, and dialed. "There's a man in Ludwigsburg who wants to have a chat with you," he said. He put the telephone to his ear. "Have you cut this off? If you have, I'll drill you here and now."

Roschmann shook his head. "I haven't touched it."

Miller remembered the fallen branch and the pole lying across the drive. He swore softly.

Roschmann smiled. "The lines must be down. You'll have to go into the village. What are you going to do now?"

"I'm going to put a bullet through you unless you do as you're told," Miller snapped. He dragged the handcuffs out of his pocket and tossed them to Roschmann. "Take these to the fireplace," he ordered. "I'm going to lock you to the wrought-iron scrollwork there while I go and find a phone."

But Roschmann dropped the handcuffs at his feet, bent as though to pick them up, and instead gripped a heavy poker and swung it viciously at Miller's kneecaps. Miller stepped swiftly back and whipped the barrel of his pistol across Roschmann's head. "Try that again and I'll kill you," he said.

Roschmann straightened up, wincing from the blow.

"Clip one of the handcuffs around your right wrist," Miller commanded, and Roschmann did as he was told. "You see that metal branch in front of you? Lock the other bracelet onto that."

When Roschmann had snapped the second link, Miller cleared the area around him of all objects he could reach.

Outside, in the driveway, the man called Oskar pedaled toward the house, his errand to report the broken phone line accomplished. He paused in surprise on seeing the Jaguar, for his employer had assured him that no one had been expected.

Quietly he let himself in the front door, then stood irresolute, hearing nothing through the padded door to the study.

Miller took a last look around and was satisfied. "Incidentally," he told the glaring Roschmann, "it wouldn't have done you any good if you had hit me. I left the complete dossier of evidence on you in the hands of my accomplice, to drop into the mailbox, addressed to the right authorities, if I have not returned or phoned by noon. As it is I can phone. I'll be back in twenty minutes, and the police will be no more than thirty minutes behind me. You couldn't be out in twenty minutes, even if you had a hacksaw."

As he talked, Roschmann's hopes flickered. He knew he had only one chance—for the returning Oskar to take Miller alive, so that he could be forced to make the phone call at their demand and keep the documents from reaching the mailbox. The clock on the mantelpiece read ten forty.

Miller swung open the door and found himself staring at a man a full head taller than he. Roschmann screamed, "Hold him!"

Miller jerked up the gun he'd been replacing in his pocket. He was too slow. A swinging left backhander from Oskar's paw swept it out of his grasp. At the same time Oskar's right crashed into Miller's jaw and lifted him off his feet. As he fell, his head slammed into the corner of a bookcase. Crumpling like a rag doll, his body

slid to the carpet and rolled on its side. From the back of his head a trickle of blood flowed onto the floor.

"You fool," yelled Roschmann when he had taken in what had happened. Oskar looked baffled. "Get over here."

The giant lumbered across the room.

"Get me out of these handcuffs. Use the fire irons."

But the fireplace scrollwork had been made in an age when craftsmen intended their handiwork to last for a long time. Oskar's efforts merely bent the poker and a pair of tongs.

"Bring him over here," Roschmann told Oskar at last. While Oskar held Miller up, he felt the reporter's pulse. "He's still alive," he said, "but he'll need a doctor to make him come around quickly. Bring me a pencil and paper."

He scribbled two phone numbers while Oskar went for a hacksaw blade. "Get down to the village as fast as you can," he told Oskar when he returned. "Ring this Nuremberg number and tell the man who answers it what has happened. Then ring this local number and get the doctor up here immediately. Now hurry."

As Oskar ran from the room, Roschmann looked at the clock— ten fifty. If Oskar made the village by eleven, and was back with the doctor by eleven fifteen, they might get Miller to a phone in time. Urgently, he began to saw at his handcuffs.

In front of the door Oskar grabbed his bicycle, then paused beside the Jaguar and peered through the window. The key was in the ignition. His master had told him to hurry, so, dropping the bicycle, he climbed behind the wheel of the car and gunned it into life. He had got up into third gear and was boring down the slippery road as fast as he could take it when he slid around a curve in a spurt of gravel and hit the pole.

Roschmann was still sawing at the chain linking the two bracelets when the shattering roar in the pine forest stopped him. Straining to one side, he could peer through the French windows, and although the car and the driveway were out of sight, the plume of smoke drifting across the sky told him at least that the car had been destroyed by an explosion. He recalled the assurance he had been given that Miller would be taken care of. But Miller was on the carpet a few feet away from him, his bodyguard was certainly dead, and time was running out without hope of reprieve. He lowered his head and closed his eyes.

"Then it's over," he murmured quietly. After several minutes he resumed sawing. It was more than an hour before the specially hardened steel of the military handcuffs parted. As he stepped free, the clock chimed twelve.

If he had had time, he might have paused to kick the body on the carpet, but he was a man in a hurry. From the wall safe he took a passport and several fat bundles of new, high-denomination bank notes. Twenty minutes later, with these and a few clothes in a bag, he was bicycling down the road, around the shattered hulk of the Jaguar and the remnants of a body in the snow, past broken pines, toward the village. From there he took a taxi to Frankfurt airport. He hurried to the information desk and asked the attendant, "What time is the next flight for Argentina—preferably within an hour? Failing that, for Madrid?"

16

IT WAS one ten when Mackensen's Mercedes turned off the country road into the gate of the estate. Halfway up the drive to the house he found the way blocked.

The Jaguar had evidently been blown apart from inside, but its wheels had not left the road. It was slewed slantwise across the drive. The center section was completely missing. Bits of it were scattered in an area around the wreckage.

Mackensen surveyed the wreckage with a grim smile, then walked over to the bundle of scorched clothes and their contents twenty feet away. Something about the size of the corpse caught his attention, and he stooped over it for several minutes. Then he ran at an easy lope up to the house.

He tried the front-door handle. The door opened, and he went into the hallway. For several seconds he listened, sensing the atmosphere for danger. There was no sound. He reached under his left armpit and brought out a Luger automatic, flicked off the safety catch, and started to open the doors leading off the hall.

The first was the dining room, the second the study. Although he saw the body on the hearthrug at once, he did not move from the half-open door until he had covered the rest of the room. Warily he glanced through the crack between the door's hinges to make sure there was no one ambushed behind it, then entered.

Miller was lying on his back with his head turned to one side. For several seconds Mackensen stared down into the chalky white face. The matted blood on the back of the head told him roughly what had happened.

He scoured the house, noting the open drawers in the master bedroom, the missing shaving gear from the bathroom. Back in the study, he glanced into the empty wall safe, then picked up the telephone. He sat listening for several seconds, swore under his breath, and replaced the receiver. He found the tool chest, took what he needed, and went back down the drive, leaving the study by the French windows.

It took him almost an hour to find the parted strands of the telephone line, sort them out from the entangling undergrowth, and splice them. When he was finished he walked back to the house and called his chief in Nuremberg.

He had expected Werewolf to be eager to hear from him, but the man sounded tired and only half interested. Mackensen reported what he had found—the car, the corpse of the bodyguard, Miller unconscious on the floor. He finished with the absent owner.

"He hasn't taken much, Chief. Overnight things. I can clear up, and he can come back if he wants to."

"No, he won't come back," Werewolf told him. "He called me from Frankfurt airport. He's got a reservation on a flight to Madrid, connection this evening to Buenos Aires—"

"But there's no need," protested Mackensen. "I'll make Miller talk; we can find where he left his papers. There was no attaché case in the car wreckage, and nothing on him, except a sort of diary lying on the floor. But the rest of his stuff must be somewhere not far away."

"Far enough," replied Werewolf. "In a mailbox."

Wearily he told Mackensen what Miller had stolen from the forger, and what Roschmann had just told him on the phone. "Those papers will be in the hands of the authorities in the morning, or Tuesday at the latest. After that everyone on that list is on borrowed time. I've spent the whole morning trying to warn everyone concerned to get out of the country inside twenty-four hours."

"So where do we go from here?" asked Mackensen.

"You get lost," replied his chief. "You're not on that list. I am, so I have to get out. Go back to your flat and wait until my successor contacts you. For the rest, it's over. With Vulcan's departure his whole operation is going to fall apart, unless someone new can come in and take over the project."

"What Vulcan? What project?"

"Since it's over, you might as well know. Vulcan was the code name of Roschmann, the man you were supposed to protect from Miller." In a few sentences Werewolf explained to Mackensen why he was supposed to have eliminated Miller. When he had finished, Mackensen uttered a low whistle.

Some of the old authority returned to Werewolf's voice, and he seemed to pull himself together. "*Kamerad*, you must clear up the mess over there. You remember that disposal squad you used once before?"

"Yes, they're not far from here."

"Have them leave the place without a trace of what happened. Roschmann's wife must never know. Understand?"

"It'll be done," said Mackensen.

"Then make yourself scarce. One last thing. Before you go, finish that bastard Miller. Once and for all."

Mackensen looked across at the unconscious reporter with narrowed eyes. "It'll be a pleasure."

"Then good-by and good luck."

Mackensen replaced the receiver, took out an address book, thumbed through it, and dialed a number. He introduced himself to the man who answered and told him where to come, and what he would find.

"The car and the body beside it have to go into a deep gorge off a mountain road. Plenty of gasoline over it, a real big blaze. Leave nothing identifiable about the man—go through his pockets and take everything, including his watch."

"Got it," said the voice. "I'll bring a trailer and winch."

"There's one last thing. In the study of the house you'll find another stiff on the floor. Get rid of it. A long, cold drop to the bottom of a long, cold lake. Well weighted."

"No problem. We'll be there by five and gone by seven. I don't like to move that kind of cargo in daylight."

"Fine," said Mackensen. "I'll be gone before you get here."

He hung up, slid off the desk, and walked over to Miller. He pulled out his Luger and held the gun at arm's length, pointing downward, lined up on the forehead.

Years of living like a predatory animal had given Mackensen the senses of a leopard. He didn't see the shadow that fell onto the carpet from the open French window; he felt it and spun around, ready to fire.

"Who the hell are you?" growled Mackensen, keeping the man covered.

He stood in the French window, dressed in the black leather leggings and jacket of a motorcyclist. In his left hand he held his crash helmet across his stomach. The man flicked a glance at the body at Mackensen's feet and the gun in his hand.

"I was sent for," he said innocently.

"Who by?" said Mackensen.

"Vulcan," replied the man. "My *Kamerad*, Roschmann."

Mackensen lowered the gun. "Well, he's gone."

"Gone?"

"Heading for South America. The whole project's off. And all thanks to this little bastard reporter." He jerked the gun barrel toward Miller.

"You going to finish him?" asked the man.

"Sure. Werewolf's orders."

"Werewolf?"

A small alarm sounded inside Mackensen's mind. He had just been told that in Germany no one apart from Werewolf, and now himself, knew about the Vulcan project. How would a man know Vulcan and not know Werewolf? His eyes narrowed.

"You're from Buenos Aires?" he said.

"No."

"Where from, then?"

"Jerusalem."

It was half a second before this made sense to Mackensen. Then he swung up his Luger. But half a second is a long time, long enough to die.

The foam rubber inside the crash helmet was scorched when the Walther went off. But the slug went through the fiber glass without a pause and took Mackensen high in the breastbone with the force of a kicking mule. The helmet dropped to the ground to reveal Josef's right hand, and from inside the cloud of blue smoke the PPK fired again.

Mackensen was a strong man. Despite the bullet in his chest, he would have fired, but the second slug entering his head above the right eyebrow spoiled his aim. It also killed him.

MILLER awoke on Monday afternoon in a private ward in Frankfurt General Hospital. He lay for half an hour, becoming slowly aware that his head was swathed in bandages. He found a buzzer and pressed it, but the nurse who came told him to lie quietly because he had a severe concussion.

So he lay and, piece by piece, recollected the events of the previous day. He dozed off, and when he woke it was dark and a man was sitting by his bed. The man smiled.

Miller stared at him. "I've seen you," he said at length. "You were in Oster's house. With Leon and Motti. Josef, they called you."

"That's right. What else do you remember?"

"Almost everything. Roschmann?"

"Roschmann's gone. Fled to South America. The whole affair's over. Finished. Do you understand?"

Miller slowly shook his head. "Not quite. I've got one hell of a story. And I'm going to write it."

Josef leaned forward. "Listen, Miller. You're a lousy amateur, and you're lucky to be alive. You're going to write nothing. For one thing, you've got nothing to write. I've got Tauber's diary, and it's going back home with me, where it belongs. I read it last night. There was a photograph of an army captain in your jacket pocket. Your father?"

Miller nodded.

"So that was what it was really all about?" asked the agent.

"Yes."

"Well, in a way I'm sorry. About your father, I mean. I never thought I'd say that to any German. Now, about the file. Why the hell couldn't you have let us have it? We could have used that information to best advantage."

"I had to send it to someone, through Sigi. That meant by mail. You're so clever, you never let me have Leon's address."

Josef nodded. "All right. But either way, you have no story to tell. You have no evidence. The diary's gone, the file is gone. If you insist on talking, nobody will believe you except the Odessa, and they'll come for you. Or rather, they'll hit Sigi or your mother. They play rough, remember?"

Miller thought for a while. "What about my car?"

Josef told Miller about the bomb. "I told you they play rough. The car has been found gutted by fire in a ravine. The body in it is unidentified, but not yours. Your story is that you were flagged down by a hitchhiker, he knocked you out and went off in your car. The hospital will confirm you were brought in after a passing motorcyclist called an ambulance when he saw you by the roadside. They won't recognize me again; I was in a helmet and goggles at the time. That's the official version. To make sure it will stay, I rang the German press agency two hours ago, claiming to be the hospital, and gave them that story."

Josef stood up and looked down at Miller. "I wonder if you realize how lucky you are. I got the message from your girl friend yesterday noon. By riding like a maniac I made it to Roschmann's house in two and a half hours dead. Which was what you almost were—dead."

He turned, hand on the doorknob. "Take a word of advice. Claim the insurance on your car, get a Volkswagen, go back to Hamburg, marry Sigi, have kids, and stick to reporting. Don't tangle with professionals again."

Half an hour after he had gone the nurse came back. "There's a phone call for you," she said.

It was Sigi, crying and laughing. An anonymous caller had told her where Peter was. "I'm on my way this minute."

The phone rang again. "Miller? This is Hoffmann. I just saw a piece on the agency tapes. You got a bang on the head. Are you all right?"

"I'm fine, Herr Hoffmann," said Miller.

"Great. When are you going to be fit to work?"

Miller thought. "Next week. Why?"

"I've got a story that's right up your alley. By the way, that Nazi hunt you were on. Was there a story at all?"

"No, Herr Hoffmann," said Miller slowly. "No story."

"Didn't think so. Hurry up and get well. See you in Hamburg."

JOSEF's plane came into Lod Airport, Tel Aviv, as dusk was settling on Tuesday. He was met by two men in a car, and taken to headquarters for debriefing by the man who had signed the cable: Cormorant. They talked until almost two in the morning, a stenographer noting it all down. When it was over, Cormorant leaned back, smiled, and offered his agent a cigarette.

"Well done," he said simply. "We've checked on the factory and tipped off the authorities—anonymously, of course. The research section will be dismantled. We'll see to that, even if the German authorities don't. The scientists apparently didn't know for whom they were working. Most will destroy their records. The weight of opinion in Germany today is pro-Israeli, so they'll keep their mouths shut. What about Miller?"

"He'll do the same. What about those rockets?"

Cormorant blew a column of smoke and gazed at the stars in the night sky outside. "I have a feeling they'll never fly now. Nasser has to be ready by the summer of 1967 at the latest, and without the teleguidance work from that Vulcan factory, they'll never mount an operation in time."

"Then the danger's over," said the agent.

Cormorant smiled. "The danger's never over. It just changes shape. This particular danger may be over. The big one goes on. We're going to have to fight again, and maybe after that, before it's over. Anyway, you must be tired. You can go home now." He reached into a drawer and produced a polyethylene bag of personal effects, while the agent deposited on the desk his false German passport, money, wallet, and keys. At the door Cormorant shook hands. "Welcome home, Major Uri Ben-Shaul."

The major took a taxi to his flat in the suburbs and let himself in. In the darkened bedroom he could make out the sleeping form of Rivka, his wife. He peeked into the children's room and looked down at their two boys—Shlomo, who was six, and the two-year-old baby, Dov.

He wanted badly to climb into bed and sleep for several days, but there was one more job to be done. He quietly undressed, then put on his uniform. His trousers were cleaned and pressed, as they always were when he came home. His khaki shirt had razor-sharp creases. He slipped on his battle jacket, adorned only with the glinting steel wings of a paratroop officer, and the five campaign ribbons he had earned in Sinai and in raids across the borders.

Last was his red beret. When he had dressed he took several articles and stuffed them into a small bag. There was already a dim glint in the east when he got back outside and found his small car parked where he had left it a month before.

He drove eastward out of Tel Aviv and took the road to Jerusalem. There was a stillness about the dawn that he loved, a peace and a cleanness that never ceased to cause him wonder. He had seen it a thousand times on patrol in the desert, the phenomenon of a sunrise, cool and beautiful, before the onset of a day of blistering heat.

When he had climbed up the last hills to Jerusalem, the sun had cleared the eastern horizon and glinted off the Dome of the Rock in the Arab section of the divided city.

He parked his car a quarter of a mile from his destination, the mausoleum of Yad Vashem, and walked the rest of the way down the avenue flanked by trees planted in memory of the gentiles who had tried to help, and to the great bronze doors that guard the shrine to six million Jews who had died in the holocaust.

The old gatekeeper told him it was not open so early, but he explained what he wanted, and the man let him in. He passed through into the Hall of Remembrance and walked forward to the rail.

By the light of the Eternal Flame he could see the names written across the floor, in Hebrew and Roman letters: Auschwitz, Treblinka, Belsen, Ravensbrück, Buchenwald . . . There were too many to count, but he found the one he sought. Riga.

He did not need a yarmulka to cover his head, for he wore his red beret. From his bag he took a fringed silk shawl, the *tallith,* the same kind Miller had found among Tauber's effects. This he draped around his shoulders.

He took a prayer book from his bag and opened it. He advanced to the brass rail, gripped it with one hand, and gazed across it at the flame in front of him. Because he was not a religious man, he had to consult his prayer book frequently.

> *"Yisgadal,*
> *Veyiskadash,*
> *Shemay rabah . . ."*

And so it was that a major of paratroops of the army of Israel, standing on a hill in the Promised Land, finally said *Kaddish* for the soul of Salomon Tauber.

A Letter from the Author

It would be agreeable if things in this world always finished with the ends neatly tied up. That is very seldom the case. People go on, to live and die at their own appointed times and places. For instance, of those characters who appear in my book under their own names, Simon Wiesenthal still lives and works in Vienna, gathering a fact here, a tip there, slowly tracking down the whereabouts of wanted SS murderers. Lord Russell also is alive and well and living in Dinard. As for Eduard Roschmann, so far as it has been possible to establish, he is still in Argentina.

The rockets of Helwân never flew. The fuselages were ready, along with the rocket fuel, but all forty preproduction rockets, helpless for want of electronic guidance systems, were still standing in the deserted factory at Helwân when they were destroyed by Israeli bombers during the Six Days' War. Before that the German scientists had disconsolately returned to Germany.

At the end of 1964 Chancellor Erhard, shaken by the exposure to the authorities of a list of names which became known as the Odessa file, issued an international appeal for all those having knowledge of the whereabouts of wanted SS criminals to inform the authorities. The response was considerable. Recently a lawyer and investigator of the Z Commission in Ludwigsburg was able to say, "Nineteen sixty-four was a very good year for us."

Of course many characters in the book could not appear under their own names, but they and all those who helped me get the information I needed are entitled to my heartfelt thanks. If I do not name them all it is for three reasons.

Some, being former members of the SS, were not aware at the time that what they said would end up in a book. Others have specifically asked that their names never be mentioned as sources of information about the SS. In the case of others still, the decision not to mention their names is mine alone, and taken, I hope, for their sakes rather than for mine.

FREDERICK FORSYTH

P.S. YOUR NOT LISTENING

P.S. Your not listening

A wise, funny, strangely

moving story about

nothing more than love

A CONDENSATION OF THE BOOK BY
ELEANOR CRAIG

ILLUSTRATED BY JOHN McCLELLAND

Douglas, Kevin, Jonathan, Eddie, and Julie were
five kids who'd had more trouble before they
were ten than they—or anyone else—could handle.

Mrs. Craig, a gifted teacher who took them on
in a public school's Special Education class,
had no idea what she'd let herself in for.
The love she'd given freely to her own four
vigorous children as well as to hundreds of
normal pupils was held suspect by children who
had never known love. When they threw chairs
she ducked. When they assaulted each other
it took all her strength to restrain them.
When they withdrew into their shells she tried
again and again to reach them with patience,
sympathy, and gentle humor.

How she evolved a discipline that worked
in this most unusual of classrooms is a
rewarding and unique story. It is all true.
Only names have been changed and locations
disguised to protect those who for so long were
protected by no one.

I FIRST learned about a new program for maladjusted children when I was teaching at Hosmer School. It had come into being in anticipation of a state law which would mandate an educational plan for such children.

Three years earlier, Mr. and Mrs. David Beecher had realized that the city could offer no educational plan for their son. Donald was nine at the time and was both severely disturbed and neurologically impaired. His parents discovered that there were many other children who could not attend regular classes, yet did not belong in programs for the retarded. The Beechers formed a parents' group, which pressured the local school board and the state legislature for action.

The school board made an investigation, which showed that at least one hundred children in the city had problems that could not be handled in existing classes; a pilot program could accommodate only five or six.

Where to begin? After lengthy study a committee agreed that the logical start would be with the younger children, ages seven to nine. But Donald Beecher was almost thirteen now, and the committee had to inform his parents, who had paved the way, that their son was too old to be included in the first class for the socially and emotionally maladjusted. Not until two years later did the state legislature enact a law mandating education for all children, regardless of their handicaps. Many states still have no such law.

MARIE Collins, another teacher, and I were having coffee in the faculty room and read a notice about the new program on the bulletin board:

Department of Special Education seeks master teacher for pilot program with socially and emotionally maladjusted children. Please contact Jim Hanley, department head.

"Who'd want that job?" Marie remarked.

I didn't try to explain to her the excitement I felt at that moment. I had always loved working with children. I enjoyed teaching, but knew, without ever having considered Special Education before, that this was the opportunity I wanted.

When I told my husband, Bill, about it that night, his reaction was similar to Marie's. "But why?"

"Honey, don't you see? It's my chance to learn. Besides, when have I ever had a class without disturbed children? To teach them separately, where their behavior wouldn't disrupt twenty-five others, would seem like a privilege!"

"Maybe. But with four vigorous children of our own, I'm afraid you'll find it too demanding. Please don't rush into it."

I thought about it for days and finally went to see Jim Hanley.

"As yet there's no specific teacher training for this type of class," he said. "The person we're looking for must have certain characteristics that don't necessarily accompany a degree in psychology or education. We need someone with insight and understanding. But don't pursue the job if you're looking for a sense of personal gratification. Challenge, yes. Gratification, no."

For weeks after, members of the Transitional Class planning committee interviewed me and observed my classes. Two months after the first meeting with Jim Hanley, I received a letter from him informing me that I would teach the class starting next year at Central School.

Bill and I celebrated at Mario's that night. "Congratulations." He lifted his glass in a toast. "I hope it won't be too tough."

Too tough. Nothing in those interviews had prepared me for a child like Douglas.

CHAPTER ONE

DOUGLAS and his grandmother arrived early the first day. Mrs. Grant was a heavy, weary-looking black woman wearing a shabby print dress and wrinkled elastic stockings.

"You Mrs. Craig? Well, Doug's here, but he don't want to come in. He's behind the door." A low groan from that direction. "He scared 'cause he wasn't allowed in no school last year. Some schools you've got! Can't even handle a nine-year-old."

"Douglas." I peeked at the huge boy—all of one hundred pounds at age nine—crouched behind the door. "Come choose a desk. You'll have first choice."

"Boy," his grandmother pleaded, "your teacher wants you in that room. Now you git yourself in there."

She reached down to pull him up, but he kicked her cruelly in the shins. "Ooooh." She swayed in pain, biting her lower lip. Douglas grinned at her anguish. After a minute or two she spoke softly. "You got the devil in you, boy. That devil sure in you."

"'You got the devil in you, boy,'" he mimicked as she headed toward the exit.

Looking down at the handsome brown-skinned child, I was tempted to help him up, but angry black eyes warned against it.

"It's time to come into our room now. I'll be waiting for you." Five minutes dragged by as I pretended to be writing at my desk. Finally he crawled into the room as a baby would and sat on the floor, glaring. I stared at the untied shoes, the faded patched jeans, the too-small blue shirt, bare belly bulging. I found it unbearable to maintain contact with his fierce eyes.

"Which—ahhh—which desk do you want?" It was a relief to find myself able to speak. "Since I had no idea you'd be so tall, we may need a bigger chair."

"Oh God!" He laughed and rocked on the floor. "Ideyah! Chayah! Oh God, what an accent! She can't even talk right. Ha-ha-ha! You talk just like Kennedy!" He stood up at last. "Okay, I'll choose my chayah!" He picked up a chair and began to spin around, holding the chair out with one hand.

I headed toward him. "Put that chair down!"

He twirled faster and faster. "Can't you see? Oh gosh, what a nut! I am putting it down!" The chair shot out of his hand and slammed against the cork bulletin board.

He sank to the floor. "Dizzy, mmmm, dizzy," he murmured. I leaned against the wall for support. I'd had one student for ten minutes, but already felt as if I'd been through a harrowing day.

In screening children for our pilot class, the admissions committee had waived an important qualification for Douglas. It had been stipulated originally that no child be accepted unless his parents agreed to be available for weekly conferences with the school's psychiatric social worker.

In Douglas' case this was unrealistic. His young unwed mother had first given birth to a severely retarded child, Luke, and less than a year later to Douglas. When Douglas was four, she suddenly called the welfare department to say she was leaving her children. When the caseworker arrived at the housing project, Douglas was leading his brother from unit to unit in search of their mother. Neighbors supplied the information that she had left with another woman's husband.

Luke was sent to a state institution for handicapped children. Douglas spent two years in an excellent foster home. Though he grieved for months for his mother and brother, his social worker felt he'd made a good adjustment. Finally a welfare worker made contact with his maternal grandmother in South Carolina, and she came north to make a home for the two boys.

But at six, this second major upheaval was too much for Douglas. He became unmanageable in school and at home. In the second grade he had bitten and kicked his classmates and nearly stabbed one child with scissors. After that he had an instructor, who provided one hour of daily tutoring at home.

Douglas' intelligence measured in the near-superior range; yet the prognosis was guarded. Hopefully he would adjust to our small group and eventually return to a regular class. Otherwise he might have to be removed to a residential treatment center.

As Douglas rolled about on the floor, the other member of my class—Kevin Hughes—appeared at the door with his mother. They both froze in horror at the sight of Douglas.

I tried to smile encouragingly. "Mrs. Hughes, Kevin, I'm Mrs. Craig. And this is Douglas Miller."

Kevin's mother was a large-boned, austere woman in a mannish brown tweed suit. In contrast, her son had a delicate, sensitive face, soft blond hair, and timid brown eyes. Although he was eight, he looked closer to five. The psychiatric evaluation described him as depressed and withdrawn.

"All right, son, here's a place for you." Her large hands on his tiny shoulders, she maneuvered him into a seat. "Pay attention. Don't forget your lunch box. I'll be waiting when the bus brings you home. Good-by, Mrs. Craig." She looked at Douglas with unconcealed disgust and hurried out.

Kevin sat rigidly with his hands folded in his lap and his head bent down. Douglas got up now and looked at him. "What's wrong with this teacher? Didn't even tell us to put our things away." He swung open the coat closet. "I'll take the first hanger. This is the other kid's." He stared at Kevin.

Kevin rose obediently and hung up his jacket. But with incredible speed, Douglas grabbed it, darted across the room, and hurled it out the window. He turned to face us triumphantly. Kevin looked away. Infuriated that his victim did not react, Douglas ran to his side before I could stop him and shook his chair until he dumped him onto the floor. "Are you retarded or something? Get outta my seat." Kevin moved.

"Douglas, you will not be allowed to—"

"Hold it," he interrupted. And he sat down calmly with his hands folded. "Okay now, I can't work, see? I get all shook up. So what are we gonna do here?"

I decided to forget the jacket for a moment and began again.

"Let's start with introductions. I'm Mrs. Craig." The yellow chalk squeaked on the green board. MRS. CRAIG.

Douglas pounded his fists on the desk furiously. "Oh wow! Don't you even know that Mrs. has three S's in it? Can't you hear them? MiSSuS! MiSSuS! Maybe they spell it that way where you come from, but you better learn it has three S's in this part of the country."

"We'll spend time on spelling later, Doug. The first thing is to learn each other's names. Now would you like to draw pictures of what you did this summer?"

"Are you kiddin'? Would Macy's tell Gimbels?" he yelled. Douglas then spent the rest of the morning dismantling the toy closet. By noon the floor was littered with crayons, trucks, and Lincoln Logs. Kevin continued to sit with his head bowed, even when I pulled up a chair and tried to talk with him.

Kevin's record contrasted sharply with Doug's. He had never been excluded from school. In fact, it was to his teacher's credit that he had been referred to guidance at all. His parents insisted at first that he had no emotional problems. He was so passive and withdrawn that a less perceptive teacher might have described him as a "terribly good boy, one of the quiet kind who never get into trouble."

Kevin was the only child of a couple who had married late. From a previous marriage his mother had a twenty-year-old son, now in the army. His father was a burly man who wanted a "real boy"—one who would play baseball and someday work with him as a mechanic. Instead Kevin had had a difficult infancy. He developed allergies that required frequent hospitalizations during his first year. There was no way to determine whether his illnesses were so traumatizing that his ability to relate was impaired, or whether his parents were unable to accept this scrawny baby and deprived him of their love from those earliest days. After initially denying such feelings, both parents admitted that he had never brought any pleasure or satisfaction into their lives.

Though he rarely cried, he never laughed or smiled either. None of the neighborhood children would play with him. At home he spent much of his time sitting in his room silently arranging and rearranging a set of small plastic soldiers.

I wondered if Kevin would be more approachable after he began his sessions with Ceil Black, our psychiatric social worker. She would be seeing both boys individually each week. Every Friday after school, she and I were to confer.

BEFORE lunch, Douglas went to the bathroom. There were a few minutes of peace, suddenly broken by the angry voice of the custodian. I looked down the hall in time to see Mr. Jakowsky chasing Douglas, both running at full speed. It was the first of many times that Douglas hurled wads of sopping toilet paper to the ceiling of the bathroom, where they stuck. Douglas fled into the coat closet. Mr. Jakowsky, now chagrined at his own behavior, turned away, muttering softly.

At lunchtime, Douglas gobbled his entire meal while Kevin was still meticulously spreading a yellow napkin over his desk top. "Hey kid, let's see what you've got." Douglas unwrapped Kevin's sandwich, then sank his teeth into it. "Ugh! Salami!" He spat the entire mouthful into Kevin's lunch box.

No reaction from Kevin. "That's enough!" I yelled, starting after Douglas. He led me several times around the room, then took off down the hall.

I refused to satisfy him by giving chase. In fact, it was a relief that he was gone. Perhaps now I could draw out Kevin a little. "What would you like to do this afternoon, Kevin?" No answer. "Hear a record?" A silent no. "Then let me read to you." If he heard the story, his frozen face gave no indication.

We didn't see Douglas for the rest of the school day, but exactly at dismissal time he sauntered in, collected his jacket and lunch box, and waited at the door. "I'm first in line."

"But you weren't even ready to stay with us today! Tomorrow you must not touch Kevin's lunch. You must remain in the room."

He looked at my face as if he were considering these demands, then lowered his eyes. "I could bite you, you know."

When Doug and Kevin were gone, the principal peeked in.

Carrie Silverstein was a tiny, dynamic woman who was always available to calm an upset child, encourage a poor performer, or counsel a new teacher. This time I really needed her.

"I can't even get started with these two," I said. "They're not ready for workbooks or play therapy. What shall I do?"

"You can't expect to start either right away. But workbooks might be part of the therapy."

"But I'm so concerned about these boys being together. I understand the theory of an aggressive child and one who's withdrawn balancing each other. But when I see this in practice, it seems that we're just victimizing Kevin."

"It's too soon to tell anything. I'm betting you're in for some surprises. Anyway, it won't help to have you brooding about them. Now go home to your own."

MY OWN, my own. Ann would already be home. Junior high was out at two. Still, with luck I might beat the elementary school bus and arrive before Richard, Billy, and Ellen.

But traffic was heavy, and it took twenty minutes just to cross town. Although my husband was at home, I was upset at not being there to greet them myself on their first day back in school. It's the inescapable guilt that makes working hardest for a mother, I thought, as I finally turned into our drive.

Richie and Billy were in the yard playing football with several friends. Richie broke from the huddle and ran toward me. "Hey, Mom. Guess what! I get to play soccer this year, but I've gotta get a gym suit. The coach says we have to be ready if we want to go out on the field tomorrow."

Richie was now in fifth grade and Billy was in third, both at the same school where they'd started kindergarten. Their teachers and classmates were familiar to them, and I expected no major problems. Our youngest, Ellen, was beginning second grade.

My main concern was our oldest, Ann, thirteen, and suddenly so pretty. All summer she'd become increasingly apprehensive about entering junior high. I went into the house. Ann and Ellen were in the kitchen, sharing a bag of pretzels.

"Mom, Mom, I got Mr. Spitzler, the worst science teacher! Everybody hates him. We've already got three chapters for to-night. I'll flunk, I know I will!" Ann went on to detail the horrors of junior high. But the recital ended with the advantages of the cafeteria. "We get chocolate milk, ice-cream sandwiches, all kinds of good stuff." I smiled. She would be all right.

Finally seven-year-old Ellen got to talk. Her teacher gave prizes for each finished workbook. Robin, her best friend, was in her room again, after all. They'd been afraid they'd be separated.

Bill came down from his study in the attic and joined us at the kitchen counter. "Annie, would you put the coffee on? And what about Mother's first day?" He stooped to kiss my forehead.

"Ya, Mom. Tell us about your kids. What are they like?" Ann asked as she filled the kettle.

"I feel sort of numb. To give you an idea, the custodian chased one of my pupils down the hall." I expected some sympathy, but they all laughed, and then it seemed funny to me, too.

The kids all decided to bicycle to the store for school supplies, and I was glad for the chance to have a quiet cup of coffee with Bill. I worried about him. His dark hair and beard had become almost totally gray since he'd begun writing full time, about a year ago. His original plan had been to work all day as a salesman, writing a history book evenings and weekends. But as his research on the Second World War progressed, the need to devote full time to it became urgent. Luckily, I had been able to return to teaching. Our income was severely reduced when Bill left his job, but we had no regrets about the gamble we'd chosen to take.

Bill went back upstairs while I raced to do the laundry before dinner. Then there were dishes, more laundry, ironing. When the kids were in bed, I went up to the attic.

"Ready for bed, dear?"

"Boy, am I," Bill said, stretching his long arms over his head. "I feel like I could sleep forever."

I felt that tired too. Yet when the house was finally in darkness I lay in bed restlessly. Why, I wondered, were my last thoughts of strangers' children and not of my own?

CHAPTER TWO

WE MADE no progress toward an academic program on the second day. Douglas started the morning by spinning in circles until he fell from exhaustion. Kevin again sat silently. When there was any pressure to conform, Douglas would run out of the room. He was spinning out on the playground when the mothers arrived to pick up their kindergartners. I approached him and caught his hand. "You belong in our room," I said sternly.

"No, no!" he yelled, and suddenly flopped down on the black-top, pulling me down with him. Mothers grabbed their children and began to run, staring back at us. I struggled up and gripped his hand so tightly that he screamed, "You've broken my hand. Why? Why? You've broken my hand!"

At the door I discovered Miss Silverstein had witnessed this drama. She whispered, "You'll have to contain him in the classroom or we just can't have him here. It's too dangerous for the other children."

"I know, but how?"

"He's testing you. Why don't you gamble that he really wants to be here, and tell him that if he leaves the room he may have to stay at home for a while?"

The second day's lunch was almost a repetition of the first. Kevin was still setting out his food when Douglas took the apple and cookies from Kevin's desk and munched on them arrogantly.

"Douglas, you may not continue to take Kevin's lunch. His mother packs it for *him*."

"Boy, the trouble with this teacher—she always wants her own way. Gosh, what a nut."

After lunch we toured the building, visiting the nurse, the library, and taking a look at the enormous furnace. Our last stop was the custodian's closet. "We may want to come in here to borrow a broom or wash out paintbrushes."

"Wow, that's boss!" Douglas enthused, and I turned just in time to see him slam the door. The lock clicked and we heard

Doug's laughter, then his receding footsteps. I fumbled unsuccessfully for an electric switch. Kevin began to whimper.

"It's all right, Kevin. Doug is playing a trick. You help me call for Mr. Jakowsky." I yelled while Kevin began to sob.

"Dark, dark," he cried.

"Don't be afraid. The dark can't hurt us." I reached for his thin shoulder, but he shook my arm away.

"Dark. Where's Mommy?" he whimpered. "Where's Mommy?"

"We can sit down and wait. Someone will come soon." He sank to the floor. I sat too, and he edged closer.

"Douglas is bad," he said. "I hate Douglas."

I felt encouraged that Kevin had finally begun to express himself. I put my arms around him. "Maybe you and I can help him to be better. We can show him that he can't tease people anymore."

"No more teasing," and he leaned against me, sucking his thumb.

We sat this way about twenty minutes; then we both jumped as light flooded the little closet. The custodian was as startled as we were. "What's the matter here?"

"Don't worry, Mr. Jakowsky. It was just Douglas playing a trick on us." I guided Kevin back to the room.

Douglas, his feet up on his desk, was nonchalantly chewing on the remains of Kevin's sandwich. "Oh! Where you been?" he asked, his eyes wide with innocence. I needed a few minutes to decide how best to handle the morning's disaster. My anger at Doug's behavior was tempered by the realization that because of it I had at last begun to establish some rapport with Kevin.

"Doug, Kevin and I have decided that we are not going to let you—"

"Ugh, this sandwich has lettuce in it!"

"Now"—Kevin's voice was wavering—"now you have to bring me a treat tomorrow. And you owe me an apple too."

Douglas turned sharply to stare at Kevin. "Will you turn off the water hoses? Some people just don't like Africans. There's always some persecutor getting other people into trouble."

"Wait," I said. "You get yourself in trouble. Why not stop and think of what will happen before you do something?"

As he headed for the minibus, he rotated his index finger around the side of his head to symbolize my insanity. On the parking lot he turned to face the school and shouted, "Some class, two crazy kids and a crazy teacher!"

IN THE morning I fixed a pot of coffee for Bill and packed lunches for the kids and myself.

"Hey, Mom," Billy suggested as we were leaving the house. "Those kids in your room. Would they like a surprise?"

"Like what, Bill?"

"Take my guppies. The mother is having babies again."

ABOUT half an hour after the boys arrived, Douglas finally became too dizzy to spin around anymore. Then both of them became intrigued by the guppies, especially the pregnant mother.

"She's having babies because she's so sexy," advised Douglas. "Do you know what sexy means, kid?" Kevin blushed, pressed his nose to the fishbowl, but did not answer.

"He's retarded!" He threw an eraser violently against the closet, then tore around the room, flinging every object he could grab. Chalk, a plant, books, the blotter and papers on my desk all sailed through the air. Kevin took refuge in the kneehole of my desk. Douglas threw the fish food, and the box broke open when it hit the blackboard.

"Ha! Now she'll be so hungry she'll have to eat her babies!" Douglas ran into the closet. Next, I expected, the coats would shoot across the room. I was not prepared to hear muffled sobs. He was huddled in a corner of the closet, crying heartbrokenly.

I approached and he kicked out violently, so I sat and waited, not knowing for what. I felt angered by my own ineffectiveness.

Kevin continued to cower under my desk. Douglas wept more openly. After fifteen minutes came a small voice from the closet. "I could buy some food next Saturday."

"The fish won't live until next Saturday, Douglas."

Silence. Then, "I have an idea."

"Oh?" I went toward the closet and Doug rose to meet me.

"I could sweep it up."

I wanted to hug him as he labored to Scotch-tape the box back into shape. But I felt certain I must watch quietly, accepting his action as if it were the expected course.

I didn't know how it had come about, this miraculous change, but for the first time I felt hopeful about Douglas. Kevin did not conceal his amazement. He crept out from my desk and stared openmouthed as Douglas spent the rest of the morning brushing every visible grain of fish food into the battered container.

On Friday, Douglas arrived late. "Damn stove, damn stove. Can't make anything on that damn stove. Look!" There was an ugly red burn across the palm of his hand. "Just wanted an egg for breakfast." He was fighting tears.

"That must hurt terribly, Doug. You must feel like crying." He did cry then, allowing me to put an arm around him and comfort him until the tears subsided. We sent for Mrs. Rogers, the nurse, who led him to her office for treatment.

Kevin as usual had been a silent observer. He sat at his desk, holding out his hand. "Look." He pointed to an invisible wound. "I hurt my pinger. I hurt my pinger!"

I hugged him. "Too bad, Kevin, too bad. You and Doug both have hurts. Let's find a toy, and maybe it will help you forget."

With unusual enthusiasm he rummaged through the toy closet, emerging with a plastic baby bottle. He headed toward the door. "I get wa-wa." He hadn't spoken in baby talk before, and I felt a little uneasy about it. I was at my desk when he returned. "Up, up." He climbed into my lap, closed his eyes, and sucked on the bottle. Though unsure about permitting this behavior, I hesitated to interrupt any opportunity to improve our relationship. He drained the bottle and hurried out to the bathroom for a refill.

"Wock me. Wock me." He dragged over the child-size rocker. I wedged into the little seat and he climbed back on my lap. He lay his head on my shoulder, sucking contentedly.

Douglas, his hand now bandaged, walked in on this bizarre scene. He stared at us and went straight to the closet. Next, he too had a bottle and was on his way down the hall. Oh no! Not both of them! But when he returned he stopped, then threw the bottle to the floor. The nipple shot off and the water spilled. He hurried back to the closet and took out paste, scissors, and paper. Douglas seemed not to want to interrupt us, yet he frequently glanced uneasily in our direction as he cut and pasted.

When Kevin drained the second bottle, he returned for a refill once again. More rocking and sucking. But Doug, totally exasperated, lifted the sticky paste brush from its jar, approached us, and ran a wide streak of paste up Kevin's back. Kevin didn't even notice. He remained a baby all morning. Frustrated, Douglas took apart the entire closet, while muttering about the crazy teacher and the retarded kid. I hoped to bring Kevin back to reality by frequently commenting, "It's fun to play baby, isn't it?"

Douglas finally approached me. "I'm hungry," he said.

"Why don't we have lunch a little early today, Kevin?" I said. "You and Douglas can get ready right now."

But I had been too abrupt. Kevin looked startled, then climbed down and crawled over to the hand puppets which Douglas had scattered on the floor. He put on the rubber crocodile and began to devour me, first my arms, then my face. The attack was accompanied by ferocious growls.

"The crocodile's pretty angry at me," I said.

Douglas laughed uneasily as Kevin's crocodile turned menacingly in his direction. "You sure are blowing your stack, aren't you, kid?" Kevin growled and snapped. Douglas was unnerved. This time he pleaded, "You're bugging me, man. Turn it off. You can have half my cake if you stop."

Surprisingly, Kevin responded. He dropped the puppet and sat at his desk. I went to Doug's side. "It was kind of you to offer to share your cake."

"That's okay, nothing to it." He carefully broke the chocolate cupcake in half and deposited a piece on Kevin's desk.

When he had finished eating, Douglas put away all the toys he had scattered earlier, stacking them neatly in the closet.

Kevin just sat, ignoring Doug's offering. As the bus arrived he mashed the cake flat on his desk. Douglas looked more hurt than angry. He started down the hall beside Kevin, then returned to our door. "Wow!" he whispered confidentially. "He sure is a harsh kid, isn't he? You better start getting hard on him."

CEIL came in as soon as the boys left. I launched into a long recital of the week's events, anxious for her advice. "Is it harmful to allow Kevin to play baby? When Douglas begins to spin, should he be allowed to continue until he falls, or would it be better to stop him? How much should he be allowed to get away with before he's punished? What is an appropriate punishment? Do you believe there is any hope that either one will ever be well?"

She smiled. I was to learn that she used pauses in conversation more effectively than most people used words. Ceil had a master's in social work and a twelve-year-old son of her own. Because of her outstanding record in her department she had been assigned to this pilot program, for which she had suggested the name Transitional Class. She now said, "How could you expect anything but a long hard time with Douglas? He has no reason to trust you or anyone else. Your story about his cleaning up the fish food shows more remorse and sensitivity than we had any right to expect. About the spinning—it's something we often see in schizophrenic children. They repeat and repeat the same action, unaware of their repetition, unable to stop themselves. If you want to bring him out of it, words won't do. You'll have to touch him. Put your hand on his shoulder and lead him to something else."

We were sitting in the low chairs at the reading table. Her reddish curls bobbed as she spoke more intensely. "Look, if you didn't keep questioning yourself, you wouldn't be right for this job. But you can't assume the guilt for their problems. The damage has been done over a period of years. We won't undo it overnight.

"As for Kevin, finding comfort and security by being a baby is serving a purpose for him. He may want to do it again. Your assuring him that it's fun to *play* baby was fine. Next time, you could talk to him about babies, how they learn to crawl and then to walk and talk, and do all the things a boy his age can do.

This will help in easing him back to the present. I've made a tentative appointment for his parents to come next Thursday evening, okay? It should be very interesting to learn more about what goes on with Kevin at home."

CHAPTER THREE

BILL was hoping for a spring publication date and worked the whole weekend. Ann had looked forward all week to the first slumber party of the school year. She spent Saturday packing and repacking her case.

Sunday, Richie had a Cub Scout meeting at our house, and there was a noisy debate on different ways of raising money for an outing. I began to appreciate how important it was that those who work with exceptional children have fulfilling lives of their own. By Monday, Friday's despair was long forgotten.

I began the week with enthusiasm. Art seemed an appropriate activity—no right or wrong, just the pleasure of working with the materials. Before the boys arrived I set up two easels, each with an assortment of paints. A minute after the bus door slammed, Douglas came bounding into the room. Forgetting his ritual spinning, he approached the easels immediately.

"Oh, painting, huh? I'm very good at it. I never got a turn before, but I'm a good painter."

Kevin entered, head bowed, shuffling as if he were sleepwalking. Mechanically, he took his seat.

"Hey, Kevin, ya gonna sit there looking mean all day? Trying to spoil other people's fun? Well, man, I'm painting."

Douglas made a huge red O, then smeared the paint all over his paper and discarded it for another.

Kevin responded to Doug's prodding by approaching the easel, but he wouldn't try to paint. Finally I put my hand over his and together we brushed dabs of color on the large paper. Left on his own, he continued woodenly. By eleven thirty Douglas had produced twenty-three paintings, scattered all over the floor to dry. But Kevin had given up.

"It's almost time for lunch, Doug. Why don't you just finish up the picture you are working on?" I said.

"I'm too busy to take a break, thanks," replied the artist.

Kevin spread his napkin on his desk and unscrewed the thermos. "Can't drink," he muttered, "can't drink." He groped inside his desk and brought out the baby bottle. He poured the milk from the thermos to the bottle. "Dwink, dwink."

"That kid's at it again!" Doug moaned.

"Wock me!" Kevin begged.

Once again I jammed myself into the little rocker. He was on my lap instantly, sucking loudly. "It's fun, isn't it, Kevin, to pretend that you're a baby again. Being held and loved, sucking a bottle." He closed his eyes. The milk was nearly gone.

"Then remember, Kevin, how babies learn to do more things—to creep and crawl all around, discovering everything." The milk was gone. He sucked in air. "Then the baby gets bigger and bigger. He begins to pull himself up and then to stand alone."

He was listening. He slid to the floor, crept to the legs of his desk, and cautiously pulled himself to standing position.

"So finally the baby becomes as grown up as you, Kevin, and able to do so many things." He smiled.

"Are you two through?" Douglas bellowed. "Man, you make a person feel like a gutter. Nobody speaking to you, everybody stepping all over you. Like a gutter." He poured the paint down the legs of the easel, one color after another, then shook the final drops into the fishbowl. "There! If she dies, will it be my fault? Well, I hope she does and her babies too! You can probably hate me."

"Doug, you're unhappy because you thought we were ignoring you. I'm sorry it seemed that way. Now take the jar quickly and fill it with water. We'll transfer the fish."

Douglas didn't answer. He was in the closet, crying. Kevin hurried off to fill the jar. We scooped the guppy out with his thermos cup. In clear water, her recovery was remarkable. I tried to let Douglas know, but his sobs were louder than my words.

"Here, Kevin. Keep the jar on your desk. You watch her while I go down the hall and rinse out her bowl."

When I returned, Kevin had the guppy on his desk. He was chopping her to pieces with his ruler. Sickened, I grabbed the wastebasket and whisked the sections of fish into it. Kevin kicked the desk over, then crushed the crayons and pencils with his feet.

Douglas rushed from the closet and grabbed Kevin by the collar. "You sure have a mind for killing, boy!" He punched Kevin in the face. Amazingly, Kevin stuck out his tongue!

"Enough!" I shoved them apart. "No more hurting anything or anybody! It's all right to be angry, but *say it!* We are here to learn together. We've made mistakes, but from now on . . ." My efforts were being drowned out by the beginning of what I was later to call Kevin's "shoe language." As I spoke, he tapped and then stamped his feet louder and louder.

The bus came. When the boys left, it was my turn to cry.

DURING the next few days Douglas' moods were extreme—wild tantrums, sudden crying spells, or encouraging expressions of insight. Working with him became exhausting and disheartening. His resistance was even greater when I tried to introduce reading with each boy individually. Each time, Douglas knocked the book from my hands, then slumped to the floor, feigning sleep.

Kevin, who had so much he needed to express, now relied on his shoes to do it for him. Every time I approached, his feet would begin to tap—heel-toe, heel-toe—louder and louder. I said he must stop so that we could read. He shrugged innocently.

On Thursday, when it was Kevin's turn for "work period," he headed for the fountain outside the room.

"Just a minute!" I called. "You may have your drink when we have had a look at this book."

He eased out of each shoe and carried them into the hall, lined them up under the water fountain, then returned to his desk. Kevin was obedient—only his shoes were defiant.

THURSDAY evening Ceil and I arrived at the darkened school simultaneously to keep our appointment with Kevin's parents. While we waited for them I filled Ceil in on Kevin's recent behavior. Mr. and Mrs. Hughes finally arrived twenty minutes late, offering no apology.

We squatted on low chairs around the reading table. Ceil took the initiative. "Mrs. Craig and I feel that Kevin is adjusting to this new situation about as well as we would expect. There is really not too much to share with you at this point, but we felt that you might have some questions you would like to ask."

"Do I? Oh boy, do I!" Mr. Hughes plunged in. He looked much younger than his wife, and wore a stylish teal-blue suit and pale blue tie. "The kid hasn't come home with homework once! Is he doing anything in this place or not? What the hell kind of school *is* this?"

Ceil jarred my stunned silence. "Mrs. Craig can answer questions about the learning program better than I."

"Yes. Well—ah—part of the reason Kevin is here, Mr. Hughes, is that he *does* have a learning problem. When Kevin is *able* to work, he will receive individual attention here and progress at his own rate. We have to work together to help him reach that point of readiness."

Ceil elaborated on Kevin's feelings of inadequacy, and the importance of cooperation between home and school. Mr. Hughes shook his finger at her, then at me. "I get it! You're saying the kid hasn't got what it takes to make it. Right? In other words—*he might as well be a teacher!*" And, grabbing his wife by the arm, he left the room.

ON FRIDAY, Ceil and I attended a meeting of the Transitional Class planning committee. This meeting was to review the first two cases on the waiting list of more than fifty children that social workers hoped to place in the program. Douglas and Kevin were about to have new classmates.

The committee now included Jim Hanley, head of Special Education; Barbara Rizzo, chief social worker; Arlene Wood, the psychological examiner; Miss Knight, a junior high school principal; Miss Silverstein, Ceil, and me. Ceil summarized the case histories of the new boys.

"Edward Conte is a seven-year-old with a background of be-havioral problems since kindergarten, where he was unmanage-able, restless, provocative, and disobedient. His first-grade teacher wrote, 'He cannot go more than a few days without attacking an-other child. He just explodes for no reason.'

"Parents of Edward's classmates finally petitioned the prin-cipal for the boy's removal, complaining that their children were afraid to come to school. Mrs. Rizzo spoke to Edward's parents about his being included in the Transitional Class."

Mrs. Rizzo then told us, "Mr. and Mrs. Conte are extremely immature, with no understanding of Edward's condition. The marriage has always been stormy, and they are constantly on the verge of terminating it. There is a five-year-old sister, who so far seems to be doing all right in kindergarten. The father works in a gas station and says he spends all his free time on his motorcycle. The mother wants to enroll in a modeling school." Mrs. Rizzo turned toward me. "I would recommend that if Edward goes into your class, Eleanor, you adjust all demands to his very short at-tention span."

I shuddered at the thought of Douglas and Edward together. Ceil said, "One of our goals is to maintain a balance in the group. For that reason we had hoped to add two girls at this time, but the waiting list is made up almost entirely of boys." She then read, " 'Jonathan Bergman is an extremely disturbed eight-year-old, who is also reacting to his parents' destructive handling. Jonathan is an only child, born after his parents had been married for six years. After having Jonathan, Mrs. Bergman suffered three mis-carriages. She had a two-month hospitalization for a mental break-down after the third miscarriage. Recently she began private treatment with Dr. Gross, who feels that she is a borderline schizo-phrenic. She goes on periodic alcoholic binges. Apparently the husband is cold to both his wife and son. He is a successful busi-nessman, vice-president of a large ad agency.' "

"It's interesting, isn't it," Jim Hanley interrrrupted, "how some of these guys can function so well on the outside and be such miserable failures at home?"

"Jonathan lasted only a few weeks in first grade," Mrs. Rizzo said. "He couldn't be contained because he was so disruptive and because of encopresis. He soiled daily."

I gulped. Miss Knight read from a manila folder. "'Psychological testing indicates that this child's behavior is a reaction to many inner fears and great insecurity, to such an extent that he is unable to control his fantasies of destruction. Nor can he separate them from reality. Life must be frightening for Jonathan.'"

"There's one positive factor," Ceil added. "That is that both parents desperately want help at this time. They are all going to be seen regularly at the Child Guidance Center."

Jim Hanley said, "I frankly think this kid may be too sick even for our program. But I wouldn't want to recommend a residential placement at his age until we've given this a try."

The committee voted unanimously to accept both Edward and Jonathan on a trial basis.

ON MONDAY morning Douglas and Kevin had to be told that they would soon have new classmates. Nothing could have united the two boys more than this news. "Let's keep our desks away from them, Kev. Just you and me are buddies."

"No. My big brother can be your friend," Kevin said. "He's the best one. If you don't believe it, come over sometime."

"Can I? When can I come over, Kev, huh?"

"Maybe soon. I'll ask my mother."

"Today we are going to do something new," I interrupted, handing them folders. "These contain work for you, work you will be able to do. I'll sit with you first, Kevin, then with you, Doug, to answer questions. If you are completely done by lunchtime, we can use the gym this afternoon."

"Hey, that's boss! Come on, Kev, let's hurry up!"

Kevin shook his head. "When I hurry, I make mistakes."

"Now listen, dummy," Douglas counseled, "everybody makes mistakes. Some people say there's no such thing as mistakes."

Douglas finished early. Kevin was barely through by twelve. But both had been attentive and cooperative all morning. After lunch we went down to the gymnasium, as promised. We began tossing the basketball, but when Kevin caught the ball he refused to return it. "Right here, Kev, ole buddy," Douglas called.

"Uh-uh." He clutched it tighter. "I only play alone. I never play with anybody."

Douglas pointed to the corner. "You stand over there, *pleeeeze*, Mrs. Craig. Kevin and I have to do our physical fitness. Kevin," he demanded, "get over here!" Surprisingly, Kevin followed Douglas to the middle of the court. They threw the ball back and forth. Whenever Douglas missed a catch, he would command, "Go get it!" And Kevin would run after the ball until finally he was exhausted and slumped against the wall.

"Kevin looks tired, Doug." I left my corner. "And it's late. We just have time for drinks before the bus."

Douglas playfully slapped Kevin's back. "Good game, buddy." Poor Kevin nearly collapsed.

"Me and Kev are gonna live together on a farm someday, Mrs. Craig. Right, Kev? We don't have to get married to get our food cooked. We can do it ourselves. We can be bachelors."

By PREVIOUS arrangement, their mothers brought Edward and Jonathan half an hour early the next morning. Mrs. Bergman, Jon's mother, was thirty-four and looked closer to fifty.

Eddie's mother was in her mid-twenties. Her jet-black hair was elaborately teased and her lashes heavily mascaraed.

The two women waited uncomfortably while their boys chose closet spaces and storage cubbies. Then Jonathan's mother murmured good-by and scurried away. Her son looked pale and frightened. Eddie clung to his mother's suede jacket, begging her to stay. She grabbed his skinny wrists. "I'm sick of you actin' like a baby!" She stormed out angrily.

He wailed for almost ten minutes, then stopped abruptly. By the time the bus arrived, the new pupils were sitting quietly. Douglas and Kevin must have rehearsed their song on the way to school. They sang to the tune of "Three Blind Mice" as they defiantly dropped their coats on the closet floor.

> "*Two new punks*
> *Two new punks*
> *We hate them*
> *We hate them*
> *We hate them and they hate us*
> *We hate them and they hate us*
> *Two new punks.*"

Jonathan's pale cheeks flushed. He closed his eyes tightly and covered his ears with the palms of his hands. Eddie darted at Douglas, leaping on his back. Douglas was thrown off-balance and fell. He and Eddie rolled around the floor, legs locked, arms flailing. Kevin yelled, "Kill him, Doug, kill the punk."

They tumbled across the room until both bodies struck the hot radiator. Howling in anguish, they fell apart. Douglas raged. "Okay, Mrs. Craig, you did it. You let this little killer in."

But it was my turn to be angry. "And what did you do, Douglas? And you too, Kevin? Did you give these boys any chance at all? I'm sorry that we couldn't have—"

I was interrupted by Kevin's feet. *Tap-tap, tap-tap-tap.* Then both feet slammed against his desk, tossing it upside down. The contents rolled out. Douglas patted his ally. "Okay, okay. I don't blame you for being mad, boy. I hate her too." Kevin stamped on a pencil, splintering it.

"Come on, man. You're blowing your stack again, aren't you? Look, let's get away from the punks."

Douglas carried his desk to the corner farthest from mine. "Come on, Kev. We can sit over here together. We won't need to deal with those guys." Kevin slumped forward limply. Douglas became impatient. "Now look, I told ya we're moving, dummy." He picked up Kevin's desk and pushed it beside his own, then dragged Kevin's chair, with its occupant, to the same location.

Eddie pointed. "Look at them babies. Huh! They moved their things, so I'll move mine!" He jammed his desk against mine—a silent plea for protection.

In the center of the room Jonathan was grimacing with obvious strain. From the odor, I realized his predicament. "Let me show you where the bathroom is, Jonathan. I'm going to help you so you won't have that problem here."

"Oh no, no thanks. Don't come any nearer! I can't stand people with faces like yours."

I opened the windows, then handed Douglas and Kevin their folders, expecting vehement protests. They not only accepted the work but concentrated on it all morning.

I wanted to work with Eddie and Jonathan and get an idea of their abilities. But each time I tried to approach Jonathan I set him off. "Don't come any closer. My radar has picked you up. Pow, pow!" So I spent the morning with Eddie, while Jonathan crossed his eyes, muttered, and whistled.

Lunchtime was peaceful for almost twenty minutes; then Eddie stamped on his empty milk carton, making it explode with the sound of a shotgun. This triggered a chain reaction. When everyone had popped his milk carton, I advised that cleanup would have to be quick, since we were going to have a film, *The New Classmate*. No one else looked approachable, and Eddie was delighted to be chosen for all jobs. He threaded the projector, pulled down the screen, and turned off the lights.

"Kevin and Doug, if you move your chairs back a little you'll be able to see the screen," I suggested.

"Man, is she crazy! You've just brought in two little punks. Don't speak to us anymore, after what you've done."

Jonathan continued talking to himself. Eddie bent over the projector, intrigued by the film's progress through the machine. I alone watched the pictures, which showed how many small kindnesses had made a new pupil feel welcome.

Every day that week Jonathan soiled and burped, Eddie and Douglas fought, and Kevin and Douglas continued their self-imposed exile. Yet there were glimmers of progress. Folders were being completed by lunchtime, with the understanding that only then could one participate in the afternoon activities. We had finally established limits, rewards, and consequences, a necessary step toward self-discipline.

MISS SILVERSTEIN CAME IN after school. "Sorry I can't give you more notice, but the central office just called. Jim Hanley is coming over tomorrow to observe your class with three people from Belmere who are interested in setting up a similar program there."

The next morning Eddie ran in and leaped around the room, screaming, "I didn't see him! I didn't even see him hit my mother, and now her head's all lumpy! I hate him! I'll never call him my father again. Oh, oh, my mother's head is broken, and he's gone! When he comes back, I'll hold the door so he can't get in. If he smashes it down, I'll stab him with a knife."

Kevin and Douglas arrived together. "Do it, go ahead," I heard Kevin whisper. Then, calmly, Douglas strolled over to Eddie and belted him in the stomach. Eddie doubled up on the floor, clutching his stomach and crying hysterically.

"Douglas! How dare you?" I cradled Eddie's head.

Douglas pointed at me indignantly. "Now listen, you keep quiet. That little punk cried all the way to school about his mumma. It's embarrassing." After that speech, Douglas sat down and devoured his lunch.

Eddie was still sobbing when Jonathan began to yell. "Oh, it's here now. It followed me to school! Hurry! I have to get it with my atomic radiation gun. Pow! Pow!"

Eddie began to shout again. "He left before I woke up! I didn't hear the fight at all, then Doug has to sock me! Oh, oh."

His head was still in my lap. I brushed back his dark hair, damp from the tears. "Mrs. Black will see you at ten today. I guess it made Doug angry to see you cry on the bus. But he's going to learn soon to tell people with words and not with punches."

"Ha!" Douglas licked the frosting on his cupcake. "That little punk's too dumb for conversation!"

Eddie sprang up. "Huh! Mrs. Black thinks I'm waiting till ten o'clock, she's crazy!" He ran down the hall toward her office.

The visitors suddenly appeared in the doorway. Mr. Hanley introduced me, then all four took chairs in the back of the room.

We had progressed to the point where each child worked on his assignments while I sat with one after another at the reading table, giving individual instruction. I now called Douglas. Today he would start fractions, using a felt circle cut into quarters. "Think of it as a pie, Doug. Each person will have one-fourth—"

"Mmmm, a pie, huh? I'll have it, thanks." He stuffed each piece of felt into his mouth, then pretended to gag and choke until he spat out the last scrap. "Man, what a crummy pie! Why didn't you say you're a lousy cook?"

"Man, what a funny student!" I couldn't resist it. "Why didn't you say you're a comedian?"

Douglas looked at the ceiling. "Help her, God. She's trying to crack jokes in a foreign language. It's you'RRRRe, not yah!" But he put every bit of felt in the wastebasket.

Eddie jogged in and circled around the room, gasping. "Mrs. Black's not there. Am I supposed to wait for her all day?"

"She'll be there soon, Eddie. Sit down for a few minutes."

"I'm getting all the stuff outta her room. She's not using it with anybody else!" He left.

I looked around. Douglas had settled down and was working on his folder. Kevin was scribbling. Although he had been given short simple assignments, he was unable to work independently. "Our time to work together, Kevin." I led the way to the table.

"You seemed to be having trouble with the arithmetic. Let's start again." Just having someone beside him enabled him to complete the assignment that had been so frustrating. The contrast in papers was astonishing. "Finished already, Kevin? And they're all correct! It must make you happy to have done such a fine job."

He tried to conceal it, but a smile broke through. I looked back at the visitors, hoping they had caught Kevin's fleeting expression. They were smiling too.

At eleven Eddie returned from Ceil's office with a sketch of his battered mother and several finger paintings. His time with her had been an outlet for his tensions. He opened his folder.

"Do you think I'm gonna do all this?"

"Do you think you are?"

He started right away.

Ceil came for Jonathan, who became self-conscious walking

past the visitors. "Whew—burp—urp, I think I'm blowing my top! Whew! Here I go!" She guided him out.

Douglas finished his folder and began playing with anagrams. Jonathan burst in, carrying three play-dough monsters he had molded in Ceil's office. He arranged them on his desk.

"Hey, Ed," Kevin taunted. "Jonathan used the play dough. I thought that stuff was just for you."

Eddie exploded. He knocked over Jonathan's desk and hurled one of the monsters against the wall. "That bitch! I told her everything is only for me!" He snatched the two other models and ran toward Ceil's office, screaming.

"You know, Kevin, I'm beginning to hate you," Douglas snarled. Kevin looked stricken. Douglas picked up the remaining play dough and deposited it in Jonathan's hand, righted his desk for him, and bowed gallantly in my direction. "Okay, Mrs. Craig. Your turn to do something spectacular." Mr. Hanley and I burst into laughter. The children joined in, including Jonathan.

Mr. Hanley glanced at his watch and rose. The four men nodded their thanks and filed out. It was hard to imagine a worse day for having the Transitional Class observed.

By Friday of each week I had a list of subjects to discuss with Ceil. My major problem today concerned Jonathan's soiling. "Why does it happen, and what should I do when it happens?"

"Jonathan's encopresis is his way of expressing his inner fears," she explained. "Like Kevin when he taps, or Doug when he fights, Jon is asking us to listen. His symptoms speak for him."

"But, Ceil, the kids are beginning to call him names, and he becomes unbearable sometimes. What should I do?"

"What do you want to do?"

"I've been thinking about it. I want to send him home. I want him to understand that soiling is unacceptable here."

"Then do it. Just be sure he understands you're not rejecting him as a person. Tell him calmly that he's not ready to be in school that day, but you hope he will be able to stay tomorrow."

Then I showed Ceil the papers I had saved. Jonathan's ghost

family, which he drew on each day's folder, had Mommy telling Daddy that Junior was bad (wet pants), and she had put him underground with King Tut's coffin. Doug's stories, illustrated with magazine cutouts, were hard to read but very moving. Eddie drew himself swallowed up by a menacing-looking mother. Kevin's angry scribbling was done the day Jonathan and Eddie joined us.

We talked until four thirty. "Save those and any other interesting papers," Ceil said. "They'll be helpful when we discuss the children at the clinic. Happy weekend."

CHAPTER FOUR

TOWARD the end of October, Miss Silverstein invited the class to participate in the school's annual Halloween party, including a costume parade around the grounds. Many mothers came to photograph this colorful event. Privately, she told me that any disruption by the Transitional Class would only increase the resentment of some parents toward our being in "their" school.

"I'll be a ghost," said Kevin.

Eddie was really excited. "I'm going to wrap up in hundreds of bandages and be a mummy."

Douglas said, "I'll probably wear an astronaut's suit, with oxygen and all."

"Even with the simplest costume, it will be a special day for all of us." Miss Silverstein smiled. "Such an exciting day that we'll have to keep reminding ourselves to obey the rules. Jonathan, we haven't heard from you."

"Pow, pow! Squish, squish, bang!"

"Yes, I hear your noises, but I want to know what you might wear to our Halloween party," the principal said.

Jonathan replied, "Have you ever seen them clean out a cesspool? I love to step on the BM. Squish, squish."

AT HOME, Halloween fever was running high. Richie, like Douglas, chose to be an astronaut. For days he argued that I was unreasonable not to let him wear Billy's fishbowl on his head. Billy would be a cowboy and Ellen a cat. Ann felt too old to wear a disguise. While I sewed Ellen's costume, the kids made popcorn balls. Though I knew I'd be wiping up syrup for days, it was a pleasure to hear them talking and laughing together.

At school everyone but Douglas was giggly in anticipation of Friday's Halloween party. He became surlier by the hour. He even refused to participate in the phonics game he'd invariably won.

"Come on, Doug," I coaxed. "You can think of a word that begins with str—"

"Haven't I told you before?" he snapped. "Will you turn off the water hoses? Don't pretend you like Africans." But when everyone was stumped for a word beginning with X, "Exile!" he yelled. "Like me," he whispered.

At noon on Thursday I found his note face up at the top of the wastebasket.

Mrs Craig

_____

I would like to see you after school

Doug
Miller

P.S. Your not listening

Because Doug's grandmother had no phone, I asked the bus driver to stop at their apartment and let her know that I would drive Doug home in an hour or two.

After the others had left, I said, "I found your note, Doug. Won't you tell me what it is I haven't been listening to?"

He became enraged. He ripped all the pictures from the wall, threw chalk, erasers, books in all directions. Then he ran into the closet and began to yell. "Trying to get me in trouble, huh? You want me to steal some dumb costume? Think my grandmother's got money to spend on some junky thing just to make *you* happy?" His voice faltered. He was crying.

"*You're* the only one who could do it, Doug. Make a costume better than any store has. I'll help you."

Within an hour he had transformed a paper bag into a lion's head. He had also picked up everything he had thrown around. I drove him home, and on the way we stopped for hamburgers and French fries. "Douglas," I said, "see how much better everything was when you finally told me what was on your mind, instead of bottling it all up inside?"

"Look"—he opened the car door—"just sympathize, don't criticize." And he was gone.

HALLOWEEN at Central School was a great success, due in large measure to the skill of the parade marshal, a perfect replica of Charlie Chaplin. We didn't find out for days that it was Miss Silverstein. The party was barely over when the bus arrived, so Douglas the Lion, Eddie as Captain Hook, Kevin as an all-too-pretty girl, and Jonathan the Dragon rode home in costume.

"How about party time for us?" Ceil suggested. "We don't have to have our conference in this building. We can both get home quickly from that Italian place."

"Sounds great. I just have to get my plan book. Be right out." Doug's note was on my book.

"Look, Ceil. It's the most eloquent thank-you I've ever received."

Dear Mrs Craig
the mask work
fine and I had
a good time
Douglas M

CHAPTER FIVE

MONDAY morning, Kevin was at home with tonsillitis, and isolation proved too much for Douglas. He moved his desk nearer Eddie's, and by Wednesday they were buddies. Once Doug whispered, "Don't tell Kevin we're friends, okay? He'd get all steamed up."

Jonathan had more urgent problems. "Do you know what day it is?" he asked when I called him for reading.

"November fourth?"

"Uh-uh," he replied. "It's poop day."

It was.

"I'm sorry you're not ready to stay here today, Jonathan. Your mother will take you home soon. I hope that tomorrow you'll be able to stay all day."

After lunch, Douglas and Eddie painted together, one on either side of the easel. They became confidants. Eddie stepped back to admire his striped paper. "I'll have to show this rainbow to my mother. She thinks I'm crummy, but I'm not. I'm good."

Douglas came around. "That looks cool, man. Have you got a pretty mother?"

"Well, in the morning she's all mussed up, but when she puts on that spray for hard-to-manage hair she looks better."

They laughed condescendingly.

"My mother, too," Doug said wistfully.

"You don't even have a mother. The bus driver said that's your grandmother. I hate her because she's colored."

"Do you think that's my grandmother? Heck, that's the cleaning lady." Douglas looked uncomfortable.

"Oh yeah?" Eddie's voice became shrill. "You boog! You're colored too!" He pointed his brush at Douglas.

"Do you think I'm colored?" Douglas went back to his painting. "See, my mother was married to a colored man for a while, but he was my cousin, not my father. My real father's dead."

"Liar! Liar!" Eddie screamed. "You're going to the devil!"

Douglas painted a green stripe from Eddie's forehead to his waist. Eddie reciprocated with purple.

"The brushes are for the paper!" I moved in and, caught in the middle, was thoroughly decorated by both artists.

When the boys were too spent to continue, I tried cleaning all three of us with a damp sponge. The sponge smeared the paint.

Douglas contemplated his ruined jeans. "By the time my grandmother sees these pants, Mrs. Craig, you better be seeing your travel agent."

No TIME for the travel agent. Ceil and I had an appointment with Eddie's mother. I spent fifteen minutes in the washroom scrubbing my face and clothes. Then we waited almost an hour before Mrs. Conte sauntered in. We sat in the teachers' lounge.

"We've been concerned," Ceil began, "about Eddie's frequent upsets."

Mrs. Conte looked disgusted. "He's upset! I try to tell that kid how I feel, but he only thinks of himself." Her eyes narrowed suspiciously. "What does he say?"

"Eddie's worried about all of you, Mrs. Conte," I said. "He seems frightened."

"What's he got to be frightened about? His father hits me, not him. Nine years of this misery."

"But the situation is very threatening," Ceil replied. "He sees his father out of control."

"He started again last night, but I threw hot coffee at him, and he left. I wish he'd leave for good. He's so full of hate. He hates everyone—me, the kids, his mother. He hated his mother for drinking herself to death, but he's no better." She took a long drag on her cigarette, then spoke more gently. "I could hate too. I could hate my mother for dying when I was born. Or my grandmother for putting me in a foster home, but would that do any good?"

"You've had a difficult time," Ceil sympathized. "Surely you understand how the fighting affects Eddie. It's impossible for him to settle down here."

"I'll settle him down for you. Last time I had to beat that kid, he couldn't sit down for three days."

"Please, Mrs. Conte," I found myself pleading, "that's the opposite of what he needs. Eddie needs your love and reassurance more than ever."

"Yeah?" She rose, smoothing her sweater into her belt. "Who's going to love me?"

On Thursday morning Eddie bolted in, gasping, "Help! Doug's gonna kill me!" Jonathan ducked into the closet.

Douglas swaggered in, grinning down at the gleaming object projecting from his pocket. It was a paring knife. "Don't worry, Ed, just be a good kid. Any more talk about colored people and I'll take care of you."

"Let's have it, Doug." I concentrated on keeping my hand steady. "You're giving Eddie exactly what he wants."

He stood still, listening. "You're letting him get you in trouble. I won't allow him to do this to you. Let me have the knife."

Douglas drew the weapon from his pocket and studied it. He stared at Eddie, then at me. Suddenly he shuffled across the room and gently laid the knife in my palm.

Eddie pranced around his desk. "You're a dirty black-faced nigger," he squealed, "and so's your grandmother."

Douglas looked totally betrayed. He turned toward me. With venom he spat out, "I've got a faggot for a teacher."

I clutched Eddie's bony shoulder and forced him into his chair. "Jonathan! Douglas! To your seats immediately! We're going to settle this right now! Eddie, don't you realize there's a name for everybody, if people are foolish enough to do name calling?"

He came up with one for me. "Bitch! Take your crummy hand off my shoulder!"

"I will when you control yourself. Right now you need my help. I'm giving you a paper. You too, Jonathan and Douglas. I want you to write down what you don't like about each other. If you can't do it in words, draw a picture. Begin now. It must be done before you get your folders."

I slapped a paper on each desk. Jonathan, as usual, drew his ghost family. Jonathan hadn't soiled since he had been sent home. Moreover, he had begun to make dramatic progress in reading.

At first he had been unable to sound out the simplest words. Now he read fluently at first-grade level.

The other two drew feverishly. Soon Douglas held up his picture. "Look at this. Freckles all over him. He calls me black, but he's spotted, that's worse! His father musta been a leopard."

Eddie's portrait of Douglas was featureless, just a lopsided brown circle he was furiously coloring in. "Look at this chocolate face. He musta been dipped in Cocoa Marsh."

Eddie's imagery amused his intended victim. "How about you? Were you dipped in Marshmallow Fluff?"

Eddie's tense face broke into a smile.

"Hey, Eddie," Douglas continued, "wanna play connect-the-dots with your freckles? You get first move."

They began connecting the freckles on the drawing.

"Okay, lady, let's have our folders now. Me and my pal don't wanna be having lunch at one o'clock. We wanna have some time for fun. Right, ole buddy?"

KEVIN returned the next day, looking thin and pale. When Douglas ignored him and sat down beside Eddie, Kevin remained in the corner, often turning to look sadly toward Douglas, who worked diligently with Eddie. They encouraged each other to hurry so they would have time to play. When it was Kevin's turn at the worktable, he deliberately bumped into Douglas' desk as he walked over.

"Hey!" Douglas roared. "Are you blind?"

Kevin answered in a quiet monotone, "I'm going to tell my mother that you're not ever coming over."

"Why Kev," said Douglas, "I didn't mean no harm to you! I just have to intend to my work, but I'm still your faithful companion. You said I was coming over soon."

Kevin slumped into the chair beside me, then drooped forward onto the table. His eyes were shut.

"What's wrong, Kevin?" I put my arm around his shoulder.

No answer.

"We missed you this week. Is it hard to get back to school?"

"My mother," he murmured. "She doesn't believe me when I say I'm sick."

"Are you sick now?"

Suddenly he leaped up, darted into the closet, then began to pull the door shut on his neck.

"Don't, don't!" Douglas yelled. "You'll hurt yourself!"

"So what," Kevin answered flatly, his face scarlet. "I want to."

I rushed to the closet and yanked the door from Kevin's grasp. He crumpled to the floor, and Douglas began to whimper. Eddie, scornful of Douglas' concern, mocked, "You worried about that tomato face? That crazy tomato face is your friend?"

"See what you've done?" Douglas sobbed. "You bum!" He bolted across the room. "You've embarrassed me! Eddie thinks I've got nutty friends." He kicked Kevin in the stomach.

Kevin doubled up in pain, while Douglas went on an all-time rampage. Picking up a chair, he hurled it across the room. Two legs flew off as it cracked a section of blackboard. Coats and jackets were hurled out the window, followed by the wastebasket, papers, and workbooks. He was grunting and snarling, upsetting desks and chairs, scattering papers everywhere.

I caught Douglas' wrist, but he kicked my ankle and ran, calling back, "Shut up, shut up. . . ." He zigzagged down the hall, ripping everything off the bulletin boards on both sides as he ran.

Luckily an intercom had just been installed. Miss Silverstein's secretary answered sweetly.

"Doris, quick! Tell Miss Silverstein that Douglas is somewhere in the building, and we need the nurse for Kevin."

Seconds later Miss Silverstein and Mrs. Rogers, the nurse, rushed in. Our room looked like the aftermath of a tornado. Kevin had recovered enough to howl. Eddie was prancing around, holding the broken chair aloft. "He broke school property! Now who's a punk?" Jonathan, having taken cover under his desk, was grunting suspiciously.

Mrs. Rogers went to Kevin. "What happened to him?"

"Douglas kicked him in the stomach."

"He could have a rupture!" The nurse was a capable heavyset

woman. Effortlessly she scooped up the child. "This whole setup just babies kids. Four in a room, a waste of time and money!"

I thought of the innocent classmates these children had victimized previously, but it was no time to justify the program. She stormed out, Kevin draped limply in her arms.

Miss Silverstein and I whispered in the doorway. I tried to describe the sequence of events. She smiled knowingly. "You don't have to tell me how these kids can explode. Mr. Jakowsky and I will look around for Douglas."

I had begun to straighten up the room when the intercom buzzed. Mrs. Rogers' voice. "Kevin wasn't badly hurt, just upset. His mother is coming for him now."

Douglas hadn't shown up when the bus arrived. Frantic, I raced to beg the driver to wait a few minutes, but he was already pulling away. As the bus turned onto the road, Douglas' face suddenly appeared in the rear window. He saw me, grinned, and raised his fingers in the peace sign.

"CAN'T bear to let them go, eh?" Ceil had driven in while I stood numbly watching the bus depart. "Did you forget the meeting? Get your coat. I'm driving you over."

The meeting had been called to discuss two new pupils, this time girls. It was hard to concentrate as Sandra's case was being presented. Today's drama kept replaying in my head.

"What do you think?" Jim Hanley was addressing me. "Does Sandra sound like a good candidate to you?"

Why hadn't I listened? But wouldn't any girl be easier than another boy? "I'd like to hear about the other girl before we decide."

Claire Megan, the social worker who was making the referral, presented Julie's case. "Mrs. Neumayer is forty-seven and her husband is forty-nine. For many years they had considered adopting, but Mr. Neumayer was a master sergeant in the army and because of frequent relocations they never followed through until seven years ago."

Julie's unwed mother had kept her until she was two, making it more difficult to place her. In the next twelve months she lived in three different foster homes. Each foster mother complained about the child's tantrums and frequent nightmares. When the Neumayers first took Julie to a pediatrician, he advised them that the child was functionally retarded, but he predicted that with love and stimulation her mental development would accelerate. Mrs. Neumayer says she wanted to return the child then, but her husband would not agree.

"Julie is a nervous, whiny child with many psychosomatic complaints. Now, in second grade, she spends most mornings in the nurse's office. Even with individual attention her work is poor. She has no friends; the kids all tease her."

"How do Julie's parents feel about Transitional Class?" Mr. Hanley asked.

"Mrs. Neumayer is not happy," Claire replied. "I saw her last week. She talked at length about how Julie deliberately provokes by bed-wetting, among other things. She wants her sent 'someplace where they handle that kind of child.' She will go along with our recommendation only because she hopes it will lead to residential placement."

Mr. Hanley said, "Miss Wood, you did the testing?"

She nodded. "Psychologicals reveal high average ability, but feelings of deep depression and insecurity with inadequate defenses. There is no cerebral dysfunction."

"One thing we can do for Julie right away," Ceil said, "is to have her seen by Dr. Bialek at the clinic. If he could put her on Tofranil for the bed-wetting, it would be one break in the vicious circle."

The committee voted unanimously to accept both girls.

On the following Thursday, Ceil called after school to say the plans had been upset. "Sandra's father has been transferred. We'll look for another girl. It's far from ideal to have only one, but I don't think we should postpone Julie's arrival."

While I was on the phone with Ceil, the storm that had threatened all day broke full force. By the time I got home I was completely drenched.

The children had been soaked too and were sitting in the living room in bathrobes, watching TV. I started supper, but just as I slid the meat loaf into the oven the electricity suddenly went off.

We heard on Richie's transistor that power would not be restored in our area for several hours. Searching the refrigerator while Ann held a flashlight, I came up with a package of hot dogs. Bill brought in our biggest logs and piled them in the living-room fireplace. The kids roasted the hot dogs and marveled at how "neat" it must have been in "the old days" when people cooked all their meals in the fireplace. By morning the power was restored, but the kids were still animated, and chatted at breakfast about last night's fun.

But what had been exciting for my own children had been traumatizing for others. Kevin came to school subdued and depressed. Eddie raced around frantically. "Someone turned off the lights! We just got crackers for supper!"

My explanation of the power shutoff angered Douglas. Holding his jacket as if it were a bat, he pounded it against the wall. "So that's what did it!" he snarled. "My grandmother said we didn't have no money for the lights!"

Jonathan was most deeply affected. "All night," he cried, "rats and monsters came down from the attic! Then I saw a plane crash and it burned and burned. I got my flashlight to signal the other pilots, but their planes crashed too."

We talked at length, did finger paintings, and played records, but none of these activities soothed Jonathan.

"Oh, oh," he moaned at bus time, putting on his coat. "I hope there won't be more rats and monsters tonight!"

CHAPTER SIX

Mrs. Neumayer and Julie were waiting at school when I arrived Monday morning. The mother, a thin tense-faced woman, had parting messages for both Julie and me.

"Mrs. Craig, I will expect a progress report on this child every Friday. Julie"—her voice was cold—"you are to cooperate. We've done all we can for you. Now it's your turn."

Julie was an adorable girl, small and chunky, with dimpled

hands and knees. Her round petulant face had a light sprinkle of freckles across the bridge of her nose. After her mother left, she sat sucking her thumb.

I had told the boys last week about Julie's imminent entry, but apparently the words had been lost in post-blackout excitement. They were stunned to have a girl in the class. They devised circuitous routes to their desks to avoid approaching her. They accepted their folders almost gratefully and buried themselves in their assignments. There was an unnatural calm.

The "honeymoon" period of model behavior lasted an entire week. By Friday Douglas was becoming coolly objective. "She's a good-looking girl," he observed during his reading period. But Kevin's reaction was the most unexpected. Small gestures revealed his enormous interest—he would move his coat closer to hers or get next to her in line.

In the next school week the veneer and gallantry wore thin. Julie had episodes of weeping, then of fanatically turning on herself, biting her arms and hands. I learned to subdue her by holding my arms around her until she was calm. This depressed the boys. Jonathan returned to whistling and grunting, Eddie and Douglas to their ambivalent relationship—unprovoked warfare, sudden reconciliations. Kevin, most distressed by Julie's behavior, tapped his feet and accomplished nothing at all.

Thanksgiving became a focal point for all our activities. Art projects evolved, from brilliantly painted headdresses to a life-size canoe Douglas and Eddie created from giant sheets of heavy construction paper.

At lunch the day before the holiday the children all chose to be Indians, and I was the lone Pilgrim. Jonathan brought in his flashlight. "See? This is the original one I used to signal the planes. I covered it with red cellophane so it would look like a fire."

Douglas and Kevin dragged in a tumbling mat from the gym. "This will be our campsite, okay? Jonathan, you put your flashlight in the middle," Douglas directed.

Eddie bolted from the room, but returned in minutes, his arms full of twigs, which he skillfully arranged around the flashlight.

He and Douglas lowered all the shades. The result was pure magic, a glowing campfire. When had they changed? I wondered. When had they begun trying to get along with one another?

When the children were washing up before lunch, the mood was broken by Julie's screams. I found her in the bathroom, Douglas' arm around her neck. He and Kevin were lifting up her skirt.

"Douglas! Kevin! How dare you do this to her!"

Kevin was mortified at being caught. Douglas was angered by the interruption. "Just button up your lip, lady, and keep your mind out of men's business."

"It is my business to see that you don't take advantage of people, either of you. And protecting Julie is my business. Don't you dare do anything like this again!" The possible consequences were flashing through my mind. Should they be sent home now? Or might it still be possible to salvage the Thanksgiving celebration?

Julie's expression, frightened but somehow pleased with the attention, encouraged me to try. "I'd like to return to our room now," I said. "I'd like to forget this incident and start again. Would you?"

Kevin gulped. His face was scarlet. Douglas' bravado vanished. He nodded as the first tear rolled down his cheek.

We sat cross-legged on the mat around the rosy "fire"—Douglas and Kevin, two subdued Indians; Julie, surprisingly complacent; Jonathan and Eddie rendering bloodcurdling war cries. Then a clay peace pipe Eddie had molded passed hands solemnly.

"May we please wear our headdresses on the bus?" Douglas asked respectfully.

"And I get to take the canoe," Eddie added.

"You gotta be kidding," Douglas challenged. "I did more work than you."

"Oh yeah? I stapled the whole damn thing!" Eddie screamed.

"See you later, little punk." Douglas lifted the canoe onto his back, arching the bow over his shoulder.

Eddie lunged at the canoe and tugged so ferociously that Douglas was dragged halfway across the room before the paper tore. The Indians filed out, Douglas and Eddie triumphantly, each with a jagged section of canoe draped on his shoulder.

ON DECEMBER 11 at nine fifteen there was a blast from a horn in the driveway. Then another and another.

The intercom buzzed. "Your bus driver's having a fit. Will you see what's wrong?"

I rushed out. Kids were tumbling back and forth in the minibus. I could hear Julie crying and the boys yelling.

Mr. Dixon leaned out, his face purple. "You get this mob outta here! I never seen such little bastards."

When they spotted me, everyone scrambled for the door to be first with his grievances. They shoved and fought their way up the stairs into the building.

"You started it, Kevin," Douglas yelled. "I heard you teasing Julie and Jonathan."

"And you hit me hard," Julie added.

Kevin, quite pleased with the accusations against him, led the way to our room. Eddie danced around Julie and Jonathan and stuck out his tongue, making donkey ears with his hands. Kevin sat angelically, hands folded on his desk. Douglas had just sat down when Eddie crept up behind him and swung a metal lunch box at the back of his head. "Duck, Douglas!" I screamed. He missed being hit by a fraction of an inch, only because the lunch box broke. The container skidded across the floor. Eddie still gripped the handle.

"Okay, you broke my lunch box!" He waved the metal bar at Douglas. "You owe me two dollars!"

"That's ridiculous, Eddie," I said. "You were trying to hurt Douglas with it. It's lucky the lunch box did break."

"You're protecting him? He tried to steal my new gloves yesterday! I'm getting out of here. I'm leaving my gloves in Miss Silverstein's office. *You* can trust that boog thief, I don't." Eddie left.

Remarkably calm, Douglas beckoned to me. He confided, "I think Eddie's troubled, the way he's been acting."

"You think he tries to hurt people when he's unhappy?"

"Naturally." He nodded.

Eddie danced in. "There! She's keeping my gloves every day. I told her to put them in the safe."

I surveyed the Transitional Class. Eddie was anxious, Douglas stoic, Kevin smug, Julie tearful, and Jonathan tense, about to blow his top.

"No folders today." No smiles, either. "The Christmas program is at ten. Before we go you may write a story or draw a picture of what you would like for Christmas or Hanukkah."

"I'm not drawing a goddam picture," said Eddie, reaching for the paper.

"I ain't doin' no story," Kevin grumbled.

"Fine. Here's a drawing paper for you, too. Jonathan, which do you choose?"

"Stay away! My radar's on you! Everyone's picking on me, here and at home, too."

"Tell me." I knelt beside him.

He whined, whistled, and burped.

"Tell me in words."

"Y-y-yesterday . . . at . . . home . . . I . . . was . . . m-m-m-making a . . . big hole in my backyard." He had to force the words. "These kids came over to watch. I warned them to stay back, stay behind the tree, because my rays are dangerous, but they wouldn't!" He winced. Even the telling was painful. "They stepped out and laughed at me. I hadda chase them away with my shovel, but my father saw me and he hit me on the bottom. He hit me hard!" He was close to tears.

"Of course you don't like being hit or having kids tease you. But good for you for being able to tell about it. That's hard. And take another look, Jonathan. Your rays aren't affecting me. They didn't affect the kids yesterday. You don't have dangerous rays."

He looked uncertain but less troubled.

I collected the papers. Douglas had written a sensitive note wishing happiness to his enemy, Eddie. Julie wanted to be a dog, a dead dog, which her family would mourn. Kevin, too, wished himself dead, in a cheery coffin with curtains and a chimney. Jonathan's ghost family scolded baby for wet pants. Eddie sketched me wearing a witch's hat, about to be executed. He was holding the gun.

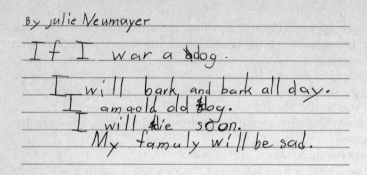

By Julie Neumayer

If I war a dog.

I will bark and bark all day.
I am a old old dog.
I will die soon.
My famuly will be sad.

I Wish I Can Die

Christmas wish
Kevin

A Wish Doug Miller

Oh Oh Oh how I Wish That Happiness Shall Come

To Other People, Like Eddie Conte.

I Know That Happiness Can Come to Eddie if He Could

Try A Little Harder in School

By now the other classes were parading past our room into the auditorium for the program.

"I'm not going," Eddie whined. "I'm not leaving this room." His tone was pathetic, as if he were afraid.

"I'll walk with you, Eddie. You and I will be partners."

He became frantic, and he kicked over the easel.

"I see how much it means to you, Eddie. If you calm down you may stay in the room. Sit here. I'll take the class to the program and be right back." He sat.

In the auditorium, I asked another teacher to watch my kids for a few minutes. When I got back to our room, I found Eddie had taken the clown punching bag from the closet. He was pounding it with his fists.

"Something happened, Eddie?"

"*He* came home last night. He just came to look for money. He put my mother in the closet and tried to find her money, but she got out. She threw the radio at him. When he left, his head was all bloody. If he ever comes again, I'll put all my strength against the door. I'll tell him, Get outta here! Don't ever come back!" Now he karate-chopped the plastic clown. "If you do I'll chop you with a knife. I'll never call you my father again." Sobbing, he draped himself across the inflated punching bag.

"Oh, Eddie, I'm sorry. It must be very hard for you."

"Shut up! Shut up! I don't wanna talk about it!"

"Okay, no talk. I'll just sit here with you."

Within five minutes he seemed calm. "Eddie," I said softly, "may I leave you for a minute? I'll be right back."

He nodded his head slightly. I hurried across the hall to my class in the auditorium. I wanted to make sure someone would see them back to the room. There was a sudden commotion, and I heard someone say, "It's one of those nuts."

Eddie had come to the auditorium door and exposed himself. When Miss Silverstein tried to remove him, he kicked her. A male teacher grabbed him, pinned his arms behind his back, and took him to the principal's office. He was still holding him when I reached the office. Eddie looked pale. His body shook.

"I'm excluding him for two days, mostly to let him know he can't kick me," Miss Silverstein said. "We'll have to talk to Ceil Black about the other problem."

"Right. But I wish we didn't have to send him home. Apparently there's been a big upset there."

Miss Silverstein was firm. "Your mother's going to come for you, Eddie."

"No, no! Don't send me home!" he cried.

"We'll talk about it. Come with me."

I walked out of the office, full of guilt for having left Eddie alone in our room. A little progress, then a big setback. Would it always be this way?

Someone jumped when I entered the room. It was Julie. "You're supposed to be at the play," I said. For a moment it didn't register that my opened pocketbook was in her hand. She dropped it.

"Julie, what are you doing? What's going on?"

She darted into the closet. I picked up the purse, shoved it into the desk drawer, and sat down, too stunned and depressed to respond to her muffled sobs. Minutes passed before she spoke. "It's because you . . . you," she cried, "you have everything!" She ran out and threw her arms around me, pressing her wet face to mine. "I'm sorry, I'm sorry, Mrs. Craig!"

"Oh, Julie, Julie. What do I have that you could want?" I stroked her hair.

"I—" She wept. "I don't have anything!"

"But you do! You're a lovely girl."

"No, no! Nobody likes me. Kevin hates me. I don't have any friends."

After a few minutes, "Come on, Julie. Let's wash our faces. We look like those Weeping Wanda dolls." She clutched my hand.

After school I began recording the day's events for Ceil. But each thought was more disheartening than the last: Jonathan's dangerous rays, the bloody head of Eddie's father. Finally, thinking of the terror in Eddie's eyes when he realized his mother was coming for him, I started to cry. Why should these kids suffer so terribly? Nothing I could ever do for Eddie, no warmth or kindness I could ever show him, would nullify his mother's cruelty.

I was still crying when I left the building. I drove home slowly, not ready to resume my responsibilities there. When I pulled into the driveway, I sat watching the falling snow gleam in the headlights. I was purged of tears, but exhausted and discouraged.

CHAPTER SEVEN

EDDIE came back three days later, ugly bruises on his arms and back. "My bottom's all purple. She hit me with her belt. Here, keep these." He handed me a paper bag full of his mother's belts.

He ran in circles around the furniture. "I've been locked in my room since Tuesday. Didn't even get any supper. Oh . . . oh . . . I hate being locked up! I hate her whipping me! I wanna knock the whole damn house down. I wanna get matches and burn it!" He was still running.

"No wonder you can't sit, Eddie. Run around three more times. Then we'll tell you the party plans."

He had circled twice when Julie asked solicitously, "Do you still have your gloves?"

"Oops, I forgot to leave them!" He headed for the office.

In his absence Douglas said, "I'll put my coat on his chair so he can sit better."

"That's kind of you, Doug."

"Duty before pleasure."

Eddie trotted in and thanked Douglas for cushioning his chair.

"Does Eddie know about next week?" Julie asked.

"Tell him."

"Next Tuesday we're having a class party. Everybody's supposed to bring a present. Wednesday we're having a party with mothers. We practiced songs to sing and—"

"Oh no! You're not inviting my mother! I'm not getting whipped in school too!"

"And my mother's not coming either," Kevin added.

"Maybe things will be different next week. Let's rehearse the songs again."

But the rest of the day went badly for Eddie. He cried that his bruises hurt, ran around wildly, and frequently provoked Douglas into punching him. "Here, boog." He flung Douglas' jacket at him. "I'm not sitting on your bugs."

As soon as he left I called Ceil. "We've got to do something quickly. Eddie's mother is working at cross purposes—locking him up, beating him, making him desperate to hurt someone else. Now he encourages attacks on himself, as if he wants pain."

"I agree with you. Would you call her and set up an appointment for all three of us to meet?"

But when I asked Eddie's mother to come in, she replied, "Well, my son has a pattern to his life. A rhythm. I do too. It takes us a long . . ." Her voice trailed off as if she were floating away.

"Mrs. Conte, when could Mrs. Black and I see you?"

"I don't know why everyone tells me to lock him in his room. . . . And when they tell me to whip him, they're making me treat him like an animal."

"Mrs. Conte." I felt desperate. "Listen, please. We want to help you find other ways to handle Eddie. What day could you come?"

"He has all this in him," she continued. "He has to find himself. I know how hard it is because I was lost for years. I want to say"—a long pause—"thanks for calling." *Click.*

THE following Tuesday our class party began at noon, with everyone eating lunch together at the reading table.

The boys wore everyday school clothes, but Julie dressed for the occasion in pink organdy with lace-trimmed sleeves.

Eddie noticed. "You look pretty, Julie."

"Your dress is lovely, Julie," I said. "Why don't you be first at the grab bag?"

The gift Kevin had surreptitiously deposited under the tree was the only one with a name tag. The label read G R I L.

Julie picked it. "This one must be for me. I'm the only girl." She tore through layers of green tissue until a tinny ring with a green stone, genus gum machine, lay exposed. No one connected Kevin with the gift.

Eddie got a squirt gun in the grab bag, Jonathan crayons, and Douglas play dough. Kevin refused to take his gift. Eddie opened it for him. "Here, Kevin, you get a comic. It's the *Fantastic Four.*"

"Uh-uh. It's not for me. Douglas can have it."

"Hey, thanks, pal." Douglas took the magazine.

The PTA contributed ice-cream cups and fancy cookies. Everyone ate eagerly except Kevin, who rejected his ice cream by shoving it in front of Douglas.

Douglas finished his own dessert and immediately started on Kevin's. "You should be glad I'm here today," he said. "I coulda been locked up in jail."

Wooden ice-cream spoons halted in midair. Julie gasped and he warmed to his audience. "Me and another kid got caught in Woolworth's yesterday. We was trying to look like salesmen so we could sneak out with this Jaguar model. It was gutsy, man, only it was too big to hide." He shot me a penetrating you-made-me-do-it look, then continued. "So the manager took us to his office, and a cop came to talk to us."

"Piggy cop," Eddie sneered.

"Piggy cop nothin', man. We coulda gone to the station."

"Hey, where's my ice cream?" Kevin suddenly demanded.

"You pushed it over for Douglas, remember?" I replied.

"I didn't mean to give it to him. I take it back."

Douglas was lapping the last sip of melted vanilla from the container.

"Too late, I'm afraid. Douglas finished it."

"Don't think you're ever coming over, Doug," Kevin said. "I've got two places to go. Saturday and Sunday."

"I'm going someplace too." Everyone stared at Jonathan, so unexpected was his participation in any conversation.

"I've got a new kind of doctor I'm going to. A kiatrist. Dr. Russell wears x-ray glasses. He can see right through me."

"He's a good doctor." I made a mental note to ask Dr. Russell if Jonathan might examine those glasses.

"Kevin shouldn't get mad, should he, Mrs. Craig? How could Douglas know it was his ice cream?" Logic from Julie, the least acceptable source, was enough to drive Kevin right into the closet. He pulled the door shut.

"Kevin is just like me," Julie said. "We both like to get ourselves in trouble."

"You like to get in trouble?" I repeated.

"That's because I don't like myself. Sometimes I try to hurt myself. I could even kill myself!"

Douglas reached for another cookie. "Julie is her own persecutor. Kevin too. Not me, man! Other people persecute me, but I'd never do it to myself."

"Well, you like yourself," Julie said. "That's different."

"Ya, well, my grandmother likes me too," said Douglas. "She likes me more than my brother. Anyway, my brother fell on a rock and died, so he won't be here tomorrow."

Eddie hopped up. "Don't worry about my mother. She has to stay home all the time now and guard the house so my father won't sneak in." He clutched his pants. "I have to go to the bathroom. Be right back."

"My brother's not really dead. Just his brain is dead." Douglas seemed to be speaking to himself.

"It's hard to have a retarded brother," I said.

Eddie returned quickly with a question for Doug. "Is it okay if I called the kid in the bathroom a nigger?"

Douglas' response was barely audible. "Don't pick on any black kid, Ed. They've had enough pickin' on already."

On Wednesday morning I went in early to fix up the classroom for the parents' party, then realized that the cans of punch still sat on our porch at home. Before I could decide what to do, Julie and Eddie burst in, breathless. "Douglas says he's not coming in!" But shortly after Kevin and Jonathan arrived Douglas straggled in, holding aloft a startled tiger cat. "Look what I found! She must be lost. Isn't she fat?"

Eddie lifted the animal's front paws and examined her stomach. "She's having babies, dummy."

"Oh, and she's lost! Can we keep her, Mrs. Craig? Please? Please?" At last, a unanimous request.

"She looks too well cared for to be lost. She probably lives near the school. Our guests will be here at eleven, so perhaps we could keep her in the room until ten thirty. If she's still around after school, we'll decide what to do with her."

"Can we make her a bed?" Doug begged. A storage carton was quickly emptied, and each child contributed his coat as part of the mattress. The cat was placed inside, and a fight began as each pulled at the box to keep it near his desk.

"She'll want to leave if you don't stop! We'll decide on turns by drawing anagrams, as we've done before."

Douglas drew C and was first. Eddie, with M, had to wait until ten fifteen. At about ten twenty, Julie and I were arranging cookies when Douglas remarked, "Will wonders never cease, the way Eddie is acting."

Eddie was holding the cat above his head, lapping her underside with his tongue. "I wanna suck your milk! Let me! Let me!"

I returned the cat to the box. "That's upsetting her, Eddie."

He looked very agitated. Suddenly he yelled, "Who's that giant at the door?"

There stood Bill with the cans of punch I had forgotten. "Oh, thank you so much! Meet Douglas, Jonathan, Eddie, Julie, and Kevin. This is Mr. Craig."

Douglas waved a casual greeting. Jonathan belched five times. Kevin lowered his head. Julie leaped up and hugged Bill around the waist. Eddie was coolest. "Mr. Craig, come see our cat." Bill walked to his desk. "Bend down, Mr. Craig. Take a good look."

Something in his tone warned me. "Bill, don't!" I was too slow. Eddie wound up and socked him on the nose.

Bill was stunned. I could see his fists clench as he fought the impulse to deal with Eddie directly. But he regained his composure and put his arm around the boy's shoulder. "Hey, you know that wasn't fair. I thought you really wanted me to see the cat."

"Listen!" Eddie was upset. "Don't you understand I can't control myself?" he screamed.

"That sounds like a cop-out, pal," Bill said. "Who's supposed to control you if not yourself? You're not hitting anybody right now, are you? You're proving you can control yourself."

Bill agreed to take the cat out with him. Julie insisted on kissing him good-by. He spoke briefly to each boy and privately to me at the door. "Interesting group you've got here."

A few minutes later Mrs. Bergman, Jonathan's mother, stood hesitantly at the door. Douglas had appointed himself official greeter and led her to chairs he had arranged earlier. The unhappy-looking woman offered a strained smile as she passed Jonathan. "Hello, son."

He jumped up yelling, "Oh! Ow! A tack in my butt! Burp-urp. Calling A-O-Five. Someone broke the radar barrier!" His mother's eyes filled with tears.

Mrs. Conte came next, with Eddie's five-year-old sister clutching a leg of her mother's pantsuit. Julie's and Kevin's mothers arrived together, chatting amiably. At exactly eleven, Douglas' grandmother and his brother, Luke, stood at the door. I caught Douglas' stricken look and went to them. Nothing had prepared me for Luke's sad condition. His mouth hung open and his tongue protruded, but his eyes shone when he saw Douglas.

I introduced the women, who exchanged self-conscious greetings. Frequently and with great confidence, Eddie had practiced standing in front of the room to announce the songs. Now, head bowed, frozen in his chair, he muttered, " 'Dreidel, Dreidel.' "

The children rose reluctantly and stood behind Julie, who spun the dreidel, a toy used in a traditional Hanukkah game, with trembling hand. Eddie and Douglas, eyes fixed on me, were the only ones whose voices were audible. Jonathan rolled his eyes and deliberately struck his hand against the blackboard behind him. Jumping on one foot, he wrung his hand in mock agony.

When the song was done, Jonathan fled to his seat and, holding invisible instruments, began surgery on an imaginary wound. His mother, chin quivering, focused her eyes straight ahead.

Douglas, as planned, picked up the drum and began tapping an introduction to "The Little Drummer Boy." At first the singers were too timid to be effective, but as their confidence increased so did the volume. Their voices were pure and lilting as they sang, "*I am a poor boy, too . . .*" to Douglas' drum.

Ceil tiptoed in and stood at the back of the room. We exchanged glances, and she put her hand to her throat as if having difficulty swallowing. I knew she felt moved, as I did.

There was a brief silence followed by applause. Douglas made a spontaneous speech: "Me and the kids and Mrs. Craig are glad you came. If you liked our songs, there's some food back there."

The party lasted forty-five minutes. Douglas remained with his grandmother and brother. Luke's hand shook as he tried to raise the cup to his mouth. As though he had done it a thousand times, Douglas took the cup and held it for him.

Jonathan's mother was the first to leave. She looked shaken as she wished Ceil and me happy holidays.

Saying good-by to Eddie's mother afforded an opportunity to ask again for a conference. Hand on her hip, she said, "Well, I'll letcha know if I can come."

Ceil moved in. "We have to be more definite, Mrs. Conte. We could meet the Friday after vacation, the eighth of January." Mrs. Conte glared, snapped her chewing gum, and sauntered out.

Douglas' grandmother was wiping Luke's hands and face with a paper napkin. "Douglas, you take him outside now. I want to thank you," she then said to me, "for puttin' my boys' names on that list for presents."

"It should be a happy Christmas," I said.

CHAPTER EIGHT

By NINE forty-five on the Friday after vacation no children had arrived. I went out to look for the bus. Suddenly, tires screeching, it careened into the parking lot. But no children were on it.

Mr. Dixon raged at me. "I warned 'em! I don't have to drive them bastards. They're gonna cause an accident! They kept fighting, so I threw 'em off." He gunned the motor and whipped the bus around in a tight circle.

"Wait!" I jogged along, calling up to him. "Where did you leave them?"

"By Francis Street! Down about a mile!" I began to run in that direction, then realized the futility of it. If indeed the kids would head for school, there were several possible routes from Francis Street.

Miss Silverstein should be told what happened, and possibly the police as well. By the time I located her on the second floor, I was so out of breath I could barely speak. After my brief tale we rushed to her office.

"Both the police and the bus company must be alerted," she said. "I wonder if that driver realizes he's responsible for whatever happens."

Miss Silverstein had begun dialing when I heard stamping, followed by Douglas' wail, "Mrs. Cra-a-a-a-aig!" I went into the hall, and he spotted me and collapsed like the movie version of a victim of the desert. "The others," he moaned feebly, "are coming."

The words were barely spoken when Eddie appeared. "Mr. Dixon kicked us off the bus. I hate him!"

"And the others?" I asked.

"Kevin is comin'. Jonathan and Julie are way back."

Eddie dropped next to Douglas. They lay panting in the middle of the hall. Miss Silverstein arrived on the scene while I was urging the boys to move. "You could get stepped on here."

In came Kevin, every freckle intensified by his deathly pallor and starched white shirt. "Jonathan—fell—down. Cut—his—knee. Julie's with him."

"I'll go after them," Miss Silverstein said.

Kevin and I led the procession to our room. Douglas and Eddie followed, on hands and knees all the way.

"Put your heads down and rest awhile," I said.

After a few peaceful moments Eddie looked up. "Are you gonna fire the bus driver?"

"I can't promise till I know exactly what happened," I said.

Each, suddenly revitalized, launched into his version of the morning's ride. In the midst of the babble, Miss Silverstein, with Julie, stood at the door. "Jonathan's in the nurse's office getting a Band-Aid on his knee. Julie"—she hugged the girl—"was like a nurse herself. She was taking such good care of Jonathan when I found them." The principal left.

"Thank you, Julie," I said.

Douglas stood and faced his classmates. Raising his hands above his head, he commanded silence. "Listen, I'm the oldest! I say Mrs. Craig tells the superintendent of schools we're *never* ridin' Bus Ten again."

"Just a minute," I said. "I'll need something in writing if you expect me to submit a protest."

With a frown of concern, Douglas dispensed both paper and advice. "Be gutsy. We've gotta convince him."

They were writing when the nurse brought Jonathan in. His face was tear-stained, but my sympathy was tempered by the thought that Julie's attention had been good for him.

"You've had a hard morning," I said. "How's your leg?"

He began crying again. "More trouble. Prehistoric monsters living in our drain! There since the Mesozoic age."

"Now, Jonathan, that's impossible. Your drain isn't that old. Will you ask your dad to check it?"

"I told him, but he doesn't believe me!"

I was still comforting Jonathan when the first anti-bus-driver deposition was completed and handed to me.

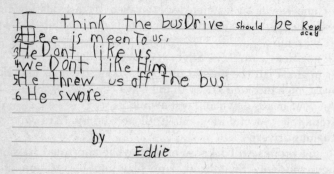

```
1 I think the busDrive should be Repl
2 Hee is meen To us,         aced
3 He Dont like us
4 we Dont like Him
5 He threw us off the bus
6 He swore.


                by
                    Eddie
```

After lunch, Julie expressed the apprehension they all felt. "How will we get home? Mr. Dixon might kick us out again."

"Let me speak to Miss Silverstein, and then I'll answer." I picked up the intercom, planning to ask permission to drive the children home. The principal had other news.

"The bus company called. Mr. Dixon walked in a while ago

and threw his keys on the boss's desk. The manager says he'll drive till there's a replacement."

The children were visibly relieved when I told them. "We knew you wouldn't make us ride with that bum," said Douglas.

I was pleased with this expression of confidence and even more with the realization that, given a choice, they all had headed directly for school!

For the rest of the month and well into February, each child's condition worsened.

Jonathan constantly talked to his pencils or scolded crayons for jumping around in his desk. In one week he was sent home twice for soiling.

Julie ran the gamut of her psychosomatic complaints. "Does my neck look swollen?" or "I think I'm getting a rash." She bit herself until her arms were covered with bruises.

As for Douglas, his tantrums in January were nearly as terrible as the outburst to which he had first subjected Kevin and me. Without warning, he would rip and shred the wall charts and room decorations. He wrote an obscenity on the blackboard in enormous letters every time he got near it.

Yet I knew that Douglas, who seemed so much more difficult on the surface, was better off than Kevin. Douglas had outlets for his anger. But Kevin harbored as much if not more hostility. Not daring to be aggressive, he was far less ready for reading and arithmetic.

Of all the children, I was most concerned about Eddie. He had begun having what I could only describe as seizures. He would suddenly slump to the floor and turn face down, his eyes closed. I tried speaking to him, both comfortingly and later imperatively. His only response was to blink rapidly. At first these attacks lasted a minute or two, but soon they increased to twenty minutes and occurred several times a day. After each episode he acted dazed and apparently had no memory of what had happened. Ceil was alarmed. "We're due for a conference with Dr. Bialek soon. Let me try to set it up immediately."

We met the following Wednesday at the local Child Guidance Center, of which Dr. Norman Bialek was director. We told him about Eddie and arranged for him to visit my class.

On the morning Dr. Bialek was to come, I put Eddie's folder on his desk and he tossed it back. "It's your work! You do it!"

"It's not my work, Ed."

"Well, you're the marker. Give me any mark you want."

"I don't get this junk!" Kevin said. His feet were tapping in a heel-toe protest.

"You little punk!" Eddie sprang at Kevin. "I can't think when your feet are yelling." His hands were around Kevin's neck.

"We do not hurt people!" I pulled Eddie away.

"Oh yeah?" Eddie spun to face me. "Nobody—nobody—can stop me from losing my temper."

"Nobody but you, Eddie."

Dr. Bialek entered and had only a brief wait to observe Eddie's bizarre behavior. I was holding Eddie's wrist to prevent him from punching Kevin when he slumped to the floor and lay there writhing. His tongue was protruding and he made guttural sounds.

Dr. Bialek came closer for a better view of the boy. Suddenly the convulsive motions stopped. His head flopped from side to side. His eyes rolled back so only the whites showed. Then he was frighteningly still. I motioned to Dr. Bialek that I would pick him up, and he nodded.

Eddie was a deadweight. I eased him into a chair and, as though spineless, he slithered onto the floor. He rolled face down, his eyes blinking rapidly. I tried all the techniques I had used before, so the psychiatrist could realize how futile they were.

While Eddie was still prone, Douglas demanded attention. "Hey! Is this paper right?"

"It's fine, Doug." I looked over his shoulder. "Except that our is o-u-r, not a-r."

"Why don't you go to hell?" he said.

"Just change that word. You'll be proud to have a perfect paper."

Julie tugged at my sweater. "Is this a nine or a six?"

Douglas spoke, hand cupped over his mouth. "Hey, Kevin, did she say sex? Don't tell anyone, but did she?"

I had to smile. "Julie asked about the number six."

It spoiled his fun. "Don't be a square, Mrs. Craig. I'm not fixin' my paper either." He tore it up.

"Would you hand me the scraps, please?" I said. "Today's papers go on the bulletin board."

Fuming, he kicked his desk away. "You make me so mad!" Then he stalked to the front of the room, snatched a fresh paper, and rewrote the work faultlessly.

Dr. Bialek coughed. I had forgotten all about him. We spoke quietly near the door. "I'm convinced this is not a physical problem. I'm going to prescribe medication that should help calm him down. Something emotional, some internal stimulus, is triggering this behavior. Let me know if the medication makes him drowsy. Call the clinic for an appointment in about three weeks."

Eddie recovered shortly after Dr. Bialek left and soon challenged Douglas to see who would finish his assignments first. They were both done by eleven thirty and played a quiet, thoroughly rigged game of Candy Land, Douglas blatantly stacking the cards to his advantage.

For the first few days after starting medication Eddie was sluggish and listless, but by the second week his behavior was as erratic as before. He was far from drowsy on the day of my conference with Dr. Bialek.

When he entered the room I was amazed at the change in his appearance. His clothes looked slept in. His face and hands were filthy, his hair unkempt.

He pulled back his chair as if to sit down, but knocked it over. "You know I don't like anyone touchin' my things! Who did this? That damn janitor?" He jumped up and down in the same spot, wailing. "I left my desk right against yours—now it's not even touching! Oh! Oh! I'm going down to see Mrs. Black."

"It's not her day," I said. "She'll be here on Friday."

"Dammit!" He pounded both fists on the desk. "When I see her on Friday I'm going to kill her with a knife for not being here."

The children continued their routine of hanging up coats, putting away boots and lunch boxes. Only Julie turned in Eddie's direction. She watched without expression.

"You're laughing at me! I see you. You're laughing at me!" He grabbed a ruler and fanned it in her face.

I appropriated the ruler. "You're upset this morning. What's wrong?"

"Oh, no! I'll never tell. I'm not supposed to tell, and you can't make me." He snatched a yardstick and in a leap was on top of his desk, brandishing the ruler.

"It looks as though you're not ready to be with us today." I approached him slowly.

"Oh no, no, Mrs. Craig!" He jumped down before I reached him. "Please don't send me home. I *can't* go home!"

"Then into the office till you show me you're calm enough to join the class."

Relieved, he took his work folder and pencils with him. The "office" no longer meant Miss Silverstein's. By rearranging furniture, I had isolated a desk between two bookcases. It faced a blank wall and was an effective cooling-off place.

Eddie was barely settled when Kevin began the next disruption. His hands cradled a paper bag.

"Kevin brought a show-and-tell," Julie said.

All eyes were on Kevin as he opened the bag and pulled out a round plastic paperweight filled with imitation snow which drifted onto a miniature village.

Eddie, still in the isolation office, tilted his chair back to see. "Gosh," he said, "that's beautiful!"

Julie reached toward Kevin. "Can I try it, please?"

"Me first, ole buddy," said Douglas.

A smile played on Kevin's lips. "Not Julie or Eddie or Jonathan. Just Douglas."

Eddie kicked the wall. "Goddammit! I want a turn!"

Douglas grabbed the paperweight, created several snowstorms, and respectfully returned the treasure to Kevin.

Julie fled to the closet. "He hates me!" she sobbed.

Kevin smiled. Eddie yelled, "He's makin' me so mad I could kill him!"

"But you're staying in the office," I pointed out. "Good for you! You won't let Kevin tease you into fighting."

Eddie considered this, and turned back to his folder.

I then sat with Jonathan as he drew his ghosts. "You have a new lunch box, don't you? I see all the boys like spacemen lunch boxes," I said.

"There's no sense telling me that. I'm not a boy, I'm a ghost."

"But look, everyone can see you talking and doing fine work. People know that only an intelligent boy can do what you do."

"You think that's what the world is all about?"

"What do you mean, Jonathan?"

"People with other people?"

"Yes, I think that's what it's all about."

Eddie worked in isolation until reading time, often the opportunity for confidences. "I'm not supposed to tell you," he began hesitantly. "I was out all night. I stayed under the porch. My mother didn't know I was there."

"She must have worried about you."

"Ha! She didn't even care! One of her boy friends came over. My sister's so dumb she calls him Uncle."

"You don't like him to visit your mother?"

"They were probably in there kissing." He covered his face with both hands as if to protect himself from the image. "I hate him. Before I left I wrote him a note and put it under my mother's door. I said, 'I hope you die tonight.'"

CHAPTER NINE

IN MARCH the school's boiler broke down. Outside it was twenty degrees above zero, and the temperature inside was rapidly dropping. The children and I, teeth chattering, bundled in scarves and coats while the custodian determined the extent of the problem.

We played strenuous games to keep warm, until finally the pipes in the old building began clanging as the steam forced its way through. Our room alone remained cold.

I sent for Mr. Jakowsky, who came in with an assortment of tools projecting from his overalls. He stretched out on his back under the recalcitrant radiator and began tapping gently on the pipes. The children, unaffected by his presence, continued their game of Simon Says until, without warning, the room erupted. Kevin had called Eddie "out."

"Liar! Liar!" Eddie was enraged. "Everyone here hates me!"

"Right!" said Douglas.

Eddie socked Kevin in the stomach. Kevin collapsed. Douglas ran after Eddie.

Suddenly a voice boomed from under the radiator. Startled, Eddie and Douglas halted in midchase as if frozen in motion.

"You kids, you!" Mr. Jakowsky pulled his head out from beneath the pipes. He sat up. "Look at me!" His face was scarlet. "I never had no nice teacher to help me. You wanna be like me? You wanna fix pipes when you grow up?"

The class was hushed. Mr. Jakowsky shook his wrench at them. "You wanna mop floors all your lives? Clean other people's messes? You better sit down and listen to your teacher."

They tiptoed to their desks. Mr. Jakowsky returned to his work. Minutes passed before Eddie, in a choked voice, broke the silence. "Don't blame me. I'm sick, ya know. And I didn't get my pill today, so I'm nervous."

"Eddie," I knelt to tell him privately, "you can control yourself without a pill."

The radiator began to hiss. The custodian pocketed his tools and left.

ON A chilly afternoon Ceil and I drove to the Child Guidance Center together. On the way I confessed to being nervous about hearing Dr. Bialek's impression of the class and of my teaching. But to my relief he was enthusiastic about what he had observed, commenting on the individualization of instruction and the built-in rewards and consequences. Then he asked if I thought Eddie's mother was reliable about medicating him.

The only pattern I could report with any certainty was a diminishing of the "seizures."

"Have you been in touch with Mrs. Conte?" the doctor asked Ceil.

"Yes, she came to the mothers' group I started last Friday. She never mentioned Eddie, but she told about the modeling course she takes three days a week."

"Well, at least she came." Dr. Bialek shrugged. "Would you impress on her that I must have periodic checks on the boy?" He swiveled his chair in my direction. "It was interesting for me to see the Bergman boy in your group. A very disturbed child, and frankly I'm pleased he's been able to remain in school. There's one encouraging note. Mr. and Mrs. Bergman have joined a parents' group here. I originally thought Jonathan might not be able to remain at home, but after seeing him in school, and now that the parents are cooperating, I feel more optimistic."

Ceil and I grinned simultaneously, then Ceil looked at her notes. "I'd like to discuss Julie. Last Friday her mother began talking again about wanting to send her away 'to a school where they keep problem children.' Yet we feel the girl is progressing."

"She still has a reading problem," I said, "but her difficulties in relating seem more social and much less severe than the other children's."

The doctor glanced at Julie's chart. "Let's see, we put her on Tofranil in December. Did the bed-wetting stop?"

Ceil nodded. "Apparently what's upsetting Mrs. Neumayer now is that Julie constantly challenges her about being adopted. She often says, 'I hate you. My real mother would be nice to me. She wouldn't be mean like you.'"

"I think it's interesting that we see ten times as many adopted children in clinics as their proportional number in the population. The adopted child's ability to learn may be hampered by the great amount of energy he invests in the longing for, the hopeless unfulfilled search for, his natural parents.

"I have approached adoption agencies about better ways for the situation to be handled, but until changes are effected, it's our job to help parents understand that some complications are not abnormal for the adopted child."

"What does he mean, better ways to handle adoption?" I asked Ceil as we drove back to school.

"I've heard him on the subject before," she said. "He feels the current practice of repeating to the young child over and over the story of his adoption undermines his establishing his identity as a person. It's better, he thinks, to have the child grow up without this burden. Because the information won't have affected his early development, he'll be better able to cope with it later."

"Isn't the big concern that a child might find out accidentally?"

"Yes, but he believes it's worth that risk, because the older the child, the better. It would be traumatic, of course, but a single trauma. Less damaging than the day-by-day effect on the younger child who fantasizes for years about missing parents, and resists those he lives with."

The morning after our conference with Dr. Bialek, Eddie came in, sat on the floor, pulled off his boots, and hurled them into the closet. I started to reprimand him for this when he suddenly clutched his hand to his throat. Then he turned and lay on his stomach, his arms and legs flailing.

"Eddie!" I had to shout above his noise. "That doesn't mean anything! If something's wrong, you have to say it!"

With a thud his head struck the floor. His eyes were closed, arms and body motionless.

"What's a matter, punk, lose your key?" Douglas taunted.

Eddie sprang up and pounced on him. "You took it! You took it! That's how you know. Where'd you put it?" Eddie seized the front of Douglas' shirt. A button popped into the air.

"That does it," Douglas growled. "I'll never tell ya."

"I knew it!" Eddie hopped around, pointing his arm at Douglas. "I knew that black boog took it!"

Douglas, incredibly cool, turned away and strolled to his seat. "You're not getting me in trouble, punk."

I planted both hands firmly on Eddie's bony shoulders and with little resistance directed him to his chair.

"When you're ready and through with name calling, we'll talk about your key," I said.

"I'm ready! I'm ready!" His voice was shrill, his face tense. "My mother's at her beauty school. I'm supposed to let myself in. I put the key on a string around my neck. Somebody musta untied it on the bus. Now I'm locked out! She won't be home till seven thirty!"

"Doug." I stood in front of him. He was nearly as tall as I. "You had wonderful control, not losing your temper when he tried so hard to make you. Do you know anything about Eddie's key?"

He shrugged innocently.

"You admitted it!" Eddie yelled. "You said you'd never tell."

"Because you made me mad." Douglas' nostrils were flaring, his temper rising.

"Did you see it, Doug?"

I had gone too far. "Oh, don't believe me, huh? Okay, lieutenant, search." He pulled off his sneakers and socks and faced the wall, holding his hands above his head.

"I don't want to—"

"Think I have it, ha?" He started to undo his pants. "C'mon, lieutenant, aren't ya gonna frisk me?"

Eddie leaped from his chair and pummeled Douglas on the back. "I can't stand people who do things to me! I'll get you for this!"

Douglas wheeled and punched him in the stomach. I got between them, but Douglas got his arm around the smaller boy's waist and flipped him. They tumbled across the room, punching as they rolled.

I reached the intercom. "Doris? Eleanor. I need help, quick!"

"You boog!" Eddie screamed. "I'm gonna kill you." He writhed away from Douglas and grabbed a chair.

I knew the chair could fracture Doug's skull. I dug my hands under his arms and dragged him out of range just as Eddie released the chair. It dropped a foot short of its mark, and two legs caved in.

When Miss Silverstein and the nurse, Mrs. Rogers, rushed in, they quickly sized things up and backed Eddie into a corner. Both women held his arms, but with enormous strength the small

boy twisted free. "Keep your dirty hands off me! I hate your guts!" Douglas and Eddie quickly locked in another struggle.

Arms around each other, they landed together on the floor. I grabbed the back of Doug's pants just as he fell off Eddie and collapsed with an agonized moan. Blood was seeping through the shoulder of his shirt.

Eddie, terrified at the sight, crawled under my desk and sat huddled. "I'm sorry, I'm sorry!" he cried.

Flushed but efficient, the nurse took off Doug's shirt. Blood gushed from at least ten separate punctures. Eddie's upper and lower teeth had penetrated deeply into Douglas' flesh.

"Help," Douglas said feebly.

"You'll be all right," she assured him. "Rest a minute. Then we'll go to my office and fix you."

"Help." His voice was stronger now. "I've got that little punk's germs in me."

"Come on now." The nurse supported the heavy boy. "Let's get antiseptic on them."

He shut his eyes and extended his hands as if groping blindly. Slowly she led him out. I stooped beside my desk. Eddie was shivering. "Let me help you. I know you're upset."

He shifted in the cramped area, turning his back to me. Miss Silverstein spoke gently. "Come and have a talk, Eddie."

Anything would have triggered him. "Gimme one good reason why I should!" He leaped up. "I hate principals like you. I hate this whole stinkin' place!"

He wrapped his hand around the heavy stapler on my blotter and hurled it at the principal, barely missing her head. Then a barrage of books, pencils, and rulers flew through the air. A book struck my hip as I approached him. Julie began to cry.

With his ammunition gone, Eddie gripped the back of my chair and propelled it first against Kevin's desk, then Jonathan's.

Miss Silverstein and I caught him on the rebound. Purple-faced, he screamed profanities and tried to bite our hands. He got away and charged at Julie. "I hate crybabies!"

This time we locked Eddie's hands behind him, lifted him by the elbows, and rushed down the hall. His feet didn't hit the floor till we reached the main office.

"Would you give us a hand?" Miss Silverstein directed her gaping secretary. "Mrs. Craig has to get back."

Mrs. Rogers met me in the classroom. "Douglas may need tetanus. I'll drive him home and ask the grandmother the date of his last shot. Let me have his things. He won't be back today."

At noon Doris came in. "Eddie's mother is in the office. Miss Silverstein wants you to talk to her. I'm supposed to stay here."

"YA? WELL, WHAT'D THE OTHER KID do to him?" Mrs. Conte was pointing her cigarette at Miss Silverstein when I entered the office. "That's what I wanna know."

Eddie stood against the wall, fearfully watching his mother.

Miss Silverstein said, "Mrs. Craig will tell you what happened from the beginning."

While I described Eddie's morning, he kept his hands over his ears. "The key was part of his upset, Mrs. Conte. Would you know if something else might be bothering him too?"

"I'm upset too, getting called out of my classes. I paid for those classes. I'm supposed to be in makeup right now." Her eyes were beaded with mascara, her brows plucked thin.

"Some children are afraid of going home to an empty house. Could someone be with him after school?" I asked.

"Listen, I got my daughter over at my girl friend's, but she's not gonna take two of them." She jerked her thumb in Eddie's direction. "How long's he suspended for?"

"Two days. From now until Friday," Miss Silverstein said. "When he comes back, we hope he'll be ready to stay."

"He'll be ready all right. I'll beat him till he's ready." Eddie began to whimper.

"That won't help him learn to control himself." I couldn't conceal my anger.

"It better!" She got up. "I'm not missing more classes for him. My kids don't have a ball and chain on me."

As she dragged Eddie out, his whimpering developed into full-scale crying.

CHAPTER TEN

BEFORE school on Friday I saw Ceil. She said, "Yesterday Eddie's mother called.

"She'd locked him in his room for the day and gone to modeling school. A policeman was waiting when she got home. One of the neighbors had seen Eddie climb out his window onto the roof. Afraid he'd fall, she called the police. But he just stood there exposing himself. The officer threatened Mrs. Conte with child-abuse charges if she locked him up again. Can you believe, she doesn't see anything wrong with that? She's just furious at the boy for getting her in trouble."

"Oh, that's so discouraging, Ceil," I said.

"I thought about him for hours." Ceil picked up her briefcase. "As long as he's in that home, Eddie may never be better."

"They're here." I heard the bus turn into the driveway.

"Send him in at nine," Ceil said.

Seeing Eddie come down the hall, I knew his two-day absence had served no purpose. He was already provoking Douglas, criss-crossing in front of him, impeding his progress. "I'll bite you any-time I want! My teeth are good weapons. I bite my sister, too."

"Use them again and you'll be swallowing them." Douglas held up his lunch box menacingly.

"Good morning, Doug," I called. "Take a look at the new puzzle on your desk." Hand on his back, I guided him in. "And Eddie, I'm glad you're back." I directed him straight ahead with the other hand.

While Eddie was with Ceil the class did creative writing. More and more our mornings were passing peacefully and productively. Rewards and prizes were less urgently sought. The satisfaction when work was well done was becoming a goal in itself.

Lunchtime was peaceful. Eddie, in fact, tolerated a brief dis-cussion about why no one liked him.

"You start fights."

"You bit Douglas."

"And you always swear."

This was the only charge he answered. "My mother swears at me. Why can't I swear too?"

For afternoon play, Douglas chose the truck and Julie the loom. Jonathan painted at the easel.

Suddenly Julie jingled a shiny object. "Look what I found in the yarn box!" The lost key.

Eddie dropped the hammer he was using at the workbench. "That proves it! I knew someone stole it. Who did it?"

He twisted Julie's wrist. The key fell. "Oh! Don't. I just found it. Help! Let go!"

Douglas headed for Eddie. I stepped between them and ushered Eddie to the isolation office. "Then it was Douglas or Kevin," he yelled on the way.

"You're a harsh kid," said Douglas and shook his fist toward Eddie. "Watch who you're accusin'."

Kevin sat back, smiling smugly, his arms folded across his chest. Then, realizing I was watching him, he lowered his head. The foot tapping began.

"Shut up your feet!" Eddie blocked his ears.

"We're taking a few minutes right now," I said, "to discuss the key. Someone knows how it got in the box."

"Listen, judge. Everybody wanted to get that punk. We're all guilty, okay?" Douglas thrust out his chin pugnaciously.

"Do you all agree with that?" I turned to the others.

"He's asked for it," said Julie.

"Yeah," Kevin whispered.

"Asked for what?" I was angry. "When someone's got a problem, he needs your help. You've all been upset one time or another. Would you like being teased about something important to you? I agree, you're all guilty. It's not my idea of why we've come together."

There was a long silence. Julie hung her head. Kevin scuffed his shoes. Eddie sat rigidly facing the wall.

"Please, God"—Douglas folded his hands—"will she always be a softy?" But he picked up the key, shuffled over, and left it on Eddie's desk.

"Thanks, Doug."

"Can Eddie play now, Mrs. Craig?" Julie asked.

"Are you ready to play without fighting, Eddie? Has this helped you understand what you do to make people angry?"

The activities were resumed. I went back to the workbooks and didn't notice Kevin walk to the closet. Then Eddie yelled, "No ya don't!"

Kevin was holding Eddie's jacket out the window. When Eddie

approached, Kevin let go. It caught on a bush a few feet off the ground.

"My mother'll kill me!" Eddie ran to the outside exit.

Expressionless, Kevin leaned out to watch.

"Will wonders never cease," Douglas said. "Why don't you control it, Kevin? You're startin' to act bad like me, and I'm startin' to act good like you."

"Luckily the bus came while Eddie was getting his jacket," I told Ceil as we sat over coffee in the lounge. "I don't know what he'd have done to Kevin if there'd been time."

"You really had a day." But her smile vanished quickly. "Eddie's no better, El, and I'm not getting anywhere with him or his mother. He's in trouble in school, at home, and in the community.

"I heard from the police. The woman upstairs has been calling the station to say the kids are often alone all night. Wednesday evening she heard the little girl screaming and went to check. The sister told her that Eddie had been playing with matches and set a curtain on fire. He managed to pull it down and douse the flames. Eddie appeared at the door with a butcher knife and told the woman to mind her own business, not quite that politely."

She paused to sip the coffee. "It might be different if his mother would cooperate. She's stopped coming to the group. She won't see me or Dr. Bialek. I finally reached her by phone today. She was high on something, talking strangely and breathing heavily.

"The police won't institute legal action if we make some other recommendation. If it should go to court, the judge's only alternative might be to place him in a foster home. In his current state, he wouldn't last a month with foster parents."

Another long pause. "Ceil, what do you think?"

"He's crying for help. More help than we can give. We should consider residential treatment for Eddie."

I wasn't surprised, nor did I want to burden her with my feeling of failure. "Where?"

"Green Valley is nearest, but I'll have to check on their intake. Would you want to see a few possibilities with me?"

251

We agreed to visit wherever openings existed. Meanwhile, we would present Eddie's case to the Transitional Class committee for review.

WHEN the meeting of the committee was called to order, I summarized Eddie's behavior, and then Ceil described her private sessions with Eddie and her contacts with his mother.

Dr. Bialek reviewed psychiatric information. "If this mother had been more reliable," he added, "medication might have helped. When the boy annoyed her she gave him twice as much, other days nothing, so I stopped the prescription."

"Thank you, Doctor." Mr. Hanley then outlined possible plans for Eddie, including foster placement and residential treatment.

After an hour's discussion the committee unanimously recommended residential treatment for Eddie.

"Mrs. Black and Mrs. Craig will report again after they visit these places." Mr. Hanley rose. "Beyond that, we can't do anything till we get the mother's consent."

AT HOME we began Easter vacation with a ravioli dinner.

"You know I hate cheese-filled ravioli," Ann complained. "I only like the meat kind."

"Cheese is best," Richie declared with his mouth full.

"Who asked you? And stop eating till we've all been served!" Ann grabbed the fork from Richie's hand.

I dropped the ladle onto the platter, splattering Ellen and myself with tomato sauce. "Stop it! Stop it this minute!" I was usually able to ignore this kind of bickering, but tonight it was shattering. Bill and the kids stared at me while I wiped Ellen's face, then my own.

Stony silence prevailed while we ate. But as food so often lulled my class, it now worked magically on my family and me. Bill opened a bottle of wine and, urged by the boys, was soon regaling us with the story of his unsuccessful major-league tryout many years ago. "I'll tell you this, kids. There's nothing I wouldn't give to put on that Red Sox uniform just once."

I chuckled, then couldn't stop laughing.

"What's so funny, Mom?" Richie put his hand on my arm.

"She's cracking up," Ann said.

"No, no," I finally gasped, "I'm just admiring your blue eyes. All five sets."

CHAPTER ELEVEN

THERE were only two facilities in our state that might be available to Eddie. Thursday morning of vacation week I picked Ceil up at eight, and we set out to visit both schools.

The first was state-run Green Valley Center, about an hour's drive. It offered residence, treatment, and education to fifty boys from six to sixteen. The second was Kirby School, a private institution near the state capital. After our visits I felt as Ceil did, that Green Valley was the more appropriate. One young man we'd seen at Kirby had been there eighteen years. I didn't want that to happen to Eddie. Green Valley, although much more rigid than Kirby, was geared to returning children to the community, and so it seemed more hopeful.

When I returned to school on Monday, April 24, Julie greeted me with, "Eddie can't ride the bus no more!"

Following her down the corridor, Mr. Sargent, who had replaced our original driver, marched angrily toward me. He had Eddie tucked tightly under his arm like a slippery football.

"No job's worth puttin' up with this." He dumped the boy at my feet. "First he makes trouble and won't sit where I can watch him. Next he opens the door while I'm drivin'. Coulda lost a kid. Tell his mother," the driver called over his shoulder, en route to his bus, "I ain't pickin' him up."

"Okay, Eddie." I put my arm around him. "What happened?"

"That driver's a bum." He twisted away from me. "If you talk about it, I'll run up and down the hall and throw everything around. I'll pollute the whole damn school."

"I see you're pretty angry." I walked into the room, expecting him to follow. He remained in the hall. None of the other children

253

in the room looked refreshed by vacation. Mechanically, Julie, Kevin, Douglas, and Jonathan put away coats and lunches, then sat staring as if we were strangers.

"Good morning, Douglas." I patted his shoulder in passing.

"Shut up."

"Eddie's not the only unhappy one," I said. "Is it because of the bus ride?"

Silence.

"Maybe we should work awhile and talk later."

I had learned that work, far more than play, helped these children pull themselves together.

Eddie finally appeared but clung to the wall, his hands and cheek pressed against it. In this strange position he gradually moved around to the reading table, where I sat with Kevin.

I leaned back to prevent him from passing. "I'd like you to sit with us."

"Get outta my way, dummy!" He pushed against me.

"See?" Douglas suddenly exploded. "Other kids know that punk's in my class! They think I'm crazy too!"

"That's corny, Douglas." Julie faced him, hands on hips. "You're crazy or you're not. It doesn't depend on Eddie."

Douglas looked momentarily confused, then apparently accepted Julie's philosophy. His folder finished, he started on a crossword puzzle. Jonathan, also finished, began to cut and tape huge sheets of white construction paper into a mysterious form.

Eventually Eddie took his folder from my desk. "I'm not workin' near these nuts." He went into the isolation office and I went to sit beside him to help him start.

"I'll drive you home tonight, Eddie. Then we can talk about the transportation problem." He said nothing, but I was certain he'd listened.

Eleven o'clock. "Douglas' turn to read," I said. Douglas had become captivated by the controlled reader, which flashed words and phrases at set intervals. In two months his reading speed had doubled. When he reached to adjust the machine, I saw that his arms were covered with a rash.

"What's wrong?" I asked.

"Huh?" He pulled up his T-shirt to expose a spotted stomach.

"Has your brother had a rash, Doug?"

Douglas studied his body in alarm. "Luke's a mutation. They don't get rashes. What is it, anyhow?"

"Nothing serious, I'm sure. Mrs. Rogers will know."

The nurse came to get him, led him out, and returned in a few minutes for his belongings. "German measles. I'll take him home."

Jonathan had taped his paper sculpture to a chair beside his own. "Oooeee. Squish, squish. You can stay if you don't wet your pants." Thus began a steady dialogue with the unresponsive occupant of that chair, a life-size paper ghost.

Shortly before two, Eddie became edgy. When the bus came and the others started to leave, he was ready to cry.

"Time for us to go, too," I said.

He darted into the closet, crouched in a corner, and pulled his sweater over his head.

"You don't want me to drive you?"

He tumbled over, lying on his side, but this time he spoke. "Whew! I thought you were trickin' me to get me on the bus."

In the car, Eddie sat as far from me as possible.

"I'm hungry," I said. "Would you like a treat?"

"If you want to. Anyway, I just had a little lunch. My mother forgot to go to the store."

We had hamburgers and Cokes at a picnic table outside a drive-in restaurant. He ate, but was unresponsive to conversation. Back in the car I said, "For a while your mother will have to arrange to transport you, but maybe the bus driver will give you another chance. If he does, should I tell him you'll not make any more trouble?" He nodded.

"Here," he said in front of an old wooden three-family house with sagging porches on each level.

"Eddie," I said, "at least the bus problem gave us a chance for a treat."

"I know one thing." He was outside, speaking through the half-opened window. "I had a good time, Mom." He ran to the house.

Eddie's mother was furious when I phoned. "I pay my taxes. They can't kick him off the bus."

"They can if he endangers himself and the others," I said. "But we can hope for a short-term exclusion."

"I'm sick of everyone pickin' on my kid. He won't be there till this thing's settled." She hung up.

But Eddie did come the next day, breathless and twenty minutes early. "Am I late?" he panted. "Where are the kids? I ran all the way." He had come three miles rather than miss school. Yet all that day he railed against being there.

MONDAY morning, exactly a week after Douglas had been sent home with measles, a star-studded envelope was lying in my mailbox at school.

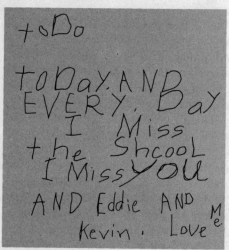

Douglas' absence occasioned a long recital of past illnesses and accidents involving his classmates.

"Once, slidin' down the hill on my sled, I crashed into a car," Julie said. "Got a percussion or something like that."

Kevin looked wistful. "When I was a baby I was always in the hospital. My mother tole me."

"Think any kids are in the hospital now?" Julie asked.

"Course, dummy. There always are," Eddie said.

That afternoon Julie said to me, "Since we sent stuff to Douglas, could we get some things for other kids who are sick? Kids in the hospital?"

"Why, that's a lovely idea! Let's talk about it tomorrow."

Julie's suggestion helped crystallize vague thoughts I'd had about the program. Total individualization had served its purpose. It was time now for group action, time for the children to become full-fledged members of the school and the community.

With Kevin carrying his books and Julie heralding his arrival, Douglas returned Tuesday morning. He delivered an enthusiastic speech on "keeping busy with a contagious disease." "And I learned to cook corn pones and grits. See, down South, my grandmother useta cook for fancy people and . . ."

When Julie got the opportunity, she repeated her idea of sending gifts to hospitalized children. Douglas appointed himself chairman of the project. "I was sick last, so I know how it feels. Not that I didn't like the puzzle you sent or nothin', but if we give money, kids can get stuff they want. Money's better."

But no one had money, so I proposed a bake sale.

"Cool. Me and my grandmother'll make raisin cookies."

From that day on, my wish for group activities was realized. Even Jonathan worked on the posters that were proudly distributed to every class. Excitement mounted. Central School had never had a bake sale. Debates were held on which class should come in first. Douglas, of course, opted for the oldest. Julie argued. "The little kids won't buy as much. Let them choose before everything's gone." Surprisingly, she won unanimously.

When the great day came, Julie dragged in a carton containing fifty cellophane bags of popcorn. Kevin's mother delivered a chocolate sheet cake cut into fifty servings. Eddie brought twenty double packages of cream-filled cupcakes, each of which he sliced in halves. Douglas ceremoniously removed the covers from the two shoe boxes he'd carried. Both were filled with plump golden raisin cookies.

Jonathan came empty-handed.

"You're the only one who forgot," Julie scolded.

"You bum!" Eddie said.

Jonathan sought solace with his paper friend. The merchants stood behind desks, on which they had spread the goods. There was a frantic search for the Magic Marker when Douglas insisted that none of the signs indicated the true worth of his cookies.

"Ten cents each," he insisted.

"For one cookie?" said Eddie. "You're flaky."

"Five cents is fair for everything," Julie decreed.

"Now listen"—Douglas thrust a cookie in her face—"these have eggs and margarine and genuine raisins. Do you know how long it takes one single grape to become a raisin?"

"They're beautiful," I said, "but if you charge too much, kids won't be able to afford them."

"Okay, okay, five cents." He held up his hands in resignation. "But for five cents they're not getting raisins."

At nine fifteen the first-graders filed into our room. At the same time, Jonathan's mother appeared with a tray of candied apples. He and his silent partner sold every apple.

By the time the second-graders arrived Douglas was in business—a mound of crumbling deraisined cookies on one desk, tiny piles of raisins on the other, both products labeled: 5¢ EACH.

When the sixth-graders left at eleven thirty, the room was a shambles. But from the beginning the event was a social success. Children who had been reluctant to enter our room found it not only safe but perhaps enviable.

"Hey, you got only five kids and all this audiovisual jazz?" one sixth-grader said admiringly.

"You're lucky, getting to have a bake sale," a girl told Julie.

I was delighted with the effect of such recognition, particularly on Kevin and Jonathan. As the morning progressed they had changed from self-effacing boys to confident salesmen.

Miss Silverstein bought the leftovers and lingered to hear Douglas announce the final tally. Eleven dollars and thirty cents.

"Boss!" Douglas said. "That's a lotta bread!"

"Will you bring it to the hospital today," Julie asked me, "and tell 'em it's from us?"

"Better yet"—Miss Silverstein paused in the doorway—"I'll call their office now and let them know how hard you worked."

Each child voluntarily shared in cleaning the room. The only fight concerned who would be first with the broom. Douglas finally surrendered it to Eddie.

Miss Silverstein called on the intercom. "I have Mr. Mollo, public relations director at the hospital, on the line. I need your opinion. He's inviting you and the children to bring the money in person, and he'll provide a tour of the hospital."

"That's great. Any day next week would be fine. I'll tell the children."

CHAPTER TWELVE

THE happiness engendered by the bake sale and the hospital's invitation lasted all Wednesday and Thursday. Friday, I was sure, would round out our first perfect week. Sunday, May 8, would be Mother's Day, and with every class I had previously taught I set aside a day before each holiday for making presents. I decided to try it now with my Transitional Class.

Before school I arranged a corner for making paper flowers, a paint and clay area, a weaving table with potholder materials, and the workbench with a variety of tools.

Eddie's arrival interrupted me. "Why'd you change the room?" He swept the weaving materials onto the floor. "You know I hate things moved!"

I knelt to look directly in his eyes. "That was okay earlier, Ed, when we didn't know each other as well. Why does it matter if furniture is rearranged? You know this is your room. Those things aren't important when people trust each other."

"They matter to me! Some man was having coffee in my chair this morning when I wanted to have breakfast. I can't stand people who take my things!"

The others came in. Julie tucked a yo-yo in her cubby. "Eddie, stop being so mean. Mrs. Craig worked hard to put that stuff out." She looked around. "What's it for, anyway?"

"For you to make Mother's Day presents."

Douglas said, "Mother's Day, huh? Then I don't have to do anything. Might as well go home." He turned as if to leave.

"I thought you'd like to make something for your grandmother," I said to Doug, but Kevin answered.

"Yeah." He looked out the window. "Every time *my* grandmother comes, I feel happier. Why don't ya make a present for your grandmother, Doug?"

Douglas clutched Kevin's lapel. "Listen, pal, just 'cause you got a mother, no wisecracks from you."

Julie said, "You're just feeling sorry for yourself, Douglas."

Douglas patted Kevin on the shoulder. "Listen, ole buddy. I'm just not used to you makin' speeches." He laughed. "You used to talk with your feet, remember?"

Kevin looked at his shoes. "My mother doesn't like me to talk."

"You mean she'd rather have you tap?"

Kevin didn't look up. "She'd rather have me nothin'."

Eddie chose some boards from the wood carton and went right to the workbench. Douglas sat on the floor, threading the loom. Jonathan, also on the floor, sat working the clay. He rocked back and forth, making sounds, "Mmmm, mmmm," as the softened material oozed through his fingers.

Julie clipped a paper to the easel and painted a radiant sun in the upper right-hand corner. "This is gonna be where I used to live. I went to a park there once, with my other mother." She painted grass and a row of yellow and red tulips. Suddenly she slashed a huge brown X over the idyllic scene. "Oh, I don't know who I went to the park with!" She tore the paper from the clips. "I'm throwin' this away. Nothin' I make is any good."

"Me neither." Eddie kept hammering. "Anyway, my mother don't like dumb presents kids make." His voice was rising. "And I know something else she doesn't like. A two-letter word—m-e." Eddie's project was beginning to look suspiciously like a machine gun. "If this doesn't work, I'm gonna get mad!"

"Blow your top if you want to." Douglas grimaced, rubbing his shoulder. "Just don't do any biting."

Kevin sat staring vacantly. "I think my mother likes me sometimes." He spoke as if he'd been debating the issue. "She lets me sleep in her bed when they have a fight. In the morning I like to put my hands in her bureau and mess up her stuff."

"I'd never do that," said Julie. Calmer now, she began another painting. "I just like to touch my mother's stuff and smell the perfume. But it makes my father mad 'cause it costs so much."

"Yeah, I know about them women"—Douglas quickly assumed a fencing position—"who run all over the place yelling 'Charge!'"

Julie giggled. "Oh, Douglas, you're funny." She had been painting steadily, but the only evidence was her work shirt, stained with blotches of every color.

Several times I had moved toward Kevin, hoping to get him started on something, but he slipped away to sit pensively in another corner of the room. By lunchtime only Douglas' potholder was close to completion.

For the past two days our class had joined others in the lunchroom, but today it didn't seem feasible. Cubby doors slammed as paper bags and metal lunch boxes were removed.

"Ugh!" Kevin spat a mouthful of sandwich onto his desk. "She knows I hate salami!"

Eddie arranged his lunch on the workbench. "I know one thing." He chewed as he talked. "If your parents aren't good to you, kids should be allowed to choose new ones."

"That's a good idea. I think my mother hates"—Julie stopped; she bit her lower lip—"little kids."

"I know how ya tell," Kevin said. "If your mother doesn't yell, it means she doesn't care."

"My grandmother really needs this." Douglas picked up the loom. The potholder was nearly finished.

"Your grandmother, your grandmother!" Eddie mimicked. "Where's your mother, anyway?"

Douglas half rose, fists clenched, but made no further move. "She hadda go away. She couldn't help it."

"Did she die?"

He sank into his chair, his head cradled in his hands. "No, she just went away. I think she had tired blood."

Julie took her paper off the easel and laid it on the floor. She had painted two heads. She dipped her hand into the jar of red paint, then knelt by the picture and smeared both faces.

She didn't stop when the paper ripped, but rotated her hands on the newspaper beneath until that too was red. "Pretend the mother kills the child," she said softly, "and they're both all covered with blood."

I asked, "Why would the mother do that?"

"She hates the child. She hates her little girl." Julie stared intently at the papers. "She just got stuck with her."

"She didn't want her?"

"Course not. The girl's real mean. She calls her mother bad words. But she feels better now. She's dead and she's happy." Julie sat back on her heels, her hands motionless. "She's not mad anymore," she said quietly.

"I see. Then she used to be mean because she was angry."

"Mmm." Julie looked at her hands as if she were amazed to find them red. "Quick! I've gotta go wash!" Arms outstretched, she ran to the bathroom.

"Kevin, why don't you paint for a while?"

He got up and went to the closet where his work shirt was kept. I was pleased that he would accept my suggestion, but stepping inside, he quietly pulled the door shut.

"You don't have to do that, Kevin. It's all right to say you don't feel like painting."

The door opened a crack. Then, one behind the other, his loafers slid into the room. Here we go again, I thought. "I'm glad your shoes are with us," I said, "but I wish you'd join them."

A hand reached out near the bottom of the door and rocked the nearer shoe. Heel-toe. Heel-toe.

"Goddammit! Everybody's always yelling!" Eddie hurled the hammer against the cork bulletin board.

"You're through there, Eddie." Trembling at the thought that someone might have been hurt, I picked up the hammer. "If you throw tools, you're not ready to use them."

"I hate people like you!" he screamed, grabbing the wooden gun. "Rat-a-tat-tat. I hate all of you!"

Jonathan, now caked with clay, scurried to his desk. Cupping his hands around his mouth, he bent to direct his words down the empty inkwell. "S-K-Five. Calling S-K-Five. They're penetrating our defenses. Check the radar."

"Who are you talking to, Jonathan?" I lifted his desk top. "I don't see anyone here."

"Whew! Good getaway, S-K-Five!" He went back to the clay.

Eddie was still shooting. "Rat-a-tat-tat!" At first I was barely aware of muffled sounds from Douglas, resting on his desk, his head buried in his arms.

"Doug, what's wrong?" He raised his head, revealing the loom. Every thread hung loose, completely unraveled. Giving a heave, he tossed his desk on its side, then leaped up, grabbing his chair by the rung. Holding it out, he began to spin.

"Douglas!" I yelled. "Put that down before you get in trouble!"

He twirled faster and faster. "I hate her. I hate her. I hope she never comes back!"

Returning, Julie heard Douglas' words at the door. "Oh, no! I didn't do nothin' to him!" She burst into tears.

Douglas began teetering. "Dizzy, dizzy." The chair shot across the room and banged against the front panel of my desk, leaving a deep gouge in the wood. He sank to the floor and sat motionless for a moment. Gradually his whole body began to tremble. He rolled back his head and suddenly burst out with a high keening wail.

Jonathan clapped his hands over his ears. The closet door squeaked. Kevin retracted his loafers.

Douglas' shrieks rose and fell with terrifying intensity. Then his words became audible. "Mother, why? Why? Oh, Mother, why?" He fell forward, hunching like an animal. "Oh Mother, Mother. Why? Why? Oh, Mother, why?" He cried a long time, venting his unbearable grief in terrible choking sounds.

When much of his sorrow seemed spent, I put my hand on his shoulder. But I could not speak.

"She'll never come back," he moaned. "Never."

AFTER school I talked with Ceil while we waited for Mrs. Conte to keep an appointment I had requested to discuss residential treatment. "I was asking them to demonstrate a love that was never there or is totally inexpressible, after you and I've worked months to help them express real emotions."

Ceil didn't sympathize. "Believe me, they expressed real emotion. More than you were prepared to unleash. Stop beating your breast. If you want penance, here comes Eddie's mother."

Mrs. Conte wore a hot-pink pantsuit. Her hair curled girlishly about her face. Skillfully, Ceil led the conference to a discussion of Eddie's behavior. I was to summarize his activities in school, his tremendous anxiety and how it interfered with his learning.

Mrs. Conte sat back, eyeing me without comment. Ceil leaned toward her. "Do you see any relationship between the upsets he's had here and his behavior at home?"

Before answering, Mrs. Conte lit a cigarette. "Listen, I don't keep records. That kid's worse every day. Every time I go out he does somethin'. Twice he's cut electric cords. Says he likes gettin' shocked. Last night I was tellin' him to watch out for his sister. He told me to get closer, like he wanted to kiss me good-by. He pissed on my best dress." She stubbed out the cigarette angrily.

"Eddie's having trouble at home and in school, even in special class," Ceil said. "We believe he needs more help than we can give. The kind of help I'm suggesting is a school with intensive treatment for emotional problems."

"You mean he should go away?"

"It's our recommendation." Ceil nodded. "That doesn't mean you have to accept it."

Don't! I wanted to yell. Say you want your son at home!

"I could've told you long ago that's what he needed." She sounded annoyed. "It's one terrible day after another wonderin' what that kid'll do next." She twisted a strand of black hair around her index finger. "Let someone else try with him. I've got other problems." She bit her thumbnail pensively, then looked up and said, "The agency told me if I cut my hair I'll get a job right away. I dunno. My boy friend likes it long."

CHAPTER THIRTEEN

ON Mother's Day a breakfast tray was carried in by four tiptoeing servants who sat on the bed to watch me eat. On the tray: a rose, bacon omelette, blueberry muffins, and coffee so black it made Bill's eyes bulge.

I stayed in bed, half reading the paper, half listening to the children's running arguments over who was to wash the dishes and who to dry.

At one o'clock, feeling sheepish, I started to dress and discovered a light rash on both arms. Within an hour my German measles were highly visible.

Miss Silverstein and I had occasionally talked of finding suitable substitutes, but invariably her final remark was, "Just don't get sick!" Now, when I phoned, she sighed.

"My plan book's in the middle drawer," I said, "and would you postpone our trip to the hospital?"

"Only if you'll get well quickly. How I'll miss you with that gang on my hands."

In spite of the fever and a very sore throat, it was nice being home. "You're not to get up," Bill announced. "I'm in charge, and we're going to see some discipline around here." Ann rolled her eyes toward the ceiling.

I read and slept a lot, but from nine to two each day I couldn't help but wonder what was going on in my class.

CEIL stopped by Thursday afternoon. "Well, today a Mrs. Hines substituted," she reported. "She brought in her daughter's guinea pig, and Eddie broke its back. Said he just felt like squeezing it. Mrs. Hines was almost hysterical."

"Poor guinea pig! Well, I'll be in Monday, I'm sure."

"Good news! Oh, by the way, we received releases from Eddie's mother to forward his records to Green Valley. Kirby is out. The city won't finance his going to a private school when there's an opening in a state institution. I'm satisfied that Green Valley's the better place for him, anyway."

"I'll have the papers ready Monday," I said.

I had thought often of the harsh discipline I had witnessed at Green Valley and the gentle approach at Kirby. Which would be better for Eddie? I was angry that we had just two choices.

Ceil put on her coat. "You'll enjoy the letters the kids wrote, and Miss Silverstein will be delighted to know you're better," she said. I read and reread their notes.

My first day back was unique for its strained silence. I sat on the corner of my desk. "Thank you for the notes. I really enjoyed them."

Silence.

"You certainly kept the room neat. I appreciate that too."

Kevin squirmed. Julie's lower lip trembled.

"I missed you all."

"Are you gonna be sick again?" Eddie leaped up. " 'Cause if you are, don't get that bitch who kicked me out!"

"Yeah. She kept hollerin' at us to shut up, but she gave us candy all the time," Kevin said.

"The reason she gave us candy," Douglas said, "is she was doin' it wrong all the time, and she didn't want to lose her job."

Jonathan jiggled self-consciously and clutched his ghost. "You forgot t' tell those people I'm a ghost. They didn't believe me."

"I'll bet that's because you're such a good-looking boy."

He flushed and crossed his eyes. "I told you! I only pretend to be a boy."

After class, reluctantly, I mailed Eddie's records to Green Valley.

On Wednesday we went to the hospital to donate our bake-sale money. All but Eddie came dressed up. He seemed more neglected than ever, in a frayed flannel shirt that lacked two middle buttons. His face and hands were grimy, his hair disheveled.

Dar Mrs. craig

I get well soon please.

I hop you feel well
bry pleas get well

Di0 you have to get sick
get well for affee one
in the class

love.
Douglas

Dear. Mrs. Craig I wish,
you can get well If you get my
wish I wish to you, I'm
giving you a surprise Love, Julie

ghost's
wish

Boo
HoaHooo0o
get Well

Dear Mrs Graig

Hi Mrs craig. I hope you feel goD.
You will get well.
I hope you can come BoK to school
Come BaK to school soon.
By Mrs Craig.
Eddie

aBy

Boo
waguu

Back

Wet
Pants

(from Jonathan)

Dear Mrs. Craig,
I love you.
and I like you too.
and I hope you get well
and I hope you come back
and I like you very much.

love.
Kevin

Kevin, his hair slickly groomed, looked handsome in a camel-color jacket. Douglas wore a white shirt, so well starched it crackled when his arms moved. Although Jonathan toyed uncomfortably with the lapel of his navy-blue suit, he looked older and slimmer. And Julie, in her "goodest pink dress," with matching ribbons on her pigtails, was very pleased with herself.

Before we could leave, the question of who should present the money had to be settled. Douglas cited his credentials, both as oldest and most recently sick. Eddie screamed that being a better reader entitled him to make the speech.

"Let's decide with anagram letters." I held the box while each child chose. Kevin won with letter C, but his victory upset him. Pale and shaken, he thrust the envelope of money at Douglas. "You give it to them. I don't wanna."

"Thanks, pal." Douglas grabbed it.

Julie donned rhinestone sunglasses to make the trip, which took just ten minutes. We parked in the shadow of the huge brick building, and the children clustered around me anxiously on the walk to the entrance. The receptionist peered over the counter and said, "Wait here, please. Mr. Mollo will be right along."

We could hear his light footsteps before he was visible. A small dapper man, he shook hands with me and each child in turn. "Ah, welcome," he said.

Douglas offered the envelope. "The kids and me—"

Mr. Mollo shook his head. "Not yet, son. Come to my office."

We trailed him through the bustling corridor to a small room where a photographer waited. "You see," Mr. Mollo said warmly, "your idea is so thoughtful and the money so badly needed that we're going to put your picture in the paper."

The children posed stiffly, except for Jonathan, who burped and crossed his eyes. After five or six flashes, the photographer nodded and left.

"Before we begin," Mr. Mollo said, "you should know you won't see any patients. But I can show you how the place runs. You can see the kitchens, the laundry, and the laboratories we have to help us get people well."

The children followed him eagerly. They marveled at the huge pans in the enormous kitchen. We cut through a storage room to the noisy, steamy laundry, where Mr. Mollo shouted statistics above the clatter: ". . . and one thousand sheets every day, plus six hundred gowns and all the baby bedding . . ."

The confusion was upsetting to Eddie, who looked ready to bolt. Although he relaxed a little when I moved closer, it was a relief to leave. We went by elevator to the basement laboratories. There a woman in a physician's smock wheeled her mobile equipment table toward us. "It's nice to see young visitors," she said as she approached.

"My doctor wears one of them," Eddie said, pointing to her stethoscope.

"Would you like to try it? Leave it on my tray when you finish." She took some test tubes into another laboratory.

I adjusted the stethoscope on Eddie. "Bar-ump, bar-ump! That's what my heart's doin'!" he shouted gleefully.

After everyone had a turn, Mr. Mollo led the way through swinging doors marked X RAY. All the children followed except Jonathan, who hesitantly tried the stethoscope again. His enraptured expression persuaded me to wait.

With his right hand he held the stethoscope to his chest. His left hand marked the rhythm he heard, as if he were conducting an orchestra. At last he placed the instrument back on the tray.

"What did it sound like?" I asked.

Jonathan replied, "I heard it beat! I heard it beat!" He kept repeating the words as I led him in pursuit of the group. We found them with Mr. Mollo at the elevator.

"Oh, look!" Julie pointed down the hall.

A masked nurse, an infant in her arms, was leaving one of the x-ray rooms. She stood some distance away, but her eyes crinkled above the gauze and she raised her elbow to make the child more visible. The dark-skinned baby was asleep, his lips twitching in a sucking motion.

"You can't tell if that kid's black or white," Douglas mused.

"Red," Eddie said.

Julie was concerned. "Is he sick?"

"The doctor just wanted his foot x-rayed. Nothing serious. He slept through the whole thing."

"It's a black kid, all right." Douglas nodded. "They're much braver."

"Ha!" Eddie's hands were on his hips. "How come you squawked like a chicken when I bitcha?"

Fortunately, the elevator arrived. We thanked Mr. Mollo and shook hands again in the waiting room. All the way back to school, babies were the topic of discussion.

"I wonder what his heart sounds like," Jonathan said.

"I bet the mother's worried about him," Julie said.

"Fathers worry too, smarty," Kevin replied.

"Or else that baby doesn't have one." Douglas flipped through a magazine he'd found on the back seat.

"What a dummy! Who d'ya think planted the seed?" Eddie challenged.

"So?" Julie, beside me on the front seat, turned to face Eddie. "That doesn't mean he'll really have a father. Besides, just because he grew in his mother's tummy, she still might not keep him. What if he's bad?"

I couldn't let the moment pass.

"Being bad would have nothing to do with such a decision, Julie." I spoke slowly. "A mother who gives her baby up does it because she's not able to take care of him. She wants what's best for the baby because she loves him so much. That's the reason she would plan for her child to go to new parents, who would also love him very much. Do you understand?"

Julie began sucking the tip of her pigtail. She nodded and cuddled close to me. In the parking lot I switched off the motor, but no one stirred.

"You should be very proud of yourselves," I said. "First you raised money for the hospital, and then you behaved so well there today." Julie sat up. Kevin's smile was reflected in the rearview mirror.

I started to get out, but Douglas dashed around the car to open my door. When I thanked him, he bowed deeply. "Anything for a lady."

"Miss Silverstein!" he yelled as we reached the first step. "Miss Silverstein! We saw a new baby!"

THE next morning, for the first time, Jonathan came in ahead of his classmates and hurried to my desk. He leaned toward me breathlessly. I had never seen him so bright-eyed.

"You're pretty excited about something."

He nodded and began hopping from one foot to the other.

"Doesn't it feel funny?" he asked.

I was puzzled. "What feels funny, Jonathan?"

"Doesn't it feel funny to wake up in the morning and say, 'Who am I?'" He took several skipping steps toward his cubby, then stopped. His voice shaking, he spoke again. "Doesn't it feel funny to wake up in the morning and be a human being?"

All day I watched him with pleasure. He would suddenly stop working to scrutinize each fingernail or the creases in his palm. When it was time to leave, he ceremoniously snipped the Scotch tape that bound his paper friend to the chair. On the way out he stuffed his ghost into the wastebasket, stamped on it once, and briskly walked away, his head held high.

CHAPTER FOURTEEN

To all members: The Transitional Class planning committee will convene in the administration building at 2:30 on Friday.

Ceil served as chairman. I felt confident about recommending Julie for transition, and Ceil discussed her contacts with Julie's parents and how much more accepting they'd become. "As they began to understand the origins of her anxieties and fears they felt less threatened by the symptoms, which in turn are greatly decreased. There's been a good chain reaction in the whole family."

I said, "We could try her first in a regular math class. That's a strong area for her. And she tested third grade, sixth month in reading on the Metropolitan Achievement Test. That's a big jump from first-grade level, which she scored in October." By unanimous vote, Julie was to be tried in a regular math class until the last day of school. If this transition went smoothly she would return to her local school in September.

Kevin, on the other hand, was seen as more disturbed than we'd originally thought. "The child has been atypical since he was an infant," Ceil said. "I've been seeing the mother all year, but I'm no closer to understanding the dynamics of the situation."

Ceil and I both requested that Kevin be returned to Transitional Class in September.

In Jonathan's case it was a pleasure to report his accelerated progress. Although he'd entered the class as a nonreader, eight months later he tested on fourth-grade level.

"Marvelous." Miss Silverstein shook her head appreciatively.

"He's not ready to work in a group," I added, "but that's coming, too."

"His problems, as we have said, are still serious," Ceil summarized, "but he's come a long way. And the family situation is more stable. I think Jonathan's a good candidate for a second year in our program."

The discussion about Eddie was sad and brief. Ceil had just talked to the social worker at Green Valley. "They'll admit him in June. Mrs. Craig and I will start preparing Eddie, and I'll continue to work with the mother."

The planning for Douglas took longest. There was chuckling as I described his behavior over the year. But I was serious about the recommendation. "Douglas needs more time to consolidate the gains he's made. He isn't ready to move out."

To my surprise, it was Ceil who took issue. "I've been seeing Douglas for a year. The remarkable gains he's made in impulse control indicate that his earlier behavior was in response to his life experiences and not triggered by any emerging psychoses. I think he's benefitted as much as possible from Transitional Class and should be tried for one hour a day in a regular group."

"He'd require a handpicked teacher, both for now and for next year, when he returns to his neighborhood school," said Doug Watson, a young social worker.

"Muriel Flynn offers the structure and support Douglas will need," Miss Silverstein said. "At the same time, she's flexible and understanding."

One of the committee said, "Could we put it to a vote?"

"I don't know what a vote has to do with it." I tried to sound objective. "It's a question of whether he's ready. I want to keep him until I'm confident he can succeed."

"There's such a thing as holding on too long," someone said softly.

The decision was eight to one. Douglas would go.

THE rest of that week, Muriel Flynn and Mrs. Tefft, Julie's new teacher, sent a pupil to escort Douglas and Julie to their respective rooms for brief get-acquainted visits. Douglas and Julie were proud of the prestige and attention this plan afforded them. Eddie was angry. "How come they get to go and I don't?"

On Friday morning, Ceil took Eddie to her office to talk about a new kind of school. Only Jonathan and Kevin were with me when he returned. He smashed the door open with a kick and it banged against the wall. His arms were loaded with toys from Ceil's office—puppets, play dough, a can of Lincoln Logs. He hurled them all across the room and yelled from the doorway, "If you and Mrs. Black think I'm goin' to a go-away school you've got your minds crossed up! I wish you'd die and burn in hell. You too, fart face." He yanked Jonathan's chair out from under, and the boy crashed to the floor.

Jonathan began to rock and moan, "Oooo-oooo."

"And I'm sick of you and your shoes!" He rattled the back of Kevin's chair, but Kevin, his eyes bulging, clutched the seat and refused to fall.

Eddie tore around the room screeching, his arms extended like wings. He escaped my attempt to block him by crawling under my desk and out the front. He propelled himself to Kevin's desk and began chomping on his shoe, growling like a crazed dog.

Kevin was trembling. I tugged Eddie from under the desk, but he writhed and kicked and I had to let him go. He was still tearing around when Ceil appeared at the door.

"I've come for Eddie," she said loudly. "We hadn't really finished when he left."

"Oh no ya don't!" He dashed under her arm and out the door.

"I'm not takin' chances on any more schools. I'll run away if you put me in that place." He ran down the hall, his voice fading. He must have gone straight to her office, because Ceil made a victory sign, then turned to follow him.

EDDIE wasn't on the bus Monday, and Ceil called later to say he and his mother were at Green Valley being interviewed.

I was grateful for an easier day. Douglas and Julie seemed to be progressing well in their new classes, and although Kevin was moody in their absence, Jonathan was blossoming. He began talking about astronauts, moon shots, and spaceships, and together we read on the subject.

On Tuesday, Eddie was better than I'd expected. "I saw that damn school and I'm not goin'." But he spoke without conviction.

"I was real scared," he said later. "All the kids looked at me. I got to see where they sleep and where they eat. Those lucky bums get hot lunch, and chocolate pudding too."

"It sounds like the boys get very good care, Eddie."

"Yeah, well I'm not goin', so cross that idea off your brain." When he'd finished reading he lingered by the table. "Did ya know they're gonna build a swimming pool up there?"

Douglas' grace period lasted till midweek. When more was expected in Miss Flynn's class, he began to falter.

"I'm getting concerned about him," she said in the teachers' room at lunchtime. "He wouldn't work at all today."

I sat beside him that afternoon. "Let's look at the work for your other class. I'd like to help you."

"That's my business." He folded his arms obstinately. "And I'm not doin' it now."

"It's my business too, Doug. I want you to do well in Miss Flynn's room."

"Will you get off my back!" he snapped. Then he added, "Look, can't ya have some faith? I'll do it. Me and Kevin are gonna play checkers now."

Julie had been invited to stay in Mrs. Tefft's class for art and music, and had come to ask my permission. "I'll be back by two." She hugged me.

Kevin watched from the corner of his eye as Julie skipped out the door.

THE next morning, Julie arrived first and reported that Douglas ate all his lunch on the bus, something he had done before on particularly anxious days. Hoping to prevent a major disruption, I waited for him in the hall.

275

"Listen," he rasped. "I have this bad cold, see? I'm gonna stay in our room. These kids are used ta my germs."

I put my hand on his shoulder. "Your cold certainly came on suddenly. Were you able to do those examples?"

"I did my homework, but I left it home."

"Doug, did you do it or not? Is that why you're upset?"

"The reason I didn't do it was I have this cold!" He shrugged my hand away. "I don't give a damn what you say."

For the first time in months he and Kevin moved their desks to the corner.

By chance, Miss Silverstein stopped in at eleven, when Douglas was to leave. I scribbled a note: "D's reluctant to go."

She nodded and approached him slowly. "I thought we could walk to Miss Flynn's together, Douglas."

"No, thanks," he said quietly, not budging.

She took his hand. "I hoped you'd keep me company."

He rose. "Okay, I'll go. Who'd wanna stay here?" Douglas glared at me. "Who'd wanna stay with the nut teacher?"

As DOUGLAS rejected me, his relationship with Miss Flynn improved. Miss Flynn soon extended his time to two hours. Best of all, he kept up with the work.

While he and Julie were gone, a new relationship developed between Eddie and Jonathan. Together they made a cardboard rocket. Eddie was still quick to turn on Jonathan, but most often he was kind.

Kevin now worried me most. He had begun to fall apart. He even looked disorganized, scuffing his shoes, leaving pants unzipped, shirttail out. Sometimes he'd pretend to hold a rifle, and going home one night he'd dropped a paper in the hall. "Remember the gun," it read.

Ceil suggested a conference with Mrs. Hughes. "He may be responding to something in the home."

But the day before we expected his mother, I was startled to find Kevin's father watching me from the doorway. When I left the desk to greet him, he folded his arms and grinned boyishly.

"Heard there was some kinda problem, so I thought I'd save my wife the trip."

"The appointment is for tomorrow. Mrs. Black wants to be here too, and we would like to see both you and Mrs. Hughes then."

"Uh-uh." His smile faded. "She can't make it, and neither can I. Just wanna know what the kid's been up to."

I invited him in and we sat at the reading table. "We don't want to upset you, Mr. Hughes. We just felt you should know that Kevin is having difficulties."

"He been telling some kind of weird story or something?"

"It's nothing he's said. In fact, I wish he could tell me what's bothering him."

Mr. Hughes slumped back as if enormously relieved.

I talked about Kevin's behavior. "When a child changes so abruptly and will talk to no one, we are naturally concerned."

"Okay, doll." Suddenly Mr. Hughes was on his feet. "You've got my permission to hit him anytime. Thanks for everything." Whistling, he strutted out the door.

I never saw Kevin again.

CHAPTER FIFTEEN

"I'm wrung out," Ceil said, after a meeting in which we tried to screen new candidates for September. "I've never heard so many difficult cases, one after another."

"I feel the same way," I said. "But, Ceil, I'm concerned about something else. Kevin hasn't been in all this week. I keep thinking of how strangely his father acted. I've been calling their house, but there's never any answer."

"They could be away. There are lots of possibilities." She looked at me, then added reassuringly, "Call me if he's still out tomorrow. Then I'll drive over to the house and see what I can find out."

As soon as the bus arrived the next morning, I buzzed Ceil to tell her that Kevin wasn't on it.

She came in after school, looking harried and bewildered. "It was so strange," she said. "No answer there, and none of the neighbors seemed to have even missed them. I decided then to call the police."

"Oh, Ceil, don't tell me something happened to Kevin."

"Well, the two officers got into the house. It looked as if they'd gone in a hurry—clothes dangling out of open drawers, a few things left in closets, even food in the refrigerator."

I felt frightened. "What do you think, Ceil?"

She frowned and shook her head. "The police don't know what to make of it either."

TUESDAY, June 18, was the last day of school. During the past week Douglas and Julie had been spending the entire day with their new classes. Both children would return to their neighborhood schools in September.

All morning Eddie and Jonathan helped me carry books and materials to the storeroom. Until today, Eddie had seemed almost relieved about going to Green Valley, but now, knowing that he'd soon be on his way, he was edgy and apprehensive.

"It's your fault, isn't it?" he asked, sweeping the floor. "You're the one who kicked me out."

I shook my head. "You know that's not true, Eddie. You understand why Green Valley's a better school for you. Think about the things you liked there, and stop feeling angry."

"Don't worry!" he shrieked. "I'm glad—glad to get outta this stinkin' place."

The bus was due at noon. At eleven, Douglas and Julie returned to clean out their desks, and then I served cookies and punch at the reading table.

Douglas gulped the drink and held his cup for more. "I miss my ole buddy Kevin today."

"I'm gonna miss everybody." Julie nibbled her cookie.

"I'll miss you, too. But I'll be seeing your new teachers next year, so I'll get to hear about you."

"The bus is here! The bus is here!" Eddie leaped up, knocking over his cup of punch. "Quick! I gotta do something." He grabbed a paper and ran into the closet. He was out in a minute and dropped the paper in his desk. "I left ya a note." He dashed by me and out of the room.

Julie flung herself at me, clutching my waist.

"Happy vacation, Julie." I hugged her. "You go ahead to the bus. I'll be out to say good-by."

That left Jonathan and Douglas, still at the table. While they were getting ready, I couldn't resist a peek at Eddie's message. Raising his desk top, I picked up the crumpled note and unfolded it slowly.

He had blown his nose all over the paper. Sickened and discouraged, I walked out behind Jonathan and Douglas. Ceil was there, standing beside Julie. Eddie sat in a rear seat by a raised window. I went to the bus and spoke through the opening.

"I got your note, Eddie. Someday you won't feel so angry. Come back and see me." He slammed the window.

Julie kissed Ceil and me. Jonathan allowed us a brief hug and hurried onto the bus.

Squinting in the sun's glare, Douglas extended his hand. "Well, it's been nice knowin' ya."

I clasped his hand in both of mine. "Have a wonderful summer, Doug."

"Summa? Oh God! It's summeRRR. Can't ya hear the R?" He hopped on the bus and shouted to Ceil, "Help her, Mrs. Black. She still can't speak our language!"

The driver closed the door and we stood waving. I struggled to maintain a smile and call out a last good-by. I was still waving when Ceil caught my wrist. "El, I want to tell you something. Let's go in."

I sat in my chair and Ceil perched on Douglas' desk opposite me. "I had a call from the police station an hour ago. They thought we'd want to know. The mystery of Kevin's disappearance has been solved."

"What happened? What are you trying to tell me?"

"He's all right. Take it easy. It's Kevin's father who's in trouble. Apparently he's the prime suspect in a series of robberies. He is being held at the county jail."

"What about Kevin?" I asked, slumping back in my chair.

"He and the mother are staying in California. That's all I know. Listen, I have to rush. Someone's waiting in my office. Sorry to upset you, but I knew you'd want to hear."

I watched her leave, then just sat. I thought about Kevin's behavior just before he'd disappeared: the sudden disorganization, his disheveled appearance, his "Remember the gun" note—all cries for help.

I began to work on the attendance records and supply sheets, but couldn't stop thinking of Kevin and his troubled future. When I finally finished, I took a last look at our room and wondered if anything of value had been accomplished there. Julie had left her rhinestone sunglasses in her cubby. Eddie's desk was pressed against mine. Doug's was at a peculiar angle, and I went back to straighten it. The motion dislodged a scrap of yellow paper, which fluttered to the floor. Reaching down, I recognized Douglas' familiar scrawl and smiled, then laughed as I read and reread his final evaluation.

MRS. C.
SHOULD
BE
PERMOTTED

Eleanor Craig

When she was twelve years old Eleanor Craig, with a friend, opened a summer day nursery in her own backyard in Watertown, Massachusetts, for a dozen neighborhood kids (one widower gladly contributed five students). Their official-looking lesson plans covered water play, sand play, and visits to the firehouse. The tuition of fifty cents a morning was largely absorbed by fruit juice and supplies, but the nursery school lasted until the two instructors were sixteen and were able to take salaried jobs during vacations.

Eleanor's sixteenth year was a milestone for another reason: in high school she met Bill Craig. They were married when she received her bachelor's degree in education and began what she calls a "zigzag progress" across the country and back. Bill sold advertising displays while he studied for his A.B. and master's degrees; Eleanor taught elementary school, and they also began to raise a family.

Then one day she saw "Jim Hanley's" notice on the school bulletin board. That began her adventure with the Transitional Class. It was essential not to become emotionally involved with her disturbed students if she expected to teach them. And teach them she did. Of the twenty-eight children in the special program, "Eddie" was the only one who was not able to return to a regular class.

What sustained her the most, she says, was returning to her own family each night. The Craig household, with two working writers and four children, is a busy place. William Craig, now a World War II historian, is the author of the best-selling *Enemy at the Gates*, about the battle of Stalingrad. Eleanor Craig hopes to do another book. Her eyes shine when she says, "I feel that I'm brimming with ideas." And no one could doubt that for a minute.

P.S. The teacher *was* "permotted." After four years with the Transitional Class, she won a fellowship to Boston University and went on to receive her master's degree at another eastern college. Today she works as a therapist at a county child guidance center.